Everything's Ephemeral
Stories from the Workshops
Volume I

Short Works

Michael-Patrick Harrington

Also by Michael-Patrick Harrington:

Deep Autumn

I See No Angels

Saving Magdalene

Sweater Girl and Other Tales of Mondauk County

The Distant Sound of Boiling Tea

Get Out, You Ghosts:
Stories from the Workshops Volume II

www.michaelpatrickharrington.com

Published by Silk Raven Press
a division of Mondauk Enterprises Inc.
PO Box 31, Ambler, PA 19002

SILK
RAVEN
PRESS

(SRP-006)

"All Dogs Die of Cancer" was included in *Glimmer Train's* Top 25 list
of Very Short Fiction 2018.

Photo by Flora Westbrook

Design by Pepper Lillie
www.pepperlillie.com

<u>A Note to my Readers:</u>

While everything may indeed be ephemeral, it doesn't mean that there isn't magic in the world. Storytelling is one way of trying to capture the ineffable joy and the tender sorrow we share with one another. All that is raw and beautiful is worth saving if someone else wants to hear the tale. Most of the stories in this book and its accompanying volume, *Get You, You Ghosts*, originated in one of the five writing workshops I participated in at Arcadia University

So gather round the fire. I have some stories to tell you.

Michael-Patrick Harrington

This book is dedicated to
Søren & Silas, the Brothers Kent,
for making me laugh and think

TABLE OF CONTENTS:

God it's so painful
when something that's so close is still so far out of reach.
— Tom Petty & the Heartbreakers

I have refused my call,
pushin' my lazy sails into the blue flame.
I want to crash here right now.
The hourglass spills its sand if only to punish you.
— The New Pornographers

And Goethe says, "All things are metaphors." Everything that's transitory is but a metaphorical reference. That's what we all are.
— Joseph Campbell

A little talent is a good thing to have if you want to be a writer. But the only real requirement is the ability to remember every scar.
— Stephen King

Everything's Ephemeral
Stories from the Workshops
Volume I

The Beatles Want to Hold Your Hand, but the Stones Want to Burn Your Town

> ...at rest, I was not at ease,
> and to be at ease, I could not rest.
> Bruce Springsteen

It seems I rarely sleep anymore. I read a lot of Hawthorne and Robert Jay Lifton and sail the high seas aboard Melville's *Pequod*, trying to avoid the charismatic Ahab's gaze. The night before our daughter is to arrive home after so long, I watch nameless shadows break the beams of moonlight that steal through our bedroom window like translucent fingers of a faraway God. In the moonlight where nothing appears real, I think saints could meet sinners and become easily confused, one party subsuming the other in time. In the moonlight, even our bedroom chair looks different, a large Gila monster with a once pretty, faded rose floral pattern. Living saints are rare, we were taught in parochial school, but there are plenty of manifestations of Satan. I tell my husband during the night, waking him up, that contrary to our most recent plan, when we confront Rachel, we must do it in the moonlight. Even if it turns out there are no real saints or even no real demons or the rooms around the three of us are full of them, one side or the other must prevail, and in the moonlight, "a neutral territory, somewhere between the real world and fairy-land," was how Hawthorne described it, we would have our best chance with Rachel. Call it what you will: bait and switch, subterfuge, a double rook sacrifice. My husband rolls over and tells me to go back to sleep, but I don't. I get up and make sandwiches until the light of the sun breaks through and puts to rest the Romantic delusions of the night, cutting little stars into the bread like I used to do for Rachel when she was younger and liked those sort of things, when the worst that moonlight could do was bring easily dispelled pre-nightmare scares (the Count in the closet, Michael Myers under the bed) that have little to do with floral patterned Gila monsters. The fact that our little girl grew up seemingly fearless and now embraced monsters instead of hiding from them under the covers would be ironic if she recognized them as such and didn't think she left the Count and his ilk where she had believed them to be. For breakfast my husband eats one of the sandwiches, liverwurst, for breakfast. He doesn't mention that it has been cut into a little star—nor does he mention my moonlight plan (or our real one).

The first reading at Mass this past Sunday wasn't from Matthew's description of Christ casting out demons (a shame, I thought); it was from the Gospel according to John. "So Jesus said to them again, 'Peace be with you; as the Father has sent Me, I also send you.' And when He had said this, He breathed on them and said to them, 'Receive the Holy Spirit.' " The holy breath: what separates saints from sinners. Sinners go to Dante's inferno, I thought in Church, and saints get boiled in oil. (Gee, what's a mother to choose?) I was only there in the pew again because I was desperate for inspiration. I had stopped attending Mass soon after all this with Rachel had begun, and my husband had agreed, saying that I shouldn't continue to go, not in my present state of mind regarding Rachel's "situation." (*Situation*—that was the actual word my husband used, as if Rachel had been caught sneaking a sixer into the dorms— as if Rachel still went to college—as if our daughter had rear-ended Mr. Nickels' new Acura.) Last Sunday's appearance was an aberration; I won't be going back. Oh, I still pray just about every night, sometimes without even cursing. Although I'd started to wonder where the Lord is in all this, God isn't why I'd stopped going to Mass before this Sunday past—it was people. My return to Assumption of Our Lady just solidified my extreme irritation. Several mothers of my daughter's high school friends who know of Rachel's current comportment, accosted me outside the church, even though I'd left shortly after Communion, which I had declined to take. (Who was I to receive the unleavened manifestation?) They offered their *sincerest* thoughts, but what they were really doing was fishing for information, a juicy morsel to carry home in their faux designer handbags so they would have a reason to interrupt their spouses' football broadcasts and bore them into somnolence. (Pre-Rachel-going-off-the-rails, a million years ago, I was guilty of similar behavior, but that doesn't make me less furious now.) The members of the concerned mothers coalition are too frightened, I guess, to dare approach our daughter on a street corner during one of their frequent shopping trips to Philadelphia to get the scoop themselves.

After my husband (taking another starred sandwich for the road) leaves to pick up Rachel at the bus station—she didn't have money to take a cab all the way home and refused our offers to pay for one; it was forbidden, she said, to take alms from one's parents unless they were in the form of a donation to the movement (our word, movement—my husband and I find it difficult to bring ourselves to call it a church)—I spend time in Rachel's old bedroom, as I've taken to doing lately, smoothing out the pretty yellow floral bedspread before sitting and soaking in all the items and markers of childhood I've seen a thousand times but until recently never truly taken the time to understand, at least it in terms of what they had meant to my daughter. I do not focus on the artifacts of her pre-school and elementary school years—the stuffed green pony her father won her on the Wildwood boardwalk or the almost complete set of Nancy Drew mysteries (still missing *The Secret of Shadow Ranch*); it is items of more recent interests that occupy my eyes. Piles of CDs. The old vinyl records my husband and I gave her. The bulletin board and the wall surrounding it festooned with concert ticket stubs. Bowie as Aladdin Sane on the back of her door, partially obscured by her robe and a distressed hoodie from the college she had dropped out of to follow whatever dark, shifting, moldy yellow brick road she is traveling on now. An R.E.M. album cover (*Lifes Rich Pageant*) stapled to the wall. A stack of books on her nightstand: *Stranger in a Strange Land*, *Illusions*, Thich Nhat Hanh's translation of the Heart Sūtra, *Interview with a Vampire*, and *The One Year Bible* (designed to allow the enterprising Christian to read both Testaments in one year; there is a bookmark in Revelation, but I don't dare look at the chapter). Newer rock posters overlap older posters (and each other) as newer tastes overtook older ones. I know from previous investigations, for example, that the New Pornographers poster covers up a Smiths one. The only unmolested poster is above her headboard and features the Beatles posed in a doorway with the legend "London Palladium, Royal Command Performance 1963." In the picture, probably taken later than '63, the Fab Four are still dressed in their matching suits, but they look serious and tired, though not worried. They appear poised to take steps, then leaps, beyond "She loves you, yeah, yeah, yeah." Still, it is remarkable how freshly scrubbed they look. Maybe they were tired of being so freshly scrubbed. Can one become tired of being a saint?

Not touching, but all around the Beatles, surrounding them, are pictures torn from magazines, each one featuring a member of the '60s-era Rolling Stones. Mick wearing an Uncle Sam hat at Altamont. Charlie, bored and menacing. Lecherous-looking Bill. Beautiful Brian, stoned out of his gourd, obliviously (and obviously) doomed. And Keith, the modern day Lazarus, embodying all the insouciant danger that even early on John Lennon desperately wanted to show but couldn't, at least not under Brian Epstein's tutelage. Sitting on her bed, the wall above Rachel's headboard looks like nothing so much as a religious tableau. Four weary angels surrounded by five barely satiated devils. One party or the other, saints or sinners, must prevail in the final scuffle in the dark, I think, still believing that in the neutral moonlight my husband and I would have our best chance. But that belief erodes with every minute of sunshine, for one party, for the moment, already has the upper hand.

("You are *all* stars," was the first bit of wisdom Rachel brought home, telling us she learned it from the Greens. My husband smiled and called her Jiminy Cricket, a cute joke Rachel neither got nor appreciated. "You are *all* stars, and stars you will all become. And stars you will remain." Here endeth today's nonsensical lesson. These are the words that trapped my daughter, the eschatological equivalent of "C is for Cookie." *Goo goo g'joob.*)

"Well, at least she's off the drugs." That's what my husband says sometimes, but he doesn't see, that like the rapture of the saints, something stronger in promise almost always overcomes something weaker in spirit. The stronger something, though, isn't always a *better* something. Sometimes it's not even a lateral move. This is why we need help. Yes, both the Forest Green Temple of Exegesis and Evolvement and our only child's previous drugs of choice—angel dust, Oxy, meth—have the potential to eradicate our daughter to where she doesn't resemble a bit all the little girls in all the little frames that dot our home. The question is: do we want her to be Keith Richards, the junkie king of yore, one hot shot away from joining Jimi, Janis, and Mr. Mojo Risin', or Keith Richards of late, the opiate-free walking dead? (In Keith's case, I know, it's hard to tell the difference, but he's the example that keeps running through my mind: Keith in a '70s photograph taken, obviously, right after he shot up, nodding out but still intimidating, and Keith in a recent picture looking like an unholy communion of my great-grandmother and Boris Karloff as Imhotep, soulless, bent over his guitar, alive but looking very much the opposite.) In the *60 Minutes* piece on the Greens, their leader spoke of how he held onto his followers' souls because they didn't know what to do with them. Which is worse, I ask my husband often, a daughter a step away from the morgue or a daughter on a street corner, not hustling her cute little ass for pocket change, but proselytizing to strangers, wearing what appears to be an FLDS prairie dress accessorized with an Indian sari, during the hours when she isn't prostrated before the Reverend Most Holy Raymond Green like a groupie about to administer a blowjob to a roadie in order to get backstage? Yes, on a slab, Rachel would be gone, but she would be solidly gone, real real gone, gone baby gone; as a Green (or a Blue Greenie, as I call them, but not to my daughter during her infrequent phone calls), Rachel is gone but still here—here being on this earth: living, breathing (more the latter than the former) but incredibly out of reach. (These are our choices as I see them, if we don't avail ourselves of the available aid, and unlike my husband, I'm not interested in a trade-off unless it's an upwardly mobile one.) Even this visit is barely a reunion—just picking up a couple of books and a sweater, really. I tell my husband that this reason sounds like a desperate, barely concealed cry for help and maybe we should call the deprogrammer (or exit counselor, rather) I've spoken with during these past few months. My husband, bless his ignorant, solidly positive-thinking soul, gives my chin a tug and says that if it came down to the Greens or the corner boy pushers in North Philly, he'd be the first to write a check to creepy, moon-faced Reverend Green, devil be damned. My husband doesn't seem to care that there are rumors that Raymond Green "marries" his young female acolytes. He says that any man who has more than one wife, like a fundamentalist Mormon, deserves what he gets. He says this with a wink, which I'm supposed to take as a sign that he's joking, and he is, but about our daughter and her potential or eventual deflowering—assuming, as all mothers *want* to assume about their daughters, that Rachel is still a virgin or at least a technical one—at the hands and other (unthinkable) parts of the sixty-something-year-old Reverend Green, who perpetually licks his lips and makes odd sucking sounds when he talks (on the *60 Minutes* piece anyway), as if chomping at the bit to dip his ancient nib into fresh ink. I ask my husband if he's worried about mass suicide or the effects of brainwashing, and he smiles that infuriating smile of his that says, don't be silly, wife, you're watching too much *Oprah*. (An aesthetic impossibility, really. Besides, a large part of my downtime is taken up with studying—Waco, Jonestown, the Moonies, the School of the Prophets. Boning up on the boneheads.)

My husband says that what I'm suggesting is a kind of mind manipulation. But I remind him: sometimes saints are made. Saul of Tarsus didn't choose *apostolus* as a career path until God knocked him on his ass from a horse and turned him temporarily blind. (The ecclesiastical equivalent of going from the Cavern to the *Ed Sullivan Show*, I think to amuse myself; my little private jokes prevent me from smiting my better half on his thick backside.) My husband shakes his head and says, "Rachel *already* thinks she's a saint," as he builds a plate from leftovers. "She didn't get that from either of us," I say quietly.

My daughter is (was) a huge music fan, something she *did* inherit from us (more from me than my husband, who enjoys a good tune but doesn't care whether it comes from Mozart or the Monkees). Long ago, parenting weaned me away from my beloved music, or maybe it happened when vinyl died; I don't remember. But our daughter picked up the torch and ran with it back and forth through the decades, sucking in Miles Davis and the Dead Kennedys and Blondie and everything in between. She loves (loved) all of them, but the posters and pictures above her headboard don't lie: two thirds of the Big Three loom large. (Whither her beloved Who?) Lester Bangs wrote, "We will never again agree on anything as we agreed on Elvis," but poor Leslie forgot his Darwin and the natural law of the jungle: survival of the fittest and all that; the Top 40 is no place for the weak, especially not for one such as the King, weighed down, as he became, in cinema *horribilis*, and consumed, as he was in his later days, by a pharmaceutical hell. Tom Wolfe had a better insight: "The Beatles want to hold your hand, but the Stones want to burn your town." It is only now, at the kitchen counter, arranging little starred sandwiches on plates, that I think understand the quote—there's always a favorite, meaning there's always a *choice*: in this case, either sing with a choir of angels or, as the Joker says, "dance with the devil in the pale moonlight." You can't do both without severe existential whiplash. My daughter would like the quote too, or she would have up until the day Becca Flanders, a sometime friend of hers, whom I suspected also used drugs more than just recreationally, turned up at our house, squeaky clean and sparkly-eyed (Becca usually resembled Pig-Pen from *Peanuts*), and told Rachel she must meet, *needed* to meet Reverend Green, just had to. And off Rachel went, open-eyed Rachel, always ready for an adventure, always willing to look under a rock without a thought to snakes. Michael Myers be damned—what was he compared to a meth dealer, anyway?

+

"Why do all the sandwiches have stars cut into them?" Rachel asks, looking at the many little plates I have put out, "and why are there, like, hundreds of them?"

I ignore the jab at my liverwurst, my peanut butter and jelly celestial designs. My husband, on his third sandwich, pours himself a glass of milk. He pours one for Rachel too. I put my empty glass away.

"Rachel, honey," I begin weakly (like a poor chess player who has forgotten all her prepared openings), "I—we—found this place. Rosespring. It's a…retreat. A retreat for people who…have gone through intense religious experiences, conversions. The people there, the counselors—well, they're not really counselors, more like experienced guides, old hands—they help you put it into context. You know, how does this or that fit into my everyday life? What does transubstantiation have to do with washing the car? How does the rapture relate to writing a term paper? Those sorts of things." I am flailing at shadows.

Rachel stops eating and stares at me with a look that I swear indicates that she feels sorry for me. Beneath the table, I clench my fists, and one nail draws blood. (Great, I think, the beginnings of stigmata; can't let Rachel see this.) My husband, of course, is zero help. He should be seeking my hand under the table, but he doesn't. He's either pretending his mouth is stuck with peanut butter or it really is—either way, it's pathetic; just as some daughters are daddies' girls, some daddies, I suppose, are putty in their daughters' hands.

I clear my throat. I shouldn't be attempting this during the day. I need moonlight. Where is Lifton's *Thought Reform and the Psychology of Totalism* (the anti-cult movement's Bible) when I need it most? Hell, where did I leave my Kasparov book? "What I'm trying to say, Rachel, is this: you can like both the Beatles *and* the Stones— *equally.*" I know this (generally) isn't true. There's almost always a favorite, which, as established, means there's a choice. (I find suspect those mothers with more than one child who claim to love them equally.) Rosespring's approach was one of *analogy*; that's what we're offering our daughter, exit counseling based on the lie of equality, while continually comparing and contrasting as a way for the patient to drag their belief system into the harsh light—of what?—of day, of course, not of the moon, for the retreat isn't exactly neutral territory, although at first it pretends to be. This is risky not just because of the faux moonlight (in which may lie our only chance) but because it all begins with a falsehood, that the Greens and, say, the Roman Catholic Church are equal theologically and spiritually, that you *can* like the Beatles and the Stones equally—which is possible, for some, sure, but most of us prefer one or the another even if we enjoy both. The Rosespring counselor I spoke with told me that one of their goals is to, in time, present emotional and spiritual freedom as (possibly stronger) options without being aggressive or dogmatic. This made sense to me. Rather than send patients into shock or further into denial or shame or send them running by immediately invalidating their experiences, Rosespring initially accepts the patients' beliefs as possibly valid, then introduces more positive points of view. Mollify the victim rather than mourn the runner.

It is Rosespring's contention that an offer of *choice* (strong in promise) almost always overcomes something chock full of *limitations* (thus weak in spirit). They understand that occasionally we crave someone to tell us what to do and where to go when we're lost, which may have been how Rachel ended up where she is, and that places the blame squarely at our feet—at least that's how I see it. Rosespring aims to help patients move from servitude to freedom without pushing, without cajoling. This can be tricky, I suppose. It isn't simply a matter of Rachel placing a White Stripes poster over her Nirvana one—not according to Rosespring. There's a danger in Rachel going from bad to worse, though I can't imagine what *worse* would look like: stripping, pornography? She could experience what the counselor called a "reverso," sliding from current bad back to past bad. Rachel had gone from drugs to the Temple, so it's theoretically possible that she could get turned around by Rosespring's approach, switch favorites, and go back to drugs—after all, there's still an Echo and the Bunnymen poster beneath Kurt Cobain and company—and maybe she would do so without experiencing the effects of PTSD, which would be expected after exiting a cult, for we never heard a peep about the hell of her kicking drugs when she went over to the Greens.

While it turns out that Rachel never completely escaped Michael Myers, it is my hope that Rosespring helps her realize that Reverend Green isn't the only one wearing a mask—would a healthy Rachel even recognize the addict or the acolyte? It is my hope they help her see that trying again is worth the effort. Second acts can exist. For instance, more second marriages make it than first marriages. (I wonder if I should say this last thought aloud; maybe Rachel would be concerned that we were getting a divorce and stay.) Sex the second time is infinitely better than the tedious fumbling of the first. (Maybe I'm getting ahead of myself.)

Allowing patients to discover on their own the inherent inequalities of spiritually abusive and spurious churches, to understand how ill-treated they'd been (by others and themselves) usually results, according to Rosespring, in better decision making thus more informed choices. New favorites, in other words. No falling back, just moving ahead. How's that for a positive spin? It sounds better than saints versus sinners: choose to be an earth angel, for there is no sympathy for those acting on behalf of the scorched. If something stronger always overcomes something weaker, it is also true, and not just for those with addictive personalities, that *something else* almost always comes along to replace the first, regardless of strength or whether it's been disavowed or given up, and while *something else* isn't always *something better* (time is the final arbiter), new favorites possibly await those open to finding out. The results can be Darwinian in scope. *Exempli gratia*: Zeppelin one-upped the Stones who attempted to outpace the Beatles who decimated the Beach Boys and the girl groups. Dylan swallowed Woody Guthrie and the latter's fascist-eating guitar. Hemingway ate Twain. Twain swallowed the Mississippi. Picasso went brushstroke to brushstroke with Matisse, leaving shattered traditions in their wake. Pauline Christianity devoured James the Just and the Nazarene Jews.

But, again, it starts with lies, from Rosespring, from us, or rather, from me. Nothing bad ever came from that, right?

"You can…," I whisper, "…equally."

I'm awash in metaphors—metaphors that I understood a moment ago but no more. Setting Rosespring aside, what do *I* have to offer my daughter? What do I have to put up against the Greens besides family, which (along with college) she escaped to become a star in the Reverend's version of heaven on Earth—though to become another notch on his belt is more like it. The Beatles versus the Stones, indeed. What I have to offer is a slightly warped Herman's Hermits LP, which is the best way to describe family, isn't it: distinctly imperfect, but not completely useless. *Henry the eighth I am, I am. Henry the eighth I am...yeah.*

"I like both bands," Rachel declares, dropping her sandwich, a falling, fractured star, onto her plate. "But *not* in the same way."

And like that, my theory, my metaphors are rendered irrelevant, dubious, absurd, the result of expecting light bulbs and sunshine to provide anything but vicious circles and dead ends. My suggestions for a moonlight confrontation went unheeded by my husband. (I couldn't pull it off by myself.) It was only in Hawthorne's "neutral territory, somewhere between the real world and fairy-land" that we had a shot in hell at retrieving our angel-girl. Now? Welcome to fairy-land.

"Absolutes?" Rachel asks. I swear she looks like she's feels sorry for me. "There are no absolutes, Master says, but the absolute that is."

I ignore the doublespeak. How many dinner table conversations had revolved around Rachel discussing the merits of *Quadrophenia* over *Tommy* or which lineup of a particular band was the absolute best? I'm struck, at this moment, by how often Rachel used the word "absolute" when she was younger and discussing her beloved records. "Terrific" she used in a variety of ways during her early teenage years, but all of them were mock weary sarcastic. "Absolute" was reserved for the men in tight pants who sang about squeezing a lemon until the juice ran down their legs. The Clash were "absolutely" the right group for the right time. The Hawks were Dylan's "absolute" best backing band. Chuck Berry was "absolutely" railroaded when he was arrested for taking a girl across state lines in 1959, violating the Mann Act. (Never mind that the girl was fourteen—so was my not very worldly daughter when she uttered this statement.) Now even "absolute" is corrupted by the Greens and their Reverend, who makes Chuck Berry look like a rank amateur. What I wouldn't do to trade this lost waif before me, quickly fading into a stranger, for the sparkler of a child—no, more like a trick birthday candle girl—who used to pontificate on the relative merits of "going country" between mouthfuls of meat loaf.

Still, it's a good sign, I think: *like* as opposed to *liked*.

"I like both and I always have," Rachel says, tossing her napkin on top of the discarded sandwich. Her face is the slightest shade of red; Rachel is still in there. "And I'm not going to some deprogramming camp. Nailed up windows, held against my will for days, weeks at a time, handcuffs even. Yeah, we learned all about your so-called cult experts. Master says they're just places for parents to pay for their denial." My daughter comes around the table and takes my hands (one of them sticky with blood, which she doesn't seem to notice). I jump back, but Rachel holds me firm. I am struck by how rough her hands feel, as if the suburban pampering my husband and I worked so hard to attain has been scrubbed completely away to the point where bones are just about sticking through. But I like Rachel holding my hands; it is like when she held my hand to cross the street when she was five and I walked her to kindergarten; I didn't know who was comforting who then either.

"I am his now, Mom," Rachel says, looking me straight in the eyes. I concentrate and try to ignore the street dirt on her prairie dress and sari ensemble. (How odd that once indoctrinated, Pig-Pen rears his dusty head; I shudder to think of Becca's current hygienic condition.) "I am his. I am one of the Master's brides. It happened on a wonderfully bright day. Master—that's the Most Holy Reverend—looked at me, and I fainted and wet myself, and when I woke, I knew: I was to be married. I was to be one of his brides. They were already dressing me when I came to, and we were married one hour later out behind the Temple—there were fourteen brides that day, but I stood closest to the Master. I am his now, Mom. There is nothing better. There will be nothing better. I can only hope and pray you and Daddy join the Greens, and then you'll see—or, rather, Master will *make* you see. Oh, won't you come, Mom? Won't you come and meet my husband? There is nothing better. Never will be."

I think, *we will never again agree on anything as we agreed on Elvis.*

"Sure, honey," my husband says after he finishes off his milk and pours a second glass. "If that's what you want, we'll come and meet him." He winks at me. "Have to meet the in-laws, right?" Not a word about cult exiting, not a peep about deprogramming, not an utterance about polygamy. At least he doesn't say congratulations.

Rachel drops my hands and spins on her worn sandals. "Can you take me back to the bus station now, Daddy, please? I need to save *three* souls every day, and half the day's gone already." Meaning:

maybe she saved her father's soul (or at least thinks she got close) but not her mother's. Cultists don't bring sledgehammers when they encounter a wall; they simply turn and bang their tambourines at another airport.

"I can do better than that, sport," my husband says. "I'll drive you to the Temple if you like."

"And meet the Master?" Rachel cries.

"If that's what you want."

Both of them turn to me, but I pick up a sandwich and throw it at the sliding glass door that leads to the deck where Rachel used to put on funny little plays. I watch the sandwich stick momentarily, before the star plunges to the floor.

"C'mon, honey," my husband says to his daughter. "I'll race you to the car." And off they go.

That night I tear down the Beatles and the Stones and burn them in the barbecue pit out back, in the moonlight, their ashes the last offering to the heavens I swear I will ever make.

-end-

Bernard's Cocktail Party

As usual, talk centered around the name of Mondauk County's most prestigious institution of higher learning.

"I don't know why they had to change the name to Arcadia. Who doesn't like Beaver?"

"Beaver—come now. Tom, Tom," Miriam nagged, "what was it Teddy said about Beaver College?"

Tom pretended to rescue something from his drink and continued ignoring his wife. These sorts of events always gave him heartburn. He didn't care for his brother-in-law attorney and resented his name being constantly inserted into every conversation. *Why, just the other day Teddy...*

"We're just cheap knockoffs of our fathers," said Ethan Dragoon, the newest, shiniest member of Arcadia University's English department. Dragoon the buffoon.

"Really," Ethan added as he autographed his cocktail napkin for no one.

The needle dropped on Dylan's *Desire*, side one.

Skip.

Tom imagined that the brief silence, a rare absence of conversation, gave birth to shared thoughts of whether Bernard would grace his own party or remain holed up with Sir Thomas Malory in an upstairs study where presumably just enough noise reached him and where no one dared bother him for long—then: the needle descended again, "Hurricane."

"Pistol shots ring out in the barroom night."

"Honestly, I don't know what he's going on about."

The room resumed and Tom's wife repeated herself, turning her head this way **and** that, half comic affect, half annoying tic. *Teddy, Teddy, Teddy.*

Carrie Ann, the Humanities professor, always the cheerleader, said to no one in particular, "Bernard invites the best people." She sat alone, had arrived alone, and would end up humming herself to sleep alone, Tom thought. At least tonight. *Probably* tonight, he amended. "Always invites at least one or two interesting single men."

"Hmm—there's a wonder," Miriam said, setting the clutch of professors and adjuncts near the corner of the bar all a-titter.

Tom rolled his eyes. As a rule, he disliked faculty parties, although he could almost give a pass to Bernard's—for a Latin and Middle English professor, Bernard cooked like an Italian mother on a tear. Lots of exotic hors d'oeuvres, plenty of entrees, and always a house cocktail, invariably pink and of indeterminate origin.

"They should never have changed it. Beaver had a certain...liveliness to it. Arcadia sounds like...Simon Le Bon."

Finger food and spirits aside, Bernard's cocktail parties were certainly no worse than any other soirée Tom and his wife had attended. More colorful perhaps—Bernard's partner Brian, a tall man with an L.L.Bean fetish and a firm, gritty handshake, was an excellent host. One year he had led an intoxicated Miriam and a few others of her collegiate back-fence yakety-yak club into learning a Spanish dance, Brian's gravel-deep voice underscoring the absurdity of watching Miriam gyrate as he bellowed monotonous instructions. (Brian was an architect, which to Tom explained the man's predilection for order.) But the Spanish dance was never to be spoken of again—at least not in polite company. It had been the fault of the pink cocktails and nothing more, Miriam claimed.

But the big talk this year at Bernard's cocktail party (besides the college's name change) wasn't strange ol' Bernard locked away with his books (he rarely made appearances at his own events; company made do with only eager-to-please Brian) or even Dr. Werner's affair with a much younger student. (Dr. Werner was in an unhappy, even dangerous marriage; everyone knew it, and the fact that she had taken a grad student under her wing and bed sheets was tacitly ignored—at least until it no longer could be.) Tonight's tipsy topic was Professor Russell Fox, whose arrival was discretely watched for by most of the scavenging faculty cows and quite a few of its bulls. Professor Fox taught freshman writing, a few 100 level literature classes, and Writing Poetry and Fiction: A Theoretical Approach. He had joined the faculty barely five years before and had quickly become a favorite. His students lined up outside of his office for an open door tête-à-tête. (The school was seventy-five percent female—"One can never could be too careful about the comportment of doors," the university president's memo had read; it was meant to be clever, but it was odd coming from such a puritan.) Not that any of the salivating female professors (Tom's wife among them) or any of his adoring students had a shot in deep hell at landing the literary fox when he first arrived at the university. They all saw the shiny, thick wedding band on Russell's hairy finger. The young professor was fond of white turtle neck sweaters and black trench coats, but it was the wedding band that brought the curly haired Adonis back to the ground, where he was just another dirty blonde.

But then came the tragedy a year and a half ago. The accident. Russell had been driving and he'd been sober; not so the driver going the wrong way up the ramp. Amy was tipsy—another faculty gathering—and singing along to the radio. Russell emerged unscathed. Amy wasn't as lucky—scuttlebutt was her head was severed from her body mid-verse. (The rumor mill also claimed she was singing "God Only Knows," an unfortunate choice, Brian had commented, prejudiced perhaps by his well-known scorn for the Beach Boys, but no one had disagreed with him.) Amazingly, Russell returned to school and carried on, earning him many more points with the female faculty. A mourning period has to be observed, they said: for a year, maybe more, he'd be just fantasy fodder; then he was open game. This was how these things went, Tom thought, eating another piece of cheese. Once the faculty cows became vultures d'amour and smelled blood, they licked and clicked their bills, double checking their caked-on Maybelline. But it had been a long year; the best the kettle could do during their self-imposed moratorium had been to circle and wait.

"Is this Gouda? Do you know if this is Gouda?"

"Excuse me?"

Pulling at Tom's sweater was mousy Virginia Plain, her name a song she had most likely never heard. He wished she'd be more careful; the sweater had just arrived from Land's End yesterday.

"Gouda. Is this Gouda?"

Virginia—Ginny to her friends, she told everyone, but no one on staff ever called her Ginny (as a point of pride, Tom thought)— was truly an oddball. Although probably pretty if she cleaned herself up a bit, lost the baggy clothes, wore a touch of makeup, she often resembled an unraveling ball of string as she tore through the corridors of Taylor Hall. She taught some literature courses, a writing for children workshop, and a mixed media course that entangled *film noir* with *roman noir*. The faculty women left her alone, shunned her even, after initial attempts to crack the shell, to transform that pupa into a butterfly (either tired metaphor worked) was rebuffed by a spotlight-shy Virginia Plain. Only Bernard, old, gay Bernard, went out of his way to invite Virginia to his parties and to make sure she attended.

"I'm allergic to Gouda, and I think I just ate a piece, and I don't know what's going to happen."

"Do you want me to call a doctor?" Tom asked, playing along. "Is it that serious?"

Virginia pulled a tissue from her sleeve and loudly blew her nose. Tom leaned away. The tissue went back up her sleeve.

"Oh, excuse me. Cat hair."

Bernard and Brian didn't have a cat. Perhaps she meant the hair came from her brood, Tom thought; she struck him as one of those cat ladies.

"Serious? The Gouda? Oh yes," Virginia said, picking up from they'd left off. "This one time, my mother said her brother blew up—not literally, of course—and turned all sorts of colors before they got him to the hospital."

"Is he okay now?"

"Yes, but he has sinus problems and lives in Iowa."

"Oh. Well, that's not Gouda."

"Oh, thank you, Tom. I knew you would know."

"True enough—and you're quite welcome."

She was a pitiful creature, that much was obvious, but Tom still didn't understand, sartorial decisions aside, why she was a pariah. Virginia was intelligent, if flighty, and her students seemed to like her, even if they did call her "The Bird Lady" or "Tippi Hedren" behind her back because of the way she was perpetually startled by the birds that sometimes perched on the window ledges.

"Ho, ho, ho. Some good little children told me there was a party of *very* bad little boys and girls here tonight, so the reindeer are parked in the snow—yes, it's snowing again, folks—and I'm here for a stiff one."

Russell Fox knew how to make an entrance.

"Don't tease me, Russell," Brian said.

Miriam reached the widower first, pulling at his coat, while Cynthia Ford yanked at his scarf, nearly choking him.

"Ladies, ladies. Plenty of me to go around. And speaking of rounds: who's having one with me?"

Drinks were proffered and Russell made the obligatory trip upstairs to give his greetings to Bernard. When he came back down, three different plates of food were shoved towards him. Ronnie Smelt's glittery fingernails were thrust into a mound of potato salad.

"We're just cheap knockoffs of our fathers," Ethan Dragoon said again. Ethan was more then a tad jealous of Russell. Fox was inventive in the classroom, Dragoon intellectually sluggish; Fox was casually sharp-looking, while Dragoon had been cultivating a spotty beard for a year in an effort, Tom guessed, to look older. But if Russell noticed the jealousy, he acted as if he didn't. Tom thought that said more about Russell's character than his stylish wardrobe. Tom could barely manage not to throw up around the Buffoon's father's cheap knockoff.

"You already said that, Ethan," Tom said in an even tone, not adding that he was pretty sure Dragoon had ripped the phrase off from a television show Miriam regularly watched.

"Yes, yes. Of course."

"Tom, old chap. Ethan giving you a hard time?" Russell asked. "Knock him out with a good conjugation. That ought to do him."

Ethan fell back, defeated, into a plush sofa.

Russell balanced his plates on the edge of the bar and scooted the cheese down. "Excuse me, Virginia, but I need a bit of your territory."

"Don't eat the Gouda," Virginia warned. "If you're allergic."

"You'll turn different colors," Tom said.

"But that's not Gouda," Virginia said, "so there's nothing to worry about. Anyway."

Russell finished a mouthful of cake (he wisely avoided the potato salad) and said, "Well, gosh, thanks for the warning, Virginia. May I call you Ginny?"

Miss Plain blushed. "Oh—I—all my friends do. Always did."

"Then I guess if you say yes, I join their ranks. I swell their numbers."

"What am I saying yes to again?"

"Me calling you Ginny."

"Oh, yes. Yes."

" 'You're so sheer, you're so chic / Teenage rebel of the week,' " Russell sang, introducing, Tom knew, the bird-and-Gouda-phobic teacher to her glam rock namesake. About time, he laughed to himself; she *was* very 1972.

Virginia Plain smiled, but her eyes shifted this way and that, as if, Tom thought, she was looking for the punch line she was sure had been fashioned with her in mind. Faculty repartee was not one of her strong suits.

"Your name." Russell popped an olive in his mouth. "Roxy Music's first single? 'Virginia Plain'? No?"

The venue of vultures carefully watched this exchange between superstar and social leper, between the highest of their species and the lowest.

"Doesn't Bernard have any other music?" whined Vivienne Wormwood, drunk already as usual. Viv's husband pretended to be absorbed in an old *New Yorker*. Miriam shushed the theater arts professor and continued to stare at Russell while pretending to consider a pig in a blanket. Tom's brother-in-law had not been brought up since Russell had arrived.

"I'd give my left nut..." Carrie Ann began, out of character, but she was sort of drunk now too. It didn't take much. A cocktail and a half and she'd be pliable and humming. Tom knew that Carrie Ann would be so hungover tomorrow, she'd barely be able to get out of bed. This was first-hand knowledge for Tom. Although he didn't find Carrie Ann particularly attractive, he didn't find her particularly *unattractive*, and at faculty functions, one thing often led to another without one thought to his wedding band. Miriam never asked where he went, which made Tom think that Miriam had more than a working relationship with Ethan Dragoon, who frequently called their house and hung up, forgetting all about caller ID. (Tom considered Ethan guilty of more than just intellectual plagiarism.) In fact, it seemed only Bernard was immune from this sort of carnal behavior; he didn't even attend his own shindig, the biggest faculty hook-up event of the school year. But Tom knew at the top of the party that this wasn't going to turn out to be a Carrie Ann kind of night (the idea of a naked faculty member had kick-started his acid reflux), and judging by Miriam's Fox-induced drool, it didn't look like an Ethan kind of night either.

Russell moved away from Virginia, and the vultures cawed collectively, even Dr. Werner. Not one of them, however, had succeeded in bedding down Professor Fox since the moratorium had ended, although many had tried while deep in their cups—or thought they had. Tales circulated of valiant attempts to scale the mourning wall of intellect and hunk, but the truth of it was that a few of them had flirted loudly, maybe even danced (poorly) in front of him, and one (Ronnie Smelt) had even leaned her elbow into a bowl of onion-mushroom dip when she broached the bar for a closer look.

"Something…Frankie Goes to Hollywood…*something*."

"Give it a rest, Viv," said Miriam.

" '*Relax*,' " Carrie Ann whispered, " '*don't do it*.' "

"It's too loud as it is," Dr. Werner added. Dr. Werner only enjoyed classical and opera and only at a reasonable volume. (A good number of male professors called her "Legs," but Tom thought they were just being kind because she was the English department chair.)

When Russell Fox returned to Virginia Plain's side with two pink house cocktails, an audible sigh drifted among the disparate collection of female professors.

"Buck up," Tom said to his wife, but he'd been watching enough the entire night to know that that was statistically impossible. (That was his job, he thought: the watcher.)

"A pink lady for the pink lady," Russell said, handing Virginia her drink. Virginia did indeed have a pink sweater draped over her stooped shoulders.

"Gracious me—I mean: *thank you*. Thank you, Russell," the pink lady replied, and Tom chortled into his napkin.

"It's impossible that *he's* interested in *her*," Vivienne stage whispered.

"Nothing is impossible, Viv," Tom's wife said, but she stared into her martini as if she wished the opposite were true.

Brian had already started side one of *Desire* again. Now it was Tom's turn to audibly sigh. Bernard and Brian and their mid-period Dylan. How it must have moved Bernard along in his work. How it must have thrilled him to know just how annoying it was to his guests. Bernard enjoyed needling his easily-needled faculty friends.

"*Your breath is sweet*," the former Mr. Zimmerman sang, "*Your eyes are like two jewels in the sky*."

Vivienne, more than a little intoxicated, went to make her play, brazenly standing right in front of Virginia so that Miss Plain was left looking at the back of Viv's heavily hairsprayed head. Vivienne stuck a cherry stem in her mouth, and when it emerged on the tip of her tongue (covered in salvia), she had successfully tied it into a knot. The performance piece was followed by her trademark smoker's laugh, which made Viv, for her final trick, swallow the stem without warning, inducing a death rattle-like coughing fit.

"*But I don't sense no affection, no gratitude or love / Your loyalty is not to me but to the stars above.*"

"Ginny, you want to get out of here?" Russell asked around Professor Wormwood's considerable waist. "I can play you that Roxy song." Vivienne was left hacking and twirling a weenie on a toothpick.

"*One more cup of coffee for the road,*" Dylan concluded. "*One more cup of coffee 'fore I go—to the valley below.*"

The over-the-hill birds of prey watched as Russell draped Miss Plain's scarf around her pale, skinny neck. Their static electricity buzzed with possibilities. Russell called up to Bernard, then Brian saw them out, Russell's hand on the small of Virginia's back. The vultures crowded the windows—they were taking *his* car!—and as the sorry widower and the even sorrier old maid tore away through the mounting snow, the record skipped again and the spell was broken and the vultures melted back into cows.

Tom returned to focusing on his food until Miriam angrily pulled him home, where he slept quite soundly except for the mildest touch of heartburn.

-end-

All Dogs Die of Cancer

The snow is still on the ground. Barley sits outside facing the sliding glass door, which is spotty with smears from his nose and licks from his tongue. When I enter the townhouse, he gets up and barks a silent movie bark. Brandi Carlile pours from the speakers at top volume. I imagine I can just about hear the dog through the glass.

> *They can kick dirt in your face*
> *Dress you down and tell you that your place*
> *Is in the middle when they hate the way you shine*

Anthony comes running through on his way upstairs, smelling of shampoo, yelling something about getting dressed before we get started, and Katie is there with a glass for me and a smile, wearing her winter shorts, she calls them, her long black hair framing a small face already lined with worry. They balance each other, these worry lines and the luminescent smile. Katie is always worried about something. Anthony calls his wife a worrywart.

There is nothing about Katie that I don't love. And it isn't just her beautiful face and her shapely thighs and the smell of her neck. I love her because I am *in love* with her and because when my Katie lit out for territories unknown, Anthony's Katie was a shoulder to cry on, staying up late with me, listening to "Layla" (of all songs) and many others, drinking until we couldn't stand, and once even kissing, her tongue a foreign invading army, her little bites on my lips artillery shells—my heart was captured Stratego-style. I surrendered.

Katie's marriage to Anthony is a problem for me, but a problem with more than one bullet point. Anthony is my best friend, has been since we were in the seventh grade. Katie is his saviour; she was his way out of the stoner lifestyle he'd become accustomed to after deciding not to go to college. Anthony would not hesitate putting me through a wall if Katie and I were to have an affair. Not that I'm afraid. I'm too blinded by love, as the cliché goes, to see past my nose—even if it's been broken. The fact is that I don't want Katie to leave Anthony. I can't break up their marriage. I just want Katie—whatever that means. An affair wouldn't be out of the question as far as I'm concerned, but another furtive, drunken kiss would be okay too. Anthony usually calls it a night before either of us does, and that was when it happened last time. That was also when we both drunkenly got on her elliptical machine in the basement, me behind Katie somehow, both fully clothed but in our socks, and I ground into her firm bottom until I thought I would die.

It's Friday night, and Friday nights we drink. Katie's taken to going to Mass on Sunday mornings, so Friday night it is. Katie has tonight's drink all mixed—Ice Picks—and beer in the fridge for Anthony. Snacks too and music. Cowboy Junkies. 10,000 Maniacs. Chick music, Anthony calls them, and that's just what he says when he hustles down the stairs, kisses his wife, and grabs a cold one. I've seen them kiss a thousand times, but each time recently is a little dagger into some vital organ, deep enough to wound but not to kill me. I shrug it off and gulp my drink. This is the way it is and nothing's gonna change it, I think. I must wait for my moments.

"You're not gonna fucking believe this," Anthony says, reappearing in a Drakkar Noir haze. "At work, Joan—I told you about Joan, right?—she catches Bob Longman making out with the new chick from accounting. What's her name, hon?"

"Stacy," Katie says, making a face, as she lowers the music to conversation level.

"Katie thinks she's a skank."

"Not 'thinks'—I know. That girl's laid more pipe than—"

"An Alaskan pipeline fitter?" I suggest.

Everyone laughs at my bad joke, and we trade work horror stories through the first two rounds. We're sitting on benches at their kitchen table, Anthony on one side, Katie and I on the other. Barley watches through the glass door, his head tilted a little so he can see us sitting at the kitchen table. Occasionally, he barks silently and his breath fogs up the glass. His tail wags whenever I lean over to peek at him.

"Can I let Barley in?" I ask. "He's gotta be freezing out there."

Anthony takes a pull from his beer.

"He's fine, dude. Dogs' coats get used to the weather. If we let him in, he'll just start puking on the rug again."

Anthony enjoys words like "dude."

Katie crumples a napkin and tosses it at the wall.

"He only does that because he's sick," she says, her words a bitter syllabic rush.

"Puke is puke, babe."

And the subject is dropped for now. Barley remains outside, his bark mute and indiscernible—is he cold, does he want to join in the fun, how sick is he?

Soon it's midnight. Barley is still sitting by the sliding glass door. Anthony announces, "We are all quite inebriated, thank you very much." I call him Master of the Obvious and he bows.

"I'm gonna go down the basement and play some guitar," Anthony says. "You wanna play?"

I shake my head no. "I'm not in any shape to be throwing shapes," I say.

Anthony heads to the basement, and soon Black Sabbath riffs tickle our feet. They overwhelm the stereo—"Magic Man" by Heart, Katie's favorite band. I move over on the bench so that there is barely any space between us. Katie's eyes are red.

"It's just so sad, so fucking sad."

I trace small circles on Katie's arm.

"What's sad, huh?"

"Barley."

"Well, let him in then. I don't know about all this 'Dogs' coats get used to the weather' thing. Barley wants to be with the gang. Barley wants to be with his family."

In a moment of silence from the basement, Heart sneaks through:

Never think of never
Let this spell last forever

With that I lean in for a kiss and find only a cheek. I stroke her neck with one hand and try to ever so gently turn Katie's head towards mine with the other. She resists.

"I'm sorry," she says. "It's Barley."

I start to get up from the bench.

"I'll let him in myself," I say, "and I mean, what's the big deal...?"

"His tests came back today."

"Barley took a test?"

I have imbibed quite a bit.

"No, from the vet. They came today."

"Today, huh?"

I sit back down and put my hand near the top of her thigh and keep it still. Why she wears shorts inside during the winter is a real mystery and a genuine blessing.

Katie struggles with her tears and says, "It's cancer. Barley has cancer."

I withdraw my hand from Katie's leg.

"Where...how bad...what's the prog...the prog...what's gonna happen?"

Katie places her palms against her eyes and says, "We can try a few different things, all expensive. Anthony's not so sure. Or we can put him down now. Put him down—did you ever hear such a cruel expression? Extermination, they should call it. Or murder."

My hand back on her thigh, I explain, "Katie, all dogs die of cancer. They just haven't evolved enough yet to beat it back in any way. All dogs die of cancer."

Katie's tears explode past her palms and some land on me. Her body hitches, and when she removes her damp hands, tears collect in her not-in-use laugh lines. She speaks in hiccups. "That was the meanest thing anyone's ever said to me."

Undeterred, my hand remains on Katie's thigh, rubbing her flesh, trying to convey sympathy but probably only tracing shaky geometric shapes.

"Naw, people have said meaner."

Katie continues to cry and I continue to rub, and when the last Sabbath riff dies away and the Gibson is retired for the evening, Anthony clomps back up the stairs. My hand flies from Katie's leg and grabs some tabletop.

"What the hell's goin' on here?" he asks, half kidding.

"Katie's just..." I begin, but I falter. Anthony is bigger than me, thicker. He has muscles and can hold his drink better than I can despite his early retirements.

"I was upset about Barley," Katie says. "About the...tests. I was telling him about Barley."

Anthony moves behind his wife, and I get up and stretch. I don't want to watch them kiss again, if that is what they are going to do. Barley is still sitting in front of the sliding glass door, his tail wagging expectantly.

"Babe, come on. It is what it is."

How Zen, I think.

"We'll call Dr. Rubin in the morning, and you'll feel better. It's better for Barley. Barley doesn't want to suffer, now, does he? It's better all around." Anthony faces her and takes her wet hands and sings, " *'Well, I...guess...you'd say...what can make me feel this way?'*"

I try to call up the sound of Barley barking; I've caught this Temptations act before.

" '*My girl (my girl, my girl) / talkin' 'bout—my girl (my girl)!*' " He finishes in a strained but sincere falsetto.

Katie pushes herself up and almost trips backwards over the bench. "I'm going to bed," she says and turns away from us and climbs the stairs without looking back.

"I better hit the hay too, buddy. You crashing on the couch?"

I'm not sure what has just happened. Barley sees me looking at him again and wags his tail. I wonder if his tail ever gets tired or if Barley ever loses hope. I think Barley is stronger than me despite his illness.

"Yeah, probably."

"Well, you know where the blankets and pillow are, dude, so help yourself."

I clear my throat. "What about Barley? Should I let—?"

"A dog's coat gets used to the weather. Don't sweat it. Too much Barley tonight. Not enough hops."

He punches me in the shoulder and I stagger backwards.

"Good night."

"Good night."

The townhouse grows quiet, and I think I will scream if I hear their bedsprings creak-creak. I sit on the couch and stare at Barley through the glass. He stares back, wagging wildly.

Fuck it, I think, and I go over to the sliding glass door and ease it open as quietly as I can. Barley bounds in, and I place a finger to my lips. *Shhh.* Barley hops up onto the couch, and I sit there and rub his cold, Labby-like ears and his lumpy belly. He licks my face, and I wonder if it will be the only warmth that I'll feel for quite some time. It seems possible. I rub Barley's mongrel noggin once more and exit through the sliding glass door.

The snow on the ground isn't thick but it's slippery. My coat is back inside the warm townhouse. I turn around and Barley is staring at me through the glass. A dog's coat gets used to the weather. I wave to Barley and descend the hill behind Anthony and Katie's. I shake. My teeth chatter. All dogs die of cancer and all drunks die of…what? I have no idea where my car is and I don't care. My skin will get used to the weather. It's gotten used to rougher storms inside the townhouse than whatever is outside. Barley was right to want to be on the other side of the glass where it's warm. Who wants to get used to pain?

I don't feel it at first when I slip going down the hill. My head hits the ice and there's some blood, but I don't feel this either and maybe I won't until I'm home. I just lie there and listen to the crackling ice melt beneath my body. All dogs die of cancer. All broken hearts never mend. All drunks die of the cold. All fools never bend.

From what feels like far away, I hear a dog barking—Barley?—no—and then I begin to fall asleep, shivering and painfully aware that I will wake before pseudo-sensations of warmth can steal my rancid breath, that I will wake without a Katie to call *my girl (my girl) / talkin' 'bout—my girl (my girl)!*

-end-

Everything's Ephemeral

Do you know what time it is? I bet you don't, not without looking. But I do. I always do.

My grandfather respected time. He said that time was more than the great through line of history. Time was the divider, he told me, between mundaneness and greatness. Talent and hard work, plain old luck even: they had their place but couldn't hold a candle to time. "What happens between the movements of the second hand," he said, "can last a lifetime—if you don't blink." More than that, "What happens minute to minute, what events conspire an oncoming change: all subservient to time." My grandfather, his thinning white hair combed back on his head, his face perpetually Irish ruddy, as if he'd just downed yet another shot of Tullamore Dew, continued, "One minute a fellow's waiting on a train. Maybe waiting for his sweetheart. Perhaps heading back to the base after some R&R. Maybe just getting the hell out of Dodge. The next minute, an eighth of an inch closer to the edge of the platform than he should be, craning his neck maybe—and BLAM!—he's so much ooze for the scrape and sweep crew. Now let's say it was an eight car passenger train going sixty miles an hour. Slower probably since it was pulling in, but let's use sixty. In order for the train to come to a full stop, it would need thirty-five hundred feet or roughly two thirds of a mile." My grandfather winked. "But all time needed was a couple of seconds." He refilled his pipe as he often did during a dramatic pause, then added, "But I guess it's no easier getting back those couple of seconds than it is to have the train come to a dead stop from a speed of sixty miles per hour. But if it were, Seth, if it were…ahh, but I suppose that's a whisper from God's mouth to Einstein's ear.

"I met your grandmother because of time, uh-huh," Grandfather Saul told me for easily the hundredth time, but I didn't mind. My grandmother had passed away eleven years before, eaten away by cancer, and if Saul wanted to reminisce, then who was I to stop him? We were leaving Assumption's rectory where Grandfather had just finished another whiskey powwow with Father Ron. My family was Irish-Jewish. When my great-grandfather returned from the European theatre, having just taken part in the liberation of

Buchenwald in 1945, the first thing he did was throw out the menorah. Far from strengthening his faith and hardening his resolve, my great-grandfather wanted nothing to do with being a Jew—or a Christian or a Buddhist or even an atheist. He told Grandfather Saul that religions and belief systems make people kill people, or at least make people want to kill you. Still, he married a Jewish girl, even if he never stepped foot in a temple again. His wife raised the children in the faith, and my great-grandfather did not object too strenuously. Grandfather Saul married an Irish lass and settled down, seemingly trading a mezuzah for a crucifix. But despite his marriage, my grandfather hung on to his Jewish faith in a less casual way than the rest of his family did; Saul studied more, read deeper, and actually went to temple on occasions other than the Yamim Noraim (but not very often—he considered the knowledge more important than the practice). What he and Father Ron had in common was whiskey and a proclivity and appetite for debate. My paternal grandparents had moved to Mondauk County from Philadelphia after they'd married, and Grandfather Saul and Father Ron had become fast friends raising glasses at McCullough's, a local watering hole. These days, they kept their drinking and arguing out of the public eye. (Which was more Saul's wish than Father Ron's, who still haunted McCullough's; Grandfather felt he was too old to be hanging around a tap room and that his stool should be kept warm by a much younger ass.) While Father Ron and Grandfather imbibed Irish whiskey (the only kind either of them drank, the priest being proud second generation Irish), they argued all things Biblical—from the preferable English translation to the mystery of the Holy Trinity to the true fate of Methuselah's father Enoch, which was my family name. I sat quietly to the side, maybe paging through one of Father Ron's many books, but always listening; my grandfather and the priest were the ecclesiastical Abbott and Costello, only God was on first and I Don't Know was banned from the game.

So we were leaving the rectory. I was behind the wheel. (Grandfather had stopped driving after his wife died. "Penance," he'd called it, sounding very Irish Catholic.) We were driving north in my VW Beetle towards the large swaths of tall yellow weeds (called the Fields, somewhat sardonically, by the locals) above which tall electrical towers rose barely visible in the dark.

"The 59 bus was late. It was 1966, and they'd just replaced the shuttles that ran on Pollux Avenue with trackless trolley buses the year before. Now I lived a few blocks from Fawn and Pollux, which was only about a half mile or so from Arrott Terminal at Bell's Corner where the trolley buses started out. But the damn things, those spring-loaded trolley poles, always kept coming off the electrical wires. Buses would just grind to a halt. Well, that was more than likely what happened this particular morning. I waited and kept checking my watch, but no 59 bus. So I started to hoof it. I was going to be late for work, but if I hurried, I wouldn't be so late as to catch any heat. It was about a mile to Cottman Avenue, where I could catch another bus that would get me closer to the El. I was no further than Griffith Street when I met her. It had started to rain, and she was just leaving the bus stop. She hadn't brought an umbrella. But I had. I recognized her from the bus, of course; she was quite the looker. I caught her arm and asked her if she would like to walk with me." Grandfather laughed and coughed at the same time. "That was just time. That was all it was. Sure, there was the factor of the 59 coming off the line. And there was my decision to walk to Cottman. But it was the *time* it took for me to make that decision, the *time* it took me to walk three blocks from Fawn to Griffith, and the *two seconds* I had to see Millie leave the corner, think about what to do, and gently reach for her arm. Of course, there was also the seconds or minute your grandmother waited before she decided she would try to make it home for her umbrella rather than go to work completely soaked. The rain was another factor. But it was really time, Seth." He pulled out his pocket watch, flipped it open, checked the time, and placed it back in his pocket. "Fortuitous time rather than time the avenger, but time all the same."

My grandfather Saul always carried a pocket watch. He didn't trust wristwatches. He thought they weren't made with the same care as old pocket watches, plus being worn on one's wrists opened up a whole slew of possible accidental damages. His pocket watch was made in 1873 and had belonged to his great-grandfather and his father before him. It was an Elgin 18s 15j with a triple hinged coin silver case that had etched leaves on the front with a flowering stem or branch at its lowest curve. Running diagonally across the case behind the leaves was a slim band, but time had worn the front so that any design or lettering on the band was so much history. The watch had the expected amount of wear and dings, and the cover wasn't completely flush when closed, but otherwise it kept nearly perfect time. (Not when compared to my Rolex, but what were a couple of seconds here and there, I thought.)

Saul also always carried an old Monarch knife with a mother of pearl handle. I asked him why once, and he answered that he'd carried a knife since Vietnam, and he would be damned if he would leave the house without one. The blade was about four inches long (sort of a fishing knife) and could probably cause some damage (assuming that Grandfather Saul could get the knife out of its leather sheath before his attackers, his muggers gained the high ground; it was, as he would say, strictly a matter of time). "That's what I'm leaving you, Seth," he would always tell me. "My timepiece and my Monarch blade. You don't need anything else." And indeed, I didn't. I was making a fairly good living managing a bank and I was single. I knew Saul had money socked away that would be distributed among his grandchildren upon his death, but I didn't want any. When that unfortunate, inevitable event happened, the only things I would want were the Elgin pocket watch and the knife. I was the only grandson. The end of the line as far as carrying on the family name went. The watch and the knife would be heirlooms I would leave to my children (if or when I sired some).

We turned west on Ryder Road, the Fields on our right, heading towards Bethlehem Pike, which we would take south for a bit before turning west again and climbing a road up to the Heights, the westernmost most section of the borough Mondauk Proper, where grandfather lived in a row home, too proud and far too sharp to move to a retirement community. ("Slow death camps," he called them, "for the diaper set.") We had the windows down, the Stones low on the radio, and there was a slight wind; the acres of tall yellow weeds between the road and Pennypack Woods in the distance undulated and rustled in the dark. The wind carried the sharp, unpleasant scent of Pennypack Creek (called the Puddle by the denizens of Mondauk Proper, who majored in sardonicism). The fetid smell, which came in intermittent bursts through the open windows, was enough to make Grandfather pinch his nose. I tried to breathe through my mouth. "One of these goddamn days," Grandfather said, "the borough's going to stop staring into their own asses, discover a new smell, and clean up that swamp. A little time and—"

A car swung off Bethlehem Pike, but for a couple of seconds all I knew of its existence was the sound of peeling tires and a vague, fast-moving shadow. Then the driver popped on her headlights—right before plowing into us. The Beetle flipped, landing with a crunch, upside down on the blacktop. The car had somehow turned around, so that I was hanging out the window with the Fields on my left. A young girl, obviously under the influence, her face a maze of bleeding cuts, ran over and yelled into my face. For a few seconds, I heard nothing, then my ears popped. "I said I called 911 on my cell phone." She pulled me from the car, and I thought she followed me, as I stumbled around to the other side, but she took off, tires squealing, her car somehow still running. A third vehicle pulled up behind the backwards-facing Beetle, and the driver kept his headlights on us.

Grandfather was in an awkward position, and his head was partway through the windshield. I went to pull him out, but the driver of the third car stopped me. "Let the paramedics do it. His spine, his neck…" The sirens were already close; it was a small town. When the firemen extracted Grandfather Saul, he was still conscious but his breathing was slow and deep. The paramedics immediately loaded him into the ambulance and told me to come with them and sort it out with the police at the ER. Holy Redeemer Hospital was a mile or so away. During the brief time we spent in the speeding ambulance, the cuts on my face were treated and my left hand was bandaged, but all I cared about was my grandfather. This opinionated, educated, time-obsessed man looked extremely frail and tiny lying on the stretcher, an IV line running into one of his thin, wrinkled arms. He looked to be in severe need of more time, which was a better way of looking at it than to think that Saul's time was running out. When we neared the hospital, I reached over and relieved Saul of his Elgin pocket watch and Monarch knife. (I wasn't being morbid, just cautious.) The paramedic cleaning my cuts, a blonde guy with two earrings and a stethoscope around his neck, raised his eyebrows, but I ignored him, stowing the watch and sheathed knife in the pockets of my torn pants as we pulled up to the hospital. "Time…" my grandfather said when I took the pocket watch. "Loses time…have to reset it…" At least that was what I thought he said. His face was covered with an oxygen mask. Before he was wheeled away, he appeared to lose consciousness

Blondie said, "That blade looks to be longer than the width of your palm. Don't let the cops see it."

My first impulse was to cut off his earrings, but there wasn't time, so I just nodded.

The emergency room at Holy Redeemer on Friday night could be a zoo. (I know from a previous visit when I'd fallen off a ladder trying to fix the clock at the bank afterhours; maintenance could never get it right; it was always off at least two minutes by the end of the day; in the ER, I was low priority and ended up waiting for hours with a broken arm.) This night, the waiting room was packed. There were the requisite number of sick children with worried parents, as well as a pair of injured drunks close to my grandfather's age and a couple of college-age kids, obviously high, giggling while one held an ice pack to what appeared to be a broken nose. Two strung out-looking women, one young, one middle-aged, cried about their friend who'd overdosed and had been brought to the ER via ambulance. (A nurse I knew who worked at another local hospital had told me that there were at least a couple of overdoses a week coming through their ER. Mondauk County, like much of the country, was undergoing an opioid epidemic, and yet another meth lab in Paradise Lakes Trailer Park was recently shut down by the police.) In one corner of the waiting room were a bunch of people who looked like they'd just fought Muhammad Ali and lost. Across the room were a couple of guys sporting Lakes Boys tattoos and three girls who also had a fair amount of ink, two with tramp stamps. (They couldn't sit still and were constantly moving about.) A gnarled biker with road burn up his leg, visible because his jeans were shredded like the Hulk's pants, had a faded Fields Gang tattoo. One of the Lakes boys kept howling in pain, and the old Fields Gang biker kept telling him to keep it down to a dull roar, pussy, or he would shove his teeth so far back in his throat, the only noise he would make would be a death rattle. An old man kept grabbing his privates, telling anyone who would listen, "They said I should call if I had an erection that lasted for more than four hours." Another elderly man, on a gurney in the hall between the exam area and the waiting room, begged for water, but when a nurse gave him a sip, he threw up emerald bile.

Suddenly: hustle and bustle. Cops and staff and paramedics everywhere.

"Big accident..."

"The train..."

"The overflow's coming here."

"...derailment..."

The ambulance bays were all filled, a nurse said. A woman with one arm and half a face was whisked past me.

Grandfather Saul's gurney had been wheeled to the exam area closest to the waiting room, just past the nurses' station and the thirsty old man, and there he stayed behind a curtain, the very bottom part of his gurney visible from where I was sitting. For five minutes, I stared at his feet. He had one polished black leather loafer on. I fought an urge to walk back to Ryder Road to see if I could find the other one. It would give me something to do; if Grandfather Saul regained consciousness and found me gurney-side, his embarrassment would swiftly be succeeded by his extreme annoyance at my hovering, which is why I remained in the waiting room for now. I also decided against calling Father Ron. What would the old, besotted priest do, I asked myself? Perform the Last Rights? Too defeatist. Besides, maybe Grandfather would think of that as an affront, being a Jew (in his own way). What if he woke in the middle of Father Ron giving him the *viaticum*? There might be hell to pay for that. But better safe than sorry?

My thoughts were shattered by the pounding of shoes on the linoleum and random shouts. It started when a machine went *beeeeeeep!* Just one long tone, one that would have been easily lost in the myriad noises of the ER, if it weren't for its persistence. "Code blue, code blue," a nurse yelled. Her voice had neither the serene confidence I'd come to expect from ER nurses (this was hardly Saul's first visit) nor the unhinged hysteria that was creeping up my throat. I knew it all had to do with Grandfather Saul. The waiting room rabble seemed to not be paying attention. As I stood up, Grandfather's curtain billowed, behind which many shadows traded places. Someone called for the crash cart. *Code blue? Crash cart?* I attempted to get past an orderly and a nurse at the top of the hallway. The orderly was very large, but eventually he stopped trying to stop me and let me go, and the nurse arrested my charge by simply holding my hand.

I could see Grandfather's pale, skinny legs.

"Clear!"

"They're doing everything they can," the nurse said, caressing my arm, and I looked at her for the first time. An attractive, harried woman in her late-forties. If I didn't know better (and I didn't, not really), I would have said she was flirting with me. Her name tag read, Peg.

"This is an odd time to be horny, Peg," I said. "Maybe some other time…" But Peg seemed not to have heard me.

"He lived a good life," she said.

She didn't even know him! (At least I didn't think she did.)

I inched closer; Peg didn't stop me.

A nurse lifted a bag valve mask off Saul's mouth.

"Clear!"

Grandfather's legs spasmed. I could see the defibrillator pads on his chest. Another nurse leaned over Saul with a stethoscope while a male technician (or nurse) stared at a machine. It was like watching a movie.

"Nothing?"

"Nada."

"Again, Doctor Andrew?"

"Code blue," a voice announced over the PA. "Code blue."

"Train…" said a nurse.

"Jesus." Doctor Andrew looked weary and disgusted and somewhat distracted. He aggressively chewed gum. "We've hit him, what, twice already?"

"We've tried everything else," the nurse with the stethoscope said.

What else had they tried, I wondered.

"Once more."

Peg leaned her head on my shoulders. I could smell her hairspray.

"Clear!"

Grandfather Saul's body jumped again, and Doctor Andrew, young, late thirties, sandy hair without a speck of grey, grizzled face like he'd been working too hard and too long to bother to take a shave, said, "I'm calling it."

I should write here that Grandfather Saul was my favorite person on the planet. My father was dead, and he'd been no great shakes. The drink got him early and never let go. Gambling got him even earlier, and he eventually lost our house. A particularly bad weekend of wagering mixed with Cutty Sark meant I was in for a beating. Atlantic City wasn't enough for my father. There were dice games in the alley behind Old Nick's Tavern. Card games with the Italians in the back of Mr. Foster's social clubs. Blackjack in the basements of Chinatown in Philadelphia. He was even picked up for vagrancy on the AC boardwalk, found like a Monopoly piece that had been tipped over. He died young, living away from his estranged wife and only son, in a filthy hooker-and-meth motel where he'd managed to pay for a night (which was cheaper than paying by the hour). To say he died penniless would be a lie. He died in the negative.

Early on, my father taught me how to play blackjack and count cards using the High-Low system. I was pretty good. (I always had a head for math, though I ended up an English teacher.) He even got me into a few underground games as a shill as soon as I turned eighteen. But when he had his gambling partner, Frenchie, vouch for me at a poker game, my mother showed up at the Foster-owned clubhouse in Rhawnhurst, bullied her way past the muscle watching the door, and dragged me out by my ear. My father waved his hand dismissively at my mother, which he shouldn't have done. The Mafiosi weren't as dismissive. My father and Frenchie got off relatively light; each received a broken arm, smashed fingers, and a lifetime ban. After he healed, my father was basically confined to small stakes games held in paneled basements or dank cellars, but he never again took me along as a shill, which, while not perfect or normal, was the only father-son relationship I knew, even if it barely resembled one. Grandfather Saul watched all of this, if not impassively, then at least objectively. (He was not a judgmental man by nature.) He helped my mother out with the bills from time to time. He took me out for a movie on occasion. But when we lost the house (my father went on the lam after trying to rob a numbers runner), Grandfather Saul went into action. First, he bought my mother and me a little place with a tiny garden. Then, knowing full well where his son was hiding (the Port Richmond neighborhood in North Philly, just outside of Harrowgate, where he said my father regularly flopped with underage whores), Saul drove to Mr. Foster's house in Anchor Hop and told the capo where his son could be found. My father had to pay for the attempted robbery. I was told Foster's boys did quite a number on my father this time, even took one of his thumbs. "It won't be missed," Grandfather said. "Trust me. Better off floating in the Puddle than stuck up his ass."

"I'm calling it," Dr. Andrew said with more determination. He looked at his wristwatch, then at a large clock on the wall.

And I understood. I understood my favorite person on the planet was about to be officially declared to be no longer of this planet.

"NO!" I cried, but Peg stepped on my foot (accidentally or on purpose, I don't know), and the large orderly held my shoulders. He may have been holding them the whole time.

"12:25 a.m.," Dr. Andrew said, and a nurse wrote it down and someone else turned off a beeping machine. The nurse handed a clipboard to the doctor, and then she pulled the sheet over my grandfather's head.

"NO!" I cried, but love-hungry Peg and the orderly built for football had a firm grip on me. "Extreme Unction! What about Extreme Unction?" My pores oozed desperation.

"Come with me," Peg said, and I swear her hand brushed past my package.

I tore myself away from grabby Peg and the linebacker, but I was turned around so that I was next to the old man on the gurney begging for water. Beyond him was the waiting room with the burnouts and the brawlers and the old Fields Gang motorcycle accident victim flashing his ink and wearing his faded colors. Grandfather's knife weighed down my pants. I took the Elgin from my pocket and squeezed it in my sprained hand; I wanted to feel pain in order to center my mind.

"What happens between the movements of the second hand can last a lifetime—if you don't blink."

I tried not to blink.

I found myself standing in the center of the waiting room, Mondauk Proper bleeding and suffering around me, as I stared at the pocket watch. I ran my finger over its familiar dents, opened it, and wiped away a smear on the glass.

"What happens between the movements of the second hand can last a lifetime…"

But this was no H. G. Wells novel. No Marvel *What If* comic book. No…

I wound the Elgin back two minutes. The scene around me slowed down. I wound it back five minutes. The scene froze. People paused in the middle of walking, talking, scratching their balls. I wound the pocket watch back ten minutes. Everything blurred. I tried to wind it back further, but it wouldn't budge. The second hand was moving though. It was 12:15 a.m.

No *beeeeeep!* Not yet. But it was coming. I hadn't been able to bring us back to Ryder Road where I could safely pull over before the drunk girl played chicken in the dark with the Beetle. But *now* was *before*. *Now* Grandfather Saul was still alive (barely).

That was when I caught Dr. Andrew in the corner of my eye. That was when I knew what I had to do and that I only had a few minutes in which to do it. Dr. Andrew leaned over a water fountain, his sandy hair falling in his eyes, his wedding ring clearly visible. *Sorry Mrs. Dr. Andrew, but your husband's days of "calling it" are over. I'm sure he was very talented, Mrs. Dr. Andrew, but there are other doctors on staff, on call, whatever, who can and will do a better job of "calling it" or, rather, not.*

Hustle and bustle. Cops everywhere. Woman with one arm and half a face. Lakes scum screaming, Fields biker hollering back. The old man begging for water.

Turned out the cliché was true: time *was* of the essence.

As ol' T. S. Eliot wrote, "HURRY UP PLEASE IT'S TIME!"

Or as Reignier, Duke of Anjou, said in *Henry VI, Part 1,* "Defer no time, delays have dangerous ends."

But I think Mick put it best when he sang, *"Ti-i-i-ime is on my side. Yes it is."*

I pushed my way to the water fountain and bashed Dr. Andrew's head down as he went for another gulp. Keeping the woozy physician bent over, I cupped his mouth with one hand and pulled his hair with the other (careful not to drop the pocket watch), leading him down the hallway. The staff appeared oblivious to our movements, the patients too, but I thought I saw the linebacker orderly blink as if something was in his eye. The last exam area was empty (which was a surprise, considering all the train derailment victims), and I closed the curtains around us. Grandfather had kept the Monarch sharp, like he knew, like he knew his only grandson would deke his way through the movements of the second hand to score a touchdown and would need a good knife to accomplish the win. The crisscrossed slashes it left on Dr. Andrew's face rendered him unrecognizable, and I clocked him to make sure he was out. It was difficult to remove his white coat, but I did it in record time and stuffed it in a trash can. My sprained hand had become numb, and I wanted to look at the Elgin, but I knew how much time was left. Every second caressed my brain stem, Peg-like, hungry measurements of time.

"*Beeeeeeep!*"

"HURRY UP PLEASE IT'S TIME!"

My hands were bloody, but it was a hectic emergency room. Train accident survivors. Whiny druggies. Old drunks. What difference would a little blood make?

Peg and the linebacker stopped me. Peg held my bloody right hand (she seemed not to notice its stickiness) and placed her head on my shoulder, then stepped on my foot (a bit early, I thought), as the orderly held me to the spot. I had a boner despite the situation, despite looking down at my grandfather, frail, impossibly white, tubes sticking in here and out there. But I knew there would come a moment soon when Peg's hand would brush my crotch. Maybe after Saul was situated in the ICU, improving every second, Peg and I could slip away to a storage closet for some after-near-tragedy sex, tearing each other's clothes off without thought to what we would have left to wear afterwards when we slunk back out.

"I don't know where Dr. Andrew is," a nurse said.

"I got it, I got it."

This doctor had black hair and was taller, but his hair fell in his eyes the same way Dr. Andrew's had. He was chewing gum aggressively.

"Clear!"

Jump!

"Nothing. Again, Dr. Mark?"

"You tried how many…?" He sighed like he'd seen too much loss tonight. "Okay, one more time."

"Clear!"

Jump!

"I'm calling it," Dr. Mark said looking at his wristwatch, then at the large clock on the wall.

"NO!" I screamed and pulled myself free of needy Peg's grasp and the big orderly's hold to look at the Elgin…and it was gone. I checked my pockets but only the Monarch was hidden there. A bloodstain was blooming on my pants.

"You can't…you can't…wait a few seconds…I can feel the second hand…just wait…"

I pulled out the knife, ready to take down Dr. Mark, but the orderly knocked it out of my hand, and it went skidding down the hall.

Another nurse appeared. "We have face lacerations down here. Bleeding bad."

"Coming, coming," Dr. Mark murmured under his breath. Out loud, he said, "I'm calling it. 12:25 a.m."

I searched the floor for the Elgin, frantic, until the orderly pulled me up.

"*Ti-i-i-ime is on my side,*" I sang to Peg. "*Yes it is.*"

But it wasn't. Not yet.

As the orderly led me down the hall, my eyes looked for the Elgin in every corner, and I checked my pockets for the umpteenth time. I just needed the pocket watch—if I did it once, I could do it again; I was confident.

(Do what exactly?)

It worked like gangbusters last time. Yes it did.

Last time—*this* time I didn't have the pocket watch *or* the knife.

I broke away from the orderly, but again I was turned around, and I found myself staring at Dr. Andrew in the last exam area, an oxygen mask over his mutilated face. Dr. Mark and two nurses leaned over him.

The nurse who was swabbing Dr. Andrew's face said, "Some of these are—"

The other nurse, as she hooked up an IV, asked, "Paperwork, does anyone know where—?"

Dr. Mark said, "Run a line and get his…"

They didn't recognize him.

Another Stones song ran through my head:

You're obsolete my baby, my poor old-fashioned baby
Baby, baby, baby, you're out of time

It glinted from Dr. Andrew's hand just as the linebacker was about to turn me left down another hall where two policemen were approaching. I looked back and it glinted again and I knew what it was. Dr. Andrew had done what I could not, what Grandfather Saul could not. Dr. Andrew had stolen time.

I managed to hinder the orderly just as the Stones hit the chorus of another number:

Well, this could be the last time
This could be the last time
Maybe the last time
I don't know, oh no, oh no

I elbowed the linebacker and knocked over Peg (sorry, darling, another time perhaps) and squeezed between the team working on Dr. Andrew.

"Get him out of here!" Dr. Mark yelled. "Someone, please!"

Grasped in Dr. Andrew's hand: the silver Elgin 18s 15j from 1873, only the hinge was damaged, the cover missing.

"Security!" Dr. Mark bellowed. "Get this man out of my..."

The glass on the Elgin was broken. Dr. Andrew's fingers gripped the face of the watch.

You know what time it showed, don't you? Oh, you do. I know you do. You know exactly where time was stopped. I knew before I looked. Now I wait in my little room every night for that time to come before I go to sleep, even though I have no watch and there are no clocks in here. But I know. Oh, I know.

It read 12:25.

-end-

Ellie Strunk
and the Invisible Man

Ever since he'd discovered girls, Francis Brodie wanted to be invisible.

+

Ellie Strunk lived a solitary life, what her favorite writer Chuck Palahniuk might call a single-serving life, before the Invisible Man came into her apartment. She didn't date; she didn't go out to clubs; she didn't even drink. During the week, she woke at exactly 6:30 a.m., had a breakfast of toast and jam, brushed her teeth, and showered. She arrived at her cubicle exactly at 8:10, after a quick commute in her sensible car. Her job was also sensible, although it required little more than common sense. A monkey could sit in her cubicle and no one would be the wiser if they could account for the excess hair. Her nights were barely more exciting. Perhaps a movie (whatever was on cable), a little dinner (initially frozen), and some popcorn (microwave variety). Boyfriends were a thing of the past, tied into memories of proms and nosegays and once a nasty fumble in the backseat of Roger Dearling's father's Cadillac. She'd walked home from that post-prom festivity, Roger neither being a boyfriend (of which she had very few as a teenager) nor particularly good looking, appealing, or well-mannered. But her virginity was not a lifestyle choice; it was a result—a result of too much good girl living and possibly not enough attention paid to *Cosmopolitan*, plus there was a hint of shyness and a general sense of being stuck in a rut. But Ellie did not weep for her virginity nor did she treasure it like a nun. It was just a fact and Ellie liked facts. She enjoyed fiction too, but she had a whole bookcase filled with atlases, encyclopedias, and almanacs. Facts were hard little nuggets, difficult to crack, and that was how Ellie thought of herself. Thirty-nine, she ignored the still-voluptuous body she sponged in the shower. (At least that was what others had called it: voluptuous; Ellie thought they'd been pulling her leg.) She pushed away any and all amorous or lascivious thoughts. She dressed conservatively, downplaying her full breasts and shapely legs. Weekends were spent playing chess on the computer or listening to her Buddy Holly records. (Her favorite Buddy song—inexplicably, she thought—was "True Love Ways.") Ellie Strunk was secure in her place in the world, and the very last thing she desired was a secret admirer, let alone one who was invisible.

+

At first he didn't believe it. It was too good to be true, nothing less than the greatest thing to happen to him in his eighteen years. Sure, he'd won the Science Fair with his Sodium Pentathol-polygraph experiment (although it had freaked out Assistant Headmaster Bogle when Mrs. Bingle admitted to fondling meat and vegetables). His acceptance into MIT was not particularly a surprise. He would graduate Hoskins High with honors, maybe even be named valedictorian. But in all of Francis Brodie's relatively short life, nothing compared to what he'd just accomplished. It was a good thing his family considered him a genius and left him alone. For one, he could masturbate in peace or play music at whatever volume tickled him. He could also immerse himself in his studies undisturbed by parental interruptions or sibling nonsense. Best of all, he could work on his experiments, some of which his parents would have deemed dangerous. The Bunsen burners alone would have gotten him grounded, straight A's or no. But what he'd discovered just a few days ago, completely by accident, was so mind-blowing he could never, ever tell his teachers. He couldn't even tell Ned, his best friend. And he certainly couldn't inform his parents. Besides, he'd already broken a few cardinal rules of science: there'd been no scientific control and he'd experimented on himself. Plus he'd run naked through the neighbor's backyard after his discovery, touching himself inappropriately. But the biggest reason he couldn't tell anyone else was this: who would believe him until they'd seen it with their own eyes (so to speak) and then who would shut up about it once they did? Being invisible was hard work. But now, just maybe, it was paying off, for Francis Brodie was in love. True, the object of his unrequited affection didn't know who he was and had probably never even seen him (pre-invisibility), but, oh boy, had he seen her. Never before had he peered at a woman so beautiful and so naked. (His knowledge of naked women was limited to a heavily-thumbed through, much passed around *Playboy* from 1972.) Being the Invisible Man had its perks and Ellie Strunk was one of them.

+

The first time she'd noticed him was three days ago while she was waiting for her frozen dinner to finish in the microwave. It had been Salisbury steak with string beans, mashed potatoes, and an apple crisp, all in one convenient package. (A Friday night tradition.) She felt him standing behind her, and later, when she went to the bathroom before turning in, she had a difficult time closing the door, as if someone was trying to squeeze his (his!) way in. (How she knew *it* was a *he*, Ellie couldn't have said.) In the bathroom, this bodiless being's breathing grew rougher, and she peed, wiped, and flushed quickly, glad to escape the heavy breathing. All night long she stayed awake, listening for more noises, but there were none. In the morning, it was no longer a concrete event, a fact, but just a weird dream—except she discovered that the hand towel was wet, and she hadn't used the bathroom during the night, not since she'd peed.

So on Monday, Ellie went back to work and tried to put the odd dream and the wet towel and the mystery of the subsequent two days out of her mind—it had been the result of something she ate, she thought (the apple crisp hadn't been the least crisp), or perhaps fever dreams (she'd felt warm all weekend)—and proceeded with her cubicle duties. Ralph Trainy was especially annoying this Monday morning (a welcome distraction, although the smell of his cologne always made Ellie queasy), trying to simultaneously get her to participate in the football pool and sell her tickets to the Mondauk County Volunteer Firemen's Spaghetti Dinner. Judy Pawlowski hovered around Ellie's cubicle, her voice a phlegmy meat grinder, a ragged afghan blanket around her shoulders, the heavy scent of the Marlboros she had smoked in her car (smoking was forbidden on company grounds) invading Ellie's space until She felt like a participant in a smoky back room deal. Judy's granddaughter had sung in the school play. *Wasn't she just a doll, hon? Cough, cough, rasp, and, oh, here's some more pictures.* The supervisor's niece, pretty Deanna Smith, dropped off some forms with her perfunctory good morning, and then she was gone, just her light perfume lingering to fight the remnants of Judy's Marlboros. A snob, most of the guys in the office called Deanna. Driven, Ellie thought—as well as a bit of a snob.

Deanna was given a nickname by some of the women in the office, Nepotism Neddie, but Ellie thought they were just jealous because none of them could wear a sweater quite like Deanna, a true sweater girl. Later, Bonnie Munch leaned over the cubicle wall, her pendulous breasts just about falling out of her blouse (Ellie could see the top of her left nipple, just below a faded Rolling Stones tongue), and told Ellie about the hunk of a man she went to bed with the night before. "At first I was just going to blow him in his pickup," Bonnie said, "but when I saw how *big* he was, I just had to break off a piece. My husband finds out, the shit'll hit the fan for sure and I'll be dead. Hand to God." But Ellie drove Ralph, Judy, Deanna, and Bonnie out of her mind whenever she could—there'd been a man in her apartment the last three nights. She couldn't deny it anymore. Maybe a ghost man, but a man. Could it all have come from her lonely imagination? After all, she would have, at one time, loved to have had a boyfriend, a husband even, but the cards had never been in her favor or she'd never bothered to pick them up; fantasy had never become fact, and she'd long ago stopped hoping. So, could she have made it all up? No, whomever it was had been real; she was just about positive. Unless he actually *was* a ghost. (In which case, she would have an entirely different problem on her hands.) But tonight she'd find out for sure. Tonight she had a plan, and if there was one thing Elle Strunk was good at, it was making a plan and executing it. A man could be a good thing, but an invisible man was another.

+

Francis loved to masturbate even before he discovered invisibility. He did it in the bathroom, the bedroom, every single room in the house. The front porch, the back porch. The neighbor's shed. He wasn't a sex freak. He just liked to masturbate. It made him feel good. It was the principle of Occam's razor: all other things being equal, the simplest solution is best. The simplest solution to finding happiness for Francis was masturbation. Other than the mess, Francis saw no downside. Of course, being with a real girl instead of one conjured up by his imagination would be ideal, but until his invisibility breakthrough, a real girl was a distant dream. Francis was a science geek, and, as Ned frequently reminded him, science and math geeks don't get laid. They don't get the girl. Francis sometimes wondered if anyone got the girls *besides* the jocks, who knew nothing about Avogadro's law or the Woodward-Hoffmann rules, let alone the difference between Galileo's invariance and Einstein's theory of relativity. This was the stuff of living, not football and basketball and wrestling. One would think the girls would be flocking to the boys with the most knowledge, not the biggest muscles. Alas, the world worked in mysterious ways not always quantifiable by data and samples. But invisibility had changed all that; when he was invisible, he could be anyone.

Ellie Strunk lived right across the driveway. Her apartment building was on the corner, and the windows of Francis' bedroom faced Ellie Strunk's bedroom windows. Many nights, he'd down the lights and stare across the drive (he didn't even know her name until he stole a glimpse at the buzzer system by the apartment building's front door), but it was a frustrating experience. She always closed her blinds at exactly the same time every night, and she always did so completely clothed. Even before he could turn invisible, he was falling in love with her—or at least he thought he was. He only knew love from books and movies, and while this love didn't fit into any of the plot devices he'd encountered, it felt real enough to him. He wrote her name in his school notebooks. He planned his nights around the time when she closed her blinds. He even followed her to the bus stop one day (although he wondered if he was being creepy) and would have rode the bus with her to work if he didn't have first period English. (Definitely creepy.) But now that he could turn invisible whenever he wanted, Ellie Strunk was uniquely available, so to speak (possibly bringing creepiness to a whole new level).

The first night had been frightening. He had to make sure he'd followed right behind her as she'd entered her apartment door. (He'd contemplated stealing her keys and having a copy of the door key made before Deck's Hardware closed, but then he remembered he'd still be invisible—the serum didn't wear off quickly—and he hadn't wanted to cause old Mr. Deck's heart any undue stress.) That first night, he didn't know where to stand and constantly bumped into furniture. (The latter issue remained a problem.) He thanked the gods she didn't have a dog or a cat. The hardest thing to get used to (and maybe the best part of the experience despite its degree of difficulty) was that he was completely naked. His serum (which he dubbed the Ellie Serum) didn't turn clothes invisible. Just skin and hair plus finger and toe nails. (He'd forgotten to account for nails during the trial phases, and at first he'd resembled a seventeen-year-old, mostly transparent, Max Schreck in *Nosferatu*.) But it worked just fine now, and as Ellie Strunk changed for bed, his invisible boner shuddered in the breeze coming from the open window. Although he had no plans for touching her—that would be dead wrong, he knew—he still almost came right then and there without even playing with it. But he didn't, not that night. But the third night—the third night he set himself up in the corner of her room in the wicker chair and did it while she undressed. Disconcertingly, his sperm was not invisible; it appeared, briefly, as a floating mosaic of white splashes. He started to ease out of her bedroom, glad that the invisibility hid his red face as well as his shameful, wilting member. That was also the first night Ellie spoke to him. As he was leaving her room, she said, "Good night, ghost," and he almost replied. But he knew if he did, he'd blow it. What he had here was special. Ned would sully his drawers if he knew. Love: exciting and new. He hoped he hadn't stained her carpet.

+

Ellie poured the olive oil in a little bowl and placed it on her night table. It was going to be messy, but no worse than what the ghost had left on her floor. She hoped the ghost (or whatever he was) wasn't in the apartment as she prepared his unmasking, but he still bumped into things, and Ellie was usually able to hear him navigating her furniture with all the finesse of a cow performing ballet, so she thought she was safe. What disturbed her as she continued with her preparations was the way her heart was beating—like it was excited. It had been that way all day. It was like she'd met some dreamboat from the bodice rippers Bonnie Munch always read. *Oh, that's just your luck, Ellie Strunk*, she thought. Getting all hot and heavy over someone she couldn't see. But she *could* see part of him, couldn't she? The seed he'd left on her carpet last night. Yes, some landed on his chest (or where she thought his chest should be), but a good amount made it to the floor, and Ellie had scraped some up and put it in a small glass to determine what it was. Because of her limited experience, sperm seemed out of the question at first, but the heavy breathing and sounds of exertions that had preceded its trajectory to her bedroom carpet made all her other conjectures moot. It was spunk, plain and simple. Man spunk. A fact. And her heart beat faster. What little fear she'd had the first night had vanished. She looked forward to his visits, even his exertions. She just needed to know he was real. Her only empirical evidence was the semen, the splooge, the spermatozoa. She reminded herself: all other things being equal, the simplest solution is best.

So it was with a near-bursting chest that she noted the time and unlatched the front door as she'd done the night before and made some popcorn to eat while she watched the end of *Little Children* on cable. She heard the door squeak but didn't turn around to look. (What would she see anyway? He wouldn't come in ejaculating.) When the movie finished, she washed the popcorn bowl. In an effort to distract herself, she contemplated the film's explosive ending—so different from the novel's. She didn't want the ghost to hear her pounding heart. Would he be surprised that in addition to literary novels and encyclopedias, she occasionally read the bodice rippers that Bonnie lent her? Would he understand that the romance novels were only for those nights when she couldn't sleep and those weekends when she was so lonely even facts couldn't help, those moments when she thought she would implode and disappear— become invisible? And yet that was what she craved sometimes: to be invisible. Because she was already, metaphorically. Judy and Bonnie would prattle on to whoever sat in her cubicle. Ralph hit on every woman within visual-raping distance, and Deanna barely looked at Ellie when she dropped off her forms every morning. (Ellie thought she and Deanna would make a great pair, best friends even, but she didn't know why.) Nobody at the office had the slightest clue of her likes and dislikes. Nobody ever asked her a question that didn't already come with a response. "Did you see the game?" "I…" "Flyers are going all the way this year." Invisible.

She washed her face and looked in the mirror—still there. She listened: floorboard squeaks, a stumble, the rustling groan of wicker. The ghost was in her bedroom chair again. She entered and undressed slowly, stretching out naked on top of the comforter. She had never felt less self-conscious about her body before. It was like she was giving all of herself to the ghost—well, at least more than she'd ever given to anyone else or even thought about giving. The ghost rocked back and forth on her wicker chair, preparing to release his ghost sperm. Ellie reached over to her nightstand, grabbed the bowl of olive oil, and threw it at the rocking ghost. And there he was! Only he wasn't a ghost—he was the Invisible Man! A skinny Invisible Man with an engorged penis squeezed in his right hand.

"Who are you?" Ellie asked.

"Francis," said the Invisible Man, his voice tremulous and cracking.

There were a couple of minutes of silence during which Francis' boner never relented.

"I'm eighteen," he said.

"Oh," she replied.

The oil seemed to drip audibly.

"I love you," the Invisible Man said finally. "I'm in love with you."

"With me?" Ellie couldn't believe her ears.

"You're so beautiful, Miss Strunk," Francis said, "I can hardly stand it."

Another minute of quiet passed until Ellie broke it. "You can finish if you want. I'll clean up."

The Invisible Man brought himself to a moaning conclusion, drops of oil glistening on his body as he did so, mixing with the inevitable spunk.

"You'll come back tomorrow night?" Ellie asked. "I'll leave the door unlocked."

"Okay," the Invisible Man said, "after I finish my homework," and then he was gone, the light from the streetlamps reflecting off the oil, as she watched from the window.

Ellie hugged herself and thought, *I have a boyfriend...after all these years. I'm going to marry him someday when he's older...and isn't that a silly thought?* But she knew it for a fact...Ellie Strunk and Francis the Invisible Man.

As she cleaned up his come with a washcloth, she sang quietly to herself: "*Sometimes we'll sigh / sometimes we'll cry / and we'll know why / just you and I / know true love ways.*"

-end-

Bernard's Cocktail Party Redux

It smells (and tastes) like stale breath and chalk. (The stale breath comes from teaching all day.) There is also a political science professor who insists upon removing his shoes wherever he is (classroom, meeting, etc.), and his feet define malodorous. The stale breath is soon replaced by alcohol fumes—no one drinks quite like college professors, especially those who expected to be on the *New York Times* bestsellers list by now, not teaching undergrads Edith Wharton and *Moby-Dick* (again). As one works the room, the fumes seem to change odoriferous colors: pale yellow hoppiness for Professor McKendrick, the chemistry chair; pink lady daintiness-about-to-be-thrown-all-to-hell for the lit professor all the men call Legs; angry Irish whiskey wood tones for Professor McGonagal, about whom it is said that if it weren't for the smell of Tullamore Dew on his breath, there would be no smell at all, he is that unnoticeable.

The host of the party and his partner only play Bob Dylan at these functions—and only the *Desire* album and only on vinyl, which means the host is constantly dashing to the stereo to turn the record over. During the rare instances when the educated mass is not jabbering to one another (the volume increasing with every sip), Mr. Zimmerman's shredded voice can be heard lamenting the fate of Rubin "Hurricane" Carter. At odd times, the hosts' excitable cocker spaniel barks his own melody for a minute or two, but no one listens. Mr. Pitzel, as usual, climbs on a chair and sings "Maneater."

The sights there are to see! Many professors came directly from a full day of teaching, so J. C. Penney sport coats and conservative, patterned skirts are the norm. But there are those lucky few who were able to run home and dress to the nines. Two psychology professors and a secretary from the biology department proudly display their wrinkled cleavage. The Latin professor (who calls himself Lucky Larry) has slicked back his hair with what appears to be Vaseline. The grasshoppers and pink ladies stand out against a sea of muted brown clothing and pale teacher flesh. The apartment was recently done over and resembles an unimaginative IKEA display. Most everything has a faux mahogany finish. The rug is red. The dog is black. The host's partner wears a peach colored shirt beneath his grey pinstripe jacket. He is easily six foot five and must duck as he moves from room to room. It is most precarious when he runs to turn over the record. On the faux mahogany bar, there is a bowl of Trojans, mostly blue, some red, almost all expired. Mrs. Marshall, the librarian, who has been alternating dirty martinis and German stout all evening, laughs hysterically whenever she catches sight of the bowl. Her shrieks disturb the dog, who moves to a corner and passes bitter gas as a response. Mrs. Marshall, an avid L.L.Bean fan, is wearing a Fresh for Fall green blouse with one button in the middle missing, her pale yellow bra clearly visible, and when she proceeds to give herself sobriety tests by blowing up several Trojans, she is a rainbow.

Soon hands used for shaking in greeting become hands used for copping feels. Everyone grips everyone else. The handsome young stud of the English department prepares to leave early with the wallflower writing teacher. While they put on their scarves, their hands touch briefly, and the static electricity is a promising visible blue.

-end-

I Like a Girl in a Dress

World is suddener than we fancy it.
Louis MacNeice

The man in the black hat kicked up dust on the road to the big yellow house. Marigold would have barely made him out were it not for his padre hat, riding high upon his head, black like the gloom that haunted every heart. No half-remembered shadow, it was the kind of black that rose up out of the dust of her dreams and threatened to overtake every single bit of color until all was as dark as the angel of death. Marigold shuddered. That dream and variations had plagued her behind closed eyes for going on twelve years, and she was only fourteen. Now here was the hat, as if conjured from her nightmares, resting atop a man of dust.

Marigold was still dressed from church in the white dress with little flowers sewn along the hem in red thread. Her arms were bare, and they were tan from working in her grandpa's fields—although they were Grandma's fields now since Grandpa had passed on. Corn mostly, rows and rows of tassels and silk and green husks. The nearest town was Anchor Hop and that wasn't real close. The farms out here in the hamlet of Maes Mawr weren't part of Mondauk County, but they weren't officially part of anything else either, Marigold thought. For example, Grandma paid the water bill to Mondauk and voted there too, but Montgomery County collected their trash and policed their roads. It was a huge swath of no man's land, though Grandma always said it was *somebody's* land whenever she paid the tax bill.

Marigold ran to her bedroom window—a better vantage point, she thought—and the man in the black hat was now fully enclosed in the dust, so not even his hat visible, but she could *feel* his approach, as inevitable as anything ever was. Marigold busied herself by pretending to put on makeup (which her grandma strictly forbade) and by reading a passage from *Pride and Prejudice*, the book she'd been gnawing over all summer. She still wasn't sure what she felt about that Mr. Darcy, but she figured Miss Elizabeth knew best.

She went back to the window just in time to see the man in the black padre hat emerge in the dust. He apparated piecemeal, hat first, followed by a white button-down shirt with the sleeves rolled up, then dirty grey jeans, and finally a pair of work boots that had seen better days. It was only through careful scrutiny of the dust for several moments that she was able to discern the occupant of the ensemble, who chewed upon a stalk of onion grass with both hands in his pockets. At least he wasn't a Bible salesman or a Jehovah's Witness—the latter didn't always come out as far as Hawkhurst Farm, although Marigold had a respectable collection of *Watchtower* magazines. No, the man in the black hat was different. He walked in a curious manner like he didn't have a care on God's green earth. But it was with a purpose too—the two combined, so that he *appeared* to be insouciant but in fact was not.

This was worrisome, but not overly so. Marigold's grandma had gone to Anchor Hop to play bridge with the ladies like she did every Sunday after church, her cardigan draped around her shoulders "in case there's a draft." Marigold welcomed the time alone in the house. During the summer weeks, she worked in the fields with Old Jake the caretaker (a teddy bear of a man) and the itinerant field hands who kept their distance, with her being the granddaughter and all. But to be alone in the house for a time on Sundays—that was heaven. She could lounge anywhere she liked, loll about with her book, no religious music on the radio, no preachers on the television. (Her grandma was overly fond of Jesus.) But it also meant she was isolated. Old Jake's house was further down the road, and the fields were empty on Sunday. Marigold was of the age where she balanced a lack of inhibition when it came to her behavior around men with a deep-seated fear of what they were capable of when given half an opportunity—at least that was how Grandma put it, and she hadn't been smiling when she said so. Marigold didn't know if it was true, for she trusted Old Jake and she had no fear around boys, who were more curiosities than threats. Still, there was a reason why she was being raised by her grandma—she just didn't want to look at it too closely.

She peeked out the window again, and the man in the black hat seemed to be gone, but his dust cloud remained—he just didn't appear to be inside of it anymore. It was more of a feeling than a fact but didn't any good fact start with a feeling? Marigold ran to the window on the other side of the room: no sign of him. This was (almost) more disturbing than if he had appeared in her bedroom. Unless he walked straight into the corn fields—at which point maybe she should run the half-mile to Old Jake's. The only other place he could be where she couldn't see him from her window was...

Marigold descended the stairs two at a time and wasn't even halfway down when she heard someone knocking upon the front door. The man in the black hat was on the porch. She hurried down the stairs, achingly aware of the fact that her legs were bare—she'd ditched her pantyhose directly after church. She didn't want the stranger to see her legs—they were beginning to look like women's legs. Her skirt would have been cover enough, but the dress was white. She thought he might be able to see through it; it was too hot to wear a slip and somehow she'd gotten away it. (Her skirt, her dress, had to be modest, Grandma said, but her arms could be bare, which made no sense to her.) The stranger knocked upon the door again, as if he knew she was in here, mentally killing time while primping her blonde hair in the foyer mirror and trying to extract her sweaty bangs from her equally sweaty forehead. She lifted her skirt briefly: no razor nicks. Good enough. *I mean, if he was to see my legs*, she thought. She only shaved the fine blonde hair that grew in fits and starts because the other girls did, but she still hadn't—

Marigold pulled the door open with both hands. He was taller than she'd expected, even without his padre hat, which he'd removed and held in his hands. He was in desperate need of a hot shower and could use a shave too—a shave and a haircut. And a fresh shirt. This one wasn't white up close. It was dusty and dirty and stained with crimson spots. She was glad the locked screen door was between them.

"Miss, sorry to bother you on this beautiful day of the Lord, but I was passin' through, goin' southerly you might say, and I was wonderin' if you might have a bit of work for a time. I can do just 'bout anythin'. I've *done* just 'bout everythin': picked apples, shucked corn, plowed fields, shod horses even. Fixed automobiles? You betcha. All of it, miss. Done paintin', carpentry, even a bit of roofin'." He paused to look at the sky before continuing. "Dug cellars *and* graves, miss. You might say I get 'em comin' and goin'. Don't matter much which."

Marigold found it difficult to say anything. He was handsome like a pirate, arresting even, like no male adult she'd ever taken notice of before. Underneath all the dirt, there was something familiar and appealing about the man—and something unsettling too, as if the familiar was the scariest thing she'd ever seen. (Maybe her grandma had been right.) She lifted her ponytail off her neck and wiped the sweat away. She knew the man was watching her, watching the way her collarbone was exposed when she lifted her arms. Taking in her bare biceps and triceps. Staring at the pockets of her underarms.

"Miss?"

She brushed an imaginary fly away from her face.

"I'm sure I know nothing about it, mister. My grandma runs the place. She's the one that does the hiring."

Marigold's nipples got hard and she crossed her arms, suddenly feeling very fourteen.

"No need to cross your arms, little sister. Them's God's way of tellin' you which way the wind blows. And when to get out of the way."

"I'm sure I don't know nothing about that either."

The man laughed a phlegmy laugh and took a pack of Marlboro Reds from his shirt pocket. After offering her one (she shook her head no wistfully—she longed to be bad, at least a little, but it wasn't in her), he lit a Blue Tip with his thumb and suddenly the porch was filled with curlicues of rancid smoke.

"Well, thank you for the information, miss—'bout your grandma. Maybe when I come back this way, I'll look her up for a job."

"That would be fine."

She was shifting her weight from foot to foot.

"Maybe I'll come look you up, missy. I like a girl in a dress."

She stopped moving.

"My name's Marigold."

The stranger smiled.

"Like this house?"

"This house is yellow. A marigold is a flower. They can be yellow *or* orange. Not just one."

"Like you, missy? Not one thing, but right in between?"

"I'm sure I don't—"

"I'm sure you do. I'm sure you know plenty 'bout it. That's why you crossed your arms. 'Cause you didn't know *why* your buttons popped."

"I'm not alone in here."

The stranger blew out a tunnel of smoke.

"Yes, you are."

And she remembered Billy Slatterly taking her to the alcove behind the holly tree, both of them eager and scared.

"You first," Billy had said, but his pants were already undone and he'd pulled it out. *That's what the older girls make a big deal over?* She'd left her underwear somewhere between Hawkhurst Manor (as the house was called) and the trail leading to the reservoir—she'd thought skinny dipping was in the offing; she was wrong. She hiked her skirt up and squatted down and before she could start a stream, Billy got so excited, he peed himself, all down the front of his trousers. She reached out to help him, maybe sneak him into Hawkhurst Manor through the root cellar, stick him in the tub and the trousers in the washer, but he ran into the night, away from her grandma's outdoor soirée, and the next time she saw him, he barely nodded in her direction. Later on in school, she heard from several sources that Billy Slatterly claimed to have seen her ginny, and Marigold figured she deserved it and would neither confirm nor deny, which just made is worse.

Best to be honest when it's hardest, she thought.

"Yes, I am," Marigold said to the man on the porch. "I am alone."

The man spit and ground out his cigarette with his boot.

"That's what I thought, missy. Just you and me, huh? Mano-a-mano, as it were."

"What's your name?"

"My name, missy? I have many names. But then, don't we all? At different times?"

"What's your name right now?"

Marigold knew the stranger was toying with her, but for some reason she was leaning into the teasing like Spike, the cat that lived in the barn, leaned into her legs.

"Right now? Right now my name is Sirius."

"The dog star."

"For the dog days of summer, missy."

"Is that your first name or last?"

"What do you want it to be?"

"Your first," she answered laughing, before clapping a hand over her mouth.

Sirius smiled, and she could see he was missing a tooth on the left side, but it did not detract from his looks.

"I could ask you a similar question," he said.

"You could?"

"Sure. Which you is the real you? But later. We have pleasantries to get through first."

"Okay."

Sirius began rolling his right sleeve up even further.

"Want to see something?"

"Yes I do."

"Here you go, missy."

On his forearm was tattooed in black the words "Memento Mori."

Marigold shrugged.

"I've seen tattoos before."

Sirius smiled.

"Do you know what that means? 'Memento mori?' "

Marigold shook her head.

" 'Remember you are mortal.' Remember you are mortal, girl. Do you understand that?"

Marigold nodded.

"Do you? I guess we're gonna find out, you and me, aren't we?" He spit again. "Not much time left: that's one way of lookin' at it. Another is: do what you want, 'cause you're gonna *expire*, missy. Sooner? Later? Does it matter? Don't matter at all, I say. 'Tis the way of the world and that there's the point."

Marigold wondered if this was her final moment, if Sirius was going to kill her here at her grandma's house. It briefly occurred to her that she could just shut the door, lock it, and call the police, but she didn't, and she no longer hid the fact that her nipples were hard. Her brain yelled, "run, hide!" but her heart, her feet seemed compelled to ignore that inner voice.

"Do you have any fresh lemonade?"

Marigold was startled. She'd thought for sure the ravishment wouldn't begin with lemonade.

"Y-y-yes," she stuttered.

"Could I bother you for a glass? Mighty hot out here." He squinted at the sky and spit. "Might even thunderstorm. It do catch up quick, don't it? Even I can't escape that. Always gotta clean up after me." He brought his gaze back to her face after a quick glimpse at her chest. " 'Bout that glass, missy? Extra sugar, if you don't mind."

Her feet could move again! With haste, Marigold fixed Sirius a glass with plenty of ice. She thought about spitting in it but didn't. It would be out of character. Her grandma had raised her better.

As she stirred in the additional sugar, she had the distinct feeling that she'd been *allowed* to go to the kitchen.

On the way to the door, Marigold paused. This was the test, wasn't it? She'd have to undo the latch and open the screen door to hand Sirius the glass. Once the door was open, anything could happen. She'd be his and the game would be up. No more guessing; it would become very real. Then again, she was raised to not refuse a thirsty man water.

For a second she thought he was gone. The porch looked empty, but then Sirius rose from where he'd been lying like a dog and revealed himself.

"Ah, now missy, that looks like a glass for a man."

"What are you going to do to me?"

"Right now, I'm gonna drink your lemonade."

"That it?"

"I double swear. Cross my heart and hope to die, stick a needle in my eye."

Marigold laughed in spite of the knot of fear pushing on her bladder.

"I'm gonna hold you to that, Mr. Sirius."

"Call me Dog Star," he said and grinned a grin that showed she was wrong: he was missing a tooth on the *right* side.

"I'll do no such thing. I'm gonna unlatch the hook now."

"Growlin' with thirst."

She opened the screen door and eased her hand out with the glass.

"This outta take care of that," she said, and Sirius grabbed her wrist and ran a long fingernail down the length of her arm.

"Close the door and lock it, Marigold. Don't open it no matter what you hear. I'll leave your grandma's glass on the porch. Don't open this door until you hear the rain."

Marigold slammed the screen door, locked it, then did the same with the front door, leaning her back against it, breathing hard. What the hell was going on? Sirius was acting like a werewolf only without the full moon. What if Sirius was still on the porch when her grandma came home? What then?

Even though she knew her heart and feet were free, she remained in that position for hours, watching the clock, listening for the rain. At one point, she heard scratching that sounded like it was coming from the other side of the front door, the locked screen door be damned, and she peed a little, but the scratching soon stopped. Exhausted, she slumped down and drifted off. When the rain finally came, when the thunder and the lightning provided the soundtrack to a real August downpour, she bolted upright, unlocked the doors, and stepped onto the porch. The glass was where Sirius said it would be. Everything looked the same, but it wasn't—or rather, *she* was different. She'd crossed over. She'd passed the test. Blood ran down her leg. She was a woman. She'd waited so long.

When her grandma found her, she was dancing in the rain in front of the house, her white dress sticking to her like a second layer of flesh. Her grandma tried to cover her up with her cardigan, for "everyone can see your naughty bits, Marigold," but Marigold just smiled and looked forward to the rest of her life: memento mori—remember you are mortal.

-end-

Tess of the Quivers

In the photograph, Mother and Father pose in front of a black, wrought iron gate, Mother proud in her cap and gown and a mere five months away from having me, fifteen months away from having my sister, a few years from their so-called marriage. If I had my druthers, if the space-time continuum allowed, I would go back to the black, wrought iron gate and tell them no, don't buy the cheapest ring they have at Maxie's (as the story goes); I would say, Mom, don't spend what remains of your college money for a wedding dress, and don't, whatever you do—you can give me away, abort me, go the single parent route—get so-called married. But of course I can't go back and change what happened. And none of us could have changed what happened to my sister. The past is murky for a reason: "the future's uncertain and the end is always near," to quote from one of my sibling's favorite songs.

My sister's name was Tess. "Not short for anything," she would tell people. "I am my own Tess." We lived in a large house in a somewhat affluent community, the town of Anchor Hop in Mondauk County. Our father was a teacher, Professor Robert L. Quivers, and he taught graph theory and combinatorics, probability, statistics, and game theory. The last was not to be confused with the rules of Monopoly or Risk or even chess as far as Tess and I were concerned—our father didn't play games. He was a balding, imposing man, who spoke slowly, as if weighing each word on his tongue, and he had little to do with us other than contributing the sperm. He was always on the second floor in his study reading or graphing or cursing at the chalkboard that stood in one corner of the room. Our mother's name was Mildred but everyone called her Millie. Silly Millie was Tess's name for her. And indeed, our mother *was* silly. Nervous silly. Nervous that we kids would bother the professor, nervous about getting us to school and picking us up (but never nervous about how we did unless one of us got an F and had to have a report card signed), nervous about how she looked and about how we looked— the professor liked a clean family, Mother said, a family he could show off at faculty dinners. But after our first one of these, the one where Tess "forgot" to wear underwear, flashing what he she called her sixteen-year-old beaver to tenured septuagenarians, Tess and I were never brought along again. That situation about sums up my family life during our teens: the professor slammed his study door after a silent ride home and locked himself in there for the rest of the night, Mother lectured Tess, gently, on what the appropriate audience for a beaver was, and I eavesdropped, a hapless virgin, eager for any news of female genitalia.

Things continued this way, the way they had for the first seventeen years of my life, for another year, the only differentiating events being my graduation and the gradual increase in our parents' fighting. When we were little, Tess used to call them "bouts of passion," and so they seemed: my mother would come out of her shell and teeter between complete submission and furious vengeance, and our father would trade (or surrender) his silence for thundering bolts of invective. As we were growing up and struggling with adolescence and puberty (I showed my first pubes to Tess and she let me squeeze her left breast—a most sorry act, one I never stopped thinking about), our parents' battles became background noise. We might be awakened from our sleep and wander to one another's rooms, but we were never scared, never concerned. Many of the fights would swiftly be followed by a violent squeaking of mattress springs, and Tess would shape her left index finger and thumb into a circle and thrust three fingers from her right hand in and out of it. Then we would go to sleep in the same bed, even when we were older, reading our favorite novel to each other until Tess started to drift off, and I would strategically try to place a hand near the breast I had once touched (in case it accidentally moved my way), but Tess would always reach down and squeeze my balls if I got too close. "A boob is a boob," a sleepy Tess would say, "but balls are forever." When I turned eighteen and Tess seventeen, the parental arguing had turned pugilistic. Mother went through a glass partition, and Father had to have stitches to his bald pate. "Don't even think about copping a feel now, mister," Tess said to me in bed. "After all this, I might just tear your balls right off and wear 'em as earrings."

When Father left later that year, it was like the house itself breathed a sigh, but still, we were concerned. "I've accepted a position at Boston College. I will be able to continue my research there as well as teach less parochial students. Your mother will receive a stipend and I should be home for most holidays. It's a two year contract." And with that, the professor was gone. Only the chalkboard remained. Tess celebrated his absence and soon browbeat our mother into getting a dog, a yellow Labrador retriever, who Tess named, appropriately, Balls, for they hung so low you feared for their egg-like delicacy every time he hopped off the sofa or bounded up the stairs. Balls' name was a reminder, Tess told me, that her boobs were off limits due to DNA restrictions.

It was a quieter house with the professor gone, but Mother's sadness, her longing, was loud enough for everyone to hear despite her careful silence and her attempts to hide her drinking. Even Balls seemed to sense it and covered his ears with his paws whenever Mother began pacing in the kitchen. (At least that's the way I remember it.) Almost anything could go on at our house now, and Tess entertained several young men who surely were granted the opportunity to touch her boobs. "I stop liking them once I'm doe, so I don't let them finish," Tess explained. "That's why they keep coming back." I nodded but both of us knew I had never come close to having intercourse. I tried to talk to Tess about safe sex and she just smiled.

"Carpe diem," she said.

"Memento mori," I reminded her.

The professor's two year contract was extended. Mother started drinking in the afternoons, and our attempts at hiding or removing the liquor had little effect. Without saying a word to us about the missing booze, Mother would drive to the State Store and be half in the bag by three. She also started to go to church just about every day. I was now attending Arcadia University, where the professor had taught, and I found the student body the opposite of parochial. Tess had left college to find work, and her latest retail experience had her selling lipstick and facial cream to Botoxed ladies of a certain age. Except for the drinking, life in Anchor Hop hummed along nicely, interrupted only by Mother taking a spill or Tess bringing home her latest manager and watching him leave shirtless, pants undone, sexually unsatisfied. Tess didn't let anyone finish, not even pull out. I know. I watched on two different occasions, and compared with the flailing of her partners, Tess looked extraordinary, in control, with Balls close by as a deterrent. What we didn't know was that the arrival of Father's household stipend was becoming erratic and soon Mother feared losing the family manse.

Our mother never wore the wedding band from Maxie's, and we never questioned it. But over a pitcher of margaritas one afternoon, the truth came tumbling out, a drunk from a taproom. The first words we understood amidst her slurring were "Stipe" and "Mason." It sounded like a law firm, I said. It made little sense that Mother was referring to Mason Stipe, who was a few years older than us and worked at the gas station just outside of town. Mason wasn't the brightest fellow. Tess pronounced that he was a few peas short of a casserole. The professor once said Mason fell out of the stupid tree and hit every branch on the way down. What Mason Stipe had to do with our mother's distress, we had no idea, but we were about to find out, and when we did, everything would be different. Mother let it all out on a wave of alcohol fumes. Mason Stipe was our half brother. The professor was actually legally married to his mother, Joanna, who retained her maiden name, Clarkson, when the professor appeared to be doing more than tutoring coeds. Of course, our father hadn't actually been a professor then. When our parents met, he was a grad student with a new name, a married grad student, who would soon be dating our mother, and she knew nothing about a wife or a child or a legally changed name—not yet. (That we were Stipes not Quivers made Tess shudder.) Mother made her pact with the devil a couple of years later when it was already too late to turn back and she had children of her own to protect. Mother accepted his explanations (which she never revealed) and pushed it out of her mind, never asking him to divorce Ms. Clarkson and never threatening to go to the authorities. The professor wrote a check to Joanna Clarkson each month, but Mother never asked for the mailing address. In fact, until the incident in the supermarket, Mother had pushed it so far out of her mind with prayer and spirits, she acted as if she had almost forgotten the situation completely. Ms. Clarkson was staring at Mother through a hole in a display of albacore tuna when the woman said, "They look nothing like you. They look like him." The end of the illusion, which is why Mother told us. Turned out Ms. Clarkson lived close by—two blocks away—and the professor didn't mail the check. He delivered it (and God knows what else) every month before he left for Boston. Now he just put it in the post.

Of course, Tess and I brought Mason Stipe to our house for iced tea and crumb cake, but the man-boy was disoriented—either that or he'd lost the ability to speak. Mother had locked herself in her bedroom after Tess informed her of her intention to introduce Mason Stipe "to proper society." (And it was all Tess' idea. I was skittish and ambivalent—curiosity aside, what did we need with a half-sibling who pumped gas and checked tire pressure?) But Mason never spoke the entire visit. Not when offered refreshments or a tour of the house. Not when shown the professor's study. Not when Balls suspiciously sniffed his. Not even when Tess lifted her shirt and showed Mason her boobs. Tess said beforehand if Mason didn't react—and he didn't, not one bit—then he must be brain dead, immune to all stimuli except the bell that rang whenever a car drove over a hose at the gas station, which is where we dropped him off, both of us disappointed and a little frightened. How many chromosomes were we away from being a silent idiot like Mason Stipe? The professor had a lot to answer for.

But in truth no questions were asked of him. He and mother rarely spoke. He was staying in Boston for who knows how long, perhaps germinating another family. Tess declared herself liberated— Mother was too weak to be a shackle of any consequence. Tess said if the professor was free, then so was she. What this meant, I didn't know yet, but the reverberations would be felt until the sorry end of her life in Anchor Hop and would continue all through mine.

With the professor's checks arriving with significantly less frequency and it looking more and more like we were the next family to be left floundering in the professor's wake, Mother decided we needed a boarder to make up the shortfall. A boarder in upscale Anchor Hop would be a scandal, but nonetheless a discreet classified ad was placed in the *Mondauk Common* and the professor's study was cleaned out except for the desk and the chalkboard. My old bed was reconstructed there and curtains were hung to give it a more homey touch. Tess and I watched from the stairs as Mother interviewed the few applicants, but most were not in the habit of steady employment, and Mother wished to have no adults lounging around her home during working hours. As the last man left, hat in his hands, Mother had her head in hers; she moaned softly, steadily. I stood up to go to her, but Tess restrained me. It was as if she knew, for the buzzer rang, and Mother ran to answer it, and Ronnie Savage stood in the doorway, a dirty black fedora cocked on his head, his thumbs jammed into his jeans. "Do you have steady employment?" Mother asked breathlessly. "Yes, ma'am, I most certainly do. Stock shelves at the supermarket down yonder. Done just about everythin' though." *Down yonder.* Tess and I, sitting side by side on the stairs, looked at one another. Where was this applicant from? "Dug cellars *and* graves, ma'am. You might say I get 'em comin' and goin'. Don't matter much which." Mother didn't even blink. Tess and I hung on every word. "The room's not much but it's cozy. Has a desk and a blackboard, which you can use at your discretion. I have children. Two. And a dog. Can you afford the rent? It's one hundred dollars a week, but it's only three hundred if you pay for the whole month." The man cleared his throat, started to say something, thought better of it and shook his head instead. "I'll take it," he finally said. "Been livin' just ahead of the storm. Time to lay some roots." And when he said "lay some roots," he turned his head and looked directly up the stairs at Tess. No one else but me noticed Balls growling the entire time—unless I made Mr. Savage up out of whole cloth, in which case maybe Balls was growling at me for having such a twisted imagination, one that would include his demise. But I'm getting ahead of myself.

So Ronnie Savage moved in with his meager belongings, which consisted of some clothes and a photo album of children's school pictures. With Tess finally clued in to Balls' discomfort, we kept a ceaseless vigil on Mr. Savage, even one day, a week after he moved in, following him as he went door to door in our neighborhood. Some of those doors were slammed in his face, others stayed open for a bit, but those more often than not ended in a slam too. Puzzled, we huddled by the large sycamore at the end of our street. We'd never seen his application. Was Mr. Savage a salesman? A bad one? Was he a Jehovah's Witness? We were debating these considerations when Ronnie Savage appeared on the other side of the tree. "Good mornin', children," he said, doffing his black fedora. "Lookin' for me?" We shook our heads and he grinned, his lips stretching over his teeth, matching the way his hairline seemed to stretch back his scalp. He was missing a tooth on the left side. "Savage sounds like a made-up name," Tess said. "I have many names," he responded. "What do you want it to be?" We knew all about men with more than one name. "Cat swingin' on your tongue? Well, I know your name, Ladyfingers." Tess stared at him. I thought it was meant to be an imposing stare, but she squeezed her legs together. "My, my. I love me some ladyfingers after supper." He ran a thumb over Tess' lips and she didn't move. Stand your ground, I thought. Good for you. Ronnie Savage popped his thumb into her mouth. "Anyone ever tell you, Ladyfingers, you got blowjob lips?" I couldn't believe he was doing this in front of me. Tess bit down on his thumb—hard. It was bleeding and Mr. Savage quickly stuck it into his mouth. "Pretty, pretty pony," he said, "I'll see you back at the homestead. I stay up late." With that, he was gone, and Tess ran across the street and knocked on a door Mr. Savage had just knocked on, and when she came running back, she was smiling wide. "He's a registered sex offender. He has to knock on everyone's door and tell them what he did." I stared in wonder. "What did he do?" I asked. "Diddled little kids, pulled out his doink on a bus, peed on a statue of the Virgin Mary," Tess said. "I don't know. But he was caught, and now he's living under our roof." I knew from the way Tess continued to smile that this information had somehow shifted the tone of her relationship to Mr. Savage, but I couldn't tell how. I just knew I had to get home. My stomach hurt like hell and my head pounded like Brazilian drums.

The night it all went down, I saw everything. How many times had I spied at the door of the professor's study? I knew every creak in the floorboards. I knew how to push open the door a crack without it squeaking. Tess knew I was watching. She knew I would not be able to resist. Before she went in, I almost said, "carpe diem" to her, but I didn't approve; I didn't think this was a wise way to seize the day. First she made Mr. Savage a glass of lemonade in the kitchen. (Mother was out again either imbibing or praying or both.) While he was taking his first sip, Tess asked him what he'd done to have to walk around the neighborhood so, and Mr. Savage did an exaggerated spit take before pretending to compose himself and smiling at me. I leaned against the stove with my arms crossed. "Well, little lady, seems someone was caught with his pants down, wasn't he?" He used his thumb to light a cigarette with a Blue Tip match, and the flame seemed to dance on his thumbnail for a moment before disappearing entirely. It was fitting metaphor for what would happen to Tess. "Come up to my room, Ladyfingers, and I'll show you exactly what I did to get Mr. Lawman all wet and messy." And Tess went with him. She brushed past me with only the slightest of looks—a look that was hungry, a look that was needy, a look that said this was the right revenge on our mousy, alcoholic mother and, more importantly, on our absentee, polygamist professor. Revenge was why she never let her romantic partners finish: Tess was angry at *all* men (except maybe me) and sperm was what drove men to evil, she conjectured, the need to seed, so she refused to be at all involved with spermatozoa. Blue balls were the best revenge, a dish best served piping hot.

Our Balls followed close behind her, and I knew she would be safe with our pooch. Balls would let nothing untoward occur with his Tess. The Lab was loyal to a fault, sitting on the bathroom floor while Tess shook the dew off her lily pad. But when I approached Mr. Savage's room, Balls was sitting outside staring at the door, which was already cracked open, and I pushed it further than our dog had done, and they were already naked, Mr. Savage's hairy back humping up and down upon my sister, his mouth greedily sucking her breasts, his hands alternately pulling her hair and choking her. Balls was beside me, growling low in his throat as if assessing the situation. Then Mr. Savage turned her over and sang to Tess, " *I'm a back door man...what the men don't know...the little girls...understand.'* " Mr. Savage spit into his palm and said, "Little lady, Ladyfingers." Tess screamed before her head was pushed into a pillow. I almost made a move then, and I should have. But Balls was ready. Mr. Savage's balls were quite visible and made an easy target. I did nothing. For years afterwards, I wondered whether it was lust or repulsion that held me back from rescuing Tess. Whatever the reason, my inaction was unforgivable. But Tess did what she always did: when she thought Mr. Savage was close (an easy assumption for he was very vocal about his progress), Tess managed to roll off the bed. There was my sister naked, the body I'd wondered about for so many of my adolescent years and beyond. Mr. Savage humped air for a couple of seconds before he fully realized what had happened, and when he did, he leapt off the bed and pushed Tess against the wall. That was enough for our dog. True to his name, Balls went straight for the balls. I heard the dog's jaws clamp shut, but he only nicked them, enough for blood to be everywhere quickly though. Mr. Savage screamed, turned around, and grabbed a knife he must have had hidden under the mattress. Balls leapt again, and Mr. Savage stabbed the Lab in the throat. When the dog landed with a thud on the bed, Mr. Savage continued to stab, almost severing Balls' head. Having screamed once, Tess never screamed again, and I pulled her out of the room, holding the door closed as Mr. Savage violently rattled the knob on the other side. Tess didn't talk to the police or our mother. The professor never called. It was up to me to speak to the authorities. The police took Ronnie Savage away, and I helped a silent Tess bury the remains of Balls under the boughs of the dogwood tree in the backyard.

And then Tess was gone, as if she were banished, but she wasn't. (My darkest fear was that she left to escape my torrid imagination.) Mother never said a word, just kept drinking until she died from cirrhosis. The professor never returned from Boston and his whereabouts today are unknown to me. No *blame* was placed on Tess, not even, I'm sure, by our murdered dog. But she left nonetheless, in the middle of the night, and ten years went by before I finally heard from her. I have no idea how she knew my address. I was a teacher by then—a biology, health, and sex-ed teacher (the virginity issue having finally been resolved by a nice girl in college)—and I had moved several times. It was a postcard. On one side, was a photograph of Tess and a chocolate Labrador retriever. On the flip side were written two words: carpe diem. Then it hit it me and I turned the card back round. Tess had a belly. And she was smiling. Tess was pregnant. She had let someone finish. For Tess, it was over.

For me, it will never be over. I relive it every night. The professor's chalkboard sits in my house, and I wrote memento mori on it when I received the postcard and never erased it. Tess told me once, while we were at a nativity play, "Don't be a Joseph," paraphrasing a line from a novel we both loved. But that is what I was and that is what I am. The bystander, the sidekick. Even my one shot at rescuing Tess ended in Balls' execution because I did nothing while my sister was raped. So today I teach kids about safe sex after having witnessed the least safe kind, and I go home at night and stare at the postcard and hope the baby will have my name and a sister like Tess if it's a boy. There is a postmark on the postcard, but I will never look for Tess. She doesn't want to be found, and besides, Josephs never do that. We sit and wait quietly, safe in our faith that someday the one whom we lost will return and our story can continue. A family of one is a family of none. Tess, baby, please come home.

-end-

Akathisia

They trudged through the snow. The crunch of their boots made the two of them sound like an invading army. The snow blanketed everything, erasing any delineation between a mailbox and a parked car. In what someone on the radio had called "a blizzard of biblical proportions" (Mark was glad Jacob had been showering then), everything was equal. There was nothing decrepit, Jacob said as they walked, nothing gaudy, no one visibly rich and no one poor, maybe even no good or evil, a snow globe Garden of Eden.

"Don't tell my parents I'm a Christian," Jacob said, as the muscles in his face jumped, first one side, then the other, and again; his arms shot out in front of him, and he appeared to bless the snow repeatedly when Mark bent down to retie one of his friend's boots.

Even in a blinding snow, there may still be a difference between crazy and not, Mark thought. Then again…he *was* walking practically in step next to His Holiness (as others in their dorm called Jacob), red noses dripping, eyes watering, the works, because his friend wanted to "feel" what God had wrought upon the town during his reluctant homecoming rather than take a cab (if they could have even found one).

"It hadn't occurred…I won't say a word," Mark replied. As if Jacob's parents didn't know, he thought. As if everyone didn't know. Jacob Ambrosia's true major at school had become Jesus. But Mark wasn't his best friend's evangelist partner; at most, Mark identified with Mary and Martha in the gospel of Luke, possibly horny and almost definitely looking for a man. (That had always been his interpretation anyway; he often didn't pay close attention to the content of his best friend's sermons; if Mark was around when Jacob preached to his flock, he usually didn't last longer than the opening reading.)

Jacob's favorite biblical passage was Genesis 32:30: " '…for I have seen God face to face, and my life is preserved,' " which Jacob son of Isaac said after wrestling the angel. But whenever Mark feigned ignorance of the existence of his namesake's gospel (which he did at times just to annoy his self-anointed roommate), Jacob liked to quote Mark 14:51-52, which concerned a young disciple who'd possibly witnessed Jesus' arrest or its aftermath: "And there followed him a certain young man, having a linen cloth cast about his naked body; and the young men laid hold on him: and he left the linen cloth, and fled from them naked." Mark blocked out most of what his friend said about Jesus, but he liked the naked part in this passage—only in Mark's daydreams, it was Jacob who was running around naked. It was a daydream he'd had in one form or another since they'd met freshman year. Not that his friendship was anything less than sincere, but he was in love with his college's resident prophet. (Typical—why should college be any easier than high school where he'd had a crush on the starting quarterback *and* the Advanced Chemistry teacher, Mrs. Calabrand?) Not everyone in the dorm knew of this love, but it seemed most suspected it, and maybe the only reason, Mark thought, he wasn't ostracized (or beaten up) was because Jacob was considered so holy everyone knew the roommates weren't shacking up after lights out.

I'm not the man they think I am at home
Oh, no, no, no, I'm a rocket man
Rocket man—burnin' out his fuse up here alone

His internal radio was interrupted when Jacob stopped them to obey a traffic light even though they hadn't seen a car on the road since they'd left the train station. He took his hands in and out of his pockets and rocked back and forth while they waited. "It would be just one more thing. My parents, they pay for everything, all that stuff. I have to answer to them for everything too, all their questions." His irritability was visible as he spoke, the next second: gone.

"Of course."

Only Jacob never answered for anything. Mark had been called many times by Mrs. Ambrosia (and sometimes Mr. Ambrosia). The only reason he answered the phone in their dorm room anymore was in case it was them. If they didn't reach Mark right away, their next panicked call would be to the RA, or worse, Jacob's cell phone. They trusted Mark; their son didn't talk to them anymore—not about anything they considered significant. It gave them desperate comfort to know "our Jacob was still enrolled in college," they told Mark. The rest of their statement—*and not out proselytizing on the streets, living among the urchins and bag people*—went unspoken. But if they called Jacob directly, a great row would ensue, and Mark would end up cutting his classes for the day in order to sit at his friend's bedside and wipe his forehead with a damp washcloth. (As much as he enjoyed playing nurse to Jacob, he could ill afford to miss many more classes.) "Do they not know that Joseph and Mary losing Jesus for three days is the third of the Seven Sorrows of the Virgin Mother? Do they not know that Joseph and Mary then finding Jesus in the Temple teaching the elders is the fifth Joyful Mystery of the Rosary?" Jacob would ask, setting aside his usual disdain for anything vaguely Roman Catholic, and Mark would shrug. (Mark didn't know from rosaries or the Seven Dolors of the Virgin Mary; he was Jewish by birth, and his knowledge of Jesus and the gospels, as well Martha and the various Marys, were due to his immersion in all things Jacob.) His friend would be nearly naked beneath the covers following a parental phone call, and as he comforted Jacob, Mark would resist touching himself, but the way his hard-on, begging for release of one kind or another, pushed insistently against his jeans as he talked his friend down, made those moments painful in more ways than one. (Love, Mark had learned, was not a many splendored thing, but a thing with many spikes and thorns; one either learned to love the pricks—no pun intended—or died upon the very thing desired most.)

The last time his friend's mother had called, Jacob had asked her, " 'How is it that ye sought me? Wist ye not that I must be about my Father's business?' "

Mrs. Ambrosia either hadn't quite heard the quote or had ignored it. (Mark believed the former.) If the Ambrosias had caught their son's most recent campus act—trying to resurrect a dead cat, Oreo, that lived with the girls in Knight Hall, a feline who Mark strongly suspected had been dispatched by Jacob for the sole purpose of his miracle training—they would have clutched their good hearts and gone straight to committing their remaining son to a psychiatric facility like Friends Hospital. (Although maybe not Friends, maybe Quincey Hospital instead, as Friends was founded by the Quakers; the Ambrosias—"cafeteria Catholics on their best day," as Jacob put it—might be a little gun shy when it came to Christianity of any stripe, especially a denomination as foreign as the Religious Society of Friends. But, as Jacob was fond of pointing out, his Jewish mother had converted when she'd met Jacob's father—not the most sincere reason for religious defection, he reasoned. Sex and love rarely were, Mark thought, but there were nights when he believed he would feign conversion just for a chance to be baptized semi-nude by His Holiness, for he'd once watched his best friend christen a man stripped to his underwear in a baby pool.) That Jacob may have been responsible for Oreo's death seemed to elude campus authorities, leaving only Mark to ruminate on the connection between this situation and the animal abuse perpetrated by Ted Bundy, David Berkowitz, and Jeffrey Dahmer early in their careers. No one looked for a semi-loner (Jacob at least had a best friend) with fetishist behavior or a marked Messianic complex.

Love always had its downside.

The snow, despite his boots, numbed Mark's toes, and when the friends glanced at one another, their teeth chattered in time.

...no one visibly rich and no one poor... Shivering, Mark thought the unfortunates freezing in alleyways in the city or shaking beneath their blankets in putrid shelters would beg to differ.

+

Anchor Hop was the town (or borough) in Mondauk County with the largest houses, the most expansive backyards, and the newest, most expensive cars parked in triple garages or at the end of long (gated) driveways. The Ambrosia house was imposing: four stories, a corner property at least a block away from any neighbor with a couple of acres that ran from the back of the house to the edge of Pennypack Woods.

Mark looked Jacob over as they walked up the drive. There were dark bags beneath his friend's eyes—evidence of his recurring insomnia. They gave his countenance a grave aspect.

" 'Verily, verily, I say unto thee,' " Jacob whispered to Mark, as the latter knocked on the door. " 'Except a man be born again, he cannot see the kingdom of God.' "

"If you don't want them to know, just keep it in your pants, okay, pal? Everything's gonna be fine. Just a routine, holiday-oriented visit." Screw identifying with Mary and Martha; Mark felt he was auditioning for the Judas role: he'd promised to deliver Jacob to the Ambrosias for a holiday dinner, and while that hadn't been an easy sell to his friend, Mark knew he also had to present a relatively mentally stable Jacob—the Jacob he'd painted in his many phone conversations with the Ambrosias. But tonight Mark would be lying to himself if he didn't admit that he wanted the visit to go smoothly for another reason, a fantasy really: maybe Jacob's parents would insist that they stay over because of the severity of the storm, and he and Jacob would have to share his best friend's childhood bed.

Maybe snug as two bugs in a rug, there would be a conversion of another sort.

But the real reason Mark agreed to accompany Jacob like a prison guard to his friend's childhood home was that he suspected the Ambrosias were on the verge of throwing in the towel and forcing Jacob to withdraw from college. His erratic grades and wild behavioral swings, from fervent preaching to sequestering himself, had raised all sorts of alarms. Mark didn't think he could live with Jacob gone. Anything but that.

Mrs. Ambrosia opened the door. She was very thin, her hair an orangey-red, a vague old lady scent coming from her exposed, post-middle-aged wrinkled cleavage. Her hug lasted too long, and Mark wasn't even her son. The one she shared with Jacob seemed impersonal, as if both parties were afraid to commit to the hug—for very different reasons, Mark was sure. Mr. Ambrosia, in his blue sweater vest, squeezed Mark's hand hard and called him son. In the eggshell white foyer, photographs of Jacob's brother Jareth lined the walls in matching silver frames. Jacob grinned from a couple of them, the Norman Rockwell little brother.

Dinner was just the four of them. Jacob's frequently visiting cousin Jackie, she of the red hair and freckled bosom, was unfortunately not in town for the holidays—what holidays there were. No Christmas tree blinked from a corner, no stockings hung above the fireplace with care, no presents glittered in a pile. No wreaths, no Johnny Mathis, no eggnog, no outside lights. The Ambrosias, according to Jacob, had given up Christmas as easily as they had given up Christ. They'd been Easter and Christmas Catholics before Jareth's death; afterwards they had abjured everything to do with Jesus and His teachings. The holidays were just another excuse to gather together, like Thanksgiving. At first Jacob didn't mind, he'd told Mark. He'd never felt particularly close to his faith, and the rituals were more of a pain than anything else. He'd wished for a sister to take over assisting with the cookie baking and other nonsense. Jackie didn't quite fill the bill, helpful as she was— she was too much the rebel, dating older men, dying her hair outrageous colors, justifying multiple sex partners. Jacob had confessed to Mark that he'd frequently masturbated about Jackie before he found Christ. He wasn't the only one, Mark had thought. It was a total nightmare: he jerked off to both Jacob *and* his female cousin, but Jackie mostly because she seemed so slutty that Mark imagined she wouldn't so much take his virginity as devour it, maybe even, as doubtful as it seemed, bring him back to heterosexuality (if he'd truly been born straight). As doubtful as that scenario seemed, it would certainly make life easier, he thought—and if he was with Jackie, married her even, he'd always be close to Jacob.

While they ate their salads, Mark watched his friend's legs march in place; during the main course, they shot straight out. Jacob seemed unaware of the movements going on beneath the table, as if parts of his body still wrestled with the angel. Mark hoped Jacob didn't get a charley horse, a frequent occurrence that often lasted up to twenty minutes. These (and all symptoms and side-effects) Jacob interpreted as afflictions from Lucifer. He was to bear these for Christ, he'd said to Mark, but he couldn't help but struggle to be free of the pummeling, tortuous spasms. Someone had told him to squeeze his earlobes to help end a Charley horse, and Mark often found his friend laying on the floor, one leg or both raised straight out, his face a portrait of pain, squeezing his earlobes until they were blood red.

Mrs. Ambrosia passed the peas for a third time to her son, who angrily waved them away. He wiggled in his chair; she shimmied and shook.

"So no more Cymbalta, yeah?" she began, and Mark wished he could leave, but this was why he was here. "Abilify, right? Now what's that, Father? Anything like my Wellbutrin?"

Jacob looked pained.

"Abilify. Atypical anti-psychotic, I believe," Mr. Ambrosia replied, his eyes canvassing the table, as if looking for that last piece of cake; his receding gray hair was carefully combed; his manners were meticulous too, "though it's used for the treatment of bipolar and major depressive disorders as well." Mr. Ambrosia was a chemist at Merck and very knowledgeable when it came to pharmaceuticals.

"Good for ADHD too?" she asked her husband, focusing on the least troublesome of her son's problems.

"Off-label maybe," he answered as his eyes settled on the candied yams. "But a study—"

"So what's that doing for you, Jacob? Abilify?" Mrs. Ambrosia asked. "How's that going?"

Jacob spit out his peas. "Peachy-keen," he lied, his face red.

Without blinking, Mrs. Ambrosia snatched away Jacob's plate and replaced it with a clean one from the breakfront.

Mark avoided his friend's gaze. Jacob hadn't taken his medication in at least a month, despite Mark admonishing him. Peachy-keen, indeed.

"You don't need—what you need is a good job, right Father?"

Mr. Ambrosia nodded, and between mouthfuls of food, he said, "Get him a job down the plant. That's where I—"

"Mark—what are you up to, darling? How are your grades?"

Mark cleared his throat. "Just fine, ma'am. B+, A range."

He didn't like talking about himself, but at least the conversation was moving away from psychotropics.

He looked at his friend, and Jacob seemed to be spinning in his chair.

+

Christmas a year ago, and the homeless person they knew as Beggarman had approached them at the outdoor mall in Rhawnhurst. He didn't want money this time though; he wanted to spread the Good Word. He focused on Jacob as if he knew, barely glancing at Mark. (Did his demeanor scream bisexual to the non-panhandling preacher, Mark wondered.) Beggarman called Jacob a sheep and told him that in order to find his true brothers, he had to become a shepherd. He gave Jacob a card, said the number of the shelter he was currently staying at was on the back, which was where Jacob could probably find him unless he was walking the mall or the seedy Strip between the towns of Rhawnhurst and Mondauk Proper. That was how it began: a homeless man with a stained, creased, Jesus-flavored business card. (Mark wondered how Beggarman could afford to have business cards made, but upon closer inspection, he could see they came from someone's printer and were cut out from a page with scissors.) As bizarre as the whole thing seemed, Mark told Jacob he should look into it; his friend had been walking around campus talking to himself again, his penchant for shoplifting had returned, and he'd announced that he preferred going to the bathroom outside.

Jacob hung onto the card for a good month before Mark noticed that it was no longer pinned to their bulletin board. A surreptitious meeting was first (Jacob told him after the fact) and was followed by involvement in one of their services, and one day Jacob came back to their dorm room dripping wet.

"I've been baptized."

"I thought you were already baptized."

"Not where I had a choice."

Since then, Jacob couldn't sit still. At first Mark thought this might be due to a recent med change, but it continued even after Jacob stopping taking his medication. It seemed his friend was suffering side effects from something else entirely. At first Jesus found His way into every conversation, every answer in every class, even every date, if Dolores Dirigo was to be believed. (And why not? Dolores may have had a campus reputation for being easy, but she was not loose; Dolores was discerning and whip-smart, just very horny.) Jacob never proselytized to Mark, as if he knew he would be rebuffed in a hurry. (Mark had little patience for organized religion, especially one born in a homeless shelter that came to fruition in an outdoor mall aided by a sympathizer's dot matrix printer.) Even after his initial exuberance was down to a dull roar, Jesus was never far from Jacob's mind. He just didn't want his parents to know. After Jareth was gone, they had abandoned God, and having their only remaining son embrace Jesus in such an extreme manner would maybe be seen as spitting in Jareth's face—or theirs. Mark wasn't certain—he just wanted to make sure he left the Ambrosias tonight and returned to college with Jacob in tow. It had been difficult preventing Jacob from dropping out to tend to his flock (whoever they may be—Mark avoided all contact with Jacob's coterie of converts, but he imagined it consisted of more of the coffee-cup-change collector crowd than penitent college students). With the Ambrosias, independently of Jacob, apparently weighing whether or not to keep their son in college, Mark thought that was something to pray for: Jacob staying in school, still sharing the same dorm room, even if his love for his evangelical best friend was weighed down, tainted, by wet dreams (the kind twelve-year-olds had) of Saint Jacob's private parts.

+

Mrs. Ambrosia passed the peas again, and Mark watched as she plastered a smile on her kisser whenever she spoke to Jacob. It was painful to watch. (When Jacob would look away, the skin on her face sagged, and all the Revlon in the world couldn't hide the deeply etched wrinkles and the half-circles beneath her eyes, so dark it was as if they were tattooed; Mark wondered if mother and son were aware they had matching baggage.) He knew from numerous telephone conversations that Mrs. Ambrosia would push Jacob, but only so far. There was no telling what her son was capable of doing. Not that Mark thought Jacob possessed the capacity for physical violence (possible feline felony aside); it wasn't Jesus' way, but his parents, especially his mother, seemed, if not a tad fearful, at least extremely careful, which made sense: Jacob was more than just a fragile egg; he was a cracked one—and all the king's horses and all the king's men and everyone on the king's psychiatric staff couldn't put Humpty Dumpty together again.

The way Jacob told it, he'd been the one to push the wooden storm doors shut on Jareth in the old root cellar on an overcast October Saturday morning. The root cellar was a good ways from the house, next to the old curing shack, and its double wooden storm doors were almost flush with the ground. The boys used to use the otherwise forgotten and empty root cellar as a hideout, headquarters, or a clubhouse. Jacob had been the one to lash the handles of the doors with his bike chain (it had broke the day before), something he forgot about in the ensuing hours as he held in giddy giggles during the initial search for Jareth, the first born, the golden boy. Jareth did this, Jareth did that, trophies, ribbons. But he who laughs last and all that—although he couldn't be sure those thoughts went through Jacob's head at the time; he'd told Mark he didn't remember thinking anything; he was just having fun.

The game (and that was all it was) proceeded swimmingly. Jacob didn't give up his brother on the second day. Or the third. Or the seventh. Or ever. He spoke not a word, not even when they finally found Jareth, his nails gone from trying to scratch his way out. When he wasn't scratching, he apparently had been pacing around while he still physically could, so much so that he'd worn down the bottom of his sneakers and his feet shown through. Jacob overheard one policeman say to another, "It's like he never stopped moving," and he said it like Jareth deserved an award for being, what, restless? Jacob had told Mark he considered his family stupid for not even thinking of the old root cellar during the seemingly endless search. It hadn't been used for its true purpose in years, but that was no excuse for forgetting it existed. But as Jacob described it, the area was basically ignored, abandoned. The old curing shack was missing half its roof, and the vegetation was overgrown, as if Mother Nature had reclaimed what was originally hers. The one clearing had piles of forgotten firewood. The cellar storm doors were covered over with ivy and partially hidden by weeds; still, Jacob hadn't wanted the game to be too easy—he'd moved one of the many piles of firewood atop the doors and against the dilapidated curing shack.) They didn't find Jareth until the firewood shifted during a fierce storm and afterwards someone saw the bike chain glinting on a bright, crisp fall morning. (Jacob confessed to Mark that before they found the not-so-golden boy, as tension settled into resignation, he grew nervous and promised a bully in school that he'd do his math homework for a month if he found—or stole—a bike chain and put it on Jacob's bike, which he did right away, saving Jacob the trouble of ditching it in the woods or throwing it into Neshaminy Creek.) The police, for whatever reason, never followed up on the bike chain, which went missing anyway, or the removal of a pile of firewood from one place (where the earth was bare) to atop the storm cellar doors. (Silence and ignorance can be bought, and Mark wouldn't put it past the Ambrosias, described by Jacob as severely private; they would rather not mourn in a courtroom.)

But Mark thought Mrs. Ambrosia acted at times as if she knew what had gone down that overcast fall day. It had been so long ago. The boys had been nine and ten, as captured in the photographs that hung in the foyer. It was enough to make a husband and wife more than just repudiate their Christian beliefs. Mark figured it made them susceptible to the whims of the perpetrator; Jacob became a little god, in his own words, precious, so the Ambrosias parented across a divide of fear—fear of losing their remaining child and fear of what they feared most. But the little god never assumed the lustrous mantle of his brother and the bright lights shined on him only on occasion. There were no graduation photographs of Jacob anywhere in the house that Mark could see, no pictures of any kind except those of when he was nine, a year younger than the brother who mugged for the camera, Jacob's age arrested inside the house of his childhood. Still, Jacob had maintained there were advantages to being the child in the shadows. Jacob said Beggarman had looked inside him and saw the great weight he was carrying which only holy absolution would eradicate, telling him the path to forgiveness started with baptism. In fact, according to Beggarman, it was the weight which made Jacob, a sinner who understood sin, the perfect shepherd. From the moment he'd been baptized, Jacob said he viewed his doomed brother as a lamentable stepping stone to taking the mantle—not of the golden boy, but of one previously fractured, recently made whole, a shepherd gathering to him the lost and, yes, those deemed, by themselves or others, as doomed.

So maybe Jacob was culpable in his brother's death, if it had not been an unfortunate game, as Jacob claimed, an infelicitous joke. But as much as he could be a loose cannon, Mark still didn't think his angel-wrestling best friend could harm a fly, possible juvenile manslaughter aside.

Mark took some more peas, and Jacob smirked. " 'Have I not chosen you twelve, and one of you is a devil?' " he whispered loudly.

"So, Mark, tell us about our son," Mrs. Ambrosia implored, pretending Jacob hadn't said anything about the devil, and Mr. Ambrosia put his fork down as his wife went on. "Tell us what the quiet one is up to. Leave nothing out since Jacob won't talk to us. Girlfriends, grades, drinking—oh, we know you boys drink—tell us everything. Help us understand what makes our boy tick."

Mark bowed his head. Here it was. Showtime! The Ambrosias were obviously afraid of Jacob, especially Mrs. Ambrosia. Mark watched his friend rub the edge of the tablecloth over and over. Even though Jacob had recently stopped taking his medications, he'd been so sensitive to his legally prescribed psychotropics (including the aforementioned Abilify as well as Prozac, Klonopin, and lithium), Mark doubted Jacob could get it up if even cousin Jackie walked into their dorm room buck naked and horny as hell, declaring herself adopted. Jacob's problem drinking (really a freshman phenomenon) had faded away to a flinty sobriety since the coming of Jesus into his life. There was not much to tell—or not much he was allowed to tell. Jacob had asked him not to mention that he was a Christian. (The Ambrosias were many things, but they were not completely oblivious, not entirely blind.) Other than the dead cat incident, there wasn't much to report, and Mark planned to keep the cat under wraps. He didn't even hear Jacob masturbate anymore after lights out, and Mark always tried to stay awake as long as he could so he could just listen to his friend's frenzied strokes and choked gasps.

"Well, let's say Jacob's not gay of bi or anything like that," he began. (Well, it was true, sadly.) Mrs. Ambrosia giggled and Mr. Ambrosia pounded Jacob on the back (which Mark was sure Jacob would interpret as the beginning of some sort of persecution). "He's doesn't much like beer," Mark continued, the lies sliding off his tongue more easily than he'd expected. "Gives him a headache and doesn't mix well with his... In the dorms, we call him the Biblio Master. Head always in a book, the library his second home. Frisbee nut. Crazy about animals. That's your boy, Mrs. Ambrosia."

Frisbee? Jacob gave him a sidelong glance.

She clapped her hands three times. "I knew it! College was just the thing. Pretty soon, you'll be off the meds entirely and then who knows what? Find a nice girl, get married, start a family. Your father would make a—"

"Mom, we have to go," Jacob said, and Mark realized it was only the third time his friend had spoken since they'd arrived. "Last train leaves in half an hour."

(The prophet lied! The train ran till just after midnight.)

"Let Dad drive you."

"No, no. Can't ask him to do that. Besides, we like riding the rails."

"It's a Kerouac thing," Mark croaked, feeling stupid and rude for leaving before dessert and coffee.

There were kisses and hugs at the door and adjustments of scarves. Mark avoided looking at the photographs of Jareth.

"Well, goodbye, son," Mr. Ambrosia said.

"See ya, Dad." Jacob and his father didn't look each other in the eye as they shook hands.

"Thank you both for having me," Mark said.

"Anytime, Mark," Mrs. Ambrosia replied. She was having a hard time keeping her paws off her Jacob, but every time her jittery hands reached for her son, Jacob moved back or to the side. "You're like another—. Anytime."

"Merry Christmas."

"Same to—merry Christmas."

Mark noticed the door didn't close until they'd walked down the steps and reached the pavement. When it did, he thought: mission accomplished. Praise be to God. Or whomever.

+

The wind had kicked up and it was snowing harder if that was possible, making their walk back to the train station a slow trek through Anchor Hop. Jacob's scarf had come undone, and it trailed behind him like a tail.

"Why couldn't you just tell them if it's so goddamn important to you?" Mark asked, not worrying a whit about taking the Lord's name in vain. His mood had turned during the walk. He was tired of being party to hiding what he assumed the Ambrosias knew anyway; he was weary of pretending and didn't like lying to Jacob's parents when they called, telling them that he was in the library when he was sitting across the dorm room or out proselytizing barefoot on Market Street or even on Lancaster Walk. He definitely didn't feel comfortable staying quiet about Jacob no longer taking his meds. So what if he'd successfully paraded Jacob in front of the Ambrosias as a healthy, horny college kid and saved his friend from a room at Quincey (at least temporarily)? So what if Mark now had Jacob for at least another semester? Jacob would eventually quit school to minister to Philadelphia's street kids or wander the country like Caine from the old television show *Kung Fu*.

Jacob's eyes were on his boots. "Because it would be like God killed him," he finally answered.

Mark massaged his temples. *What the hell does that even mean?*

They walked in silence for a couple of blocks. The crunch of the snow and ice beneath their boots were the only sounds filling the air around them.

"What if He did?" Mark asked suddenly. "What if God sacrificed Jareth for something bigger? Sounds stupid, but so what if He did?"

Jacob threw a snowball into the branches of an ancient and frozen-looking sycamore and an icicle fell, missing Mark by inches. The pavement looked like it was littered with diamonds. Mark moved next to a utility pole to avoid slipping on a temporary gemstone, as he finished what he was saying.

"What if He did? That doesn't make you His handyman. It still just makes you one messed-up guy who did a fucked up thing when you were a little kid—when you were just a boy, Jacob."

Jacob punched the utility pole, creating its own short-lived snow shower as it shuddered. Mark didn't react, didn't even change his facial expression. This was for show, blowing off steam from the visit with his parents. He still believed that Jacob wasn't capable of real violence (fratricidal infraction aside).

On a corner ahead three kids huddled around a trashcan fire, warming their hands. It was like a scene out of a movie and totally out of place in Anchor Hop, although they were close to the train station—as if that explained anything, Mark thought. He felt the very fabric of reality rend just ahead, out of his reach. He held onto what he could.

Jacob pulled out his red Bible. "You go on. I'm going to spread the Word."

"You'll miss the train," Mark said. He was at a loss and exhausted. Something had just slipped from his fingers. Maybe he should have kept his mouth shut.

"I can always go back home," Jacob said.

Mark shook his head and stared up at the falling snow. "You would do that?"

"I could sleep in the root cellar."

And like that, it was gone.

Mark realized he understood nothing. He couldn't tell the pieces of the past from the flakes of the present. Maybe Jacob's parents were better off in the dark; knowledge leads to pain when you realize you understand nothing.

Mark took his time walking to the station. They had left the Ambrosias earlier than necessary. If he missed this train, there would be one more in an hour. Maybe Jacob would have finished proselytizing by then. Maybe he would think twice about returning to…and head towards the station.

Mark stepped into two snow angels before deciding to skirt the third. He paused and turned around, checking both directions to make the streets were empty. Then he added a fourth angel, and the snow, under the streetlamp, shone brightly and hurt his eyes. He imagined the falling snow was pregnant with hundreds of drops of angel semen. He thought of Jackie. Jackie he could get (probably). He should think of her more, he decided. A U2 song went through his head: "*In the locust wind comes a rattle and hum / Jacob wrestled the angel, and the angel was overcome.*" Not Jackie—he didn't want sugar and spice and everything nice (even if those things came packaged in a mini-skirt and ripped black nylons). He had to think more like Jacob thought, to not just admire his head but to crawl inside it, poke around, look for clues; there had to be a reason Jacob's wires were in such a tangle. Mark paused. Did he want to be Jacob's savior—and what would be the reward for that? Snips and snails and puppy dog tails? His internal radio was insistent: *"You plant a demon seed / You raise a flower of fire..."* No, he didn't want to be part of the myth, especially since he couldn't be one with the man. (He assumed love came with blinders.) But if he helped further the myth by encouraging Jacob when his interest in religion was piqued (or reawakened) in an outdoor mall in Rhawnhurst (Mark never thought Jacob would actually *join* Beggarman), what right did he have on his friend? If he thought Jacob would be more pliable (if less likely to sleep with him—at first anyway; faith would be just another phase for his attention deficient friend), then he was no better than his prey. Opportunity is often the father to the sin.

When he stood up, he was snow-blind and disoriented. After a few seconds, the confusion dissipated, which had not been the case, he was sure, for Jareth. He must have been constantly on the move once he realized he was trapped in the root cellar, maybe only stopping when he became too weak to do anything more than moan and only starting again when goaded by hope and the frenzied belief that this didn't happen to good little boys. How far his mind must have bent before it broke, Mark imagined, if he could hear the muffled shouts of his name from various search parties, but no one could hear his pounding and punching on the doors, which he did until the skin was scraped from his hands. How the empty root cellar must have taunted his slowly atrophied imagination, teased his parched throat and empty, convulsing stomach. How ferociously restless, how frightened he must have been in the darkness that threatened to absorb him even before he became nothing but a shadow. The marks he left behind were a feral epitaph.

Jacob suggesting he could rest his restless body where Jareth's had been found, shriveled, deteriorated, not so much at rest as abandoned by whatever passes for a soul, seemed like some sort of penance conjured by Beggarman, who constantly tested Jacob's faith (as he in turn did to members of his flock). But the insouciant manner in which Jacob threw out the suggestion made him seem less like a chastened supplicant and more like a masochist with a Goth streak. Mark knew better; a phone call from Mrs. Ambrosia could send Jacob reeling for days, but his questioned behavior never changed, and upon figuring out that Mark had facilitated his appearance at dinner tonight, his best friend referred to him as Judas. Jacob played for keeps—always had apparently. Beggarman offered him forgiveness, but Mark doubted Jacob needed it or wanted it until he'd immersed himself in contemplative prayer and remembered the feel of a greasy bicycle chain and the thrill of the secret horror of his will—and even Beggarman's absolution did nothing to lessen Jacob's agitation and distress, let alone the restlessness it caused, which had always seemed to be there but was made worse by the side-effects of one psychiatric medication or another, until, meds gone, it became Jacob's defining characteristic. Sometimes he paced all night in their dorm room, which more than once sent Mark to the hallway to sleep, the persistent thud of Jacob's feet on the floor echoing Mark's vision of Jareth's final days, the ten-year-old's screams and pounding muffled by the firewood, his escape hindered by a bike chain, the insistent thud of his sneakers counting out the minutes and hours, tearfully missing his family, wondering why they didn't rescue him, never for one second, Mark thought, never thinking this was a game of his brother's, a game with consequences but a game nonetheless. *Thud, thud, thud…*

And why? For cat-killing-like kicks, or was Jacob acting the part of the biblical Jacob who tricked his old man, Isaac, into giving him the blessing meant for his older brother? Mark doubted if Jacob even knew. But what to say of a man who proposed going back to what some might refer to as the scene of the crime? Callousness or an admittance of an unforgivable sinister design? Beggarman's forgiveness didn't reach the old root cellar. The Ambrosias were in such denial that Mark was sure they never even boarded it up. Inside the root cellar, Mark imagined, it was warm, or at least warmer than it was on the outside. Temporarily trapped cats accounted for recent scratch marks on the door and the only cries were those of pregnant rats. Before he started for the train station again, Mark erased the snow angels with his boots. Nothing of beauty lasts for long, he thought, even if it wasn't all that beautiful to begin with. Four people were changed by what happened in the root cellar—that's how fragile, how ephemeral true beauty was, beauty of the soul, and how easily stained if not simply erased.

When the train arrived, his car was empty, and he cried all the way back, even as others got on at various stops, all bundled up, then later disembarked and disappeared from his life, like erased snow angels. His legs were spastic, and he clenched and unclenched his fists over and over without forethought. It was like he couldn't stop moving, and he fought urges to constantly change seats or bolt at every stop. In his thoughts, he paced to and fro; in his mind, he couldn't stop scratching at the root cellar door.

-end-

It's the Way Your Shoulders Shake and What They're Shaking For

———A Scene———

> It's the stupid details
> that my heart is breaking for.
> —Elvis Costello
> & Attractions

EXT. GRASSY STREET CORNER – DAY

A Wednesday in November. The sun is beginning to sneak away. NATHANIEL, sixteen years old, is pulling political signs out of the ground, piling them near the curb. He is slight, fair-haired, and determined but not very strong, and he struggles to yank out a couple of the signs.

BRETTA, seventeen years old, rides up on a red bicycle. She is busty and on the short side with brown, shoulder-length hair. Unlike Nathaniel, Bretta is not wearing a jacket—she wishes to show off her low cut blouse—but there is a thin red scarf around her neck.

Cars occasionally take the corner at high speeds, their headlights splashing over new shadows.

> BRETTA
> So *that's* who picks those up. I always thought the political party machine fairy did it.

> NATHANIEL
> It's just a part-time thing. Obviously.

BRETTA

Sorry about the fairy comment just now. I take it back.

NATHANIEL

My folks are very into volunteer work, as you know, so it was either this or the soup kitchen.

BRETTA

And we all know how you feel about soup, Nathaniel.

NATHANIEL

I bet you remember what kind of floss I use.

BRETTA

I'm sorry…I didn't think Puck liked to floss. Oh, there I go again. I take back Puck too.

NATHANIEL

Can you imagine putting that powerful memory of yours to use on a social studies exam, Bretta?

BRETTA

How could I forget soup? Remember when we were little your mom used to say that we were the only ingredients in each other's soup?
        (surveying the signs)
We Young Republicans always vote. "Vote drive" is our middle name—and confirmation name.

NATHANIEL

The Young Republicans Club. Youth rallies. Book burnings. BYOG.

Bretta undoes her scarf and adjusts her bra straps.

BRETTA

Elucidate.

NATHANIEL
BYOG. Bring Your Own Guns. Leave your stem cells at home.

BRETTA
I take back all my taking back. Sylph—no, no: fay.

Nathaniel is clearly tired of the conversation but is unable to stop himself.

NATHANIEL
Elucidate.

BRETTA
Shakespeare., dummy.
          (clears her throat)
"Either I mistake your shape and making quite,
Or else you are that shrewd and knavish sprite
Call'd Robin Goodfellow. Are not you he
That frights the maidens of the villagery…?"

NATHANIEL
And you can't remember who won the Battle of the Bulge.

BRETTA
Thinking back to the summer afternoons of yore spent jumping off the dock at Finch's Landing, that would have been *you* winning that particular battle of the bulge. Although Joey "Johnny 'Wadd' Holmes" Bosko ran a close second. It was like a volunteer firehose company diving into the Puddle back in those days. Then—*poof!*—it became just you and me and my red bikini at Finch's Landing last summer.
          (pushing up her breasts)
Who knew boys would rather get caught throwing keggers in the woods than store up masturbatory fantasies for later?

NATHANIEL
Both are equally dangerous it turns out.

BRETTA
All three you mean.
(counting on her fingers)
Keggers. My left boob. My right—

NATHANIEL
(trying to change the subject)
So who'd you vote for in the mock election?

BRETTA
Whoever you voted for. Your guy. Your man—
sorry—your *candidate*.

NATHANIEL
You'll be old enough to vote for real next year, and it
won't be a joke.

BRETTA
(ignoring his last statement)
So where ya been lately? I haven't seen you haunting
the record store or huddled up with a dusty volume in
the school library with your mom or even mooning
over me at the Brew-Ha-Ha. Hell, I haven't seen
much of you at all since school started. Dodging me?

NATHANIEL
I always hated dodge ball.

BRETTA
Ahh, but you were so good at getting hit.

Nathaniel gives her a withering look.

BRETTA (CONT'D)
I wanted to call, but...

                    NATHANIEL
Probably not the best idea.

                    BRETTA
And how *is* your mom?

                    NATHANIEL
"White hot with anger" is the first answer that comes
to mind. Other than that, the usual.

                    BRETTA
Half pain-in-the-ass, half ATM, right? Goddamn
school librarians. She should just have "repressed"
tattooed across her forehead.

Nathaniel stops to take a long look at her. Bretta thrusts out her
chest. Straddling her bicycle, she walks with it as Nathaniel continues
on with his work until her front wheel is in the street.

                    BRETTA (CONT'D)
And your brother? How's Tommy? Kickin' ass and
takin' names?

                    NATHANIEL
Are you off your meds?

                    BRETTA
Since forever. But you knew that. You know
everything about me. Remember that time we snuck
sneak outside after our parents were asleep to meet
up and pee behind the Duffys' garage?

                    NATHANIEL
We were little.

                    BRETTA
Old enough to pee, old enough for me.

She reaches out and lifts the bottom of his jacket.

> BRETTA (CONT'D)
> Grew a bit since then.

Nathaniel brushes her hand away, but Bretta grabs and squeezes his fingers for a moment.

> NATHANIEL
> I really need to finish this before we go to…

> BRETTA
> Go? Go where? Whose "we"? You, Davey, Joey Wadd, and Greg?

She shakes her head while watching his expressionless face

> BRETTA (CONT'D)
> No, no. Not the boys, not the Five Cent Gang? Not a nickel between ya—that's what old Mrs. Whitehall used to yell when you guys would cut through her yard or masturbate in her shed.

> NATHANIEL
> We never masturbated in Mrs. Whitehall's shed.

> BRETTA
> I must have just imagined all the sweaty exertions I heard. Hell, I pictured the four of you in a circle with a cookie in the center.

> NATHANIEL
> A cookie.

> BRETTA
> Yeah. Classic circle jerk. Last one to come on the cookie eats it.

> NATHANIEL
> It's a good thing you were never a Girl Scout, Bretta. No one would ever buy your Thin Mints.

A car tears around the corner, barely missing Bretta's front wheel, and squeals to a stop.

DRIVER #1

Will you watch—?

Bretta makes like she's going to chuck a moon. The driver gives her the finger before speeding away.

BRETTA

Girl Scouts—bunch of lipsticks trying to pass. You know: doily dykes.

NATHANIEL

Right. Well, I haven't been around much because I've been concentrating on my studies. Prepping for the SATs again and such.
(beat)
Plus I just needed some time alone.

BRETTA

Oh, how Oprah! Well, despite my Young Republican membership, I completely respect your homosexuality.

NATHANIEL
(the words slipping out before he realizes it)
I've been seeing someone.

BRETTA

Another shrink? Didn't your family wring that rag for all it's worth already?

NATHANIEL

No, I've been *dating* someone. Sort of.

BRETTA
(hurt but trying not to show it)
You stud muffin you. Oh—this is not just one of your secret crushes like the one you've had on me

since the day your hormones began ting-a-ling your ding-a-ling is it? Wait—does he even know?

                    NATHANIEL
She's not...

                    BRETTA
What's his name?

                    NATHANIEL
...a he. Are you hanging around here for reasons other than phantom gay bashing?

                    BRETTA
Just thought I'd see if you needed a lift.

                    NATHANIEL
          (pointing to her bicycle)
On that?
          (pointing at the pile of signs)
With those?

                    BRETTA
We could just ride around and look for empty trash bins or bitter Libertarians' lawns.

                    NATHANIEL
Guy comes around in a truck and picks me and the signs up. Where's the Gremlin?

                    BRETTA
The Red Lady? Confiscated.

                    NATHANIEL
Confiscated. Impounded?

                    BRETTA
          (shaking her head)
Parents clipped my wings.

NATHANIEL

Catch you drawing testicles on your mom's framed
picture of Kennedy again?

BRETTA

Only a gay man would know the contents of my
mom's dressing room.

NATHANIEL

You're a laugh riot.
(gesturing towards the street)
You should take your act on the road.

BRETTA

I'll be here all week, folks.

NATHANIEL

So your crime, Capone?
(realizing he's getting sucked in again)
Forget it. I don't want to know.

BRETTA

Bad grade on Mrs. Forch's paper. My Tom Joad as a
nascent Nazi thesis didn't quite light up Forch the
Torch.
(beat)
You know, Tommy thought I was a laugh riot. Yeah,
as I remember it, Tommy thought I was good enough
to eat—or rather, he thought I was *more* than good
enough when I ate him.

Nathaniel stops pulling signs.

NATHANIEL

That's quite enough.

BRETTA

Only instead of a standing ovation—which in one
way, he gave me in advance—or roses thrown on

stage, I was gifted with his geyser of love. His *first* geyser of love, I believe.

NATHANIEL

You know he didn't go back to school this year? My parents, they still have him in an outpatient program. He's got a therapist and a social worker and a psychiatrist who gives him medications. We have to go to…we have to go to family counseling once a week. Used to be twice a week at first. And they blame *me*, my parents. Me. So don't talk about Tommy. Don't even *think* about Tommy. Just don't. If my parents even saw me talking with you… You know, they talked to the police and a lawyer. They were seriously thinking about filing charges of some sort.

BRETTA

But me being underage too put the ol' kibosh on that, huh, Oberon? Your parents always overreact. Okay, yes, your brother's on the spectrum, but that's got nothing to do with—I bet he's just fine. Probably choking Kojak more often than any other ten- or eleven-year-old around, so besides stained sheets and a couple of socks that stand up by themselves, your folks should be happy at least *that* part of him is normal. Their real sorrow will come when they find out their other son is a *massive* Freddie Mercury fan. *Poof!*

NATHANIEL

Have you ever been tested for a heart?

She fondles her left breast.

BRETTA

Wanna check? Maybe I can turn you, if it's not too late.
      (giving her breast one last squeeze)
I'm no Tin Man, mister. I developed early.

Nathaniel returns to his signs.

> BRETTA (CONT'D)
> So who ya takin' to the Fall Fling?

Nathaniel doesn't answer.

> BRETTA (CONT'D)
> Well, I just hope they play our song.

> NATHANIEL
> We don't have a song.

> BRETTA
> (ignoring his last statement)
> So, Slutty Sophie's taking a mechanic from Pep Boys, but what did you expect? Bebe's taking Oliver, of course. And Annie's going with Tourettes Tim, if you can believe it. That should be good for a hoot. She bought this horrendous yellow dress. Annie's so chunky—a big-boned girl, as my mother would say— she'll look like a squash on fertility drugs.

> NATHANIEL
> No.

> BRETTA
> I didn't ask.

> NATHANIEL
> Still no.

> BRETTA
> You were watching.

Nathaniel drops his signs.

> BRETTA (CONT'D)
> I mean, you and Tommy shared the same room, how could you not? 'Course, you could have walked out,

got yourself some milk and cookies, watched a *Martha Stewart* rerun, or gone back to your knitting, but you didn't. Standard Bretta sleepover: me on the air mattress between your beds. You said your mom thought you and I were getting too old to sleep in the same room, what with high school around the corner and all, but *Nightline* probably had a *really* interesting piece that night on gay teens or maybe it was on MLA documentation or perhaps a spotlight on librarians who work all day with vibrators shoved in their granny panties, *buzz buzz buzzing* in the stacks, constantly shushing the kids in order to concentrate on the mantra of the Pocket Rocket. So your mom was otherwise media occupied.

NATHANIEL

Stop.

BRETTA

Why? You didn't stop me? Not with Tommy you didn't.

(beat)

So after lights out, I unleashed the girls. And you looked, didn't you? You did more than look. You actually touched the right one. Gave it a little squeeze like you were considering the heft of a nice, corpulent water balloon. Then that was it. And what did I do? I did what a girl has to. Fuck *O* magazine—I read my mother's *Cosmo*. I whipped off your sheet, yanked your little red shorts down—how cute is it that you sleep in shorts?—and there he was: Nate Junior, vibrating like a stop sign in an earthquake.

(tenderly)

I know the way you look at me. I know the way you've *always* looked at me. And that time in Jackie Obie's basement, remember? Seven Minutes in Heaven? Okay, so you bolted after like seven seconds, but you did put your tongue in my mouth—and on my chin, my cheeks, almost up my nose, but you were a newbie: your aim was off. That sleepover this past summer: I just wanted to show you, since we're not kids anymore, how I feel about you. That I feel the same way you do. So I figured I'd polish your knob. But no. No, no, no. Almost broke my nose pushing me away while you pulled your shorts up. But you know what I learned in *Cosmo*, Nathaniel? You know what I learned? I learned this: a girl can't just cut her engine once it starts purring. There's no kill switch other than bad breath and professional soccer. Tommy had just finished, what, fifth grade? If there's grass on the infield, play ball, so I woke him up and gave him a blowjob with all the amenities. Look Ma, no teeth!

Another car just misses Bretta's bicycle. The driver blares his horn, slows down to yell, but never stops.

DRIVER #2
Get out of the street, you goddamn crazy...

NATHANIEL
There's something really wrong with... You need to go.

BRETTA
Very appreciative, your brother was. Not even really shy about it the next day. He told me he wished it'd lasted all summer long. Summerlong Bretta, he called me.

NATHANIEL
He did not.

BRETTA
Uh-huh. Summerlong Bretta. Like an all-day sucker.

NATHANIEL
I'm starting to wonder who the real sucker in all this is.

BRETTA

Ooooh, not so boiled Ramen after all. Mommy starch your BVDs or is that stiffie divining its way to my wading pool? Well, believe me or don't, it matters not. Tommy was as grateful as a lemon in a glass of iced tea, and he didn't harp after me every day for another summer hummer either. One and done.

NATHANIEL

That's because my parents found out.

BRETTA

That's because *someone* told your parents. No matter. You were jealous. I forgive you. But don't tell me to stop. Don't you dare. Because you didn't tell me to stop sucking your little brother off, did you? No—no, you watched. You stayed all the way to the bitter-tasting end. Good to the last salty drop, right? Yes indeedy, you watched me make wee Tommy money-shoot his brains out, and I bet your hand never left the inside of your shorts.

NATHANIEL

Go.

BRETTA

Can't stop this—you and me, us—even if you wanted to. Not in your nature. You're a Joseph, not a Jesus.

NATHANIEL

Now.

BRETTA

You can't stop it, so why don't we just cut through the formalities? Why don't we just proceed like you've already asked me to the Fall Fling and we're just finalizing the details? This year's theme is "A Red Carpet Affair." Spoon gag, right?

NATHANIEL

There's no...

Bretta pushes her bike further into the street.

BRETTA

Last chance for a slow dance.

NATHANIEL

Blow it out your ear.

BRETTA

You have to make everything so hard. No pun intended.

Bretta wheels her bike in the middle of the street. She drums her fingers on the handlebar. When headlights begin to swing towards her, she looks placidly at Nathaniel, who stands still on the grass surrounded by signs. A car flies around the corner and brakes inches from her bike.

DRIVER #3

Are you *trying* to get hurt, young lady?

Bretta straddles the banana seat and waves at the car as it pulls around her.

BRETTA

(to Nathaniel)

A Joseph.

(as she points her bike towards home)

My dress is this red taffeta number. You can pick up the wrist corsage at Precious Petals the day before. I already called it in. Only $24.99, so you're getting off cheap. Ha! That's funny. "Getting off." Get it?

Nathaniel doesn't respond.

BRETTA (CONT'D)

Hey, if you're a good boy, maybe I'll even let you get lucky.

(beat)

I really hope they play our song.

Bretta pedals away, and Nathaniel returns to the job at hand as the sun resigns the day.

-end scene-

Michaelmas

"Who is like God?" (Hebrew translation of Michael)

Driving home from his grad student's apartment, Phillip's mind wandered to the Michaelmas mass tomorrow night at Assumption of Our Lady. It was late September with the whole town sliding on a slippery slope of dead leaves towards what the fishermen called Deep Autumn: that time when the clocks were turned back and, in their part of the world, darkness was allowed to devour what it could of the day. Phillip always thought of Michaelmas as the start of the slide (although it landed a few days after the autumnal equinox). His students would tell him it was all downhill come September, and there were years he would agree. This was one of them. While visitors to Mont Saint-Michel in Normandy, France, would be dining on the traditional Michaelmas fare of Mère Poulard's omelettes prepared over a wood fire, his sweet Mary would be sucking down a nutritious meal consisting of a specially balanced formula of carbohydrates, protein, fat, vitamins, and minerals—through a tube. Despite Michaelmas being the feast day of the archangels, Michael in particular, the "chief prince" who defeated Lucifer during the war in heaven, which one would think would inspire not enervate, Phillip saw every fallen leaf as an addition to a grave blanket that only he could see.

Finding what he did last night was the only reason he'd accepted his student Elizabeth's latest invitation. After declining all previous offers (including dinner in the dark atop the small castle that anchored the campus of the college where he taught—she knew the best way to sneak up to the turret, but they'd have to eat fast), he finally agreed to go to her apartment tonight. He didn't ask himself why (he knew), but he was sure he was breaking some rule or other regarding student-teacher relationships just by going over to her place, even though she was twenty. He had no reason to be there other than to kiss her stomach, her neck, maybe even her waiting lips. But he kept himself in check. Instead of a bottle of wine, he brought *Middlemarch*, and after some Thai food, they went over the novel that had seemed to give Elizabeth so much trouble, if that was to be believed. (He doubted she was as dewy-eyed as she appeared to be.)

Elizabeth wore a short skirt, and soaking in occasional stolen glimpses of her thighs was like receiving communion when he was a kid: totally transforming for seconds, even minutes at a time—and thinking about the night now as he drove back to his empty house (he'd been a gentleman but promised a return appearance) brought him back to the Michaelmas service tomorrow night. He'd promised Father Dave he would be there. Father Dave, Assumption's pastor, visited Mary almost every week, and Phillip had become one of his most loyal acolytes, helping with the collection baskets or the readings on Sundays. But Elizabeth had said her roommate (who'd interrupted their studies, their heads close together, with an embarrassed "No way!") was heading home for the weekend, and it was oh so tempting. Since Mary's crash and during the hell before that, he'd remained faithful in his heart and with his body—no physical human contact unless sympathetic hugs and firm, meaningful handshakes counted.

When he got home, he stared at Mary's desk, the open drawer, the strewn papers, and his very bones shuddered. Her desk— and the irony was not lost on him—seemed like a living thing, pulsating, daring him to again open the folder which lay in the center of the mess and read the advanced directive and other papers within. The night before he'd been trying to organize the bills and such, which had always come under Mary's purview, only these were mostly medical in nature, and that was when he'd discovered it. He imagined he could smell Elizabeth's perfume lingering on his shirt, as he sat down at Mary's desk and gazed into the now-empty deep drawer on the right where he'd found the folder, eventually taking everything out of the other drawers to make sure there wasn't anything else.

…look what I just found among Mary's papers…

The documents were in an unmarked folder. He again read through them several times. She'd left everything in his hands, which shook at the thought of his power and her trust.

…look…

They called it pulling the plug, but why did the very thought make him feel untethered?

…just look…

Immediately he began to question his role as Mary's guardian angel, a grandiose title, he knew, one of which he was not worthy, but the obligations had fallen to him nonetheless, even before he discovered the folder. (Mary was estranged from her family.) But he told no one about what he'd found, just called Elizabeth to say that he would meet her tonight, which he'd done without incident, but sin was in his heart, on his tongue, in his groin. *Intent.* Although he'd behaved himself tonight, it didn't mean he would next time.

...stuck in the back of a drawer...

That was it, wasn't it? He couldn't make love with Elizabeth while Mary was still, technically, alive. He wasn't about to cheat on his wife. He knew he'd inched close to the line tonight, almost daring himself. And why not? Hadn't he surrendered his hope every time she landed back in the hospital or, lately, when another procedure failed and reality smacked him in the face? He couldn't remember a time when it wasn't an uphill battle just to get out of bed.

Oh, if Mary only knew how strong she really was, how until tonight's *intent*, how strong he'd been. It didn't appear that Mary was going to be shrugging off her severely damaged mortal coil anytime soon. She'd come out of her coma once, struggling to master basic motor skills, grasping for even her name, only to suffer cardiac arrest a week later, causing her to retreat back into her dark world. Was it frightening in there or was it like a warm bath? The feeding tube, so recently removed, returned, and it was accompanied by a ventilator, for the firecracker he'd fallen for in college was no more than a spark and could not even flicker on her own.

...sniffed his shirt...

Part of him just shut down. Meeting with Mary's doctors, he barely heard a word they said. More machines were brought in as more of Mary stopped functioning. For years he'd clung to her, castigating himself for being unable to protect Mary from her worst enemy: herself. But he'd been worn down. Before the crash, he used to research every diagnosis from BPD to dissociative identity disorder, and even after, he printed out articles on everything from range of motion to cognitive impairment, but then the diagnoses became more ominous and he stopped looking them up. Traumatic brain injury, subarachnoid hemorrhage, persistent vegetative state. Mary was not just submerged; she'd gone deep.

The first time he heard the words *long-term acute care*, they struck him as insidious, sounding suspiciously like *end of the line*. These were the words that brought the house down around his head, words that told him to no longer expect to encounter his Mary thistle in this lifetime. He barely remembered the transfer from Holy Redeemer

Hospital to Hillcrest Healthcare. The first student to come to his office at the start of the semester was Elizabeth, who wished to show her sympathy with a hug that lasted way too long; he didn't know who was at fault there—but she let go before he did, so he was he kidding?

    …it was all about letting go…

It was in his hands, always had been apparently—the machines, the feeding tube, all of it—even if nobody knew yet. Father Dave once said that six of the Ten Commandments were directed against sins of selfishness. Phillip used to think: if it was selfish to let Mary go, even when every examination was a mere sounding, wasn't it also selfish to keep her alive in the name of God? Now Mary's wishes were crystal clear. Why then did he feel so guilty?

    …just want what's best for Mary…

Taking up one corner of Mary's desk was a large photograph of the two of them from the summer after college when they'd gone on that trip to New England. From within the silver frame, they looked happy. He focused on Mary's red hair and the freckles that were spread across her face like a lost constellation or a treasure map. Her lucent green eyes, flecked with yellow, seemed to be looking out of the frame, just beyond him, over his shoulder, through his chest. Mary in the photograph watched over the sad circus of him lost in the mess on her desk but refused to catch his eye. Mary in the picture was as out of reach as she was in what passed for real life. When thoughts of his student mixed with memories of his romantic sojourn with Mary, he laid the silver frame down flat and tried to ignore his hard-on. This was no time for an erection. Not now. Not on the eve of Michaelmas. Not with Mary's last day within reach. It was a terrible burden and despite all efforts to the contrary, he masturbated until he cried.

+

At that time there shall arise Michael, the great prince,
guardian of your people…
        Daniel 12:1

On Michaelmas, it smelled like snow all morning into the afternoon, but snow never came. (It was fall after all.) Father Dave stopped Phillip in Rex's Pharmacy the afternoon before the special evening mass. Phillip had just come from Hillcrest, but he hadn't visited his wife. He couldn't.

"There he is," Father Dave said, "the defender of the 'lesser' archangels."

"Gabriel and Raphael are only 'lesser' because Michael was a war hero."

"Yet the feast is called Michaelmas." The priest shrugged with a smile.

Phillip chuckled despite the instant fear that manifested itself as an itchy rash across his chest.

"Spelled M-i-c-h-a-e-l-m-a-s," said the young girl behind the counter, "but pronounced mi-kəl-məs, right, Father?"

Phillip looked around the pharmacy trying to find an escape route, as the priest gave the girl the double thumbs up. A man in a black fedora with a tattoo on his forearm that read "Memento Mori" sucked on his lips as he perused Rex's lubricant selection. Phillip assumed he was a drifter because of the dust on his shoes and the bottom of his pant legs. Father Dave paid the stranger no mind.

Phillip's mouth continued to work while his eyes were pinned on the tattoo. "Michaelmas was a quarter day in England. It was a day for settling accounts and rents. It was a day for the merchants and moneylenders of the temple to strut their stuff."

When Father Dave laughed, his red beard opened to reveal a mouth of startling white teeth. Phillip stared at the floor.

(Was that "American Pie" playing over the pharmacy's tinny speakers?)

"You always manage to find the sin and the sinners in everything," the pastor said.

"I call 'em as I see 'em," Phillip muttered.

When he looked up, the man with the tattoo was gone, leaving behind just the echo of the bell that hung above the door. The pretty cashier's face was crimson. More than likely the stranger's sexual aid purchase had embarrassed her or he'd said something crude—or just maybe the message of the drifter's ink had shaken the young girl's Catholic faith for a moment or two.

"That's why the parish needs you, Phillip. You are a true teacher."

"No, I'm an adjunct professor at a small *secular* college."

"Regardless, you watch over young souls and see them through."

"I think they see through me."

Father Dave peeked into Phillip's basket, but Phillip had stuck the condoms in his jacket pocket. This was his first attempt at a five-finger discount, but he felt he had no choice; it was a sin of necessity. Everyone in town knew his wife was on life support. If he got caught, he hoped Old Man Rex would just take him aside. Hell, he didn't even know that he'd need them, but better safe than sorry, his mother used to say (though he was sure she never used the idiom in reference to prophylactics).

" 'The ego is not master in its own house,' " Father Dave quoted (percipient as ever it seemed).

Phillip knew this game well. " 'The goal of all life is death,' " he quoted back.

" 'We are never so defenseless against suffering as when we love,' " Father Dave returned.

"You win," Phillip conceded, anxious to get out of there, to go home and read over the papers he'd found yet again. He pretended to sneeze, turning his head away to make sure Old Man Rex was behind the pharmacy counter. He wasn't.

"Ah, Freud."

"But psychology is the new priesthood, so careful there, pastor, or you could find yourself ordering a couch quicker than you think."

Father Dave laughed again. He was the most educated man Phillip knew, way more interesting than most of the English department faculty.

"Long as I see you before seven tonight, Phillip, my boy, that'll be enough to keep me off the Prozac."

"Of course, I—"

"Still remember your Emily Dickinson? ' "Hope" is the thing with feathers.' "

Phillips sighed. He wondered if the pastor played this quote game (or some version of it) with everyone.

" 'Faith is the highest passion of man.' " It was out of his mouth before he knew it, a verbal reflex, one that would get him busted in front of his pastor if he lingered much longer.

"Ah, Kierkegaard," said Father Dave. "Feathers and passion, passionate feathers."

"I love Emily Dickinson," said the girl behind the counter.

Trojan Bareskin—40% Thinner!

Father Dave's countenance turned sober. "How's Mary?"

"She's—"

"We'll make sure to add an extra prayer for her tonight—and one for you."

Old Man Rex appeared at the far end of the aisle.

"Thank you, Father."

"I don't like Sylvia Plath much though," said the cashier. "Do you know she…?"

Was the pharmacist coming towards them? It was as if the condoms were glowing from his inside jacket pocket.

"What do you think I should use tonight: the Nicene Creed or the Apostles' Creed?"

Phillip mumbled something. All he thought about was moving to another town if he got nabbed.

Father Dave winked at the cashier. "Phillip wishes the Mass was still said in Latin. Giving him a choice blows his mind."

Phillip blinked. Should he make a run for it or—?

Old Man Rex coughed and knelt to straighten up a shampoo display at the top of the aisle. He nodded to the pastor—he didn't want to interrupt, Phillip thought—then headed towards the pharmacy counter in the rear of the store, giving Phillip a brief approximation of a smile as he passed.

Father Dave punched his shoulder. "Even the Archangel Michael had to make a choice. The Lord or Lucifer. See you tonight, you soldier for Christ. Gonna be a good time!"

Phillip paid for his toiletries and walked out with the Trojans still in his pocket, waiting every second for an alarm to go off, for Old Man Rex to collar him. But nothing happened, and the crisp, fall air smacked his face. He'd gotten away with it.

Saint Michael was the defender of the faith. Phillip considered all his attempts at emulation to be spectacular failures. The machines at Hillcrest went *beep, hiss, beep, hiss, beep*, as if he needed reminding. A psychologist once told him, "We truly defend only when it is in out self-interest to do so"—Phillip reached into his pocket and felt the heat coming off the Trojans—"otherwise, we just act and react, selfish animals."

Don McLean thundered between his temples.

He knew what he needed to do.

+

The archangel Michael, the prince of the heavenly host,
appeared glorious and terrible against the sky.
James Joyce

When he got home, he called a lawyer. It never occurred to
him that he would need one, but he didn't know how much
rigmarole to expect. He wondered if he meant the call to be a stalling
tactic; if so it didn't work. The lawyer told him that once they met
tomorrow, "it was as good as done." It sounded cold but Philip
hadn't expected a hug or whatever passed for one over the phone. So
both he and Mary had another day, one long enough to encompass a
lifetime—or at least it felt that way.

"Drove my Chevy to the levee…"

Mary had quoted from her favorite song in her (last) suicide
note, which he'd found just before the police called. He'd hoped he
never had to hear that song again, but it always seemed to lurk in the
background, at the dentist's office, at the supermarket; eventually
he'd come to think of his brain as a radio station with only one
record.

"…but the levee was dry…"

He felt like he'd been dying right alongside Mary from her
first suicide attempt up to now. It was only when he'd found the
folder that he realized he wanted to live. "As good as done" was
good enough for him, he told himself. But when he hung up from
the lawyer, what had been merely bruised and cracked, shattered, and
he found himself on the floor trying to find his breath. By the time
he did, the sun had moved in the sky. He took the shirt he'd worn
the night before out of the hamper and buried his nose in it,
searching for hints of Elizabeth's perfume.

…her bright, wet eyes offering what if not deliverance…

His next call was to his student. Was it irony that the love of
his life was about to reach the end of hers, and he was at half-mast
waiting for Elizabeth to answer? (He'd have to ask his students—
right.) Between calls, he'd begun sweating through his clothes, and
once he'd gotten hold of Elizabeth, the phone kept slipping from his
slick hand and ear.

When he hung up, the radio in his head blasted its sole song
at top volume, and he screamed until it was down to a dull roar again.
Yes, Mary's machines would go *beep* through the night, but it was all

over except for the wailing, so maybe he didn't have to wait until Mary was actually gone. Maybe, maybe tonight, he'd get to tune into a new frequency and bathe in the glory of a new song that didn't feature a Chevrolet.

+

> Yet the archangel Michael, when he argued with the devil
> in a dispute over the body of Moses, did not venture to
> pronounce a reviling judgment upon him but said,
> "May the Lord rebuke you!"
> Jude 1:9

Elizabeth had black hair and burnt sienna eyes. She was short and toned but not overly muscular. Her skin always looked…toasty. She had two birthmarks. One on her cheek, the other on her neck, neither raised. These were the color of dark chocolate and appeared to have subtle swirls. There was a light layer of peach fuzz above her upper lip that Phillip thought she probably waxed semi-regularly. The fact that she hadn't for tonight's rendezvous made her even more beguiling to him. A basket of crab apples sat on her tiny kitchen table, and candles were lit and distributed throughout the apartment.

Michaelmas mass was going on without him.

He couldn't completely loathe himself for what he was going to do tomorrow at Hillcrest—and what he wanted to do tonight. He knew the consequences beyond releasing Mary's soul. Forget everything else: this decision had been put in black and white by Mary; she didn't want machines doing God's work (she'd always been very devout), thus he had a moral obligation to bring her wishes to light—but that wasn't why he was doing it, was it? After tomorrow nothing would be the same—not with Father Dave, not with the faculty, not with a single person he knew, in fact (though if he was discreet about seeing Elizabeth—he would try to be careful, but that wasn't the same thing was it?—he might not be seen as a complete villain). And still he couldn't despise himself. God would take care of that, he thought. God would despise him enough for both of them.

Look at her thighs, the flesh. Her slim wrists and her perfectly shaped B-cup breasts. Her smoky hair. Drink deep the smell of her skin. When he saw her ass, he thought he'd lose it right then and there before he even unwrapped a Trojan, staining his boxers like some horny teenager during his first heavy petting session. Above her bottom was a downy patch not unlike the one above her upper lip. Did Elizabeth know of its existence? He pressed his nose into it.

Oh, how long had it been since he'd last had sex with Mary? Six months since the crash. Maybe another two and a half years before that—hard to be intimate when your beloved was in and out of mental health facilities like Friends and Quincey; hard to catch a romantic moment when you're counting out meds and locking up sharp objects or calling 911 because somehow Mary found the pill bottles that he'd tried to hide or because she bought over-the-counter sleeping pills, took them all, and overdosed yet again. She was an inpatient, she was an outpatient. She was Mary, she wasn't. She was covered, she was in danger of maxing out. Then—BAM—Mary drove the Chevy into a utility pole, and her jaw was wired shut and her front teeth were gone and the coma became home for months: nice and cozy maybe. Now, after a brief surfacing, she was back inside and all the safety rope had been let out. So Mary got what she wanted (or soon would). Why shouldn't he? He had Mary's notarized and witnessed advanced medical directive that he'd found in her desk two nights ago, along with papers which gave him durable health care power of attorney (unnecessary really; her wishes were explicit). But after the shock wore off and guilt settled in the pit of his stomach, he thought twice about having shared his discovery with the lawyer. He decided he wanted to dip a toe in first. So on Michaelmas he'd gone to Hillcrest before he went to Rex's Pharmacy (one sin at a time) and tracked down Mary's physician: *If such papers did exist, Doc...?* Without blinking, without so much as looking up from his charts: *Make sure the documents are up to snuff, then...*

The pen is mightier than the ventilator.

He couldn't bring himself to visit Mary after speaking with the doctor, and he left the facility clutching the part of his chest that he believed had once housed his soul.

"Drove my Chevy to the levee, but the levee was dry..."

Phillip unwrapped the condom slowly, as if it might explode before it ever reached his penis. He had Elizabeth in two of his classes: The Nineteenth Century Novel and Writing Fiction: A Theoretical Approach. She was a good student, better than most, but not without lazy habits. Late papers, excuses out the ass, but still good for the occasional A. Her fiction was an entirely different beast: wonderful, striking prose written with a surgeon's incisiveness and an innate ability to create multiple layers of understanding. He'd wanted to fuck her when she first entered his writing class—that too tight t-shirt (I ♥ Geeks) showing off her excited nipples, engorged from rubbing against the slight fabric—but he didn't become obsessed with Elizabeth (something he'd cop to) until he read her first short story in the workshop. By the time she submitted her paper on *Moby-Dick* ("Thought Reform in the Cult of the *Pequod*"), he was a goner. If one could masturbate to undergraduate literary insight, then he did, night after torrid night.

Now, with her breath slightly rancid from the wine they'd drunk, he kissed her, and her tongue suddenly seemed like everything he had ever wanted, her naked body: a wish granted. He started rolling the condom down, but his penis wouldn't cooperate. (Mary was still, technically, alive; the process wouldn't start until tomorrow at the soonest—and maybe that was the problem; maybe he'd been right before: maybe Mary needed to be real, real gone before he could enter the young woman splayed on the bed. (Just when he thought he couldn't hate himself more...) Phillip smiled to Elizabeth, who hugged a pillow. "Just a sec." He started wacking off—and still: nothing. "Do you want me to put it in my mouth?" she asked, sounding slightly bored. Phillip nodded yes, but it was hopeless, helpless, sincerely fucked. Elizabeth's boredom began teetering between irritation and distraction, and Phillip saw, maybe for the first time, just how young his student really was. He kept trying anyway.

"*And them good ol' boys drinking whiskey and rye...*"

All he'd done to be here (and what he planned to do to stay), all the sacrifice to come, only to be betrayed by his penis. Cursed by God.

"*Singin' this'll be the day that I—*"

No, no, it was another organ altogether, wasn't it? His penis hadn't betrayed him—he'd betrayed his heart. Mary had once called him her guardian angel, but it became apparent to him lying naked on Elizabeth's bed that perhaps he'd abandoned his post long ago. He was giving in rather than giving up (or was trying to), but did it matter? He was about to forsake his Mary thistle, or so he told himself.

Elizabeth asked him if he had a Viagra, and Phillip pulled on his pants. On his way out, as she reached for a bottle of nail polish and her phone, he reminded Elizabeth to watch how she used free indirect discourse in her latest short story. He checked his watch seven times between Elizabeth's door and the car. His hands shook as he stuck the key in the ignition. The unrolled Trojan lay on the passenger seat, the folder from Mary's desk on his lap, one a reminder of how close he'd come, the other of how close true failure really was.

+

Then war broke out in heaven; Michael and his angels battled against the dragon.
Revelation 12:7

He would kill himself if he wasn't in time. He'd do one better than drive a Chevy into a utility pole. He'd jump from the castle at the university, his body landing with a thud on the grassy common, perhaps interrupting a game of night Frisbee.

Every single traffic light was red, and every one became a crimson blur in his rearview. All the way to Hillcrest, he had to force himself to stop looking at the car clock. He didn't even bother turning the motor off when he abandoned his car in front of the facility, taking the folder with him.

Credo in unum Deum, Patrem omnipoténtem...

The Nicene Creed dripped from his inner tongue as he dodged nurses and pushed through a pair of orderlies. Despite being one of Father Dave's disciples, Phillip was an old school Catholic at heart (though a little shaky on the fifth, sixth, and ninth commandments). "If it's not in Latin," his grandmother used to say, "how will it make any sense?"

...factórem cæli et terræ...

He could feel the second hand of time tickle his neck, and before he could look at it again, he ripped off his watch. Whether he made it or not was in God's hands now. He'd been given tests and been found to be lacking. He was suddenly choked with guilt for every F he'd ever given when a D would have sufficed.

...visibílium ómnium et invisibílium—

It was the machines that undid him, every single time. The blinking lights, the monotonous beeps, the dials and cords and wires. But somehow the tubes, seen and unseen, were the most frightening. Feeding tube. Catheter tube. Endotracheal tube. Tubes for God knows what. Not a tube he could talk into, not a tube he could use to communicate with Mary's hibernating brain—Hillcrest didn't have that kind of tube.

He couldn't avoid looking at the big clock behind the nurses' station when he entered the unit. It was 8:52. He'd made it by the skin of his teeth. He didn't know if visiting hours applied to spouses anyway, but he wasn't about to ask—the thought made him wince: *not knowing* told the tale of how often he'd been in that room. It was redolent of antiseptics and bleach desperately trying to hiding a rancidness.

"She sort of squeezed my hand earlier. Just a reflex, but it was nice."

Phillip jumped.

The grey-haired nurse laughed quietly as she checked an IV line. "I know I'm scary, but it's not Halloween yet."

"No," Phillip replied, "it's Michaelmas."

"Michaelmas?"

"Michaelmas. And I won. Mary's still here. There's an unused condom on the front seat of my car, and my Mary's still here."

"Mr. Lucas, you better get some sleep. My nephew, when he doesn't get his eight hours…well, that little cutie tells me—"

"Can you leave us now please?"

"If you're staying, talk to her. Sing to her. Something. I'm sure she misses you. I'm not even here."

And then she wasn't.

Phillip pulled up a chair next to his wife, nestled among the tubes, and listened to the soundtrack of beeps and hisses that passed for living. Mary's face was expressionless and severely drawn. But it was still Mary. The Mary of the many nights spent listening to classic rock and drinking Yuengling like they were going stop brewing the stuff at the stroke of midnight. The Mary who loved to sing to the Monkees while she cooked. The Mary who had slowly been going batshit crazy (a term he never said aloud) right before his very eyes. She was the Mary who was losing her marbles while her psychiatrist and psychologist diagnosed her with everything under the sun, the former pumping her full of drugs, the latter eventually telling her she was coming in too often. Then suddenly she became the Mary whose marbles lay disturbingly still. Now she was the Mary whose spattering of freckles and tousled red hair had become a muddy palette of fall colors that matched the autumnal hues of the panoply of daily psychotropic drugs she no longer had to take, a palette that was starting to turn sallow and wan, as she was ensconced in her coma.

...stuck in the back of a drawer...

He took the notarized papers from the folder and stared at the last page. He didn't recognize the witnesses' names. Odd. He read through the document for what seemed like the hundredth time, and it hit him: it was as if Mary was forcing his hand to finish what she'd begun.

Michaelmas was a celebration of convictions over selfishness. Michael the archangel drove Lucifer out of heaven for daring to covet. Phillip knew he was no longer Mary's guardian angel; he'd failed at that job long ago. He didn't know which of the Ten Commandments he was about to break, but if it was one of selfishness, he could live with it. Call it a selfish conviction. And it had nothing to do with Elizabeth, although he'd be nipping a different kind of sin in the bud. Elizabeth would go on to beguile another faculty member or perhaps find a geek of her own to ♥. As far as the Church's stand on this sort of thing, Mary's papers, he didn't care; it didn't have any effect on his decision—and, besides except for the lawyer, they would never know, and he'd never confess it.

...it was all about letting go...

Phillip tore the advanced directive into tiny pieces. He was done with letting go. He'd apologize to Mary later.

Dickinson and Kierkegaard both had it wrong: the thing with feathers is fear, flapping frantically, for faith is relative, passion ephemeral. The things we do not to be alone, the things we do in the dark when we are—these are what define us. The rest: just stray feathers, floating and landing, floating and landing.

This is who I am, Phillip thought as he rained down the pieces of the advance directive and other papers into the toilet and flushed them away.

In New England, the aster novi-belgi—Michaelmas daisies—stood strong against the frost. In Ireland and the Hebrides, Catholic families shared Michaelmas bannock, a quick bread blessed on the feast day, as their children shrieked, searching for the lucky silver coin hidden in one of the loaves.

... beep, hiss, beep, hiss, beep...

Father Dave would forgive him for missing Michaelmas; he was in the forgiving business after all.

Mary squeezed his fingers. It was just a reflex, he knew (if it even happened), but the nurse was dead on the money: it *was* nice.

Phillip closed his eyes and what started as a whisper turned into a howl:

"*So bye-bye Miss American Pie. Drove my Chevy to the levee, but the levee was dry, and them good ol' boys were drinkin' whisky and rye, singin'…*"

Although his voice echoed in the unit that was otherwise quiet except for the beeping machines, no one came to ask him to keep it down, and he soon forgot the words and fell asleep in the chair, clutching his wife's hand.

-end-

GFE

He'd come there to write, but the drink found him before he found the words. It wasn't the first time, and he considered himself in good company: Dylan Thomas, Truman Capote, Sinclair Lewis, hell most of the Lost Generation of writers in the '20s. It started innocent enough, just a couple of beers at a local watering hole (this time a joint called McCullough's). Maybe a bourbon before he went to bed. Then a nip at lunch. Nothing extravagant. A quick shot of vodka or Irish whiskey. Those led to martinis—dirty martinis—also at lunch and maybe before dinner, which he started eating in McCullough's, sitting at the bar. Before long, as had happened in the past at a few other drinking establishments, he became a regular, shooting darts, playing cards, swapping stories with a besotted Roman Catholic priest, a fixture of the tap room. The bartenders knew him by his first name and always made him a vodka and tonic (his starter drink) as soon as they saw him walk through the door. Despite his somewhat meager funds (he still had a little money left over from the novelization he did for that sci-fi movie), he always tipped big. Maybe the barkeeps liked him for that, but he preferred to think it was because he was such good company. He didn't talk usual bar-speak. (My wife/girlfriend hates me. My job sucks. How 'bout that game? Goddamn refs.) When a bartender was near, washing a glass or pouring, the writer would ask after his or her significant other or children, sometimes querying the barkeeper about local customs (never politics or religion, never in a bar his grandmother had told him). But maybe it was just the tips. It didn't really matter once he was good and drunk. They poured a good drink at McCullough's (especially Duane, the red-haired bartender) and its working class clientele made him feel like less of a prick—writing for a living sometimes made him feel like a big one (especially after the sci-fi movie novelization, which cried sellout, but, fuck it, the money was good).

Before long, there was dust on his keyboard and computer screen and the dinner tray he used as a desk. The seat of his chair too. (The housekeeper at the Franklin Arms, the motel he currently called home, didn't dust.) He'd once revealed to Duane that he was a writer, and the barkeep asked him what he was working on. He just grinned at Duane—he couldn't remember. Oh, he had notes. Voluminous notes and timelines and character sketches. If he sobered up for a day or two and took a peek, the whole story would come back (usually) and images of a Pulitzer would dance in his head once more like visions of sugarplums. But usually, once he squeezed himself this far down the bottle, he didn't come out unless he was rescued or the bottle broke and he ended up back in the ER, babbling to himself or passed out cold and bleeding on the street. After last call, he stayed up all night drinking in his room and slept till noon. His former writing habits had him up and at the desk before dawn. Now he didn't bother getting showered and dressed until he left his room for the bar around six or seven at night.

Yes, the drink found him before he found the words, but the words found him before he hit bottom. It started out with just a few adjectives giggling behind the shower curtain, a couple of adverbs hanging on the edge of the sink near his seldom-used razor. Then one afternoon, after a particularly rough night, he stumbled from his bed to vomit in the toilet a little after three and found the letters i and e chasing each other around the rim of the bowl in a contest to see who came first. "Chicken or the egg, gentlemen," he called out to i and e, but they paid no attention to him, and he soon grew bored watching the racing vowels and threw up some more. It was the participles dangling from the ceiling fixture reading his rejection letters out loud that undid him.

"Oh, here's one: 'We have read it carefully and found that it does not fit our current editorial needs.' "

"Which means: read our magazine, stupid, before submitting."

" 'We are sorry, but we don't think we are the appropriate agents for your inquiry.' "

"Which means: what the fuck were you thinking sending this shite to us?"

" 'We currently have a very full clientele and must be highly selective about the new projects we pursue.' "

"Which means: if you think you belong up here with us, you must be a full-blown drunk."

"One more, one more. I *love* this one. 'We're sure another agent will feel quite differently about your material though.' "

"Which means: every huckster has his mark—and we're not it."

The writer brushed aside a pile of gerunds he swore were trying to have sex with their own –ing suffixes and reached for a bottle.

The only thing worse than this, he thought, would be if Nancy was still around. Pure of heart and very much in love with her man of letters, the woman was a Puritan and became an irritant when he drank, like a constant buzzing in his ears. He didn't notice she was gone until two weeks after she left, and he only truly missed her when he was sober (which was never for very long; AA meetings made him nauseous, something about the combination of whining, stale coffee, and addicts sucking hungrily on cigarettes) and then he missed her terribly. But in his cups, Nancy was part of the tapestry that included the nuns in elementary school, a nasty case of crabs he caught once from a pickup in New Orleans, and his ex-wife, Sylvia, a super c-word if there ever was one. The only thing Sylvia was interested in these days was the same thing she was interested in when they were married: money. As long as he kept that monthly check a-comin', all was well in Sylvia's land of faux Fabergé and semi-swank dinner parties for people who used to be his friends. (He should have waited until the divorce was finalized to take the novelization gig.) A real nightmare, the women in his life, from nuns to Sylvia to, yes, even Nancy, whom he loved like no other.

He'd been lucky to find a publisher for his latest project. But one blurry evening, right before he left for McCullough's, he glanced at a calendar and was surprised to discover the deadline for his manuscript was in a week. So, flicking away a pair of conjunctions that were nesting near the phone, the writer did what he thought was best since things had reached this point. He would never be able to finish the book otherwise. Time for another woman. Fuel to the fire, he thought, enjoying the cliché. Let the nightmare be complete. He opened the back of the local weekly paper and called an escort service.

+

"I tell all the girls starting out the same thing: you can't get your hands wet unless you stick 'em in the sink. Of course, the opposite is usually more like it: who knows where you gotta stick 'em to get 'em dirty, but they ain't gonna get that way on their own, and dirty hands get the filthy lucre.

"It all comes down to this: you can work the streets or you can pole dance and do bachelor parties, giving blowjobs in the back of cars for an extra twenty bucks, or you can work for an agency. Now, an agency is good; it's really the way to go. You get a little protection for your kickback plus, of course, steady work. But you have to be careful there too. I've worked for my share of agencies, and I'm not knocking any of 'em, but you gotta know what's expected of you and what you gotta do when you get to a client's. I mean, 90 percent of the time you're working out-call unless you got a place you don't mind strangers traipsing through, or unless the agency's putting you up in a hotel (which they might do for a week in the city or in Valley Forge if there's a convention in town—all the cologne hounds away from their wives for a weekend). The thing is you don't know *what* the hell you're gonna get doing out-call. Used to be they sent someone with you, someone big (usually black or Latino too 'cause most of your johns are gonna be white, and nothing scares a white guy and hurries him along like a big person of color waiting for him on the other side of the door), but good men are hard to find, so most times, you're on your own, honey.

"I tell 'em all the same thing: you have no idea how many famous people started out working on their backs. And I'm not talking about just porn stars, although them too. You know that newswoman—come here, I'll whisper her name to you; you never know who's listening—yep, her. Believe me? She worked out of an agency in Old City, the Society Hill area. French was her specialty: no quit, no spit, if you get my meaning. Well, there are lots of TV stations out that way, and this gal had a degree in communications, if you can believe it. (You'd have sworn she majored in *en français*.) Started escorting in college for money. So one day she dresses up all sharp and business-like, and she's got a stack of envelopes with her. Resumes, you'd think. She goes around to each station in the area and a couple in New York and noses around until she finds someone among the higher-ups who'd engaged her services before. Word is that in each envelope was a resume and a copy of her ad from the *Philadelphia City Paper*. Honestly, she didn't have to look too hard; she was popular with the semi-affluent 'cause she didn't look like a common whore or a bus stop babe and clients could take her out on the town; she was good arm candy. Got herself seen that very day and was off her back and on the air within a month. True story.

"Now offering the girlfriend experience—there's no better way to make the big bucks (except ghostwriting a celebrity's book). First things first though: you better be a real looker; no butter faces. Now this is important: you gotta be okay with kissing. That's a *big* part of a GFE. Helps, it goes without saying, if you speak Greek; Lord knows wives don't; nothing's requested as much as Greek. Russian's good too, but if a guy's ordering up a GFE, he's not thinking Russian. Asian maybe, but not Russian. You know I'm not talking about languages here, right, honey? No? Christ almighty, get in the game. This isn't freshman comp. Look, you gotta use super secret lingo in the weekly paper ads. The johns know all the slang. French is head. Russian is when a guy rubs his pencil (often just a nub) between your boobs. Usually get a pearl necklace with that one. (Lucky us.) Asian is anilingus—salad tossing. Takes a special girl or a whole lot of tequila to go back there. And Greek is…well, let's just say after a long date conversing in Greek, you're not sitting down the rest of the night unless it's on a bag of frozen peas. BBBJ's are a must for a GFE. (Unsafe though they may be, it's not like he's *humping* you bareback.) BBBJTC—even better. (It's a caveman, chest thumping thing. Dominant gender and other myths, right?) Sometimes, though, if you're the girlfriend experience, they won't come in your mouth out of respect. (*Really* lucky us!) But most other times, it's what they expect. (Wives don't swallow, they tell us.) That's why you gotta be open and straight with 'em as soon as you get there. Sometimes the agency will do that for you, but they gotta be so cautious about what they say on the phone, so often they don't. You just tell the clients what you do and what you won't. Boundaries.

"Some of these high rollers, they want you to blow on dice and stand beside 'em looking pretty while they play in Atlantic City. (So always make sure to pack more than lingerie and a thesaurus.) Sometimes they want you for the full night or even a whole weekend, but that's rarer and rarer these days. (Guys never watch *Pretty Woman*, and girls should avoid that flick like the plague. No sense, I tell the girls, thinking you're her and looking for him. Not without lots of testing, a boatload of lies to tell his family, and a rock solid pre-nup.) To afford a GFE, the johns usually have some bucks, which is good; you can avoid the riffraff and such. But that also means they usually have wives somewhere, and even if they're from out of town, they gotta go home sometime (which goes back to what I was saying about Julia Roberts.) Speaking of out of town, I tell all the girls, don't go roadtripping with a client unless you get at least half the money up front. Funeral costs, I tell 'em. You leave the area, you lose what safety net you have. But for God's sake, if you feel you gotta go with him, tell someone. That way at least one person will be able to let the authorities know where to start looking for your body. But if nothing else, here in the city and the surrounding 'burbs you got *some* protection because the mob, they're behind a lot of the operations, money-wise. Doesn't mean a girl can't get hurt, but it does mean that the tough guy john, when they find him, will get hurt worse. Yeah, they're behind most of the high class escort operations. They even run most of the skanks in Chinatown and North Philly, the Strip over in Mondauk County, even the under-the-El crowd. Most of the working women.

"But you gotta have rules, I tell the girls. You can't decide you want to work the GFE angle and not have rules. Even the whores working the Strip have got *some* rules. I mean, what are you gonna do? Everything? You can't. No woman can. Me, I don't speak Greek. Never have. You gotta save a hole for your man. I'll do pretty much anything else. I'm accommodating. Pee on me. Cornhole you. Threesome with another chick—that's a biggie. I don't mind. I know all the girls, so it's just like shaking hands or giving a hug. Light bondage—depends, you know? You have to feel that one out. Tie a john up? Sure, no problem. Hand me a rope and a Boy Scout manual. Tie me up? I really gotta feel that this ain't no Green River Killer or Hannibal the Cannibal. Mondauk County, they got their own freak of the week. The Red Ribbon Killer, they call him. *Loves* hookers. But mostly the Strip variety. He slits their throats, then ties a red ribbon 'round their wrists. You never can tell. But even if I do let 'em, I carry my own silk rope in my purse. Fits snug in there right between my Bartlett's and the MLA Handbook. I practice, you know. The johns, they can tie it tight, use pretty much any kind of knot, but worse comes to worse, I can usually pull a Houdini if things start to get out of hand. So it's like grammar—you gotta have rules.

"Of course, companionship and sex isn't really why the scribbler set hires us. No, we get hired because we do what they can't—we wield our words fearlessly."

+

It was Friday evening.

The escort was only ten minutes late, but those ten minutes, *phew*, what doozies. During that time, the writer managed two more shots in between pacing back and forth. He had a week. A week to hand in the manuscript. He landed this publisher without an agent, which was almost unheard of, but his last agent split when the writer couldn't get past page two of a second novelization. The agent said he couldn't sully his own good name. Good name! Hah! Half the agency's writers wrote movie novelizations. The guy wasn't exactly repping Michael Chabon or Joyce Carol Oates. But it mattered not: the writer wanted to work on his own stuff anyway.

When he'd called the escort agency, he wasn't put on hold like he usually was when he called *anywhere*. The woman on the other end of the phone was pleasant and gentle; she sounded like a school nurse and said her name was Gloria. He told her he wanted a GFE. She said no problem. He asked if he could talk particulars. The woman answered yes, but she would stop him if she felt the conversation was veering into graphic territory.

"Our girls," she said, "are the best the area has to offer, and they will shine bright on your arm and make you look like a million bucks. But they won't do anything illegal."

The writer knew the drill. "I'm looking for a specific type," he explained. "Nothing out of the ordinary."

"Languages? Romance and Germanic: we offer most of those."

"Not important. I don't need a copy editor either. No spell check chick, right?"

"I understand," the woman from the agency said. "Full length or article?"

"Full length. Novel, actually."

"Deadline?"

"Manuscript due in a week. The publisher already read an outline and—"

"Full weekend booking then—maybe a little more. Blonde, brunette, redhead maybe, or do you want me to surprise you?"

"Brunette. Shapely. Doesn't use plot wheels."

"*Magister Artium*?" she asked with a curious cluck in her voice.

"Higher," he answered. "MFA and hot as hell on fire."

He gave the address of the motel and asked when to expect his visitor.

"An hour," the woman said. "An hour and a half."

"Has to sharpen her pencil, eh?"

"Something like that." Then she hung up.

+

Being ten minutes late no longer mattered: the girl at the door was significantly better looking than he expected. A cross between Irish and Italian, he thought. Straight delicate nose with a cute rounded tip, an elegant yet sinewy neck, soft brown eyes. Not much in the chest area, but from what he could see, thighs built for holding a man tight and an ass he imagined would be sweet as cherry vanilla ice cream. She didn't smoke—a big plus, since most working girls did, even the ones who offered GFE. He hated kissing a smoker; his ex-wife had smoked. He'd rather kiss a blender.

"Okay if I put my stuff down here?" she asked.

He nodded.

She placed her jacket and the stack of books beneath her arm, which included *The Chicago Manual of Style, 16ᵗʰ Edition*, on a chair and embraced him, her lips grazing his neck. He could feel himself beginning to grow hard.

"Show it to me," she said and he did. "So you're not a cop."

"Writers usually aren't," he responded, feeling stupid. It was difficult, he knew from experience, to say anything of value when he had a hard-on, even if it was weak from the booze.

She whispered a dollar amount in his ear, and he nodded. "That's till Monday morning, champ. So sayeth Gloria." He turned away and stuck a large number of Benjamins in an envelope, which he placed on the nightstand. He'd expected this to be an expensive endeavor, but he was desperate and so just about drained his savings account.

"Trusting," she said. "Some girls, they'd wait till you went to the bathroom or passed out, then rip you off."

"But not you."

She crinkled her nose.

"Show it to me," she said, pointing to the dinner tray.

"There's not much to show. A couple of chapters. An outline."

She sat down at his desk and began scrolling through his Word documents. "A *bildungsroman*. I can work with this. Shaky right here though. Dialogue stilted too. Started drinking heavy around the second chapter? Uh-huh. My name's Lisa by the way. I have an MFA from Rosemont. So, due in a week, huh? I understand they've already read the outline. Expected length? Tsk. We're gonna have to get right to it, but, hey, listen, it's your dime. You want to make love? Take a shower? You want me to blow you?" She smiled. "Four years of Latin; I don't speak Greek. Everything else is open for debate."

She had an easy, throaty laugh.

"That would be nice. Making love, I mean," he said. "But I've been drinking…"

She laughed and unzipped the back of her dress. "Hundred proof breath. I never would have guessed."

When they finished (which took some time considering his inebriated state, but Lisa was patient), the writer fell asleep. When he woke, Lisa was sitting in the nude, her fingers flying over the keyboard.

"You need a MacGuffin, first off, and, hey, you really want the priest to be the one to molest the boy? A little much, don't you agree?"

He nodded.

"I think Mr. Stelznick makes a much better villain—maybe a kidnapper with as-yet-unknown motives."

"Kidnapper." He scratched his chest. "And who, um, who is Mr—"

"Stelznick. Harry's fifth grade English teacher. I just added him to the roster."

"Oh," the writer said. "Sounds good. Stelznick."

"He seems innocuous. The red herring is the math teacher, who's a bit touchy-feely. The reader won't expect Mr. Stelznick. He's been a mentor to young Harry."

Lisa's bottom looked good in his chair, and her small but perfectly formed breasts bounced along as she typed.

"I made you a sandwich," Lisa said, not taking her eyes off the screen. "It's in the little fridge."

"Mentor. Sandwich." He tried to sit up but found the bed to be part of a runaway carousel. "Wait, you brought cold cuts?" He slumped back down.

"Shazam!" Lisa stopped typing and spun around in the chair. "You alright? I read your novelization while you were asleep. I'm a speed reader. Pretty good for what it is. You have real talent. I think this book will knock 'em dead. Hey, you want to come before you eat."

"No thank you," he answered.

She gave his penis a squeeze. "You just let me know when you're ready. We can try that position again if you like. Meanwhile, I'll just keep plowing ahead. I don't need much sleep. Never did. I know the publisher already read the outline—and a sample chapter at least—but I tossed most of it. I thought the arc was shaky, and the dénouement wasn't strong enough, to be honest. With a *bildungsroman*, you expect some kind of psychological or moral growth, some kind of knowledge gained, even if the knowledge just leads to (more) heartache. It can have an open-ended ending, but it has to feel definitive on *some* level."

"You're the one with the MFA," he said, brushing the few remaining split infinitives off a chair. Most of the grammar-related scamps had disappeared from his room when Lisa arrived.

She laughed. "All this and reverse cowgirl too. I'm a catch. Come here, honey." She tongue kissed him. "Leave everything to me."

And he did. He left everything to her. She never slept, it seemed. When she wasn't writing, she watched PBS or made him food or mixed him a drink. She went with him to McCullough's and held her own through the stares and cat whistles, and she drove them back to the motel when he fell off a barstool. Halfway through the second day she was more than halfway finished with the manuscript.

It was a rather a blur to Monday—lots of sex, lots of (Lisa's) typing, lots of pages piling up (electronically). They did everything (except Greek), even a few things the writer had never tried and decided he never wanted to again. (His backside still hurt.) She didn't make him wear a condom when she blew him, only when they had intercourse. He had screwed more during the past two and half days than he'd had in the past two and a half years. (And one of those years he was supposedly happily married.) When Monday morning arrived, he woke with a whiskey-flavored burp. Lisa was getting dressed. She had done her hair and was putting on a fresh shirt. She was still bottomless, and he gave her ass a good long stare. He knew he'd never see her again. She threw something at his head.

"They're for you, wordsmith," the escort said. "To remember me by. Olfactory fantasy."

He took her underwear from his head.

"They're dirty," Lisa said. "Now, look, I added a minor character towards the end. It's not like he just drops out of the sky or anything, but you really needed *someone* to witness the final transition besides the reader or it won't have the desired impact, you know what I mean?"

He nodded and sniffed the underwear. They were indeed dirty and smelled like all the secret parts of her. A predicate adjective fell out of the panties and ran around the messy sheets looking to modify something, anything.

Lisa laughed. "Could've been worse." she said. "It could have been a synecdoche. Nothing worse than part of something scooting around the place referring to a whole you know nothing about."

She could see this? It wasn't just in his head? Or was she part of the possible hallucination?

"What are you, angel?" he asked, placing the underwear on his head. "The pinch hitter with legs that start at your feet and end up at heaven?"

She grinned as she pulled on a pair of snug jeans. "Should use that line in your next book. Oh hey, I used your e-mail. I hope you don't mind."

He shook his head. "What's mine is yours, sweetheart."

Lisa grabbed her bag and her books and headed for the door, snatching the envelope from the nightstand with the barest of glances at its contents, which was what he'd counted on. He became worried for a second when she pretended to weigh the envelope in her hand—until she smiled. "Generous. Thank you," she said in a perfunctory manner, presumably talking about the tip she thought was included.

He blushed and started to say something but stopped. What would happen if he confessed and threw himself at her mercy? A beatdown from some goombah for even trying—or worse?

The door stopped as it was closing. "You got it wrong though, scribbler."

"How's that?" he called from the bed, her underwear still pulled over his morning hair.

"What's *mine* is yours," Lisa said and closed the door.

He didn't think of her again until seven months after the novel had been published. He was a shoo-in, his new agent said, to win the National Book Award. Word was he was on the short list. The book tour had gone swimmingly—in more ways than one. He contemplated writing a book on how different it was to be drunk in different cities. But even his drinking had slowly begun to subside. His career was finally going well. He was meeting interesting women. He stopped dreaming of Nancy. He hadn't called for an escort since Lisa. The novel had topped the *New York Times* Best Sellers List for four weeks running. Though he hadn't begun his book, he knew it would be his masterpiece.

Sometimes he felt guilty. If it hadn't been for Lisa... He didn't worry for one second about anyone finding out, but Lisa would have known by the time she reached her apartment or maybe even in the cab that the envelope contained the full fee but a paltry tip. The standard gratuity, he knew, for a girlfriend experience with someone who has her Master's is 30 percent. Steep, but he figured the girls remembered you. Thirty percent of the agency's fee for the past two and half days would have been significant. Instead he'd given Lisa the equivalent of what he would leave a waitress at a diner. It wasn't that he was cheap. He'd been near broke and knew he would be leaving the room once those two and a half days were over; he needed to find a cheaper place. A motel room along the Strip perhaps, outside the city—but maybe that would be too close to the working girls, he thought. (Not high-end escorts like Lisa, but word about deadbeats, he supposed, wasn't kept to just one class of hooker.) He moved out of the Franklin Arms in a hurry that morning and settled for a room that defined shabby in the Grays Ferry neighborhood of South Philadelphia, extremely close, he knew, to the heart of *La Cosa Nostra*, but he reasoned it was the last place Lisa or the escort agency would look for him (if indeed he was being looked for). But becoming a bestselling author changed his life and his zip code; with the new influx of cash came a new condo in the 'burbs. It also made him a public figure; no more hiding, but he believed his hiding days were over. He often thought of calling the agency (he still had the number in his wallet) and seeing if Lisa still worked there. She might have taken a teaching post. But if she was still plying her trade, maybe he could find her and give her the money he felt he owed her—plus. Let her enjoy some of his flushness.

But he never did.

And he never checked his e-mail outbox either.

+

"I tell my girls what E. M. Forster wrote about the difference between plot and story, 'cause they just don't know, some of them. And these are girls who've been through the system, the ringer. Workshops, professors who tell them how it is and how it should be, stuffy MFA programs, dead-end teaching jobs. See, a story, I tell 'em, is that 'the king died and then the queen died.' Presto. Shazam! But a plot, a plot is 'the king died and then the queen died of grief.' That Forster for you. Causality.

"In the old days, when I was out hustling, before I had...all this, I had two rules: I don't take it up the ass and I don't do Dostoevsky. Can't stand him. Started when I was still doing term papers and theses. All that existential hoo-ha—road apples, I say. Almost six hundred pages of Raskolnikov whining? Give me more Porfiry Petrovich. Now there's a man. For the undergrads, I had sort of a third rule (but I'd break it if the money was right): no *Moll Flanders*, no *Madame Bovary*, no Hester Prynne. Why remind myself of my place in the world? (That was what I saw in the mirror back then: the fallen woman.) You want to know why so many high school and college kids commit suicide? *A Catcher in the Rye.* (Or *I Am the Cheese* for the younger set.) It hints at who they might be and reminds them of where they are.

"I tell the girls, when you sit in front of a computer for a john (or a typewriter if he's one of these old fuddy-duddies), post-modernism is all right for kicks, but anything with even the *scent* of Kerouac, head for zee hills!

"It's about character, I tell 'em. And I know, *believe me*, I know. I walked the stacks for years, did the ol' Strunk and White, until this fell in my lap. Sure, sure, any girl worth her hot salt lick can give head, and there's no guy in the world whoever had a bad orgasm, but it takes *character* to do it justice. To blow their minds, not just their cocks. To get them the A or the book deal.

"But there are other common sense rules of the road, one of which is: count your money before you walk out of the door—do it in front of the john if he's new. Guess this fella, well, he was the last one I ever made that mistake with. Forget a cab ride, he didn't tip me enough to take the El. I usually could just tell by the weight of the envelope. *Felt* generous. But I was beat. Almost three straight days of writing and screwing. (Well, most of the latter time was spent trying to help the poor sap raise Old Glory.) Another important rule (besides counting the money and making sure someone knows where you are, especially if the john suddenly wants to change locations or hit a university library) is make a backup. I once read about this writer, she finished her novel, then her house caught fire. The novel's ash and the computer's melted—*but so was her backup.* Now here's where it gets unbelievable. She was backing up her novel to an external hard drive, which was kept on her desk…wait for it!…next to the computer. Can you imagine? Enough to make you want to go write advertising copy or teach Steinbeck to high school freshmen. So what did I do for this cheap bastard? I did what I always do: I made a backup, in a way. See, the john, when he wasn't trying to hump me with his broken wiener, was passed out cold. Big drunk. So giving him a backup drive would have been pointless—he'd just lose it, and he didn't seem to use a cloud service—so I e-mailed it to myself, everything from his anemic initial chapters to my drafts. Jesus though: not so much as a 'thank you' in the book. Just thanked his mother and some bitch named Nancy.

"Now I've had a couple of success stories in my past. No, I won't name names, so don't ask. But if you look close enough, you'll find my name or one of my aliases in the thank yous of books or in the end credits of movies. One screenplay I did—no, I told you, I'm not telling—it won Best Original Screenplay. I'm not kidding. The film won Best Picture too. Surprise win, really—the Best Picture Oscar, I mean. They always find a way to thank me. Never any back-end points though. That would be nice. Tacky maybe, but nice. I was hired for a job, I did it, 'nuff said. But this fella, he can't even tip me for what I did for him (which was fairly disgusting as far as the sex went); he can't tip me for my work, for my mind. But I had that e-mail. That backup copy. When I surfaced, he went down hard. *The New York Review of Books* ate him for lunch. *Time* and *The Paris Review of Books*, among others, savaged him. An afternoon talk show host berated him on national television. (Why he showed up is beyond me.) He was stripped of the National Book Award. (I don't know why it didn't automatically go to me!) Hit the bottle with a vengeance, they say. The way I hear it, he's in a locked unit at Quincey, a psychiatric hospital, punching at reciprocal pronouns and double genitives. Would be sad if he wasn't so bitter towards me. I held up my end of the bargain, boy. The ironic part of all this, of course, is that his heroine—*my* heroine (I changed the gender)—is a reformed prostitute who tries to make good on the backs of her johns. It's funny, for all the years I spent avoiding Moll, Emma, and Hester, the fallen woman archetype had sunk into me anyway. Sometimes we can't help but stumble over a cliché, pick it up, put our ear to it, and hear more than the ocean. I tell my girls—don't print this, but I have my own stable of fillies now, all with an MFA, although one hottie has her PhD—it's not a cliché unless you use it like one, and the fallen woman isn't truly down for the count unless she was actually knocked out.

"So, yes, I'm back in the game, in a different capacity, a madam, if you will. See, at first, after he went down, no agent or publisher would touch me—until some of them realized they had. But I didn't blackmail anyone; I kept my mouth shut; that's part of offering the GFE. It's all about respect on some level; we offer discretion; the johns leave us more than the cost of a soft pretzel. I would never have gone public if my envelope contained more than a little respect—or any at all. But I keep my hand in the game because girls need to enter the room with more than just their *Garner's* and their garters; they need an experienced hand to guide them around the has-beens and those that never were, an editor-in-chief who's spent time tied to a bed in between trying to untangle some stream-of-consciousness dribble.

"What's that? No, you haven't been paying attention.

"The girlfriend experience isn't for everyone. Sometimes it's for the lonely hearts who can't (or won't) find a girl of their own. 'Course there's always the fat cats who just want to show off at the craps table, then get their rocks off in a comped hotel room. But a true GFE is for a guy who needs someone to help him be the best part of himself, the part he's long forgotten or long abandoned. (Women rarely engage our services; a woman wants to get laid, she goes out and gets laid; she wants to write a trilogy, she sits down at a desk and writes one.) But the clients, they don't always appreciate our services. They just want to pass that course or sell that article to *Esquire*. But every once in a while, the guys who truly appreciate good art (whatever that is!) and good head will take care of you, stick something extra in the envelope on the nightstand, something significant (more than 30 percent), or give you a half point on the gross. Your job, I tell the girls, is to be the muse—though today, more often than not, it means being their pen. But, hey, I tell 'em, that's okay. We're not here for us; your time will come, I say, just like mine did, though not everybody will hit the same heights. Simon & Schuster, they…well, how did New Jersey's true poet laureate put it? 'Because the record company, Rosie, just gave me a big advance!' But that's rare. It's hard to make it. (Though for our friend, only the fall was hard, but I bet my bottom dollar that in the hospital, all medicated up, there's nothing ever gonna be hard again, wink, wink, nod, nod.) We're here for them (until they *really* fuck us). The girlfriend experience is a fantasy of what should be, in their heads, the perfect female companion, a doggy style cliché who swallows, Cliffs Notes in high heels, a Playmate with a thesaurus. We're grammar's bitch, and while they play at being Hemingway or Faulkner, we cross the t's, dot the i's, and turn their creaky plots into compelling stories. And we do all this naked.

"Now, two girls, collaborations—well, that's extra, mister.

"Are we done here? Can I go?"

-end-

Rageful

I couldn't tell what her face looked like, and it wasn't like I wasn't trying.

A redhead. Gorgeous? Skin like vanilla ice cream with freckles for jimmies. Fleshy but fit. Thighs you just wanted to squeeze through so you could curl up and spend the night. Red all over? The curtains *and* the drapes, the way I remember. Eyes so blue, oceans were jealous. Daphne was the name she gave me, but I knew better. But what's in a name? She didn't recognize me at first—I'd gotten heavy—or pretended she didn't.

Was it *carpe diem* or *memento mori* tattooed on the back of her neck, hidden under her thick red hair, accessible only to those with whom she shared a certain level of intimacy and, of course, her hairdresser? I could never remember, but it added up to the same thing as far as I was concerned: time was ticking away, bud, better live it up.

"Combinatorics, ma'am?"

She nodded her head, and her hair, still wet from the shower, fell into her eyes.

"Tommy used to teach it up the college, before the incident there with the student. She hollered it up quite a bit, and Tommy, he didn't stand a poor man's chance. Said it was about problem solvin', combinatorics. Said it was the study of the finite, the discrete. Mathematical secrets, I said. Secrets that done him in."

"Uh-huh. Right in his own bathtub."

Daphne nodded her head again.

"But *your* hair's wet somewhat. You take a shower *before* the bad guys come in?" I bit my lip. Not like me to give the witness a possible answer to a question.

"My nightly ablutions, after which I went to our room and played the radio while I took my face off. That's why I didn't hear nothin'."

Her face looked on to me. Her lipstick appeared to have been recently applied, as if it was put on for someone other than the dead guy, as if it was put on for us, for me.

"You from around these parts, ma'am?" I asked even though I knew the answer.

"My people are from down Mississippi way." She sighed. Real practiced—real good too. "Guess that's where I gotta head back to, sort my life out. Tommy was always so good to me."

It was my turn to nod my head—for appearances sake. Bennie, my partner, knew to stay away when I was locked in. (Although I was quite the opposite—I just looked the part of the laser-focused dick.) He diddled around with the ME in the bathroom. In addition to being drowned, Tommy LaMastro had a curtain rod shoved into his rectum about a quarter of the way up the rod. Bennie always did have a strong stomach for these types of calls. Me, I was doing what I was good at. But I was being a bad partner. I hadn't told Bennie that I knew her, that we'd grown up together here in the county, and that we'd been best friends for two summers when we were in our early teens. That was how I knew the curtains matched the drapes.

"What did the deceased—what did Mr. LaMastro do for a living since he wasn't teaching mathematics anymore?"

Daphne lit a cigarette and offered me one. I declined. Quitting was hard enough the first time around—and the second.

"This and that. Tommy was a resourceful kinda guy."

"This and that, hmm-mmm. Did Tommy ever have any new friends that you met, friends that didn't look quite right, friends that looked…dangerous?"

"If you're talkin' Mr. Foster, that was over with. Tommy was just helpin' out with the numbers, see, nothin' big. Just accountin'. But Tommy started to play his own book as it were. Mr. Foster's point man—goes by the name of Slater—it's Slater runnin' the operation, and this whole thing don't go over too good with Slater. What started as a seed sprung up as an evil. So Tommy got his self out."

"With a substantial nest egg."

Daphne laughed. "Look around, detective. You see any nests? You see any Frabergé eggs? Tommy walked away with his skin, which is all he walked away from that college with too—just his chicken liver skin."

It wasn't that I couldn't *see* her face, but it kept changing. One minute I'd focus on the little indentation on her nose, the next on her high forehead, then the way her hair fell around her ears. When we were thirteen and the only kids our age, it seemed, in the hamlet of Blue Bell in Warminster, which consisted of burgeoning housing developments and still-large farms, we told each other what we'd never told anyone else before and unlocked even deeper secrets. Her name was Callie back then, short for Calliope, and she'd come up from the South with her family to make a new go at it, the South having been particularly unkind to her father's financial excursions. The North was equally unkind, it turned out, and our friendship ended with her father's heart attack right in front of her while he was opening yet another notice from the IRS. Or so the story went. The next day she got the tattoo after she had one of the older boys who were always sniffing around forge the consent slip. When she came back, she bent her neck and flipped her hair for me to see, but I barely looked because she wasn't alone. I never saw Callie after that unless you count the faraway glimpse I got of her at her father's burial, but I stayed pretty well hidden behind a tree. Until today, I never knew Callie had stayed in (or moved back to) Mondauk County. I figured she and her mother went back south when they moved. Yet here she was with her boyfriend gored in his chocolate starfish with a curtain rod, lying facedown in the apartment's bathtub.

Interestingly, the apartment's few windows were curtainless; they just had shades that looked new.

"How did you get that, ma'am?" I asked, pointing to an impressive shiner around her left eye. There were also older bruises on her left cheek.

Daphne blew some smoke and put out her cigarette. "That's hard to say, detective, what with circumstances being as they are and all."

"Sometimes even the nicest guys," I explained, "can be assholes."

"I ain't gonna think like that."

She was quiet for a moment and I let her be. That was how it had been back when we were thirteen. It was always better to let Callie find her own way to something.

"He was rageful, is all," she explained. "Got his self full up a-rage and whiskey. Firewater, he called it, just like Pappy. The drink of the devil."

Firewater. She actually said firewater.

"Did Mr. LaMastro hit you often, ma'am?"

"Hell, no. I wouldn't put up with it if he had. He just got a wee bit outta hand this one time—maybe twice. Smacked me but good. Had it comin', I guess. I was runnin' my mouth."

Oh, do I remember that mouth! Callie could give an earful of invective before breakfast and have plenty left over for lunch.

"So Mr. LaMastro was drinking tonight, ma'am?"

Callie rubbed away a crocodile tear and smiled. Oh, did I know that smile. The jig was up. I looked around to make sure Bennie was still occupied with the late Mr. LaMastro and the medical examiner.

"You can cut the 'ma'am' shit, Charlie. I know who you are as much as you know who I am. No, no, stop—and I know you're rememberin' that time 'neath the old willow when I lifted my sun dress and showed you my coochie. I know who you are. How I recognize you 'neath all that *you*, I don't rightly know, but it's you all the same, Charlie Walsh, just times two."

"You doing the mathematics now, Callie?"

"Yeah, but it don't add up, does it, Charlie?"

I shook my head to clear it. I was sweating pretty bad.

"Tommy—he go to McCullough's tonight, Callie, or another tap room? That where he got all liquored up?"

Callie shook her head and strands of her drying burnt orange hair caught the dim light of the solitary lamp and temporarily blinded me with color.

"Didn't have no time to do that, what with catchin' the train and stoppin' for the lottery. Had-ta come home right on time. Johnny-on-the-spot. He was like that. Must-a had it on him."

I studied my notebook for a second. Callie was right: *something* didn't add up.

"He didn't have any bottles secreted on his person," I said, "and you don't seem to have any alcohol on the premises." If he was still involved in anything…mathematical, I figure he'd want to be pretty sober for that.

Callie shrugged. I knew that shrug. It wasn't as insouciant as it seemed. It was the same shrug she'd given me when I'd told her that I loved her, right before she lowered my head to her lap and caressed my hair and I fell asleep listening to my heartbeat pounding in my ears, wondering if I could smell her secret place from where I was.

"And you—what are you doing employment-wise these days?"

Callie laughed and lit another cigarette. "This and that. Secretarial. Temp work mostly."

"You do any temp work for Mr. Foster?"

The new cigarette was angrily stubbed out.

"That's none of your damn business, Charlie Walsh." She sighed and the anger dissipated. "Just 'cause Tommy couldn't get his self straight with Mr. Foster doesn't mean I can't. If I wanted. But I don't. So the answer is not at the moment."

"Until Tommy's debt becomes yours with the vig running."

She ignored me. "I go through a temp agency sometimes."

"Any pay stubs we can check out, Callie? The boys at the station just love a little extra paperwork."

Callie pushed her hair back with her fingers. God, she was still so...and then for a brief moment I was back with her in the fields behind her house, cicadas in the trees, lying on our backs, chewing onion grass.

"Shit outta luck, Charlie. Don't keep 'em."

"Ain't that just my luck. How 'bout that ring there on your finger—that new?"

I thought I saw her blush, but it was hard to tell in all that red.

"This old thing? Gift from my grandmother."

"Both of your grandmothers are dead."

"A bequeathment then."

I scratched my head and looked quizzical. I always do this to hopefully throw the interviewee off track.

"So Foster wanted him dead but couldn't get to him? Or wouldn't fuck with him because then they wouldn't know where that substantial nest egg was hid? The only person besides Tommy who knew was probably—you, I guess. And of course, there was a finder's fee. Probably a nice one too. Wow."

Callie laughed and placed her hand over mine. "It's still red, you know."

It was my turn to blush, but I didn't. With deep regret, I removed my hand from under hers.

"I guess I only got one question left."

Callie leaned back on the sofa. "Shoot, chummy."

That was what she used to call me back then in Blue Bell: chummy. Shit. Concentrate. Concentrate. I'm so close.

"Why did it happen tonight?"

Callie blanched.

"Did it happen because it was my shift, me and Bennie's, because you somehow knew that we'd catch this case?" Silence. "I guess that was more than one question. And here's a third: was this you being *rageful* or was it a hit with you as the hitter?"

She stared at me, and for a few seconds there I felt like I was thirteen again, drowning in her twin oceans.

"Yes," Callie answered "Both." She ignored my first two questions. "But being rageful facilitated the second." It wasn't planned but she'll take the reward from the mob (assuming they don't role over the interest from Tommy's debt to her)—or she'll dig up the nest egg and beat it out of town before Foster's men show up.

My stomach churned and my hands got shaky. *Facilitated*, I told myself; it wasn't premeditated—according to Callie. A Beatles lyric spun around and around my head: *And when I touch you I feel happy inside / It's such a feeling that love / I can't hide, I can't hide, I can't hide.*

I flipped my notebook closed and reached for her hand again, but Callie was gone; Daphne was busy lighting another cigarette and took no notice.

Bennie came out of the bathroom, toothpick dancing in his mouth. "Forget about it. Total pig fuck in there. Excuse me, ma'am."

Daphne barely registered a response, so lost was she in her grief. Callie, hidden again, waited to see how I would play it.

"Whatcha got out here, eh?" Bennie asked.

We shouldn't be having this conversation in front of her, but it was for show; even my partner, who hadn't exchanged more than two words with her, could smell that something was amiss.

I sighed and tried to take one more glimpse of my long lost Callie, but I couldn't see her anymore.

"Foster hit," I answered Bennie. "The vic was crunching numbers for them, then split with a score. So Foster had him clipped."

"Jesus God, what the fuck, huh? Didn't split very far, did he?"

I have to give Bennie credit for not making the joke: they'd hit him where the good Lord split him. But he was looking at me kind of funny, or maybe that was just in my head.

"Well, at least it won't be an all-nighter anyway," my partner said. "Hey, I was gonna go out for coffee."

"I'll go, Bennie."

"Gettin' to ya?"

"Makin' me see red."

"Right, make mine black, okay? I'll keep an eye on the damsel in distress."

"Right."

I never saw her again. I drove by the apartment once, but she was gone baby gone. But not from my head. Every night she put me to bed and every morning she was there to wake me up. But we exaggerate our childhoods; our best friends become our blood brothers, our afternoon adventures become lifelong quests. I hope Daphne's okay, but I hope Callie comes back, although I pretend it doesn't really matter. Rageful I am for you, Callie, and in the best way, full of the raging beat of a scarred heart, but I will bide my time. We've got a secret again. True colors always shine through in the end, and I've got yours. No guilt, just a color, and a color is all I need.

-end-

The Basin

Something into nothing, Mr. Davidson thought. *Then something out of nothing.*

Five o'clock on Saturday nights during the summer, the fathers in the neighborhood, cigarettes dangling from their mouths, would each spray lighter fluid, drop a match, and stoke the charcoals to start their grills. Mr. Davidson was no different except that he didn't smoke. He was not a fan of grilled food either, but his children and wife were, and that was enough. The ritual was the same every pretty much Saturday summer night. He'd wave to Mr. O'Shea next door, maybe lean over the fence and talk jazz. He'd yell over to Mr. Runyon on the other side, and they would shoot the shit about last night's ballgame. Mr. O'Shea would acknowledge Mr. Runyon with, "Ted," and a slight nod. Mr. Runyon would half wave and pretend to be preoccupied with his grill or one of his many kids. Mr. O'Shea and Mr. Runyon were not fans of each other. Mr. Davidson thought it might have something to do with Mr. O'Shea having three girls and Mr. Runyon three boys (and a daughter) with only Mr. Davidson's family of four—one boy, one girl—between them in a neighborhood of twin houses. (Mr. Davidson shared his twin with Mr. Runyon, thank God. He could only imagine if the O'Sheas and the Runyons were separated by only a thin wall and a leaning fence.) Every late Saturday afternoon, Mr. Davidson's wife would pop her frosted head out of the back door and announce they were out of pickles, mustard, red onions, buns, something, and she was running to Sol's to replenish. (She'd have to walk today; she'd dropped her car off at the mechanic's on Thursday, and he couldn't find his car keys.) His son, if not playing street hockey, was usually up in the dogwood reading a book. His daughter would often come running into the yard, her face flushed, with the youngest of the O'Shea girls. The O'Shea family's yellow Lab would gamely try to keep up, but the old gal was too well fed to ever truly succeed. This Saturday promised more of the same. His son was in the tree with *Treasure Island*. His daughter practiced her pig Latin in the driveway with the leggy O'Shea girl while the panting yellow Lab sat and watched attentively. His wife was on her way to Sol's by now. (They were out of marshmallows; the kids had already picked out their sticks.) It was mid-August, and Mr. Davidson had yet to grow tired of the ritual, which had been broken only by the annual family vacation at the Jersey shore.

The only difference in tonight's backyard cookout exercise was that he and his wife were expecting guests. Two other couples, both childless. (One couple wasn't married.) Mr. Davidson wasn't looking forward to their visit. Instead of watching the kids play Freeze Tag as the light drained from the sky or taking part in a wireball game under the sickly glow of the streetlight with his son and the younger Runyon boys after the marshmallows had been burned and eaten, he'd be sitting in the coming gloom with the two couples, drinking sangrias and listening as they traded humorous stories that weren't very funny (to him) and tragic ones that, *thank God!*, the women would exclaim, happened to someone else. He'd planned on working on his sketch book after playing with the kids, but now he'd have to settle for banal banter with the leading lights—at least in his wife's eyes—of Mondauk County. She seemed consumed with their imminent presence. Mr. and Mrs. Abbott were ultra-conservative Christians from some Protestant church or other where Mr. Abbott was a reverend. (It might have been Phil Abbott's church for all Mr. Davidson knew.) Mr. Davidson had heard that the corpulent Reverend Abbott could be loquacious while on the mount, but he said very little whenever Mr. Davidson encountered him, what he said was usually muffled, as if he spoke into his second chin, so large it could easily be mistaken, at a distance, for the head of a conjoined twin. He'd rarely spoken to the reverend's wife, who deferred to her husband on most things anyway. Her Roman nose and her bosom were the only features that stood out and mostly because her nose appeared to be so heavy, her head seemed to be forever bent in supplication towards her enormous boobs.

The other couple was considerably more complicated. Meryl Payne was a retired romance novelist. (Independently wealthy, some said, but if so, Mr. Davidson wondered what was she doing still living in the eastern part of Mondauk County?) Her escort, her male friend (boyfriend being a young person's term), Feargal Finnerty, had emigrated from Northern Ireland as a boy and was now a homicide detective in Mondauk. Whereas the Davidsons had been host to the Abbotts a number of times despite the latter being poor conversationalists and the Davidsons being nominally Catholic (they were friends of his wife's from community meetings), they had never had Detective Finnerty or Ms. Payne as guests before. Mr. Davidson had to admit that his mind had gone elsewhere (to the pool, to the Basin) when the detective's name first came up and so never found out how he and the retired writer had come to be invited to their home for a late Saturday cookout. His wife was a pushover, so Finnerty could have invited himself (or had Meryl do it), or it could have been just an unlucky coincidence. Either way, it didn't bode well. Not after the events of two weeks ago. *Had it been that long,* Mr. Davidson thought. *Gee.*

Carol Conway, according to the *Philadelphia Inquirer* and the *Mondauk Common,* was a model student, a senior, the member of several clubs at Father Hoskins High, and an avid fundraiser for various environmental causes. But what the papers failed to report was that among other kids, Carol was called Cherry—and not because she still had hers. Mr. Davidson knew about the ironic nickname (which had nothing to do with her red hair, he'd learned the first day he'd watched her) because he managed the Mondauk Proper Recreational Center. (Eventually he came to learn that she was a natural redhead; he'd assumed it was a dye job.) The Rec included a concrete playground and two baseball diamonds that adults used to play softball while they drank beer on Sunday afternoons and local little league teams used to battle clubs from the other boroughs. A football summer camp was held here. But the Rec's real attraction was its Olympic size pool. During summer weekdays, mothers sat on the grass outside the fence that surrounded the pool, the heavy-set ones under the trees, the comely roasting in the sun reading *Cosmo,* occasionally watching their kids splash and cavort and piss in the pool. A few different groups of high school girls hung out there as well. One-piece bathing suits were out and, thank the heavens, bikinis were the norm among the prom and lockers set. Mr. Davidson watched them from the concrete maintenance building's small windows, his breath racing away from him, his pants often around his ankles (after double-checking that the door was locked) when he wasn't furiously trying to capture in his sketch book the insouciant way Cherry's red hair cascaded past her shoulders whenever she leaned over to give to boys an eyeful. Although it was an oven in there even with the door open and his body would be covered in sweat when he emerged (especially after his exertions), the windows afforded him the best surreptitious view. That was how he "met" Cherry Conway. That was how he came to know she had lost her cherry to Sal Greco sophomore year in Sal's parents' basement next to the water heater. It didn't hurt at all, Cherry had claimed in a cavalier manner to her girlfriends. That bothered Mr. Davidson a little, and he lost sleep trying to figure out why—why it bothered him and why losing her virginity hadn't hurt. He decided either Cherry was lying or she'd had intercourse before. He also learned of subsequent couplings with Derek Gallagher (who had rancid breath and a baby's penis) and Mark Eliot (who was packing but liked to bite). Mr. Davidson also came by the knowledge that Cherry claimed to prefer blowjobs to sex. ("Less messy," she told her gal pals, "unless …you know…you spit it out.") That day Mr. Davidson didn't leave the maintenance building for three hours, and when he arrived home, he was chafed and limping.

And so here was the problem with Detective Finnerty's unexpected invitation: Mr. Davidson had taken (as in "seized" not "absorbed") Carol "Cherry" Conway when she'd scurried to the bathrooms at the Rec during a somewhat intense thunderstorm. (It was enough of a storm that no one there, not even her companions, thought she was missing at first—just keeping out of the rain somewhere else perhaps. "Heck," classmate Deborah Fuller told the *Common*, "we were all running for shelter.") After disseminating his seed, he kept her in the maintenance building, hidden behind the pool equipment, for more than just a little while, which wasn't smart, as the Rec was soon crawling with parents and a few cops looking for Cherry after the storm had passed. (When they found the small maintenance building locked, they luckily—and stupidly—went on.) But he couldn't risk moving her until long after dark when the search parties' were just bouncing flashlight beams in the acres of tall yellow weeds known as the Fields. Then he could pull his Subaru up and load her in the back along with other bags full of sports equipment. Plus, waiting until past midnight gave him time with her. (He told his wife he'd been taking part in the search and had lost his phone in the dark.) Although he had no intention of violating Cherry (while she was alive)—he was many things, but he wasn't one of those sick bastards always profiled on the news, he'd kept telling Cherry over and over, but half the time she was unconscious—he needed to have her tell him (when she was with it) the stories of Sal Greco and the water heater, Derek Gallagher's microphallus and the biter Mark Eliot, and especially the advantages of swallowing over spitting. Extracting those words weren't easy. But he needed to hear these stories again (and told to *him*, not Cherry's regular giggling gaggle), so he could pleasure himself over her words one more time, maybe get it out of his system. He needed Cherry to witness his self-manipulation so she would see what she had driven him to do, what her wanton behavior had wrought. She needed to see the kind of man—a sweaty, red-faced, moaning ghost of a man—she had created. She'd always used condoms, she told her girlfriends, and was careful about stray sperm, but she'd been responsible for some nonetheless—*his*—and here was the proof, he thought then, right in front of her striking blue eyes. Here was truly stray, wandering spunk, messing up her pretty red hair. Here were random splashes of escaped gametes, and they were his, exploding pieces of what remained of him, seeping down past the outer trappings to her bones, hungry for resurrection. Once her hair was held back by the dragonfly barrette Mr. Davidson had bought for just such an occasion, he sketched her one last time before he took her apart.

+

Mrs. Davidson arrived back from her walk to Sol's just in time to great their guests. (It was so unlike his wife to cut it so close, and he thought she looked as if she'd been crying. Poor woman; she didn't have much luck with cars: she'd borrowed his the week before to go on a Costco run—she had a Prius—and had gotten a flat, in the rain no less. She changed the tire herself though; she could be one tough cookie though he usually thought of her as a pliable dollop of dough.) She was the perfect hostess and made sure everyone had drinks before they even parked their rears in lawn chairs. Mr. Davidson asked the detective how he liked his burger cooked. "Almost walking," was the answer (as if he'd been asked how he liked his steak) and everyone laughed, even Mr. Davidson, but it was just something he'd learned when he was younger: lift your head and open your mouth; others would provide the sounds. Mr. O'Shea leaned over the fence and asked to borrow some lighter fluid. The Runyon boys sent lightning bugs to insect heaven with their Wiffle ball bats. Mr. Davidson's young children sat with their parents and their guests, balancing paper plates on their scabby knees, politely answering questions about the impending start of school and the Phillies until their mother gave them the signal that allowed them to scamper away to finish their game of Freedom with the O'Shea girls.

The gloaming gave way to darkness.

Mr. Davidson knew it was coming—the opening gambit—and though it would be put before the group, it would really be directed at him. He'd watched enough cop procedurals to know to scrub the floor of the maintenance building after he'd folded Cherry Conway into a sports equipment bag, and he also knew from the movies how gumshoes worked their suspects. Detective Finnerty did not disappoint: it was just about dark when the detective asked the Davidsons and the Abbotts, "Still go out to the Basin?"

(A song buzzed in Mr. Davidson's head.)

The Basin had been a pond that had been drained a generation or so ago. It was located on the western edge of Pennypack Woods in the borough of Mondauk Proper, not far from the creek that everyone called the Puddle. (Pennypack Creek was infamous for its usually awful stench.) During extremely heavy rainstorms, lengthy and raging (the one during which he'd had his quiet time with Cherry was far too brief to count), the Puddle would become swollen and would overflow, filling the Basin and temporarily turning it back into a pond. Ducks would float in it; frogs would hop around its edges. Dragonflies, the kings of its kind, buzzed majestically across the surface. Mr. Davidson had come to believe this ephemeral pool was the most beautiful sight he'd ever seen (and he'd witnessed the birth of his children). *Something out of nothing.* Was there anything more beautiful than that, he wondered. There'd been an emptiness after the first couple of girls; he knew there had to be a purpose to what he did; he just didn't know what it was, and while trying to figure it all out, he found he liked to drive out to the Basin there during thunderstorms; he'd just park and watch, ignoring the retreating picnickers, capturing a bit of the beauty in his sketchbook. He'd visit there as often as he could after a big storm and the subsequent alluvion, sometimes staying for hours (which required more lies to his increasingly inquisitive wife), sketching dragonflies until his fingers cramped. But in the weeks after the rain stopped (the length of time depended upon the weather), the pond would be gone. Desiccated. The water evaporated. The ducks and the frogs, the dragonflies and the damselflies: all departed. *Something into nothing.* He'd proved he could accomplish the same, but *something* out of *nothing*? So far, his children were the closest he'd gotten, but they'd come from his jizz infiltrating one of Mrs. Davidson's eggs, hardly *nothing*—plus both he and his wife been alive during the couplings. What happened at the Basin after it was flooded by Pennypack Creek during days of heavy rain may be a natural though temporary event, just displaced water—but: presto change-o nonetheless!

(*It was a fleeting visit, all too brief,* went the song stuck in his head.)

That was why he had buried Cherry Conway's body, bespattered with his ejaculate, in the Basin—to see if he could make *something* out of what was now nothing but a heap of forensic clues. (Cop shows be damned; what did forensics show of passion and love? Yes, love—for he had loved Cherry Conway; for a few, shining, splashing moments, oh, how he had loved her.)

"Not often, not anymore," Mrs. Davidson answered the detective with the slightest hint of—what?—curiosity in her voice. Mr. Davidson was glad he couldn't see her face well beneath the string of dim party lights she'd made him hang in the backyard or that she couldn't see his well either. He'd begun to suspect, for no good reason (and that was more worrisome), that she knew of his Lazarus-tinged activities. If she did, there was no way she understood the reasons or implications; regardless, he didn't want to have to hurt the mother of his children if she decided to open her trap. He shook his head to clear the nonsense: most likely it was a non-issue no matter what she thought she knew; she was too enamored with the regularity of their life to ever utter a peep. "My Larry," his wife continued, touching her husband's hand (*and didn't it feel like touching dead flesh, honey,* he thought, *for I'm transcending this world*), "he used to love taking me there when we first dated. You used to go all the time when you were young, right, hon?" He nodded but he doubted anyone could see (there wasn't much of a moon)—except Detective Finnerty who struck a match to light his cigarette just at that moment. "Now we usually just cookout at home. My Larry says it's easier than hauling everything out to that dead old pond, isn't that right, hon?" Mr. Davidson coughed and Detective Finnerty shook his match out. "As rain," Mr. Davidson replied to his wife, trying not to grin at just *how* right she was. The rain made *something out of nothing* in Pennypack's Basin, and he'd made *something into nothing* inside the Rec's sweltering maintenance building, near the chlorine-heavy pool, as thunder rattled the windows. *Right as rain, honey bunny!* Where else would he have taken Cherry, sown with his seed, but the Basin? If the weather reports were to be believed, a three day storm was coming, and the Basin was where eventually water from the heavens and the muck of the Puddle (the glorious and the tainted) would mix with his seminal fluid and her bones (through what skin and hair he'd left attached)...*something out of nothing.*

The Basin, when not a temporary pond (which it was at least once a season), was part of a picnic area, its central feature in fact. No one knew why the pond had been drained. Years ago, the Mondauk County Water and Waste Department had argued before the County Council that the area should be made into a permanent retention pond to store rainfall runoff from the nearest acres of tall yellow weeds known as the Fields. (Having nowhere else to go, the water would often overwhelm the sewer system, which would wreck havoc in the Narrows, the neighborhood along the northwestern banks of the creek (whose location made it already susceptible to flooding). A retention pond would be, they claimed, an efficient and cost-effective land drainage system that would prevent erosion and naturally filter the water before it drained into the Puddle, but the banks of the creek nearest the Basin sloped *towards* it, ensuring the opposite, and the Council just didn't have money in its budget for altering the terrain. (Up until recently, Mr. Davidson still thought a retention pond was a good idea; the runoff from the Fields could make the Rec a hell of a mess, but after the inspiration of the old well in Spring House—and despite the failure of that first attempt—he'd become convinced that the Basin's aperiodic transformations were intrinsically related to what he knew were his latent metamorphic faculties.) As a consolation prize, the County Council had (generously, they said) given Mondauk Proper money to purchase picnic tables and such (most of which were set up adjacent to the Basin, but a few were actually in it; sometimes Mr. Davidson could make out the tops of the picnic tables whenever the Basin was becoming a pond again; *becoming* was Mr. Davidson's favorite word). Also purchased were swings and a large, flat piece of wood that became a sign dedicating the site to some long dead politician, the name burned into the wood. But the top of the sign remained blank. The borough officials could never decide on what to name the picnic area. Everyone called it the Basin, so of course they couldn't use that. The Catholics wanted to name it the St. John Nepomucene Rest Area after the patron saint of running water, among other things. (He was martyred by being thrown off a bridge and drowned.) Besides the absurdity of naming a drained pond after the drowned sainted protector against floods (and calling it a rest area—the borough hadn't seen fit to build even a small bathroom facility), the Catholics, although definitely the majority Christian denomination in the town, were, as always, faced with the very vocal Methodist minority who wanted give the Basin the name Wesley Park, an obvious enough Methodist name—obvious enough to piss off the Catholics and their powerful lay Faith Board who largely controlled the Council (but not completely). So the Basin remained unnamed—but Mr. Davidson knew its true appellation was Metamorphosis.

"Why do you ask, Detective?" Mrs. Davidson said, clearly no longer interested, her husband thought, but being polite all the same. "About the Basin." His wife, Mr. Davidson assumed, wanted to spend the cookout gossiping with Meryl Payne. (The Abbotts offered very little in the way of interesting conversation; their only mildly amusing story this evening involved some new hymnals that were missing a page.) Who could be more scintillating than a retired romance writer involved in what appeared to be a deep romance with one of Mondauk County's most eligible bachelors, the rough and ready homicide detective? But the time for the genders to split off (as usually happened) had passed with nightfall, so now they sat in a tight circle in the Davidsons' backyard as the noise of children running, laughing, and scaring each other surrounded them. Occasionally they would hear a parent call a child in, but not the Runyons or the O'Sheas or the Davidsons. On their piece of the street, they believed, their children were safe from predators and the like.

"Been working a case," Detective Finnerty began, and Meryl lightly admonished him. ("Do you think *now's* the time?") "My partner, Paulie—Detective Masconi—he says it's a snatch-and-batch..."

"*Honestly!*" Meryl said, practiced annoyance shading her tone.

"...an *inappropriate* term that means the perp abducted the victim, did his...business, ditched her, and went back to cooling his heels, that is until the itch becomes too much to bear. In these cases, the victim if often found alive—and found relatively quickly. Once he's spent, the girl is just an inconvenience; her presence may even fill him with a kind of guilt, so he just leaves or dumps her off somewhere. Maybe the guilt—or the satiation—makes him incapable of murder, or maybe he's just not wired like that. I don't know. But all of this makes it SVU's case, we figure. The captain figured different and gave it to us because she hasn't been found yet, and the

MO *seems* to match at least one other teen abduction that didn't end well. Here's the odd thing: even though this other case involved sexual assault before the girl was murdered—sorry, Meryl—there was no...fluid and no evidence of...at least not by...no evidence of penile penetration. The psychologist we consulted says the perv is most likely impotent, which doesn't bode well. Lots of anger issues."

He shook his head or seemed to.

"I apologize, folks. Meryl knows I get to talking when we're working a case. I tend to think out loud."

Nobody said a word. Mr. Davidson couldn't even hear the kids anymore. His heartbeat thundered in his ears as if it was trapped in a conch shell.

Evidence? Impotence?

No fluid?

Lies, all lies. Bones don't talk.

"Sometimes the deviant takes off with the victim—unless, of course, he has her holed up somewhere: basement, garage, shed. Either way, it's bad news for the young lady. In the latter situation, sometimes a perp keeps a woman, a girl, in captivity because he wants her more than once—not to be crude—or maybe because he believes he's in love with her. But sometimes he takes her to his lair, violates her, then splits. Never chains her up or anything. Often the woman finds us before we find her, sad to say. Now this would fit Paulie's theory somewhat, but the amount of time she's been missing doesn't. Maybe our guy is keeping her longer because of his sexual dysfunction. Needs time. Or maybe, it all goes down quickly, and we just don't find their bodies right away because he hides them. Well, we've only found the one; the others were discovered in Bucks and Montgomery counties respectively. The connection between their cases and ours are...well, there are *some* similarities."

His wife leaned in, but Mr. Davidson knew Detective Finnerty wasn't about to divulge that sort of information—or was he? Mr. Davidson couldn't figure out Finnerty's play.

"I mean," the detective continued, "if the bodies weren't all found in the Philadelphia suburbs, I would say the perp's probably two states over by now. Paulie is inclined to agree with me there. But these are crimes of convenience—he may not have known the girls, but he saw them frequently, if not every day. The girls had similar...looks, and they were all taken in public places. The psychologist suggested that these young women, in his twisted mind, teased him and brought out a rage stemming from his impotence—or reminded him of someone who'd been important in his life. Paulie though, he thinks the resemblance is coincidental; he still thinks the latest is a snatch-and-batch gone wrong. He believes the cases—even ours—are tenuously linked, and except for the amount of time the latest girl's been missing, he's not completely... Either way, Chief Hagen might have to call in the Feds soon."

The FBI?

"As to why he murdered the first girl we found—if they were indeed taken by the same person—it seemed like some kind of..."

"Ritual?" gasped Mrs. Abbott. She sat directly below the least dim of the party lights, and Mr. Davidson could see her clutch the cross that hung just somewhere between her weighty nose and what he assumed was her sadly neglected bust.

"This is about the girl from Hoskins High?" Mrs. Davidson asked, now riveted. She shivered. Mr. Davidson hoped the detective appreciated the theatrics of a good hostess. "How terrible." Mrs. Davidson's voice took a turn: it sounded edgier or about to take flight in a flurry of hysterics; he wasn't sure which or why. "And the girl in Bucks—she was a redhead too, just like the one in..." Was that a choked sob? "...and the girl you found in the old..." (Unintelligible.) "They were all—"

Meryl Payne cleared her throat. The author clearly wanted the conversation to come to a close—or wanted the group to think so. Mrs. Abbott started to say something, but Mrs. Davidson was undeterred; she wanted something to chew on and share with her coffee clutch, her husband thought. But now her voice was tight, almost accusatory. Was his dollop of dough hardening? Just who were the theatrics meant for anyway?

"You think the Basin is important why?" she asked. Mr. Davidson smiled to himself. His wife wasn't *completely* oblivious.

The song was back—no, it had never left: *It was a fleeting visit...*

Their law enforcement guest didn't answer, but, just as the bug zapper buzzed on (the timer was broken), Mr. Davidson detected a shrug that seemed to signal that everything he'd said was all a bunch of hunches. The party lights didn't help him to read the detective's body language, though he was glad that they made his equally inscrutable.

His wife whispered: "I mean…maybe it's just…" Was that regret on her tongue? Despite the darkness, he thought he could see Ms., Payne gripping his wife's hand. "What did I…?"

Mr. Davidson ignored his spouse (he thought she was overdoing it a bit) and reached for a potato chip. "So, you don't agree with your partner's theory," he asked the detective, "or do you?"

The orange coal of Finnerty's cigarette danced as he shrugged again and took a deep drag at the same time. "Neither, I suppose, but Paulie's gotta nose for this sort of thing." In the glow of the cigarette coal, his face looked old. "Gotta defer to Paulie on this one, I think."

"You have evidence of some kind that suggests more than…a snatch-and-batch," Mr. Davidson asked, "but not much more or you'd be less apt to talk about it, yes? And connections between—"

"Who am I to question Paulie the bloodhound?" was Finnerty's response. "When it rains, I see water; Paulie sees that everything's wet."

What did that even mean?

Water. Fluid.

Mr. Davidson thought of the shovel in his trunk. He should have washed the shovel like had his boning and fillet knives.

"Could she have run away?" Mrs. Davidson asked. There was desperation in her voice that Mr. Davidson found convincing enough to make him uneasy until she righted the ship with her wide-eyed schtick. "God, Meryl," his wife went on, swallowing her despair, "this is like something from one of your novels." It wasn't—Meryl Payne had written supermarket checkout bodice rippers, not thrillers—but Mr. Davidson knew his wife had never read any of Ms. Payne's books.

"Not unless she ran away in her bathing suit," Detective Finnerty replied, tapping his ash. " 'Course she could have taken off with a boyfriend, but according to her gaggle, there wasn't one on record, though there'd been more than a few in the past. She was happy at home by all accounts. No diddling stepfather or late night visiting uncle. Good grades. Applied to Penn, Brown. Popular."

"But not a virgin," Mr. Davidson said without knowing why, other than he wanted to see if the celebrated detective (he was much lauded by the local press) knew as much as he seemed to, but he hedged his bet (also without knowing why): "Isn't that what you're implying? More than a few boyfriends, popular, as if maybe her behavior—"

The bug zapper accepted its first victim.

Mrs. Davidson glared at her husband (it was hard to tell in the dark, but it *felt* like a glare) and hissed: "Don't you *dare* say she was asking for it."

Mr. Davidson realized he was sitting forwards, gripping the armrests. He leaned back and tried to casually wipe the sweat from his forehead and upper lip.

"Can only go by what her friends say," Finnerty said. "Girls don't tend to brag and make shite up." Ms. Payne elbowed him. (Mr. Davidson could make that out.) "Sorry ladies. My mouth…"

"Oh, it's fine, Detective," Mrs. Davidson lied, "we curse around here all the time."

"Well, boys brag, tell tall tales. Men too for that matter. Sexual conquests, et cetera. But not girls usually. Let's just say her experiences—the ones we know of—were normal for her age."

They sat in silence and watched two of the Runyon boys hop the fence into the Davidson yard, catching lightning bugs and sticking them in a jar. The youngest Runyon followed his brothers, clumsily scaling the fence, then whacking at the fireflies with a Wiffle ball bat. Swing and a miss. Low and outside. He connects! *Something becomes nothing.*

"Boys!" Mrs. Runyon yelled from her back porch. "Your father says it's time to come in!"

Mr. Davidson realized he could no longer hear the squeal of kids punctuating the summer night. It must be later than he thought. He could hear Mrs. O'Shea yell for her daughters out front, but his wife didn't make a move.

"Where are the kids?" he asked more out of curiosity than concern.

"My sister picked them up about a half hour ago."

Mr. Davidson said nothing. Maybe he'd known about his and had forgotten; his mind was on the coming rebirth he'd set in motion than his actual conjugal creations.

"Thinking of taking of ride out there tonight," Detective Finnerty said. "The Basin. Been out there already, of course. Been everywhere, but I'd like another look-see—in the dark. Was anybody here a Boy Scout or a Girl Scout? Sitting around a campfire or in a tent, whispering late into the night with your buddies or best girlfriends, well, it always seemed to be the perfect night for spilling secrets. The perp more than likely did his dirty work after the sun went down. The Basin's pretty empty after nine o'clock or so. Most of the families will have packed it in by then to get home and catch their shows. The high schoolers and JDs pull their keggers deeper in the woods or drink down at Finch's Landing. And even though it was raining the day we assume the girl was taken, it doesn't mean our guy wasn't careless. Maybe he left something behind—a drop, a splotch, a hair clip with a partial print—at the Rec, where she was last seen, maybe in the dimly lit parking lot there or in the woods or even in the Basin. Places that might be isolated after dark. A murder ground, a killing floor, on any given night, secrets are spilled. We've been over every inch we could—probably twice—but things look different in the shadows, and during the thunderstorm the afternoon she went missing, it would have been pretty dark. The abduction *appears* spur of the moment—Paulie convinced me of that much right away. Oh, our man had his eye on her for a while, like I said, but he probably didn't wake up that morning thinking: this is my day. No, opportunity in the form of a brief, but intense thunderstorm, a harbinger of what's coming perhaps, got this guy off his arse. If so, he would have been in a hurry and possibly nervous, which would lead you to think he'd run right to his safety zone with the young lady, the ol' homestead—but not if he lives with Mommy or a wife. Then he takes her somewhere familiar and close. But our guy, he can't get it up, right? Sorry, ladies. So this place is temporary, just some place to abuse then dispatch the young lady. No, he has destination in mind for her final resting place—"

"Like the Basin," Mrs. Davidson said. There was a sense of finality in her tone.

"Might be the whole point of thing, where she ends up."

Did he say hair clip or barrette? Were they the same thing? Despite his predilections (and having a daughter), he didn't speak girl.

Partial print? Couldn't get it up?

The detective blew out a smoky tunnel of embarrassed exasperation. "Oh hell, I'm talking out of school. Let's just say that whatever happened or wherever she is, we won't get lucky twice. Was a bunch of kids who found the Spring House girl. Big storm's coming in; rain's supposed to start tomorrow morning, if not sooner. Would wash away most evidence that survived the storm the day she went missing, if there is any."

"Is that true?" Mrs. Davidson asked. "I thought I read somewhere that—"

"True to a point, but that's assuming we found something and could protect its integrity, but so much depends upon the intensity of the exposure," Finnerty said. "The elements can make that difficult, especially in a place like the Basin, but I say it's always best to start working a smaller area—smaller than all of Pennypack Woods or the Fields anyway. Odds are we won't find anything."

You won't.

"But the Basin," Mrs. Davidson said, her voice aching—for what, her husband didn't know, "would be a pretty poor place to hide a body, I would think."

Then stop thinking.

"Cookouts, kids running all over," she continued, "plus it gets flooded."

"Maybe he doesn't want to really hide the body," Reverend Abbott said into his chins. Another Encyclopedia Brown heard from!

Detective Finnerty nodded, or at least the ember of his cigarette went up and down. "If he did, he could have just dumped her in the creek; the Puddle's seen its share. But we dragged Pennypack Creek. No, this is something else. In our other case, the girl wasn't exactly hidden. I mean, she wasn't in plain sight, but she wasn't where no one could ever find her. The doer didn't make an effort, but it didn't seem sloppy either. Just a gunny sack floating in the old—"

The detective laughed gently; Mr. Davidson thought it sounded fake. "There I go: off the reservation, as Paulie would say."

Mrs. Davidson inserted herself into the investigation: "Maybe it symbolizes something. Maybe it means something. Maybe—" She stopped short. Mr. Davidson could almost taste her crocodile tears. *My God,* he thought, *she's good.* "I apologize—I'm not—"

Meryl Payne patted Mrs. Davidson's arm before holding her hand. He didn't need party lights or more than a paltry moon to see this doubles act. What was this fresh hell?

"Maybe, maybe. Paulie's says I'm pissing in the rain, if you pardon the expression."

Ms. Payne put her arm around Mrs. Davidson, who shivered in the heat.

"As we say at the station: Paulie knows all."

Maybe it symbolizes something—maybe *it means something.*

Mr. Davidson tossed the half-eaten potato chip back in the basket and took a sip of his soda. As quick as she could be sometimes, his wife wasn't putting it together, but her lack of understanding was his least concern, as was whatever dance she and Meryl Payne were doing for hunky Detective Finnerty. Out of the Irishman's mouth: *Spring House girl…gunny sack…we won't get lucky twice.* Bekka. The detective was talking about Bekka O'Keefe from the next town over, Spring House. The only thing he didn't say was *old well,* but he almost did, Mr. Davidson was sure. But: …*we won't get lucky twice.* Troubling, but even if they'd discovered his DNA—if that was the evidence the detective had referred to—he didn't believe he was in any sort of database, and he didn't work at the school where she'd been last seen. (He snatched the half-eaten chip out of the basket and clung to his soda can in case the detective had any ideas.) The others before Bekka were just others, street trash; he'd just wanted to possess them and see their insides. Everyone has to start somewhere. He hadn't been aware of his potential power, or, rather, the potential power of Mother Nature if he made the right offering. But the nothing he'd turned Bekka into had remained nothing, a literal bag of bones partially submerged in a shallow well, found by some boys long after he'd given up hope of renewal, nay, regeneration. That was his first mistake: he should have kept some flesh attached to the bones, so his seed could find purchase. *Partially submerged:* he bet that was where he went wrong in the end. He'd already gotten better with Cherry, he thought (he'd scrubbed the maintenance building floor with bleach before they departed)—perhaps even perfected his method, for he hadn't even considered the former pond when he took Bekka apart in Pennypack Woods (after he extinguished the girl and penetrated her over and over, fuck you very much). Before he even made her acquaintance, he'd watched mosquitoes emerge from the old well during a hike and thought: *something out of nothing.* It was a distillation of his rapacious extracurricular activities. Wasn't that what he'd lacked up till then? But the well turned out to be just a bacteria-laden breeding ground; it was nothing like the Basin's magic, its miracle. Nothing at all.

It wasn't about hiding what remained of her body; that much the detective got right. But Cherry had to be submerged, so with the big storm coming, burying her remains beneath a picnic table in the Basin was the safest place for her, really—and the most perfect. If the storm was as fierce as they predicted, the Puddle would overflow and fill the Basin. *Something out of nothing.* Come you dragonflies and witness the rising of the new woman, who will answer not to her maker—Mother Nature could care less; ducks and frogs come, ducks and frogs go—but to the facilitator of her rebirth.

He thought again of the shovel in his trunk—and his sketch book filled with renderings of dragonflies and redheads, hidden beneath the spare tire. His mind lingered over each sketch, each potential rising they represented, and he became erect.

Mr. Davidson thought that for Detective Finnerty, the Basin was a just something to check off a mental list; the detective believed his partner had a better handle on the case. Finnerty was a dreamer; Masconi was a realist. He'd said as much, hadn't he?

Rain's a-coming, detective. This time, all the luck in the world won't—

"You…you think Carol Conway was taken to the Basin because…" Mrs. Davidson began, her voice fluttering. She sounded very tired. "My Larry, he came home from work, from searching, just soaked," she said, as if by rote.

"Muddy, I'm sure," Mrs. Abbott said in her muffled voice.

"Soaked to the bone," was Mrs. Davidson's reply.

To the bone, Mr. Davidson thought. *Think back: you remember the bone, don't you, honey bunny?* After he'd first seen Bekka, back in her street shorts, after a morning summer basketball league game at Assumption of Our Lady, there'd been no more boning for Mrs. Davidson. Not after he saw Bekka's thighs. But that was just the surface. All he was really interested in was Bekka O'Keefe's bones. (The others had been just anatomy lessons.) Her school's team had been handed a beating, he assumed, for Bekka was trying hard not to cry, or perhaps some girls had been cruel to her. She stood outside the gymnasium, her hands on her knees, her long red hair still tied back, ignoring her teammates who'd already boarded the bus back to Spring House. He watched her from the edge of Lawndale Fields behind the school. He'd just closed up the Rec after the seniors' water therapy session had ended, and he had to prepare for the pool to be open to the general public, but he'd been on the hunt, so to speak, since discovering the well, where a dragonfly had alighted oh so briefly upon his hand. From his vantage point, he swore he could hear Bekka's bones sigh under the onus of guarding her trapped soul. It took him all of a day to find out her name and every impermanent thing in her life. By the next sunrise, her bones had been wrenched from her flesh, her soul sent screaming to who knows where.

Detective Finnerty stood up. Ms. Payne tried to make him sit down, but Mr. Davidson could see that this had already been planned in advance; Ms. Payne was playacting—poorly. "I don't know anything for sure, Mrs. Davidson. A good detective never does until all the evidence is in. Nothing's for sure until it's a fact, right, and we have very few of those. I'd call it a hunch, but I'm not sure I believe in gut feelings much anymore. The times they've up and gone a-changin', know what I mean? So let's just call it a shot in the dark, all apologies to Inspector Clouseau. Paulie's gonna think I've gone off my rocker when I tell him tomorrow. What do you say, Larry? Phil? Up for a ride?"

The Abbotts said they had to get home—the reverend had to finish his sermon for tomorrow morning. Thus the pawns were eliminated. Mr. Davidson smiled. He knew Detective Finnerty couldn't see it in the dark. "Sure, Detective. Always been interested to see how you fellows work."

"Going to be a wee bit different than working at the Rec, I would think," Detective Finnerty said. "It'll probably be as boring as all get-out, but if you don't mind… Good. Meryl, why don't you keep Mrs. Davidson company then, and the menfolk will be back shortly."

The bug zapper took two at once, and Mrs. Davidson jumped.

+

Mr. Davidson had known nothing about digging a grave. (He'd meant to look it up on the Internet but had forgotten.) He didn't even know that six feet wasn't the standard grave depth in Pennsylvania, but it didn't matter: he could barely make two feet, so he'd just folded up Cherry even more and covered the hole with rocks. When the anticipated heavy rain fell and the Basin became a pond again, the loosely piled rocks would shift, and the body would unfold like an accordion and float around (washed clean of evidence, he hoped) until she was discovered or the water evaporated—unless: *something had risen out of nothing.* But if the body was found before then, he thought—if the body was found tonight, say—then there would be enough DNA (all over what remained of her flesh and hair) to put him away *in perpetuum.* Of course, before the big storm arrived and the flooding began, if he felt that Cherry's interim resting place was in jeopardy (or he was), he could retrieve her late at night when his family was asleep with minimum effort (being only two feet down or so); then, however, he would have no choice but to sacrifice her remains to the Puddle. (Finnerty was right about that; it wouldn't be his first choice, for transformation, he assumed, was a delicate process.) Then it would be bye-bye Cherry unless they dragged Pennypack Creek again—or unless, pre-disinterment, in the throes of an early arriving storm and ensuing flood: *something had risen out of nothing* (which he didn't believe was possible outside of the Basin, particularly in the swift, dirty Pennypack). But while the detective's fixation on the drained pond was dead on the money, the cookout wasn't a fishing expedition; it was, as he suggested, one frustrated man talking the through. Masconi was leading Finnerty away. If the detective wanted to bark at the moon, let him howl away. It might be fun to watch. Mr. Davidson knew he just needed to keep his excitement down, but it was difficult not to scream in the detective's face: the times haven't even begun a-changin' yet, know what I mean?

+

On his way out, Mr. Davidson stopped and asked, "Where's my car?" He usually parked on the street so he wife could pull in the driveway. "I know that I—"

"Normally park out front?" Detective Finnerty asked. "Guess someone beat you to your spot."

Indeed, there was a black Ford Taurus that he didn't recognize parked in front his house.

"No, I'm sure I—"

"You probably parked it up the block. We're taking my hunk of junk anyway." Finnerty laughed a little. "I'm a detective, Mr. Davidson; we'll find your car before the night's out. But let's get going. Meryl'll get P.O.'d if we make a night of it."

+

The drive to the Basin was quiet, just the squawk of the police radio. They seemed to be taking a circuitous route. Finnerty asked him to ride in the back. ("Paulie's got his shite all over the place up here.") He had no idea that detectives took their cars home. Had Meryl sat in the back on the way to their house, or had they taken separate cars? He'd have to ask his wife when he got home.

"Not a nice view from back there, huh?"

It occurred to Mr. Davidson that probably more was going on here than just a nighttime visit to the Basin. Had he read the detective all wrong? No, it wasn't possible. Mr. Davidson had the ability to reanimate. What did the detective have? Mind games? Instinct?

"Here," Finnerty said when they arrived, "the doors don't open from the inside."

He didn't realize how much he was sweating until he got out of the car. Instinct—perhaps he'd minimized its importance or at least its influence, because his told him to take off into the woods or to try to make it to the Fields. But he slowed his breathing, reminding himself that divine intellect always trumps intuition.

(Buzz, buzz, buzz went the song in his skull.)

What's the difference between instinct and intuition, he wondered.

(Buzz, buzz, buzz.)

Detective Finnerty handed Mr. Davidson a flashlight (though the moon seemed bigger and brighter than it had looked from his backyard), and when he flicked it on, he wasn't surprised to see the Irish detective's Italian-American partner leaning on a picnic table (*the* picnic table), the key chain with Mr. Davidson's lost car keys swirling around his finger. Snatch-and-batch—right. Detective Masconi greeted him warmly although they barely knew each other. "With the formalities already—call me Paulie, right?" He threw an arm around Mr. Davidson's shoulder and started telling him a story about how some kids coming back from fishing for God knows what in the Puddle two weeks back saw a man carrying a bundle—"a hockey bag, they called it, a hockey bag with long hair (stickin' out, I guess)"— into the Basin. "The guy's car, the kids said—what was it, Feargal? It was kind of like yours, I guess. What are you drivin' now? A Subaru Outback Wagon, right? Yeah, that's what the little shits say they saw." He paused and shined his flashlight on Mr. Davidson's car. How had he failed to notice that Finnerty had pulled up next to his Subaru?

And on the side of his car—it couldn't be—a black Ford Taurus. "Also said they'd seen someone sittin' in maybe the same car, all by his lonesome, on a couple of occasions by the Basin last time it was a pond, but not watchin' folks havin' picnics and doin' whatnot; no, just sittin' there. Probably whackin' it. Salutin' the ol' general. Sick twist, no?" Mr. Davidson felt Detective Masconi shrug, as he watched the beam of one of their flashlights bounce and illuminate briefly the top of the picnic table. There was his shovel, his knives—and his sketch book. How did they—didn't they need a warrant or something? "Kids probably high as kites, right?" He nudged Mr. Davidson, almost causing him to fall. Detective Finnerty was suddenly on his other side, holding him up. "Feeling okay, Mr. Davidson?" He didn't have an answer. "Told you we'd find your car," Finnerty said. "Did they just leave it here?" his partner asked, tossing Mr. Davidson's car keys to Finnerty. "Tsk."

All his time, all his seed, all for nothing. Betrayed by the living, fraught with nescience for the dead, unable to see the pond for the grave. Mr. Davidson started dry heaving. Detective Masconi laughed a phlegmy laugh. "Maybe it's the scene of the crime and all that. Got a nose like a bloodhound, do you? Well, lead us right to her. Divinate! On the way, you can tell us all about the other redheads in that there book and about the super clean maintenance building at the Rec. Perfect night for spilling secrets, wouldn't you say?" They let go of him but stayed close. Mr. Davidson almost walked into a picnic table, but the detectives steered him clear. He had no idea where he was going. "Gotta forensic team coming to scour the Basin and the Rec. Shoulda had 'em all over the maintenance building as soon as we smelled the bleach, but with all the chlorine in the air…ah, well. Luminol, Mr. Davidson. They use it to detect trace amounts of blood. They'll use it on the walls, the floor being bleached and all, 'cause blood splashes. So does semen. And who knows where a drop will end up. Liquids are funny like that." Mr. Davidson threw up a little in his mouth. "Hell, mick," Detective Masconi shouted to his partner, who walked slightly ahead, kicking stones. "I could hump your hunches. Jesus. That's good police work for you: makin' somethin' out of nothin'. Let's make something', shall we, Larry?"

And he would have. He would have led the wiser-than-he-expected detectives right to the small mound of stones under the picnic table, but just as he turned back towards it (resisting the urge to grab his sketch book), the sky lit up, just for a second (long enough for Mr. Davidson to see that Detective Masconi had pulled out his revolver), and a loud crack shook the surrounding trees. Detective Finnerty quickly pulled on a pair of latex gloves and removed Mr. Davidson's property to his car.

"Shit balls," Detective Masconi said, and the heavens opened up (cliché or not, Mr. Davidson thought it was true enough tonight), and the thunderstorm forecasted for tomorrow morning came tonight, sudden and violent. The sky shook its fist at the folly below. "Raining' tomcats and stray dogs," Detective Masconi said. "Puddle's gonna flood for sure this keeps up the way they say. You oughta go meet 'em at the Rec, mick—unless Larry here has something to show us…"

Mr. Davidson stood with his mouth open to the sky. The song—Fleetwood Mac's "Dragonfly"—played so loud in his head, he thought it would shake the trees of their leaves, unsettle the very earth beneath their feet, and tickle the amniotic sac that the purblind would call a grave.

And when the roses are half-bud soft flowers
And lovely as the king of flies has come
It was a fleeting visit, all too brief
In three short minutes, he had been and gone

"Gonna be too muddy for two dicks with flashlights," Detective Finnerty said with true disgust. "Leave it to the forensic team. If there's anything left here of interest after this storm, they'll find it." His hair was plastered to his head like everyone else's, but unlike his annoyed partner, who kept swiping at his, Finnerty appeared to barely notice; he looked as if he knew a moment of possible significance had passed.

Paulie holstered his gun. "Look at him—he practically has a hard-on. He ain't showing us nothin', and until they process the shovel and the knives, the book's not enough to hold him."

"We shoulda turned over the stuff right away…"

"We just got it tonight, mick."

"…but the theater of the thing, I thought for sure…"

Mr. Davidson never remembered feeling so…blessed—at least not since he gnawed one of Bekka's bones, a small one, in the backyard under the moonlight, as the sound of his children giggling while they played a board game inside mixed with the song whose elusive tune was just beginning to take root in his brain; he had it all, and after he replaced the bone in the sack, he would have more, or so he thought, until he would realize the inherent dynamism of the evanescent pond. Rain filled his waiting mouth. Before the Basin was flooded (and wasn't that inevitable?), he hoped the rain watered his Cherry, and the same magic that transformed the Basin (back) into a pond also struck—

"We'll talk again soon, pal," Detective Masconi whispered in his ear.

Detective Finnerty had somehow gotten behind him and said, "Paulie will drop you off. Meryl drove herself." As Detective Masconi led him to his car, Mr. Davidson turned to Detective Finnerty, who stood with his back to them, probably listening to the rain filling the fetid Puddle or to the uncountable drops landing in the now-miry Basin.

Mr. Davidson thought of Yeats, but just the last two lines of a poem he had to learn by heart in school, too familiar to most who heed not its warning, for *it* is not deteriorating (not anymore) nor expiring:

And what rough beast, its hour come round at last
Slouches towards Bethlehem to be born?

"Something out of nothing," Mr. Davidson yelled over the rain, and Detective Finnerty waved him off without turning around.

"Damn right," Detective Masconi said, as he opened the car door. "And back to nothin'."

-end-

Meet-Cute Valedico

——————A Scene——————

LIGHTS UP:****

The shades are drawn. The overhead fluorescent tube flickers. Dust motes dance in what light little there is. Two people sit separated by a worn table in a small room. CONSTANCE, a middle-aged woman, sits across from someone whose face is obscured by shadow.

CONSTANCE

Did you ever notice that in the movies no one ever says goodbye on the phone? They never do. They just hang up. Anymore, it's not just the guys with the poor phone etiquette. A few of those female mover-and-shaker types answer the phone, "Yeah?" Even Sonny Corleone in *The Godfather*—you've seen it, right?— even Sonny, when Sollozzo calls to say he's kidnapped Robert Duvall, answers the phone, "Hello?" But no one in the movies ever says goodbye when they hang up. Doesn't matter if it's a father and son, boss and mid-level flunky, two people who are supposedly deeply in love, or a pair who just danced the featherbed jig the night before. But love, it's all convention, right? The uptight guy, he spills his coffee on the pretty geek girl in the office elevator. She's annoyed, but he's surprisingly gallant. Even carries a handkerchief to help blot the stain—except that the stain is across her chest, so she slaps his hand away, but not too hard. Then, I don't know, she notices his NRA membership card fall out of his pocket, and she's wearing her PETA underwear that day. But nonetheless sparks fly. Not meaning a word, she says, "I hope I never run into *you* again in an elevator." And she doesn't. Not in an elevator. Nope. But the cafeteria. The train platform. On their way to the lavatories. One day, outside the office, they both notice a kitten run under a parked car. It's raining cats and dogs. Not literally—that would be crazy, right, and that's not why I'm here. I'm here about how no one in the movies ever says goodbye on the phone. Oh, what happened to the potentially amorous office workers? Well, I would like to tell you that the backs of their hands touch as they rescue the kitten and a blockbuster rom-com ensues, but I can't, because in real life no one gets rescued, so why should the kitten.

    (beat)

Did you notice this too: when someone in the movies, married or single, goes to the food store, they always leave with exactly one brown paper bag of food—plastic bags are verboten apparently—and there's always a loaf of French bread sticking out of the top? I mean, who's eating all that bread? You're telling me all those size twos and fours are major carbohydrate fans? Right. Oh God, there's a million cinematic clichés and tropes. I was telling the detectives some. Thunder and lightning almost always happen at the exact same time in the movies. No one waits for an elevator; it's always there—*unless* they're being chased by a bad guy. Clues and incriminating evidence can always be found by looking in the second to last drawer or by knocking on the wall to discover the hollow spot. Coughing usually indicates a terminal disease. The final photograph developing in a darkroom tray is invariably the most important, for evidence always floats. Man oh man, there're so many. L-shaped bed sheets that cover a man's lower torso and a woman's upper body, because, heaven knows, boobs are bad. Tough guys who walk away— in slow motion no less—from an explosion they just set off and never look back. The divorced hero still in contact with his ex-wife who tells him she left because she loves him too much. Movies are drowning in clichés, which doesn't mean that they're not true somehow. No siree. But no one ever says goodbye on the phone. They just hang up, sometimes staring at the receiver, but no goodbyes. I could never figure that out. I think about it every day. They wouldn't even have to show *both* characters saying it. Just one. But they never do. They never say goodbye. Oh, and pregnancies in the movies! Ever notice how like nine times out of ten, babies come out the size of two or even three-month-olds? Clean, often with dry hair. No misshapen heads ever. And pregnancies are almost always announced by having the woman vomit, and the guy, he's always surprised, as if the worst rocking the Casbah could ever get you is waking up with a monster or sleeping on the wet spot—and guys *never* sleep on the wet spot. You don't see anyone dispose of a condom either, and no one ever has bad breath in the morning; they just kiss as if they're fresh as daisies, as if their breath doesn't smell like a rotting corpse or milk that's turned. That's not all. Hardly any pregnant women are given an epidural in the movies. It's all Lamaze classes, which the significant other stops attending because either he's too busy closing that big deal or the firm's Japanese clients just flew halfway around the world to be dazzled by an architectural pitch. You'd think they couldn't write copy or build an outhouse over there. See, men, they marry their jobs, live with their wives, and nail anything in Jimmy Choos under the age of twenty-five. That's a truism. I used to work, you know. I used to teach literature at a college, but now I just watch movies. Well, not here, of course. I think in the dayroom here, they get three channels, period—oh, and PBS. So if it's not *Sesame Street*, it's all *Cagney and Lacey* reruns, if you get my drift. But movies: movies mirror real life more than most people know, despite the distracting and troubling tropes. Exaggerations is all. Movies are more real than classic literature like *Moby-Dick* or *Pride and Prejudice*. Have you ever met a Captain Ahab or an Elizabeth Bennet or even a Huckleberry Finn—a real one? How about a true Mrs. Dalloway? What did she say? Oh yes: "There was an embrace in death." But jeeze

Louise, look who I'm asking. I suppose in your line of work you've run into all these characters at least once. Well, let me tell you: Virginia wasn't all that wrong. There *is* an embrace involved with death, but it's *before* not *in*. And that's my point: movies aren't that complicated, not really. Whatever tree branch the hero is perched upon is the one the villain will pause under. It's the rule of the inevitable: if it's possible then it's possibly probable, and if it's probable and one believes in the probable long enough, doubt, the lifeblood of faith, erodes away to so much fairy dust, and what was once merely possible becomes inevitable. It only takes seconds and it's usually the hero's doing. Wishful thinking will be the death of us all, the movies are telling us—even if the villain usually moves on from the hero's tree. Nothing's as good as you think at first: doggy style, laser discs, motherhood. That's why movies are closer to real life than books. Novels detail life, sometimes explain it, other times strip it bare, but movies just put it out there for all to see. Don't look behind the shower curtain! Don't split up to search the haunted house! Don't drop the soap! Now, take death. In the movies, the people with the greatest hopes and aspirations, especially in Vietnam or Compton, say, get killed first. When a good character dies, his partner, if he's a cop, or his best friend will close his eyes, but when a villain dies, his eyes remain open, staring into the great void. Oh, and if your partner or spouse dies, no one calls 911 right away, although they might bark for someone else to do it. No, they just hold that person's hand until he or she is gone. Of course, not everything in the movies is true, metaphorically or otherwise. I know that much. In real life, in my old life before this anyway, people usually said goodbye when they hung up the phone. If my mom called to check up on the kids and me because Robert was traveling again for work, or if Sally next door called about something she saw in the latest L.L.Bean catalog, they said goodbye. You know when someone doesn't say goodbye in the real world? Do you know? When he's breaking up with you, dumping you, throwing you over for some young hussy named Emmy he met in a conference in Des Moines, of all places. In the movies, the person doing the dumping usually says some claptrap like, "I love you but I'm not *in* love with you," or "It's not you, it's me," or my favorite, "You want more than I'm prepared to give." But when you're dumped during a scratchy long distance phone call, you don't even get that much and there certainly isn't a goodbye. You prepare for these things watching movies, not studying Dickens or Edith Wharton. You try to prepare for the day when someone who was once a hello won't give you so much as a toodle-oo when they ring off. But I'm a slow learner, especially when I'm in over my head.

    (beat)

You know the romantic comedy formula, right? The meet-cute, the infatuation, the pop song montage, the contrived mix-up, the angry break up, and the final clinch? Well, they're cautionary tales; they don't translate to real life, but artifice is easier to spot in the movies than in novels. Of course, neither *really* tell you the ugly truth about being a parent. Once I had kids, I had to quit teaching. I tried to keep working after the first one, but two was one too many, and three, well... Robert was always in *some* country with *some*one, so it was just the kids and me in this huge house adjacent Neshaminy Creek. Big deal. Who cares, right? So I quit teaching—I could on his salary—and since I've read a thousand books or more, to no avail, I started watching movies. Sometimes two or three a day. I have to tell you though: eventually it stopped working for me—cinematic magic, that is—especially after the shit flew right past the fan and smacked me in the face over the wire. I'd read just about every important work, and I watched every kind of movie I could, but in the end, since no one ever said goodbye, and there are no phones in *Medea*...

(softer)

Here's one for you: in the movies, a dying person's last words are always coherent and usually significant. Not in real life. If it *is* real. I mean, if you can really call this a life.

(beat)

I will say this much: when I drugged the children, before I walked each one down to the shore, before I walked each out into the Neshaminy, which is swift and considerable, more like a small river than a creek, and held their pretty heads under, I said goodbye. But I knew it wasn't a movie. I mean, they were quiet, the kids. They didn't say a word or pitch a fit or even put up that much of a fight, not one I noticed anyway. 'Course, I'd given them an Ambien instead of a Flintstones vitamin a half-hour before, so they were a bit...subdued. Even the little one didn't go off, and the third child is always the loudest. Just watch the movies; you'll see. But he didn't cry or anything, not even when I put a plastic bag over his head before I carried him into the creek. Well, I had to; I didn't know he wouldn't scream his cute little head off. Going last can be tough. Not that it would have mattered if he did. The nearest neighbor is a half mile away at least. Like I said, I knew it wasn't a movie; I knew it was real, but it *felt* like one, you know? Not a made-for-TV kind of movie—although it will probably end up as one, I suppose—but some grainy, indie film no one saw but everyone says they did. See, the whole thing was about saying goodbye. When it was finished, when I said to each of my children the goodbye that was never said to me—at least not the right kind of goodbye, if one had to be said, not the one I wanted to hear at the end of a scratchy phone call—I trudged back to the house, locked up against the coming storm, and popped in a movie. *The Wizard of Oz.* The 1939 version, of course, with Judy Garland, not the creepy 1925 silent one with Oliver Hardy as the Tin Man. Click your heels three times, you're going to say, but I was already home. No, I wanted to watch the winged monkeys one last time. I love the winged monkeys, even though they used to scare me half to death when I was little; now I think they're cute, but I knew I wouldn't be seeing them again anytime soon. I wanted to say goodbye to them too. There's something the movies get wrong: evil is rarely adorable, at least not for very long.

(beat)

So what's the opposite of a meet-cute? Answer me that, doctor. I'll shiver my shackles like Marley's ghost and see if that helps you, if it doesn't bring in the guards—but don't say slasher movie; don't you dare. If a meet-cute is when two opposites meet accidentally under comic circumstances, what do you call the convention where people in the name of love are torn apart by their own hands, so that there's nothing left but decaying flesh and floating bone, maybe not even that, maybe no anima, not even a soul? In your office, you have a bunch of degrees on your walls, yeah? What do they tell you? What's the opposite of a meet-cute? Well, if you don't know, I'll whisper it to you: it's a goodbye.

(beat)

Are we finished? Can I go?

LIGHTS FADE.

Telford Bridge
(Memento Mori)

"The screen door slams,"
and that song plays again
as we tie the large hooks
behind the boat.

"Floater," the Chief said. Anonymous tip.
It's before sunrise and blind as bats
is the phrase thrown about.
That and sinker, not floater.

Telford Bridge is damp, green stone,
and that's where the Erin girl took a header back in '96.
Among the graffiti is "memento mori,"
remember you are mortal.

When a body goes down,
it starts moving with the undercurrent of the creek,
and if it doesn't catch on something,
it can go a distance.

The boys swap fresh sandwiches
and trade stale jokes about a stiff one,
but generally there's respect
among the draggers and divers.

Boy Named Sue even turns off his little radio,
and the cicadas and the odd owl compete with
the police radio and the sonar, but beneath it all
is the *drip drip drip* of water from our lines.

They're saying this one was pretty,
short brown hair, decent grades: Anna.
Last week there were two boys, tweekers,
both dead before they hit the water.

Our girl here went missing a week ago,
last seen laughing with a red-haired man,
the contents of her backpack found in the woods
with her blood on her math homework.

If the pretty girl went in the murky Puddle,
she hasn't shown her hand yet.
Memento mori, the graffiti mocks, and
carpe diem, Anna, must seem like a taunt from the gods.

The sun creeps up and we catch on something.
As we pull up the lines, Howard says,
"Have to go now," his ginger hair fire in the light,
and there she is, on the end of a hook.

Howard is already gone, splash,
but they'll pick him up soon enough,
and for a second it's like the girl winks,
and Boy Named Sue turns his radio back on.

When All the Men Smoked Cigars

The machines beeped and hummed and kept him alive. Salvatore Abandonato had enough money stashed away to keep the machines beeping and humming for the next ten years if he lasted that long. He even owned his own dialysis machine. The doctors were always repulsively optimistic; not a sour grape among them. Money will do that, the old man thought. Especially cash. No, the grapes in his life were the seedless red ones he insisted upon when he could speak, which wasn't every day, and then just when he wanted to, which wasn't very often. The oxygen mask, he felt, made talking an effort. They were switching to a nasal cannula soon (due to his recent diagnosis of COPD), which the old man believed would make him look even more vulnerable, but he supposed having kidney failure and cancer made him appear weak already in the eyes of his own kind.

He drifted off and he was back, back, back, before he punched his first ticket, and Ronnie was reading poetry to him, which she did sometimes when such things like sonnets and school still excited her.

Call the roller of big cigars,
The muscular one, and bid him whip
In kitchen cups concupiscent curds.

He woke noisily, the poet's name dancing away from the end of his tongue. *Wallace, was it?* He'd ask the nice nurse who usually came in the afternoons to look up *concupiscent*. It sounded important.

Call the roller of big cigars…

He'd made sure he had a nurse twenty-four hours a day; he had four in rotation. Paid in cash. The old man also owned the beeping and humming machines (renting was for suckers); they'd fallen off a truck and he'd purchased them at a deep discount. That was what forty years of loyalty gets you, he thought. That and not much else. There was no retirement party for their thing, no symbolic gold watch, nothing symbolic actually unless two in the back of the head or a garrote around the neck counted. He supposed he was lucky despite the beeping and the humming and the overly optimistic doctors who smiled when they told him they thought he might have a year rather than six months. How many guys like him—a wiseguy, a goodfella, whatever—got to rise from the streets of South Philadelphia without a pot to piss in to being a *capodecina*, a *caporegime*, a buffer or two away from the boss?

The Philadelphia *Cosa Nostra* being such a pig fuck since 1980 (not that New York had it all that much better, but Philadelphia had a larger number of singers), he'd served under seven bosses (and whomever currently ran things) since being made in 1969. The Gentle Don, Angelo Bruno, was the only boss he ever genuinely respected. The man earned it. Bruno became a made guy in the early '30s, then in 1959 took over the family from Joseph Ida (who'd fled to Sicily after the Apalachin raid) but not without opposition. Acting boss Antonio "Mr. Migs" Pollina saw rising star Bruno as a dangerous rival (rightly so) and ordered him taken out. But Bruno went to New York (either to see Vito Genovese, who'd controlled the Philly branch in the late '50s, or Carlo Gambino, who was an old business partner) and the Commission soon deposed Pollina and placed Bruno on the throne. The Commission asked the new boss what he wanted done with Mr. Migs. Did he want him out of the way—permanently? Bruno said no, keep him around so the troops, who'd served under Pollina for a year, would have a smooth transition and not be riled up by his murder. Bruno was a real stand-up guy. But Abandonato (a significantly younger man then, now hooked to machines like a schnook) rarely saw the don, being just a button man in the family then, and a lowly one at that; seldom did men of Bruno's level even acknowledge soldiers let alone those near the bottom of the chain of command; it was safer that way. After March 21, 1980, when Bruno's head had an extra hole blown in it while he sat in his car, it was open season. Philip Testa, the Chicken Man, took the reigns first. Testa's death almost a year later (he was killed by a nail bomb when he opened his front door) was so famous it made it into a Springsteen song. Then came Little Nicky, Nicky Scarfo. Little guy syndrome all the way. You couldn't piss right in front of this guy. You couldn't look sideways either, but you had to have eyes in the back of your head, that was for sure. Nicky upped him though, gave him his own regime. Somehow Nicky's RICO trial and the whole underboss turncoat situation passed by the old man, now dying in his bed. (Even then they were calling Abandonato the old man; he laughed, thinking the Feds must have it noted as his mob nickname in a file or organizational chart somewhere.) His regime remained relatively intact through the subsequent bosses: Stanfa, Natale, Skinny Joey Merlino (that prick), and Uncle Joe Ligambi, the street boss when Merlino was in the can. Word was that Uncle Joe was putting himself on the shelf—a retired boss!—so the old man honest to God didn't know who was running the show; Merlino was back inside but still calling the shots, so there had to be an acting boss. He was sure Frankie Joe Bones had told him (probably more than once), but he didn't care: seven bosses had been enough. The time when all the men smoked cigars was long gone. Oh, all wiseguys still smoked, but usually just cigarettes. Some lit a cigar from time to time but none knew how to enjoy one; they puffed on it like they were sucking a cock, like the act itself made them big guys in the neighborhood, but it was nothing more than an accoutrement necessary for the roles they played; it was dress-up with real guns and bravado to spare. His first notice of the lack of cigar aficionados among the boys coincided with the start of the downhill slide in the '80s. Scarfo got the ball rolling: every man for himself, so much so, that when someone got pinched, even a guy far up the chain, that person sang like Tiny Tim with his balls in a vise.

It had been a couple of years since the old man had actually led his regime and its crews. He was captain, *caporegime*, in name only, out of respect. He was involved in no grudges, so the family (until recent events) appeared willing to let him drift off in a haze of morphine while cancer ate away his lungs, his pancreas, his brain— that is if you could call the Philadelphia *Cosa Nostra* a family; in the old days, your street family came before everything, even your family at home; now nothing came before saving your own ass. Frankie Joe Bones, who, in effect, ran his regime, came by every couple of weeks with an envelope stuffed with cash and a card he made the guys sign. The card was stupid if sincere, but the cash was nice. He knew Bonesy was skimming, but such was the nature of their thing. If you can't dip your beak, then why play by the water? The smart move for Bonesey would be to bump off his dying captain so the big envelope would be his (assuming he could get the nod and keep his rivals at bay), but he knew the man was steadfast almost to a fault; Frankie respected their thing and took his oath of loyalty seriously.

But the old man's grandson: he was another thing altogether, a real thorn. If anything could get the dying capo clipped even while he lay imprisoned in a room that stunk of bedpans and medicine and old man—and it was looking more and more like a possibility, according to his ears on the street—it would be his daughter's kid, Donnie Baratta, twenty-nine going on nine. At least Ronnie had had the good sense to marry a man of Sicilian descent (his parents had come over), not some fourth generation wop whose great-grandfather waltzed out of the mountains of northern Italy with blue eyes, blonde hair, a green card, and a baby's works between his legs. That her husband turned out to be an utter shit was no surprise; Ronnie made bad choices like some people made sandwiches or made love: quick and often. Ronnie was no rocket scientist. Still, she knew what her father did. The husband, Artie Baratta, was in aluminum siding, but he wanted in the life. He always made sincere jokes about making the old man an offer he couldn't refuse (missing the point altogether). "Don't put a horse's head in my bed, Dad," he said. Abandonato hated when his son-in-law called him Dad. (He hated bad *Godfather* jokes even more.)

     Artie ran up gambling debts so high, his daughter's house was eventually in arrears. The old man had to step in. He wouldn't vouch for his son-in-law though; Artie Baratta was too much of a wild card for the old man to put himself out there like that for him. But he slid enough cash to Ronnie so she could catch up on the mortgage. Artie tried to get to the money, but the old man had Alonzo Vinci (known for his persuasive argumentative skills) visit the mutt on the job and suggest to him to direct his efforts elsewhere. Didn't stop Ronnie's husband from continuing down the asshole path in other ways. Artie greased back his hair. He was already fat; he got fatter. He started in on pills—OxyContin and tranquilizers; even got Ronnie hooked for a bit, but the old man stepped in again and helped Ronnie get her act together. How could she raise a kid while she was walking into walls and napping all afternoon? Alonzo, bless his heart, offered to escort Artie out of town on a one way ticket, but those kinds of things didn't work when the schmuck was married to your daughter. Artie wanted to be part of a crew. Unless there was some pillow talk (doubtful if he knew his daughter, aside from a little bragging early on), Artie's knowledge of the old man's activities was constrained to what he read in the newspapers. Still, some things can't be hidden, he assumed, but Artie, part of a crew? *Impossibile.* He even got word from above to rein the fanook in. That was the last thing the capo needed. At the time, they were in the middle of an internal war in the streets of Philadelphia that looked to be worse than the Riccobene War. Button men were on the streets twenty-four seven. The old man spent two weeks sleeping in a motel in Connecticut. The Philadelphia *Costa Nostra* was a joke. They were quite literally the gang that couldn't shoot straight.

(Oh, the papers had a field day. A hit man brought the wrong shotgun shells to a job. Another mutt called off a hit because he had to report to his parole officer. A pair of geniuses, Philip Colletti and John Veasey, managed to put down one of their targets—but only shot Skinny Joey Merlino in the ass—and set their getaway car on fire just a few blocks away from the scene; the police and fire department responded quickly and the cops were able to trace the car to a leasing company in Jersey with Colletti's name on the contract. Equally helpful in the investigation was that Veasey had reached back into the flaming car to retrieve some coins and severely burned his hand. Not wanting to go to the hospital right away, Veasey, who'd been made by Stanfa despite being only of half Italian heritage, went into his backyard, doused his hand in lighter fluid, and set it aflame, telling his neighbors he'd burned it lighting the grill. Even Hollywood couldn't make this stuff up.)

The family, if you could call it that, mattered little during the war, if at all; what mattered was what corner you came from. It was fucking awful. But in the end, the old man had a bit of luck: Artie went back to gambling, ran up sizable debts on one of the old man's books, then another bookie's, then a DeCavalcante family book up in Elizabethtown, New Jersey, till he couldn't do more than buy a lottery ticket. His drug intake also increased, and he started buying on the streets in North Philly. Finally, out of frustration or perhaps during a drug binge (the old man never knew the reason and never asked), his son-in-law worked on Ronnie's face, knocking her cold, and she had to go to the hospital. He'd hit her before, the old man knew, but it wasn't his place, his late wife had said, to meddle in his daughter's marriage, and, besides, Ronnie always denied any allegations of violence on her husband's part. But Ronnie was under no blood oath (whatever that was worth on the streets post-Bruno): she eventually told her father everything, even things he'd known nothing about, and Artie hightailed it out of town all on his own. They never heard from him again. The old man had reached out to New York and Florida and Vegas, even to the Chicago Outfit, in case Artie showed up in one of those places, but no one had seen him.

Probably beating the shit out of a two-bit hooker in Bumfuck, Idaho. But he was gone. Easy divorce, no custody battle. (Though no child support either.) Now all that remained of his mess was a clingy daddy's girl and a grandson who seemed destined to follow in his father's footsteps—or worse.

+

Donnie Baratta remembered how it all began: some petty thefts, a couple of b & e's. Just things he did for kicks with Dom and Draco. They called themselves the Catharine Street Crosses. But their last job had gone to hell in a handbasket quick. The owner had been still in his office, counting receipts and whatnot. He had a dog, a German shepherd that no one knew about. (Dom was supposed to be the scout, but he was often dusted.) When the cops came, Donnie was pinned by the dog and the owner had a gun on him. At the initial hearing, his grandfather's mouthpiece showed up. In the end, Donnie kept his trap shut: suspended sentence.

Since then, he felt invincible. His grandfather's muscle was behind him, he thought. The streets knew it, and if they didn't, Donnie made a point of telling them. He flaunted what he believed was his new found power, acting like he'd just been straightened out, made, though he'd done nothing to earn his button—the streets knew this too. He realized he ticked a lot of people off (and he was careful to never claim he'd been made, just imply it by his bold actions), but to get to the top, a lot of heads have to be stepped on, he reasoned. His father had wanted to be a wiseguy, but he was an oaf, a drug addict (like Dom eventually became). His father couldn't rub two cents together to make a nickel because he never held onto two pennies long enough to have anything to rub. His old man used to beat Donnie's mother, which made Donnie see lightning bolts of red, but his father was bigger than him and not above serving up a knuckle sandwich. Donnie prayed his grandfather would step in, do a Carlo Rizzi on the senior Baratta's surly ass. He even thought about asking the capo, then decided it was probably against protocol; besides, his father never really bruised her face, so maybe the old man didn't know.

Donnie started making runs for some people at the very bottom of one of his grandfather's crews. While he fully expected to someday (soon) become an associate, then get made, eventually (in his fantasies) taking over his grandfather's regime when the old man couldn't hack it anymore (an eventuality that seemed nearer and nearer every day), he had enough smarts to know that to step on the toes of those he might one day serve directly under (or rule over) could be bad for him down the line. Wiseguys are like elephants; they're big and they don't forget. But one day, Donnie's father up and disappeared. His mother looked like Rocky Balboa at the end of the first movie, but the palooka was out of both of their lives. Donnie had always felt that his father had been preventing his rise in the ranks anyway. If the aging *caporegime* had disappeared Donnie's old man, so be it. His father was a greaseball whose acts made him criminal. Donnie was a criminal who wanted to be a gangster. There was a difference.

Donnie knew his grandfather was at odds with Mr. Foster, another capo, who either reported to Merlino's current street boss or to one of the five families in New York (the Genovese family was always sniffing around), maybe even to, God forbid, the DeCavalcantes of North Jersey—Donnie didn't know; no one knew it seemed. Foster operated out of the Mondauk County suburbs, far enough away from the city to avoid any kind of major attention whenever the Feds poked around South Philly, but close enough to have a couple of toes in the City of Brotherly Love. Donnie thought that if a turf war broke out, it would be a good way for him to make a name of himself. But whatever ill will existed between the old man and Foster simmered rather than boiled over, and it was business as usual all around. After some time passed, time during which Donnie made sure to kick a taste of whatever he made upstairs (whether it got there was another question), it became apparent that no one was in a hurry to even go on the record for him, make the old man's grandson a connected guy at least. But there was some forward motion when he began to occasionally work closely with Pete "Little Big Peter" Conti and Conti's brother-in-law, Ambrose Gallo, known on the streets as Needlenose for his work with needlenose pliers on degenerates who didn't cough up the street tax. But neither Conti nor Gallo, both members of his grandfather's regime, used Donnie on anything of significance. He would hear whispers of a big haul or a nice scam and see Conti flashing new clothes and jewelry, and he would know he'd been left out in the cold on another juicy operation. He wasn't a kid anymore, but all the guys he did jobs for all called him just that. The way it was going, he would never get vouched for, let alone get made. Hell, he was almost thirty. The youngest wiseguy he knew was about forty-five. The traditional way up wasn't working. Donnie had to take things into own hands.

Dom was lost to heroin. Good riddance, Donnie thought. He didn't need the dead weight. But Draco was a guy he could count on, and he was turning into a halfway decent second-story man. Donnie quickly added five other guys from the neighborhood. He didn't trust all of them, but he knew they would get the job done and keep their mouths shut (because of his grandfather) and their noses (and veins) clean. They bypassed an alarm and hit a jeweler on Market Street. Kicked a piece upstairs. (Again, if the tribute was ever received, Donnie never knew, and there was no one he could dare ask since he was acting independently.) A few more jobs and their reputation grew. The Catharine Street Crew, folks were calling them (which was good: the Catharine Street Crosses now smacked of the Jets or the Sharks, he thought). All this pissed off more than a few people, Donnie knew, but he had to attract the higher-ups' attention in some way. Dash and flash were the watchwords of the day, as far as Donnie was concerned, but when they planned the candy store caper, dash was the only word four of his crew seemed to know. They turned their heads and made excuses like the pussies they truly were. It was down to just Donnie, Draco, and Christopher Ricci. Yeah, Donnie knew who hung out in the back of the candy store, but that was the beauty. It would be a bold move. He would even give back what he stole. He just wanted to show the leadership (especially his grandfather) he was more than a good earner: he was a doer. And the candy store heist wasn't all he had planned. It was going to be a full night.

Pip's Candies and Sundries didn't even have an alarm. It didn't need one. This was South Philly. Most people didn't even lock their front doors at night in the Italian section. Everyone in the neighborhood knew whose candy store it was: a capo firmly entrenched, a real old school fella. Trouble was there was nada to steal. The cash register had fifty bucks in ones, fives, and change. The back room, done up nice with an AC-style card table and a small bar, had zip too. Just the booze. Draco and Christopher looked to him for instructions, and Donnie shrugged. Break the bottles, he told them, and that was when they realized they were surrounded: there were guys at the entrance to the back room and the exit to the street. Donnie laughed and pulled off his ski mask, and one of the guys surrounding them pulled a gun. Draco shot first, and he went down quicker than liquor. Christopher dropped to the floor and covered his head and cried, "I give up!" Donnie wasn't about to do either: take a bullet *or* surrender. He threw a couple of bottles at the guys by the exit, and as they all dove to get out of the way, Donnie made his move, sprinting past them out to the street, over a low wall, and into the night. Most of the muscle back at Pip's were too out of shape to follow.

Donnie knew he was going to have to pay for the candy store job. He had shown his face: a dumb move (though not as dumb as Poor Draco's). There was always a chance the guys that had seen it didn't recognize him; it was dark. Christopher wouldn't sing. But Donnie had one last card up his sleeve, one last thing he could do to prove himself and maybe wipe the attempted candy store heist off the books. Dom had become a liability. To feed his habit, he was going into hospitals, taking morphine from patients, right from their IVs. Dom's father had been a wiseguy. (He'd passed from stomach cancer a few years back. Thank God too, Donnie thought; he didn't have to see the pathetic weakling his son had become.) Dom was hitting neighborhood houses as well—a big no-no. He would run right in the front door, grab whatever he could, then run away. His mother had thrown him out again. (She would take him back in—she always did—and while Dom promised to kick, she would sit on the stoop with him sharing a bottle of Carlo Rossi Sweet Red.) Most mornings, Dom could be found in the park or sometimes just on the corner, huddled against a wall. He was an embarrassment both to his family and to the family. So Donnie did what he thought was right and what he figured would square him for the candy store fiasco. (He had planned it as his grand finale anyway.) He stalked the streets, sticking to the shadows until he found Dom. (It wasn't hard). He discovered his old friend at the back of someone's house, huffing gas from their grill's propane tank. When Dom caught sight of Donnie, his eyes didn't seem to recognize him, and he crawled backwards on his back, an upside-down crab. Then he relaxed and said Donnie's name, followed by "So…" and nothing else. Donnie knelt down and pushed his friend's dirty hair back. Then he put two in his brain. After pulling his car around, he drove to Olde Bridge in Mondauk County (which connected the boroughs of Mondauk Proper and Spring House), dragged his body on a tarp through the woods to the red dirt of the eastern bank beneath the bridge on the Spring House side, and dumped Dom in the deep, swift, and dirty Pennypack Creek. No one would miss a junkie.

When it all came down, it came down hard. Unlike he thought, Christopher sang to the skippers about the candy store; oh, it was a cabaret show the way Donnie heard it. Christopher's body was found three months later in the Delaware River. Singing, no matter the reason, was bad news; no one could think to trust him again. But whacking Dom—that was a genuine shit storm. Who knew Dom had been spoken for? Yeah, he'd been dropped from the active roster and no one used him as soon as his habit had spiraled out of control, but someone had stepped up once and gone on the record for Dom, which made him a connected guy. Even though he'd been blacklisted, no one could touch Dom without his sponsor's say-so (or his sponsor's captain). And how could Donnie have known Dom, that gas huffing, morphine stealing street scum, was protected by none other than the mysterious Mr. Foster, who, it turned out, knew the family. No part of South Philadelphia was Foster's turf, but the capo didn't seem to care much about protocol. Just who Foster answered to was a mystery (he belonged to someone—everyone does eventually, wiseguy and citizen alike), but whoever it was let Foster run his regime the way he wanted to, and he usually did so somewhat quietly in Mondauk. Now Donnie had taken out a Foster associate. There was only one person he could turn to. That was when the dream began: looking up at Olde Bridge from the murky waters of the creek with his recently deceased friend as his grinning companion. He couldn't remain in hiding much longer; it wasn't in his nature, and, besides, when he ran out of hiding places, where would he go? He'd avoided approaching the old man thus far. He'd wanted to prove himself beyond his bloodline (which included his deadbeat father). The clock was ticking; the old man was dying, tethered to machines. Donnie had to go in on his knees now or get a close look at the bottom of the Delaware (or the Pennypack creek) himself. It was real goombah shit. Donnie almost loved it.

+

The old man knew from ghosts. He had fourteen hits under his belt—he'd made his bones when he was barely out of his teens— and he'd ordered or passed the order on for at least twenty-five more. (Did that make him a serial killer or just good at his job? He didn't give it much thought. He considered trash like Manson and Bundy to be not just sick and twisted but ultimately men without a code.) The capo knew the dead, or rather, the *murdered*, didn't simply lie down and die, end of story. Sometimes he would wake up in the middle of the night and one of them would be at the end of his bed, cleaning his nails or clipping a cigar. The dead all smoked cigars. It was as if, once expired, the murdered put childish acts behind them. The ghosts, the old man thought, were what separated the real wiseguys from the wannabes.

No one had ever told him about the ghosts, he mused. But after his first hit, maybe after his second, he noticed a flutter in the corner of his left eye. A window would be open that he swore he'd closed. His trigger finger would suddenly go freezing cold. So many long-time guys in this thing of theirs were so fucking dumb, he knew they'd they never noticed the ghosts. They held their shit together with Silly String and spaghetti and waited for their turn to get whacked or incarcerated (or, in Philly at least, sing). The ones with a snapping synapse or two either held their ground against the ghosts, the old man figured, or lost their marbles. The latter group included guys who suddenly robbed a bank in the middle of the day with no mask, blasting at every citizen who sneezed or muffled a scream, until the police took them down. Suicide by cop. These were the guys who ate one of their own bullets or hung themselves from their ceiling fans. These were the guys who'd get paranoid, dig up a body, and move it to the most conspicuous place possible, like Richie "Baby Arm" Carmandi (his nickname stemming from his legendary prick, big and thick as a baby's arm). Baby Arm dug up this mutt he'd clipped two years before. Must have stunk like hell's bunghole. Baby Arm gathered up the bones in a blanket and buried them on a construction site, normally not a bad place to bury someone provided it was an area that wasn't being dug up. But Baby Arm didn't worry about which way the big shovels were facing or which areas had begun to sprout foundations. No, Baby Arm just dug a hole and left a burial mound. *A burial mound.* Construction workers found the shallow grave the next day, and the cops used DNA from the blanket to tie Carmandi to the bones. Twenty to life. Shived in the laundry room after he'd served two. Even the wiseguys inside didn't want to protect him, he was that stupid.

The old man had faced down his ghosts they, those he had done himself and those he had pushed the button on. (They usually just one appeared at a time, thank God.) Sometimes he'd face a ghost for days or even a couple of weeks in a row before it would disappear for a spell. Now they came around less and less. Whether this was a sign that they knew he was going to die soon from his multiple diseases or that he was going to get clipped because of his grandson, the old man didn't know. The ghosts never said. But they said other things, and the old man knew the ghosts well enough, had made peace with those that let him, and he knew he could count on word being passed along to those in charge of such things, for there is always a boss.

(His mind wandered back to the poem Ronnie had read to him ages ago. *Stevenson? Robert Louis Stevenson? No, no, he wrote the pirate book, the one with Blind Pew and the black spot.* The poem: he remembered wenches dawdling in dresses and boys bringing flowers wrapped in old newspapers. And the emperor. He could never forget the emperor.)

The Donnie situation was bad. Mr. Foster was incensed, Frankie Joe Bones told him, and the ever-loyal Sally Rossi informed him that Foster wanted the kid's head. Let him have it, the old man thought, except he knew Foster was a ruthless son-of-a-bitch who'd turn his attention to the old man if Donnie wasn't found right quick. Foster might even break the code and go after the kid's mother. It wouldn't be right, but the Philadelphia *Cosa Nostra*, though in the process of righting itself, was still such a mess, it wouldn't make a difference, even if someone in New York objected. After two internecine wars in fifteen years, the heads of New York's five families tended to keep their distance from Philly (other than to exact a piece of AC and most South Jersey jobs). Too many canaries, not enough wolves. But to take out another capo required the okay from that captain's boss or sometimes from the Commission. Who was the dying *caporegime* to whichever mook wore the crown? Almost a mustache pete. But knowing Foster, he wouldn't get the hit sanctioned; he would just take the old man out, and if a noise was made, he'd point to Dom. Eye for an eye. All that Exodus shit. Truth was neither Philly nor even New York fucked with Foster much. Someone had to be holding the reins, but it often seemed like the man ran his own family. (Not for the first time, the capo wondered if Foster was his real name; he'd never heard of an Italian named Foster; sounded Irish, and no mick would ever be made, let alone be given a regime; at most he could be part of a crew but never a leader of any kind over those of Italian heritage. *Dio non voglia!*)

He could always hit the kid himself when he came—and he would come, the old man knew, but to make it official and quicker, he had Donnie sent for; when you were sent for, you came (or, again, in Philly, you ran to the FBI). The capo didn't think his grandson was stupid, but he was no Einstein either (though he thought by now the kid would have accrued some common sense, but, sadly—and considering his father, predictably—no). And for sure he wouldn't stand up under questioning. The old man thought Donnie would fold quicker than a Chinaman with two pair and a weak heart. But hitting the kid was a sensitive matter. The old man still had soldiers beneath him to do the work, however Donnie was family. A situation like this couldn't be farmed out or given to some freshman eager to earn his button. No, this required something a bit more ethereal. It would be best if it was showy, to shut down the Foster faction, make it clear who sanctioned the hit, but what was ethereal was rarely ostentatious—Marley's ghost didn't go door-to-door rattling his chains—and considering his daughter, a minimum of ballyhoo would make the medicine go down that much easier (along with her thrice daily intake of Ambien).

+

That his grandson would come packing was a given. The old man even gave instructions to the two goons he'd called up to sit in the living room (a luxury he rarely indulged in anymore, but appearances were everything) not to pat him down. Let the boy think he had one up on the old, dying capo. The more hubris the better.

The boy went to his bedside immediately and kissed his spotted hand.

"Grandfather."

The old man pulled his hand back and the IV line rattled against the pole. He'd sent the night nurse home for the rest of her shift; good thing too: that rattle would have sent her marching in like the Nazi Nurse Ratched she truly was.

"I'm no boss, boy," the old man said, trying to sound more annoyed than he really was. He knew the deference was partly real because Donnie was scared shitless and partly an affected gesture meant to appease a departing member of the old guard. Donnie would want to play it up the middle, show his grandfather that he was a man of mettle. Christ—the old man could hardly stand it: the kid read the situation all wrong from the word go, a real *minchione*.

His grandson stood back, straightened his shoulders, then slumped into a chair.

"I'm in trouble," Donnie whined. "I did something...we robbed the candy store over on...you know, Joey Galoshes' place...Pip's..."

Now came the tears. "Then...I did something else but—"

"Shut up," the old man said, barely raising his voice but allowing Donnie to cry as loud as he wanted. The old man didn't care if the muscle in the other room heard. Better they did: word would hit the street that the Donnie Baratta situation was being taking care of by the kid's grandfather. (Amongst themselves, even made guys flapped to each other like housewives over a back fence.) That was exactly what he wanted. Keep Foster, Joey Galoshes, whomever, even the acting boss, out of his nose long enough for him to actually handle it. This was his daughter's son after all.

Ronnie had come to him too, the night before. She'd heard things; she knew Donnie was in deep. She begged the old man for clemency, and he patted her hand and told her, "We don't even know he did what they say he did. I'll see...I'll see what I can do here, but it's up to Donnie to face this thing if it's his to face." He'd spoken vaguely not only because he hadn't known what Ronnie was actually privy to, but because, despite having his house swept twice a week for bugs—a silly extravagance seeing how just about the only orders he gave these days were for lunch and dinner—he never underestimated the Feds. They watched the movies too; they all wanted to be Eliot Ness. They spoke better gangster than all the guys the old man had served with, and those guys, he swore, had learned most of their lingo from Coppola and Scorsese. Still, the occasional business was discussed in the beeping room, but the old man made Bonesy write it down, afterwards burning the pieces of paper in a bowl in front of him. This put a bee in Nurse Ratched's bonnet and set the smoke detector off more than once, but fuck it. Price of doing business, but he rarely was that involved in the day-to-day operations anymore.

His grandson's tears (crocodile possibly, but the kid was shaking) subsided into an annoying fusillade of sniffles.

"I just wanted to show them…just wanted to make my bones, you know…I—"

"Shut it," the old man rasped, this time louder. One of the soldiers poked his head in, but the old man waved him off.

" 'Make my bones.' You wanna quote from *Scarface* now? How 'bout something from *On the Waterfront*? Oh, didn't rent that one, mommy's boy? Black and white—right, right. You kids need your stylized violence in Technicolor. Plus Elia Kazan: named names to HUAC. Broke the code of silence, eh? You don't even know what I'm talkin' about. Probably think *omertà* is a racehorse. Oh, but I betcha know something from *The Sopranos* through. Maybe you can sing me the theme song?"

"I just—"

"You just nothin'. You know what you did, and you barely know why it was stupid beyond all stupid."

The boy covered his face. The old man swore he'd just been dropped into the scene between Marlon Brando and Al Martino in the first *Godfather*. He wondered what would happen if he barked, "You can act like a man!" just like Don Corleone had to his weepy godchild.

"What's gonna happen to me?" Donnie asked when he lowered his hands. "I can't do no jail time. I ain't made out for prison."

So you'd wear a wire like the rest of them—assuming you lived that long, the old man thought.

"No, you're not."

"This Dom, he, he was a junkie, a real dope fiend. Robbin' the neighborhood. Shit like that. I thought takin' him—"

The old man held a finger to his lips. He wasn't going to prison as an accessory for this little prick.

"Yeah, yeah, right," Donnie said. "I thought…doin' that…would get me in, you know. Get me noticed. It didn't know he was Mr. Fos—"

The finger against the lips again, only this time with more than a hint of agitation.

"Yeah, yeah, right."

"Our friend up north, say."

Donnie nodded, his greasy black hair falling into his eyes, making him look even younger. "Our friend up north—"

"*Your* friend up north, you say to me," the capo corrected with a tinge of real anger in his voice. (These kids memorized the movie dialogue but never understood a word.) "*You* don't know from *our*."

"Right, right...*your* friend up...*our* friend...shit, the guy up north. I didn't know he'd spoken for—"

"Who'd he speak to, now?" he asked, cupping his ear.

"I didn't know that Dom was under his—"

"Umbrella?" the old man suggested, his mood recovering.

"Umbrella. Yeah, yeah, right."

The old man shrugged. "What do you want me to do?" He gestured to the machines and tubes and IV. "I'm just a dyin' old businessman. What do I have to do with such things?" Swinging for the fences, going for the nomination, wiseguy hall of fame.

"But you know—"

"If you angered certain people, then you should go to those people and offer to make amends. Hat in hand."

Donnie looked up, fear dancing from eye to eye, Fred Astaire with a hot foot. "But he'd...the guy up north...he'd...he would *take care of me*. I mean, why wouldn't he, right? The only way he wouldn't was if you stood up for me."

The old man tried to look incredulous, but he didn't have to act too hard with Donnie. He could have done this whole charade with puppets, and Donnie would probably have gone along and kissed Pinocchio's hand on the way out. "Me? What can I do? Stand up for you?" He asked, enjoying himself. "No, no, Donnie." He patted the bed, gesturing for the boy to come over. "These things," the old man said once Donnie was sitting next to him, "have to go a certain way."

"But will you...?" Donnie began to ask.

The old man smiled and gave his grandson's hand a little squeeze. (A little was all he could manage.) Donnie pulled a pack of cigarettes from his pocket, and the capo shook his head, pointing to the oxygen. Oh, they all smoked cigarettes, even the old man way back when, but not many of the young turks and the wannabes smoked cigars, and if they did, they thought that just sticking big penis-shaped rolls of tobacco in their mouths made them big men. It was that way with just about everything for them: food, drink, smoke, suits, shoes—as long as it made them look the part, who cared about really mattered? Those coming up today wouldn't even be able to taste difference between the house merlot and Brunello di Montalcino, let alone know *why* a Montecristo is superior to a Phillies Blunt—just as long as it cost more. They didn't even know how to properly cut the end of a cigar. (He'd seen his men use a butterfly knife, leaving the cigar looking like a botched circumcision.) Properly lighting one and priming the tobacco were lost arts. Cigarettes required no thought; they were the tobacco equivalent of a quickie blowjob from a street whore. No, the days when all the men smoked cigars and relished them the way one would a single malt scotch or a drop of anisette, were long gone; only the ghosts, only the ghosts.

"You like to bet, I hear," the boy's grandfather began. "Ponies up at Philly Parx. Poker parlors in Chinatown. Blackjack in AC. Into Sonny Reale's book for quite a few fazools. You're good for the occasional grift too, eh?"

The boy lowered his head.

"Hmm-hmm." The old man nodded repeatedly in an attempt to appear somewhat doddering. "I want to make you a wager."

"A wager?"

"I want to make you a bet," the old Mafioso said, trying not to sound exasperated.

"A bet?"

"Yes." The old man almost smiled.

"But, grandfather, I'm in such trouble. There's so much heat."

The capo gripped his grandson's wrist. "Yes, yes. So much heat." He suddenly became angry. It was what the role called for and easy enough to tap into, God knew, and for dialogue, he just had to think like the boy's pathetic father. "What? I should say of our friend up north, 'I'll make him an offer he can't refuse'? Then you'll feel safe and warm and strut like the big cock once more? Fanook."

His grandson looked close to tears again, and the old man gave himself an Oscar for Best Actor...but maybe it was best to leave that category open. He was just the conduit. The supporting actor. Someone else would have top billing.

Let be be the finale of seem...

"Listen close now, lean down," the old man instructed the boy, hoping his grandson inhaled all the smells of old age and medicine and decay. He hoped Donnie got a lungful. "I wager you a brand new existence—a better one, I think. Straightened out? Oh yes.

You'll be sponsored." *Che cazzo.* "Here's the thing: you have to successfully pull off a job for me. See, I bet—"

"What, grandfather? What's the job? Anything." Donnie's eyes widened with dumb excitement, but the old man could still see the fear tripping the light fantastic behind his corneas. It was enough to make him ignore the fact that he'd been interrupted by this *stronzo*. Hard to believe they shared the same DNA, he thought, but Artie Baratta acted like a man who had weak sperm. You can always tell.

"Oh, you wanna hear the job before you hear the terms?" The aging gangster raised his bushy eyebrows. "Okay by me. Your word is your blood." He shook his head in a dramatic fashion. "Youth. Always in a hurry." Lowering his voice to a stage whisper, he said, "There's a young joker causin' some trouble. He's been colorin' outside the lines. You need to help take him *down*town." The capo inwardly winced, but he was speaking to a child raised on Pacino, De Niro, and Pesci.

"Is he a made guy?" Donnie asked, breathless.

The old man slapped him.

"You are dirt on the shoes of a made man. Don't you forget that. You see the trouble you're in, and that junkie dirtbag was just connected, a nobody. No, this guy's not one of us. (And neither are you—yet.) He's a citizen. Not even Italian. I need you to scam him, con him—should be right up your alley—before you direct him downtown."

Donnie grinned. The old man felt sick to his stomach. Who talked like this? If the Feds were listening, he'd just given a couple of agents hard-ons.

"Not a long con, per se," the Mafioso continued. "Use no shills. No muscle. Just you and him. You know my man Frankie?" The old man gestured with his head, as if Frankie Joe Bones was next to him. "He's runnin' things for me. He's gonna point out the mark. He's gonna tell you the bunko, fill in what I leave out. You listen good, follow everything he says."

"I will, I will," Donnie said, sounding every bit like the eager beaver the old man had hoped he would be. "But, if I'm on the streets…"

The man in the bed shook his head. "Don't you worry about that. Eyes on the prize. A good confidence game relies on the mark's greed, his dishonesty. That's all you're gonna be concerned about."

The old man coughed. Donnie looked like he'd heard a death rattle. The grandfather smiled. "Lean closer."

The smell of fear and a copious amount of cologne made the old man want to take out his grandson right then and there. "Thing is, you don't actually pull the con."

Donnie looked confused.

"It's part of the game," the old man said. "You hook the schmuck, then have him meet you out under Olde Bridge in Mondauk County."

Donnie's face constricted. "That's where—"

The capo snapped his fingers and pointed to his lips, his impatience no longer part of the act. Maybe the kid was stupider than he thought; maybe it would be easier to take him down where he stood. Frankie always had a piece of piano wire, and he could tell Sally or Alonzo to go get the lime. But there was a littler matter of a promised offering in the offing.

The only emperor is the...

"It's where nothin'. Understood?" He lowered his whisper so the boy had to bring his ear down to the old man's mouth. "No one's gonna look for you or even think you'd go into Mondauk, our friend's turf, Foster's territory. So it's better than the Jersey swamps. Besides, I can't fully protect you in parts of Jersey, not without raisin' suspicions. And I'm gonna protect you—for a short time. Just long enough for the con, for our bet. You get the mark to meet you under Olde Bridge, and then a friend of ours from out of town is gonna come out of the woodwork and make sure this prick, he don't piss straight again. You follow? Frankie'll flesh it out, explain the hustle, like I said, but in a nutshell, you just tell the chump, you let him know, that's where the money's hid for safe keepin' until the swindle you're gonna pull together. Yeah, together—you and him. You tell him you're not goin' back 'neath the bridge till the big night. Then you sit on him—he'll make the move. They always do. You can't con the honest, boy. You bring him right to the spot where you, ah, *littered* with our friend's druggie associate. When it's over, you—you get gone, run like you're escapin'. You have to follow a con through to its end in case, somehow, the mark's still suckin' in air. Rare but it happens. Then..." The old man clapped his hands. "Straightened out. No problem with our friend up north. Button up. The books'll open. You follow? See, I'm bettin' you can't do it. (No offense.) You're bettin' you can. You pull it off: a new life. Respect."

Donnie nodded, and the old man tried very hard to hide his disgust. His grandson never asked what would happen if he didn't pull the job off. *Quel che sarà, sarà*, really, but the kid should know better than to agree to a wager without knowing the terms. That there were no terms set mattered little. He just needed to motivate the kid enough to get him where the old man had been told he needed to be.

"Now, go," the aging gangster said, waving a weary hand in the air. "Your grandfather is very tired. Bonesey'll give you a clean piece of hardware just in case—but no cowboy shit, hear? This mark's a real citizen, a nobody. Just pissed the wrong people off in a big way. He knew who he was workin' for. Tried to hide money, you know what I mean?" The capo shrugged. "You help take care of the final accountin'. Then someone else'll close out the books. Capiche?"

Donnie nodded and stood up.

The old man gestured towards the door where Frankie waited on the other side.

"Thank—"

"Shut up."

And it came to him, the couplet that ended the first stanza, as he heard Frankie lead his grandson outside, and a chill snaked through his wracked body, ending in a smile he could neither deny nor control:

> *Let be be the finale of seem.*
> *The only emperor is the emperor of ice-cream.*

+

The con had gone swimmingly even if Donnie didn't understand a damn thing. He'd followed Frankie's instructions to the letter and met the mark, this accountant-looking type, at McCullough's, a rough-and-tumble bar in Mondauk County, that according to intel the mark frequented because he occasionally got laid by one of the cougars still standing at last call. To get things going, he sent a busty chick over to flirt with him (after she'd loudly flirted with Donnie then threw him over; funny what you could buy with a double-sawbuck). Not exactly a meet-cute, but it didn't matter none—it was the dramatics of the thing. (That's what Frankie said anyway.) She didn't appear to be the mark's standard pickup—too young, Donnie thought at first, but she was hardly a schoolgirl when he saw her up close; it was just that her tits hadn't gotten all sloppy yet. She got the guy to buy her a drink, then hopped to the next lonely heart. Donnie slid in the stool next to the mark and offered his hand and his sympathies. Slut. Whore. That sort of thing. The accountant-looking guy—Livingston, some WASP, who said he was a recovering sex addict (and was eager to talk of his past debaucheries)—was obviously taken by the gangster talk, and Donnie laid it on thick. He didn't know if he was acting or just revealing his true self, but he didn't care. Donnie bitched and moaned about Mr. Foster (in a low voice), his street tax, the vig—just as he'd been told to do by Frankie Joe Bones. Livingston, drunk off his balls, started talking about how he's been working for Foster on one of the capo's semi-legit side deals, a front for a laundering operation, and how he'd been skimming. More than skimming—how he'd taken Foster, that bastard, for near enough to pay off his mortgage. Donnie whistled and nodded knowingly, genuinely impressed, and said he knew of a good job coming up. He leaned over and told Livingston—"only 'cause I think you're a stand up guy, a real John Wayne"—that he knows Foster's bringing in a truck with appliances, but that one of the boxes held a container the size of a footlocker with a million in cash to be laundered. The truck was all set to get lost on its way. "It's all been arranged." Livingston laughed and said he would love to get his paws on those bills. Donnie bought the WASP another scotch and water, offered him a cigarette, and told him he could be Italian, he was that aware. Livingston grinned, obviously flattered. Only problem, Donnie told him, shaking his head in sorrow, was that *his* launderer, this guy he knew from the old neighborhood, wanted twenty percent—not the usual ten 'cause this'll be so friggin' hot—up front or he ain't touching it. Donnie told the mook the job was set; the money was all but his, but he only had a hundred and fifty grand socked away—that was it. He was tapped. He'd have to call off the job if he couldn't come up with someone to partner with to make up the shortfall. Livingston made like he was waving Donnie away, and for a moment, Donnie thought it was off. The dream he kept having of looking up at the bridge from the bottom of Pennypack Creek, next to Dom's rotting corpse, suddenly seemed less like a dream and more like a genuine possibility.

Livingston leaned over and laid on the bullshit. "Not a problem, Donnie. You know what I do? I work in the count rooms. You know, at the new casino where the track is—Philly Parx in

Bensalem. Control auditor they call it. Fancy way of saying I watch over the working class stiffs who count the bills, and I make some reports. So loose down there. Swear to God. *Too* new. New managers, new buildings, new security system. Half the cameras in the count room don't work yet, and the hallway: forget it."

Believe nothing, Frankie had told him, but this was no count room clerk; he had to know *something* if he was going to come up with the money. But a casino count room without working cameras—right. "Dumb as a box of rocks," Bonesy warned him, "but really smart rocks." It wasn't Frankie's way to be cryptic, so to everything Livingston said, Donnie grinned and nodded as he'd been told.

"The hardest part will be walking out with fifty grand under my arm and even that won't be too difficult. Pay off this guard friend of mine, then just drop it in the trash and pick it up down the line. The number's so large, they'll think it's a miscount. We'll have a day, day and a half at the most. When we're done, I gotta put it back though. And quick. That'll be harder. Eye in the sky and all. Plus the rest of the cameras down there will work soon enough, even if most of them are for show. People don't know that. Thing is to know which ones are watching when. But the eye in the sky—that's the real deal. That's Big Brother and all his siblings-type shit. I kid you not. But I'll figure a way to put it back."

"No you won't."

Livingston looked confused and scrunched up his pasty face, his bulbous nose and unruly eyebrows nearly meeting somewhere in the middle. For a second, he looked more Irish than WASP. "Won't what?"

"Won't have to put it back, friend," Donnie said, lightly punching the mark's shoulder. "You won't be goin' back there. Heat's gonna be big. Gonna have to split town for at least a while. Take a long vacation. Medical leave or somethin'."

Livingston nodded. "Lam it."

And the con was on. When Donnie checked in with the guy, surprising him at his job (waiting for him on the casino floor like Frankie had told him to do), Livingston was nervous that Donnie had showed up. (He said he thought wiseguys were banned from the casino; Donnie didn't correct him, merely puffed out his chest.) But the hook was set. He got the fifty grand, handing it over to Donnie in a movie theater parking lot after midnight, sweating like he'd just fucked a fat chick in a steam room. (Could it be possible that this chump walked out of a casino with fifty large? Donnie didn't know and didn't ask.)

Like Frankie Joe Bones had told him, he let it drop to Livingston a couple of days later—days he'd spent looking over his shoulder; Foster could have eyes anywhere, even at Philly Parx's casino and racetrack—that he'd buried the two hundred grand, the twenty percent supposedly for Donnie's launderer, under Olde Bridge in Mondauk County, the bridge that connected the boroughs of Mondauk Proper and Spring House, on the western side beneath the "carpe diem" graffiti. Livingston's eyes damn near did a cartoon pop-out, but Donnie calmed him down. It was well hidden, he assured him, safer than anywhere else. They couldn't very well put it in a bank now, could they and stashing it at Donnie's place didn't seem very smart, did it? Besides, he told the mark, winking, he knew how to dig a hole that no one would ever find—other than the two of them.

Then Livingston confessed that despite all Donnie had said, he was still going to try to return the fifty grand to the casino somehow before he split. His sister had gotten him the job, and he couldn't put hers in jeopardy. (She was a blackjack dealer.) Donnie shrugged the way Frankie Joe Bones had told him too. This was the insurance policy. Donnie told the mark exactly where the money was hid—exactly. Practically drew him a map. Then he told him he was going out of town overnight before he met with the launderer. Livingston's eyes, now firmly back in their sockets, glittered in a way Donnie was familiar with—glittered with greed. Livingston was truly his.

Or theirs. Why his grandfather really wanted Livingston whacked, Donnie didn't know. Coloring outside the lines, the old man had said. But they were Foster's lines; why did the old man care? Had Livingston been skimming from Foster at the behest of his grandfather or one of the other Philly capos? And why the elaborate, fictional con? Couldn't the old man just hit the guy pretty much anywhere, anytime? All of this bothered Donnie for a couple of days but soon was pushed out by an increasing concern for his safety (even though his grandfather had said he'd be under his protection). One evening, he thought Fosters' boys were tailing him on the Boulevard in Northeast Philadelphia (a black Chrysler had been sitting on his tail for near about five miles), but the car soon turned off, and Donnie returned to his room in Frankford, where he was cooling his heels per Frankie's instructions, and washed his sweat-soaked shirt in the sink.

But at times his confidence was never higher. (It was a yo-yo existence.) The Livingston con (or setup) was just about a done deal. He would soon have won his bet with his grandfather. The pressure would be off, Mr. Foster would back away, and Donnie would be set to get his button when the books were opened (and they were opened more frequently now that the days of federal informants and turncoats seemed to be petering out—just not opened for anyone under forty, but Donnie's arrival would change all that). Little Nicky Scarfo had been one tough motherfucker, but he'd left a lot of corpses in a lot of car trunks and other places in the '80s and spawned not a few rats, but ended up dying in prison after thirty years behind bars. Since then, a lot of goombahs had tried to walk in his shoes, but only Skinny Joey Merlino had Gotti-like balls. But things didn't get better, they got worse. The old ways were chucked out the window. Merlino wanted to be a rock star (like Gotti had been). The new ways were more than just flash; they were a combination of *Goodfellas'* bravado (which Donnie didn't think was necessarily a bad thing) and the paranoia of Scorsese's Irish gangster flick, *The Departed*, where both the criminals and the cops tried to ferret out their respective mole. (To study Scorsese movies was de rigueur, of course, but Donnie prided himself on knowing they were just reflections of the real thing—most of the time.) Ratting out your brothers, which under Scarfo was seen by the weak as the only way to save their skins, became almost a rite of passage under Merlino, the witness protection program just another stop on a long El ride. Donnie remembered it making him sick when he was nine years old (he knew this life was for him even then) to watch this thing he'd longed since he could long for things fall apart at the seams (pending racketeering charges and more) while Merlino ate in the finest restaurants and went clubbing on Delaware Avenue. But things started getting back to the old ways under Uncle Joe Ligambi (a quiet, stabilizing force), and whomever was currently the acting boss, which admittedly wasn't clear, continued to keep things as they should be. (He felt that asking his grandfather who was running things day-to-day would possibly be not only be considered an affront but a question the old man wouldn't answer for fear of bugs.) The only thing that became crystal (after he read about it in a George Anastasia article) was that Merlino still pulled the strings—he just chose low-key guys to rebuild the family while he served an almost twelve year stretch, then acted the part of a citizen in Florida (until he was convicted again). Two things were apparent: since winning the reigns in '94 after a bloody war, Merlino had no intention of letting go, prison be damned, but he now clearly saw the advantage of a quieter family presence. Donnie didn't want a return to the *old* old ways— shit, he'd never last two seconds with those ancient stiff backs—but he at least wanted a fighting chance to earn and make his way.

It came as a surprise when the old man sent word to him that *he* was to take Livingston out. Donnie was thrilled to get the ticket. He wondered, briefly, why his grandfather hadn't just unleashed Frankie or Alonzo, but he didn't ponder too long. He was going to make his bones the old-fashioned way. Guys didn't have to get a kill under their belts to get straightened out anymore. But Donnie would have one ordered by a skipper, an old school *caporegime* from the Gentle Don's days. It would be a pleasure to kill for his grandfather and more of a pleasure to kill the pasty count room manager. The guy was a perv of the highest order, even talking about his young niece's blowjob lips. Oh, this would be a genuine joy. Maybe he'd even get to keep the fifty grand. Nothing had been said about what would happen to the money (Frankie told him to just stick it in a closet for the time being), but Donnie would kick up without question. He was so sure that his ascent to captain would be swift, he already thinking about where his clubhouse would be. The place where the Chink's was now maybe. He was about to go from a sap to what the *Inquirer* would call a Mafia prince in a matter of hours.

So it was curious to Donnie that there was no sign of the mark when he crept down to the western underside of Olde Bridge and crouched in the red dirt at the top of the bank near the abutment. Donnie waited and waited. Still Livingston didn't show. (Frankie Joe Bones had informed Donnie that the mark was going to make his move on the money around 12:30 that night; Donnie knew better than to ask how he knew.) The smell of Pennypack Creek seared the inside of his nose. (The creek was called the Puddle by the locals because despite its swift moving current, it smelled like a fetid puddle.) A thick fog had settled above the water. He kept checking his watch. He'd dumped Dom's body into the Puddle at half past one in the morning. It was nearing that time now, and Donnie didn't want to be anywhere near the Pennypack, Olde Bridge, or Mondauk County when the clock struck one-thirty. Call him superstitious, he didn't care—he kept crossing himself and kissing the gold crucifix that hung from a chain around his neck, his eyes on his watch. Goddamn it—he couldn't believe Livingston had chickened out (and Frankie's information had been bad), not with fifty grand of Philly Parx's money (supposedly) buried by Donnie's hands plus another one hundred and fifty (supposedly) hidden with it, all soon to be in play. That was presumed to be the insurance—Livingston had insisted he had to return the money he'd appropriated to his employer; even when Donnie told that him he needn't worry about it, he never looked completely convinced; everything else he swallowed hook, line, and sinker. Of course, the mark could have caught a whiff of *something* and skipped town with nada before the fake heist happened, but that wouldn't make sense considering Livingston's obvious greed (and his palpable fear of not only the casino gods but also Mr. Foster, from whom he was skimming; his cut, Livingston believed, would be enough for him to make up the loss before Foster noticed or just to get gone). Donnie was certain there was no way the mook wouldn't show.

At one-thirty, Donnie kissed his crucifix once more. It broke off the chain the instant his lips graced his saviour. "Bad fucking luck," Donnie whispered, and he pocketed the crucifix and tossed the chain behind him. From his vantage point on the western side, he could see any vehicles crossing the bridge, but traffic was practically non-existent this time of night, and there really wasn't room to just pull over, so more than likely, he'd be on foot—carrying a shovel. The eastern side could only be reached by walking through Pennypack Woods, but Donnie didn't think Livingston would come that way unless he knew the woods intimately. Pennypack was especially dense on that side; it would be easy to get lost even if it wasn't dark. If Livingston was coming from Philly, he'd have to approach Olde Bridge via Bethlehem Pike; there was no other way. Donnie checked his watch once more and touched the pocket where the crucifix was. He looked up and sucked in his breath; it whistled through his teeth. He could barely see across the Puddle for the fog, but now a light seemed to be within it, emanating from the opposite shore. Motherfucker! He'd have to climb up the bridge and go down the other side to check the eastern bank, which was where he'd dumped Dom—and he didn't want to be anywhere near there. Maybe the greedy, WASPy bastard had misunderstood him and was digging around in the red dirt on that side or was even just waiting it out to see if anyone was watching him. Whatever it was, Donnie had to find out—the whole thing was on his head. Maybe the light had nothing to do with Livingston; could be some kids with a flashlight looking to score or get laid or maybe a deviant searching for some private place to practice his perversion—but Donnie doubted it. Sure, the chump could have decided against stealing the money (unlikely) or even have made him (even more unlikely), but the meet with the launderer was supposedly scheduled to go down tomorrow night when Donnie "returned," so unless the guy planned to dig up the money in the daylight (tomorrow morning or afternoon), he would have to come tonight, which was when Donnie was to ensure Livingston met his maker. Besides, Frankie said the mark would be here, and Bonesy didn't fuck around.

At first the light on the far bank seemed to move here and there, but it rested in one place, as if waiting for him. He checked the .38 he'd stuck in his waistband, covered by his shirt, and started up the bridge. A poem he'd heard when he was in school danced just out of reach in his head. *Stevens?* What the fuck did he care?

As soon as he climbed down, Donnie smelled the cigar smoke. It seemed to hang in the fog. He brushed it off as just a smell coming from his clothes (although he didn't smoke cigars and hadn't been around anyone who did), but after about thirty seconds, he couldn't ignore what his olfactory sense told him. He hadn't drawn his gun yet in case the old man's muscle from out of town was still the picture and doing some professional shadow lurking; he didn't want to come up on the guy with his piece out. But why would his grandfather give him the ticket and still call someone up, and why would a pro be smoking a cigar on the job of all things—and under a bridge, where the smoke was trapped, swirling overhead like a storm cloud, before being carried forth, slowly, by the fog? When he saw it was Dom leaning against the wall (the graffiti behind him read "memento mori"), Donnie's body relaxed after the initial surprise wore off. Again he thought of the Chink's at Camac and Moore where Salvie Testa was taken out in '84—or maybe 9th and Christian where the old greaseball hair salon used to be: both good places for a clubhouse. His mind didn't seize up until he noticed the two holes in Dom's head and the way what light there was appeared to shine right through them like dusty movie projector light. But he didn't stop walking towards his childhood friend until he noticed that Dom was glowing just ever so slightly around the edges. It was a greenish glow, and the Puddle sludge on Dom's hair and shoulders and chest was shit brown. The combination made Donnie nauseous.

Drip, drip, drip.

"Donnie Salami," Dom said to him, using the street name Donnie had been saddled with as a kid because of his predilection for dried, highly seasoned fatty pork and beef sausage. He used to eat it right off the deli paper, his fingers greasy the rest of the day. But he stopped cold turkey after the time he almost got pinched because of a salami stain he'd left on a window casing of a house the Catharine Street Crosses had burglarized. Nobody had called him that for years and anyone that even started to got a punch in the kisser. "Donnie Salami," Dom said again, blowing a fat smoke ring and popping it with a slightly glowing finger. Sediment slid from the digit and plopped to the ground, crawling away. The cigar was the only thing not covered with muck. Donnie couldn't take his eyes off the two holes in Dom's forehead.

"Beauts but ain't they?" Dom asked, poking his fingers into the holes. Donnie heard a squishing sound and his stomach churned. "But you were always good up close. Weren't worth a shit from far away. Far away, you couldn't hit an elephant." Dom spat and his spittle glowed a sickening red on the dirt floor.

If her horny feet protrude, the come
To show how cold she is, and dumb.

Donnie blinked. Dom's mouth hadn't moved, but Donnie heard him quite clearly.

"The poem you were thinkin' of, your grandfather too," Dom said by way of explanation. "It's by Wallace Stevens."

"But you're…" They were the only words Donnie could get out. He felt the fog covering his skin, making everything he did an effort.

" 'But you're dead!' " Dom said, hocking up a really big one. The loogie hit the red dirt and slithered towards the Puddle, finally executing a summersault into the water. Donnie heard its splash.

As if he couldn't help it, Donnie's mouth opened (with a creak and a crack): "But, but…"

" 'But the con!' Tsk, tsk, brother. *'But' never got near to what 'so' saw.*" Dom took another huge pull on his cigar then regarded its lit end. "You remember that, Donnie Salami. Just made that up. You remember: *'But' never got near to what 'so' saw.*"

Donnie raised his gun, pointed it at Dom, and squeezed one off—the report echoed under the bridge, seeming to shake its very foundations—but the ghost gave a little laugh. "Stop. It tickles, Donnie." A pair of incandescent seafoam-colored worms tumbled out of the new hole in Dom's head.

He shot again; this new echo competed with the first, which had yet to cycle out. "No, Donnie. I mean it. Stop." Donnie's arm went limp and the gun slipped from his hand. He wondered briefly if the .38 would crawl away towards the Puddle too.

"Most of us smoke cigars, Donnie, the way we were supposed to. But some of us—some of them—don't even do that much. What's the word? *Elude.* What eluded them in life— particularly *in* the life—stays just out of reach, because they never understood the difference between smoking a cigar and polishing a knob. Even now, rather than going along to get along, respecting and becoming part of a tradition—one older than *Cosa Nostra*—'cause what the hell else you gonna do amongst the embers?—they keep acting like stick-up boys rather than made men. In the place, the other side of the shadows, you can either catch on and become a 'friend of ours'—belatedly—or you can spend eternity chasing that which is sweet but melted and, yes, cold, never to be more than a chimera. Your hands may become sticky and your clothes stained, but then if there were such a thing as true light where you're headed, you would find yourself bathed in crimson—except for the Black Spot, if you have colored outside the lines. Open your hand and see."

Donnie refused but he could feel the Black Spot pulsating in his palm, not at all like the ones drawn on slips of paper and given to Billy Bones and Long John Silver in *Treasure Island*, the only book he'd read as a kid because...

"...because it had pirates. Yes, yes, and buried treasure too, just like now. He winked and his eyelid fell off and floated towards the red dirt. "It's only fiction, mind you." The eyelid flapped its skin like wings and headed towards the woods.

Donnie clamped a hand over his mouth but removed it when his lips were pressed against the ridges of a poorly executed Black Spot tattoo. His teeth chattered without restraint, but the sound was drowned out by Dom humming to himself, seemingly more focused on the jagged melody than on his murderer. Yet as soon as Donnie's muscles began listening to his brain (*carry me the hell out of here*), his dead friend cut the tune off abruptly and smiled, his teeth translucent green like those glow-in-the-dark toys Donnie had as a kid.

"Hmm. Amongst the embers, Donnie Baratta, amongst the ashes. Ashes of what? Of most everything that was good. Sure, there's always ice cream, but it melts as soon as you see it. There's rivers of the stuff—thirty-one flavors—but you can't have any. Embrace the cigar, the mustache petes tell 'em. But do they listen, do they heed? No, these guys, they can't believe what they are and what they aren't, or maybe they can't escape who they thought they were supposed to be, so they just sit and think one thought over and over and over. You know what your thought's gonna be, Donnie? Not: what the hell happened here? *Vaffanculo!* No, your thought, Donnie Salami, is just what I said: *'but' never got near to what 'so' saw.* Over and over and over."

Drip, drip, drip.

Donnie wanted to make a break for it, but his legs wouldn't cooperate. A viscous liquid seeped from all three of Dom's bullet holes. The smell of the Puddle was now mixed with the smell of meat gone bad, then buried, then dug up again. Donnie opened his mouth but nothing came out.

"And nothing ever will," Dom said, tossing his cigar into the Puddle, where it extinguished with a hiss that seemed to last forever. "Ya see, buddy boy, you can't con an honest man—or a dead one, and your company will soon consist solely of the latter." Dom was closer to Donnie now—much closer—although Donnie had never seen his dead friend move or even shuffle or float. "Oh, there's some confidence games that rely on the grifter giving *his* confidence to the straight guy, but those are usually short cons. For something bigger, the long con or even the badger game, you gotta find a mark who's hungry for it. Or in your case, thirsty. You thirsty, Donnie? Me, I'm always thirsty. These holes, see." Dom poked them again, and when he pulled his fingers out, they were covered with luminous Puddle scum.

Drip, drip, drip.

"You remember how the Stevens poem ended, Donnie?"

Let the lamp affix its beam.

The only emperor is the emperor of ice-cream.

"You feel played yet? Sucks being the mark, right, Donnie? You were thirsty, you thought you were gonna drain the chalice, leave a little blood on the paten, then go fuck the prom queen. You were thirsty, but you can't, I tell ya, hand to God (now *that's* funny), you can't con an honest man, but you?"

Donnie opened his mouth one last time to say something, anything, but found he couldn't shut it as Dom's hand moved towards his gaping kisser.

"Don't worry, Donnie Salami: you'll never be thirsty again," Dom said. "You're gonna drink your fill and then some. You're too dumb to float." Then Dom raised his head to laugh—lucid, ooze-covered scarab beetles and coffin flies escaped past his receding lips—and Donnie felt the cold of the Puddle chill his flesh as his friend's rotting fist reached the back of his throat, propelling him to the bottom of the creek.

+

It may not have been enough, but the old man was happy. No one would guess it from the frowns of the nurses and the doctor, but the old man was content. He'd done the right thing. Problem solved. Didn't have to call on any muscle either. Just a little help from Frankie (who didn't know the whole plan and was still unwavering enough at least not to ask). Bonesy drafted someone from the dwindling Irish K & A Gang to clean up and play the mark, Livingston, as instructed and disappear back under the El when the job was done. He didn't even need to get him a job at the casino; Donnie was too simpleminded to check. It didn't take long for word to reach the old man that his grandson had gone missing. (He'd sent his daughter to visit his sister in Florida the day before it went down, so to speak, so she wouldn't find out until the police contacted her.) If the news had made it to the elderly gangster in his sick room, he knew that Foster knew before him. Still, it might not be enough; Donnie's body hadn't been found, so the kid could still be out there. (The old man knew better. He also knew a body would have been helpful, but a deal is a deal, even if it was made with a ghost.) Foster's men could still come for him, smother him in his sleep, increase the morphine drip, use a silencer, whatever. The bedridden capo chuckled.

It didn't matter. This thing of theirs, he thought, has been around forever. Sometimes beefs, real or imagined, were worked out with violence. How the dying, old creature shriveling in a hospital bed brought in special could be a threat to someone as powerful (right now) as Mr. Foster, the old man didn't know. The higher-ups might even sanction it. He'd never gotten along with the *consigliere* of his own family—any of them—and he thought the current underboss was a right prick. Besides, who was he to these once-young turks who couldn't see their future at the other end of a snub-nosed revolver, yet alone believe they'd be singing a fagola tune once they dangled at the end of a DA's hook? And there could always be some hungry twenty-year-old punk in Foster's regime who thought that taking out Salvatore Abandonato for the sins of his grandson would be the splashiest way to make his bones.

But somehow the ancient *caporegime* doubted it would come to that. Foster was cold, but just the fact that the old man hadn't made a stink of his grandson's disappearance should be proof enough that the dying Mafioso had cleaned his own house. The other skippers would see it that way, he was sure, even if the underboss did seem a tad anxious for their senior captain to die already. (When that blessed event happened, the old man anticipated that his rackets and territory would be taken over by another capo with management's blessing; they were too intoxicated by power to realize that would just be making one of their captains twice as strong and thus more likely to someday vie for the crown. The old man also fully expected the top soldiers in his regime, Frankie Joe Bones and Sally Rossi, to put up a fight if their turf was threatened by a hostile takeover. What's right was right after all.) But if they came for him now, they came. There wasn't spit he could do about it, guards or not, but his street sense told him he would be allowed to die the ignoble death of renal failure or cancer. But neither scenario, getting hit by Foster or succumbing to his body's breakdown, was part of his plan.

The old man raised himself up. It was quite an effort, but he wanted to make sure Nazi Nurse Ratched was preoccupied by the boob tube. She would smell it after a bit and, if Frankie hadn't locked the door before he left, the old man's final request, she would goosestep in, making dramatic exclamations, threats, what have you. (Par for the course even though he paid for her continued presence.) The old man didn't care what she did on the other side of the door. (He had Frankie take the key with him, but the capo was sure the nasty nurse would find a way in eventually.) He reached over with much difficulty to his nightstand, and from the top drawer, he fished out the Bolivar he'd been saving for this special occasion, which he'd begun to doubt would ever present itself. But now he cut the cigar, which took some time, and lit it, puffing with contentment. A cough threatened to escape, but he contained it. No need to distract Ratched from a PBS pledge drive; she would come running soon enough when the smoke reached her perpetually flared nostrils.

Ah, yes, he'd come up during the time when all the men smoked cigars. Now that he was on his way out, only the ghosts still smoked them the way they should be smoked. But as the time between being corporeal and being Casper closed, a good cigar—a Cuban like his Bolivar—was their link. The ghosts, he understood, could make your time after all this pleasant or hellish. He suspected his fourteen victims (plus the twenty-five others he'd pushed a button on) might have campaigned for a harsh punishment for the old *caporegime*, but ghosts were no different than most living men; they could be bought. Perhaps giving the gift was advantageous to the giver, but it was just as likely that the ghosts didn't care about the gift *or* the giver. He used to wonder: what was one more dark soul to them (for that was all he had to proffer)—until he'd discovered that if they were given a chance to make one more hit, it could make all the difference. Unlike most people, the old man listened—what else had he to do? His days weren't exactly activity-filled anymore—and one night, he listened hard enough to understand: the ghosts have to be invited to take part in the separation of a soul from its soma; it had to be a sacrifice or accompanied by one. Yes, all he had to do was make an offering (or two), and his way would be smooth as a baby's ass. It would be better than the best blowjob he'd ever received (Mary Jo DiMarco, October, 1967, in his sky blue '66 Valiant Sport), better than getting his button even. The old man tilted his chin and squinted his eyes as the cigar smoke collected and hovered around his head, all sorts of shapes and faces emerging for a second then dissipating. Yes sir, it would be better than getting made or getting head and a hell of a lot more permanent.

With great effort, he raised up the hospital bed.

When he heard Nurse Ratched's shoes approaching, the old man broke his reverie and became hyper-alert, his eyes the eyes of a young gun. The IV had been unhooked—fluorescent sludge dripped down the pole—and except for one, the machines and monitors (or whatever the surrounding equipment was) had been turned off. Beeping alarms sounded. (This all happened so quickly, he didn't even notice the alarms until instinct kicked in.) When she entered the room (there were two keys?), he somehow managed to lean forward (he felt hands on his back) and threw the Bolivar at her, hitting the nurse square in the face, sending her scrambling back to the kitchen it sounded like. Probably calling for backup.

But the roller of big cigars and the emperor of ice-cream were already here...

"Best not to disturb them while they go about their business, Ratched," he attempted to yell, but all that came out was dust. Ah well, she might learn this firsthand if she insisted upon inviting more guests to his farewell party.

One more piece of equipment to go: he watched the dialysis machine be destroyed by barely visible fists that left glowing streaks behind.

Let be be finale of seem.

He lowered the bed and returned to his pillow.

Ah, the ghosts. How greedy their embrace, how hungry, and he thought: how fitting.

-end-

Sides Three and Four

———A One-Act Play———

DRAMATIS PERSONAE:
Mickey, 41, a meat packer
Addie, 37, an erotic dancer
Alan, 39, a street hustler

SETTING:
A South Philadelphia row home.

The set is split almost evenly between the living room (the front
door, with windows on either side, is stage left) and the kitchen.
However, there is a small bathroom stage right with an adjacent slim
hallway.

The living room is simply furnished. It is neat but dusty. None of the
furniture matches. An old Emerson turntable and amplifier
component sit on an altar of cinder blocks and plywood next to a
milk crate of records.

The kitchen has a 1950s dinette table pushed against the wall.

TIME:
The present. It is autumn, right before the clocks are turned back.

PRODUCTION NOTES:
There is a screen above the stage. A lone camera, its operator all in
black, captures some smaller moments, transmitting them to the
screen. (*Exempli gratia*: Addie in front of the bathroom mirror, the
comparison of scars.)

In between these moments, the screen shows pre-recorded footage of Bruce Springsteen's *The River* spinning on a turntable. The image of the record should fill the screen. The appropriate side is always spinning.

This footage should be intentionally scratchy and old-looking and should be presented in a way that will not distract from the onstage action.

The play is timed to the indicated songs.

AT RISE:

Keys rattle and the front door opens to reveal MICKEY, a tall, once-muscular, now-vaguely lumpy man still in his factory uniform.

He notices a small, bulging black overnight bag behind the orangey recliner near the door and nudges it with his foot. He squats and starts to unzip the bag but stops. The light coming through the living room windows is waning. Standing, he looks at his watch, then the clock, which reads 5:42.

> MICKEY
> (to himself in a smoke-ravaged voice)
> Maybe there's still time. It ain't dark yet.
> (snapping his fingers)
> My pasta. She hasn't tasted my pasta and gravy yet.
> There's still time.

STAGE LIGHTS DIM BRIEFLY: It is now dusk.

In the small kitchen, Mickey wears a tatty apron spotted with pasta sauce over a poorly ironed shirt (untucked) and worn trousers. His sleeves are rolled up almost to his elbows. An open Budweiser bottle sits on the counter.

He lights the pair of candles on the dinette table that has been set for two. The plates and the silverware don't match, but Mickey has fanned out an old linen napkin at each setting.

He glances at the clock and hurries into the living room. After turning on a lamp, Mickey squats by the crate of records. Without much deliberation, he chooses Bruce Springsteen and the E Street Band's *The River*, a double album, and places the second platter on the turntable.

As he lowers the tone arm, Mickey hears the screen door squeak open, and he drops the needle in the middle of the first verse of the first song, hustling back to the kitchen as ADDIE enters.

Of Italian descent, Addie has teased black hair and olive-toned skin set off by her ruby red lipstick and chipped nail polish. She looks around with worry crowding the corners of her eyes, peeking through a window and checking her watch.

After a few seconds, she takes off her jacket and throws it on the ragged couch. She is wearing a sheer black top with a white bra beneath it, an absurdly short black skirt, and black fishnets.

She starts to remove her heels but stops and checks behind the recliner for the overnight bag. She nudges it with her shoe twice and hugs the cheap black purse that is rarely out of reach. As if she can't help herself, she crouches to peek at the overnight bag's contents.

                          MICKEY
           Addie, that you? Thought I heard the door.

Addie springs up. Mickey enters the living room holding a wooden spoon, which he raises to Addie's mouth. He sings along with the record.

                          MICKEY
                     (singing softly)
           "Well, they shot you point blank / You been shot in
           the back."

(speaking)
Here, taste this. Tell me if there's too much garlic.

ADDIE

Naw, Mick. I had a long day. The afternoon shift at Seventh Heaven ain't exactly happenin'—plus Jewels called out. I just gotta get my head together.

MICKEY

Taste. If there's not enough garlic, I got more. Fresh from the Italian Market. But if it's too much, you know, well, it's like the opposite of a haircut, right: you can always add more, but you can't take it out.

ADDIE

Mick, I been dancin' all—

Mickey places the spoon to her lips, and she smiles briefly and tastes.

MICKEY

Perfecto or down the ol' drain?

ADDIE

Mmm. No, it's good. Little more salt maybe. Garlic to onion ratio? Well, look, like my grandmother used to—like *they* say—you can never have enough garlic until it's enough, you know.

MICKEY

Yeah, well, *they* say a lot. Long as you think it's good. Music alright? It's on the moody side, yeah, but it still kicks up enough dust to remind ya you're alive, you know?

ADDIE
(gripping her purse)
I gotta go to the bathroom.

MICKEY
(heading back to the kitchen)
Yeah, alright. I'll be in the east wing.

In the bathroom, Addie takes a small baggie out of her purse and pours out a shaky line of cocaine upon a round makeup mirror. After the snort, she looks at her reflection and smears her black eye makeup across her face.

MICKEY
You fall in or what? Been known to happen, you know. Sal, he told me 'bout a gator that got flushed in Florida and now lives in the Brooklyn sewers layin' all kinds of eggs. Somethin' like that.

Addie washes her face and checks her watch.

When she walks into the kitchen, clutching her purse, her eyes take in the candles and the linen napkins.

ADDIE
(sniffling and more animated)
Schmantzy fancy. What's the occasion? You gotta date, Mick?

Knocked off his game momentarily, Mickey tries hard not to let it show.

MICKEY
No...date, no. This is...this is for you. For us, really. It's an anniversary like.

ADDIE
(lighting a cigarette)
An anniversary of what?

Addie goes to pull out a chair. Mickey wipes his hands on the apron and pulls it out first. Before she sits, she sneaks a peek at the front door.

MICKEY
At Chez Mick's, it's first class all the way.

ADDIE
An anniversary of *ours*?

She gently hangs her purse on the back of the chair.

MICKEY
(a little embarrassed)
Well, you been here two weeks now and—

ADDIE
(softly)
You know I ain't stayin', Mick. I told you that. Just
till…

Mickey turns back to his food preparation and takes a long slug from
his beer.

MICKEY
'Course. Right. Till Manny pays you what he owes ya.
You think there would be a union for dancin'. I mean
all I do is pack meat, and I got union dues.

ADDIE
It ain't just Manny.

MICKEY
What, someone else owe you money, shark? What's
the vig?

ADDIE
No, I mean, there's just—

MICKEY
(throwing a piece of radish at her)
I know. I was just kiddin', but you can't kid a kidder,
right? See, what we're celebratin' here is—

She throws the piece of radish back at him, and he rains chopped lettuce in her lap. Addie snaps a linen napkin on his leg. Mickey kneels to brush off her lap but thinks better of it and stands.

> MICKEY
>
> Well, so, it's our two week—it's your two week anniversary of stayin' here, yeah, but you went down the court today, right? The PFA? So we're celebratin' your pendin' freedom.

> ADDIE
> (the playful mood now gone)
> We gonna talk restrainin' orders now, Mick, when you're puttin' out such a spread?

Her hands reach for her purse.

> MICKEY
>
> What we got here is your bachelor special plus. Like Julia Child if she'd been born in Bella Vista. That's me. We got your two courses: salad and spaghetti, and I bought some merlot 'cause the guy in the state store, he said red goes best with—

> ADDIE
> I gotta go to the bathroom again.

She grabs her purse and runs out of the kitchen in a flurry of chopped lettuce.

> MICKEY
> Again? Well, if you gotta go, you gotta go.

Addie closes the bathroom door and leans against it.

> ADDIE
> Just shakin' the dew from my lily pad. But yeah, sounds good, the red.

                            MICKEY
                (as he picks up the lettuce from the floor)
        Lily pad. Okay, well, my mother ever heard you use
        language like that, she'd be confused.
                        (beat)
        Hey, Ad?

                            ADDIE
        Hey, Mickey?

With a grim smile, she pulls the small baggie of coke from her purse.

                            MICKEY
        You even allowed to drink? I shoulda…I didn't think
        to—

                            ADDIE
                        (agitated)
        So don't. So don't think, I mean.
                        (slightly softer)
        It's fine. It's all fine.

Through the windows, the waning sun has been replaced by the weak
glow of a streetlight. Mickey putters in the kitchen.

In the bathroom, Addie reaches under her skirt. She dips the pinky
from her other hand into the baggie of white powder and does a nail
bump as she stares into the mirror and rubs herself between her legs.

                            ADDIE
                        (whispering)
        It's all so fuckin' fine.

With a worried look, Mickey picks up the bottle of wine, puts it
down, then picks it up again.

Addie emerges from the bathroom "refreshed." She does a "happy
dance" in the hallway, then shadow boxes. The record is now midway
through the third song on side three.

Mickey pours the wine as Addie enters the kitchen and tosses her purse on the table, almost knocking over a glass. She laughs as Mickey hangs the purse on the back of her chair.

> ADDIE
> Mother hen.

She sits for a couple of seconds, then begins dancing suggestively and a little frantically.

> ADDIE
> (singing along with the record)
> "So you fell for some jerk who was tall, dark, and handsome / Then he kidnapped your heart and now he's holdin' it for ransom."

During the above couplet, Addie grabs Mickey by his apron and pushes him down on a chair. She straddles him and begins grinding into his lap. Mickey holds her hips gently like he's holding an egg.

> ADDIE
> (still singing)
> "I'm a rocker, baby, I'm a rocker / I'm a rocker, baby, I'm a rocker."

Mickey suddenly and roughly picks her up and places her back in her chair.

> MICKEY
> I gotta finish with the salad.

Addie lights a cigarette. The one she lit earlier is still smoldering in the ashtray.

> ADDIE
> You know what that woulda cost you down the club? Full contact lap dance?

> MICKEY
> No—yeah, I don't wanna know.

ADDIE

Yeah, I wouldn't wanna hear no meat packin' stories either.

They both laugh. Addie glances at her watch and leans back to check out the front door.

ADDIE

Listen, Mick, leave the salad.

MICKEY

"Take the cannoli." Get it? But, Ad, the salad's the first course.

ADDIE

(patting the seat of his chair)
Leave it. Come here.
(raising her glass as he sits)
To...whatever anniversary you were talkin' about.

They clink glasses and drink.

MICKEY

I feel like you're gettin' ready to tell me somethin'. You movin' out already? You don't have to—you know that—but if you gotta, I can help. Still, you stay as long as you want. Recuperate and whatnot. Rehabilitate.

ADDIE

(angrily)
I ain't goin' to no rehab! I ain't gonna be no three-time loser!

MICKEY

I didn't mean...I didn't even know you went back.

ADDIE
(calm again)
Yeah—no, I know. Look, Mick, you been great.
There was no one else I coulda turned to. And you
know what?

MICKEY
No.

ADDIE
There's no one else I woulda turned to.

MICKEY
We got a history, you and me.

Mickey stands to continue making the salads, but Addie pulls him
back down.

ADDIE
You remember when I first moved to the
neighborhood?

MICKEY
Straight from the swamps of Jersey, still soakin' wet
behind the ears.

ADDIE
Yeah, but you remember the day we met? What
happened?

MICKEY
'Course I do, Ad. Why you wanna go thinkin' 'bout
that again?

She pushes up his right sleeve to reveal a large scar that begins at his
elbow and travels up his arm. Mickey begins to pull his sleeve back
down, but Addie gently stops him and pushes up one of her own.
Along her forearm, there is a recent four-inch-long wound, stitched
up. She places her arm against his and traces his scar, then guides his
fingers along her stitches.

ADDIE

You can't keep savin' me, Mick.

Mickey doesn't reply. He pulls down his sleeve and stares at the floor.

ADDIE

You can't. At some point the only person li'ble for me is me.

Neither can look the other in the eye. Addie moves her chair back an inch or two so she has a better view of the front door. Mickey grimaces as Bruce sings, *I don't wanna fade away / Oh I don't wanna fade away / Tell me what can I do, what can I say / 'Cause darlin' I don't wanna fade away*. He stands and checks the sauce.

ADDIE

This album gets so fuckin' depressing.

She lights a cigarette from her previous, unfinished one.

Mickey walks to the living room and lifts the needle up. He turns the record over and cues up "Drive All Night," the second to last cut on side four, before returning to the kitchen.

ADDIE

(in a suddenly lighter tone)

Someday, if I get some money, some extra money—after I pay you back, I mean—I'm gonna buy you a CD player or a laptop to download or, what-do-they-call-it…stream. Bring you up to date. If I had some money, I would. I'd buy you speakers for every room in the place so, you know, you could listen to Bruce while you're catchin' a shave and whatnot. Or maybe I'd get you one of those iPods, if they still make 'em…somethin' you could…

(beat)

I don't know what I woulda done if you hadn't put me up, if you hadn't given me that money, stakin' me. That was a lotta scratch.

MICKEY
(placing fresh bread on the table)
I wasn't doin' nothin' with it. It's okay. And I don't
need no CD player or computer, thanks. Got my
records. Always got my records. And I don't know
from downloadin'. Thinkin' 'bout investin' in an
eight-track player though. Hear they're comin' back.

Mickey sits, as Addie runs out of the kitchen with her purse again,
slamming the bathroom door closed behind her. Mickey shrugs but
his face is grim. While she's gone, he stands a couple of times—to do
what, he doesn't know—but always sits back down.

In the bathroom, Addie checks her hair and reapplies her lipstick
before doing a line off the toilet lid. When she looks back up at the
mirror, she spits on it and watches her face melt as the spittle slowly
slides down the reflective surface.

Addie rushes back into the kitchen and collapses on her chair. She
starts talking as if there had been no break in conversation.

ADDIE
See, the thing is, that day we met: I needed savin', and
you clocked him but good. My father, he
woulda…well, he woulda broke more than my arm
that day. And he was worryin' more than my arm too.
You can look away, but you know I ain't lyin'. Sad
stripper story, right? Well, I ain't dancin' next to
Harvard chicks. It's not that much different than the
meat lockers, Mick. I know that much. Just a bunch
of damaged goods givin' a piece of ourselves away for
bread and butter money. And why? 'Cause it pays
better than waitin' tables or washin' someone's floor?
Yeah, but mostly 'cause we're not good enough for
much else, you know? I have great tits and a halfway
decent ass. That's it. I never took no SATs, never saw
the inside of no college. But I got big full boobs and
they're real and until they fall, I can make a buck.

MICKEY

Ad, I don't care 'bout none of that. I never judged 'bout nothin'. I just did what I did that day with your old man 'cause, I don't know, 'cause you don't hit girls. And I don't regret it one minute. Not one. I punched him, he cut me, and I fell and knocked my head but stupid. That's the way the cookie stumbles sometimes, I guess.

ADDIE
(starting to cry and reaching for his arm)
And look what you got in return. Severed tendons. An arm that don't work so good, 'specially for a meatpacker.

MICKEY

But I got you.

ADDIE

But that's just it, Mick. You don't. Even then, I still got shipped back home from the hospital the same day, and my father kept on tuckin' me in until my mother finally threw him out. 'Course she threw me out shortly after that too. Called me "the other woman." Had to live with my half-retarded great-aunt until I was eighteen.

They both fall silent. Mickey mouths the words of the song playing on the stereo—*I swear I'd drive all night again / Just to buy you some shoes*—before he gets up and resumes chopping vegetables. A noise outside startles Addie, and she grips her chair as she stares at the front door. After a moment, she relaxes her grip—a little. If Mickey notices any of this, he doesn't let on.

ADDIE
(sheepishly)
Now what Alan done...he beat on me some, yeah...but he didn't—

MICKEY

Alan's a…if Alan touches you again…cuts you like that…you don't need to worry none, Ad. I'll take care of you. I wanna take—

ADDIE

(slamming the table)

Are you even listenin' to me? Is this gettin' through that thick noggin of yours? *You can't keep on savin' me.* No one can keep on savin' anyone. No one's responsible for anyone but themselves—and maybe their kids, and I ain't so sure that's true neither. Alan's a…Alan's got issues too, you know? Issues he's gotta work out. Issues he's—

MICKEY

Issues he's gotta work out on your head.

He brings the knife down hard on the cutting board, nicking one of his fingers. Addie winces. Mickey goes to stick the finger in his mouth, but Addie gently stops him.

ADDIE

(as she inspects Mickey's finger)

This business deal of his went south, and me runnin' my big yap—

MICKEY

(pulling his hand back)

It wasn't this one time, Ad. I see him gettin' loaded over the bar, all chummy with Foster's boys, even Abandonato's crew at Dante and Luigi's, I hear— playin' both sides or thinkin' he is. I see him chattin' up other women too. Now, I ain't sayin' he's cheatin'—

ADDIE

(defeated)

He is. He does. Screw other women, I mean.

She places her purse in her lap.

MICKEY
Then why are you worried 'bout his "issues"?

Addie races out of the kitchen, and Mickey throws the knife at the wall and it sticks. He stares at it dumbly. In the bathroom, Addie takes out a cut straw, sticks in the baggie of coke, and snorts, making a silent scream face in the mirror when she's done. Mickey retrieves the knife just before Addie rushes back in with residue on her nostrils, which he chooses to ignore.

ADDIE
What you mean is: why did I choose Alan over you?

MICKEY
(caught off guard)
No, I didn't mean that at all. I—

ADDIE
I see the way you look at me. It's the way you *always* looked at me. You can't deny it, Mick. You ain't lookin' in some creepy sorta way or oglin' me like those pervs down the club. But I see you. I feel it.

She wipes her nose with her linen napkin.

ADDIE
Just these past two weeks. You lemme have your bed while you stay on the couch. Every time I come home from work, even if it's after the late shift, there's a TV dinner ready or Giovanni's just delivered a pizza. Now this spread you're workin' on here. And the music! Always somethin'…well, not exactly Barry Manilow, but romantic stuff just the same.

Mickey stares at the floor, clearly embarrassed. Bruce sings, *Let them go, let them go, let them go do their dances of the dead*, and Addie quietly sings along as she moves to the kitchen doorway and points to the stereo. She speaks with her back to him.

ADDIE
(never raising her voice)
Bruce Springsteen. Nina Simone. *Dusty fuckin' Springfield.* All my favorite records. I think you went and bought every Nina you could find, and no way you owned any Dusty before I came. I half expect to run into Van Morrison wackin' off in the bathroom. You think 'cause I kissed you that once when we were playin' records, gettin' drunk on your parents' peach schnapps, that you can seduce me with Nina Simone? I was in high school then, Mick. You were older and already out. I don't know what to tell you. Guess it felt like rebellion, or maybe it was just the peach schnapps.

Mickey smears a little blood from his finger on the table, but he lifts the apron to use his shirt and wipe it off before Addie turns around. He still holds the knife in his other hand.

ADDIE
(facing him)
I didn't choose Alan *over* you. I just chose Alan, and maybe I chose stupidly. But I chose and I never thought, growin' up, that I would ever *have* a choice to make. It wasn't between you and Alan. You weren't even in the runnin'.

She walks over and clutches his free hand, taking no notice of his still-bleeding finger.

ADDIE
I didn't mean it like that.

MICKEY
No, it's okay. It's alright. This gravy's only been simmerin' for like, I don't know, little more than an hour maybe. Usually takes a hell of a lot more time for a good gravy, but this here's the bachelor's special, so I figured we'd have our—

ADDIE

Some people get lucky, Mick, and hit the number or the trifecta. Other people are born so they can paint pictures or sing or write books and stuff. But most people get what they deserve in the end somehow. And I deserve Alan. In between his rages, it ain't so bad, and I got a roof over my head, and I don't have to worry 'bout much 'cept duckin' every once in a— every once in a blue moon.

She notices Mickey's blood on her hand and rummages in her purse only to come up with a crumpled, unwrapped Band-Aid, which she throws back in. She lights another cigarette.

MICKEY
(emphatically)
It's them drugs.

ADDIE

Yeah. No. Probably. So maybe it's just temporary like a PFA. Maybe "I do" meant "why not?" But either I'll clean up one day—either we'll *both* clean up, Alan and me, or we won't. I'm still a Catholic somehow—by birth, anyways—so I can't just give up on him, on us. Now, me? Who cares, right? And besides, where would I go? Here? That would never work. Not for you. Not really and you know it. I'm better for you, Mick, at a little distance.
(beat)
I never said the L word to Alan, not even when I married him. I hear it all the time down the club, but I never heard it at home growin' up, and I don't know what it means. I don't even like sayin' the word. When I'm singin' along to a song, and that word comes up—and it comes up *a lot*—I sing "fuck" instead. It's got four letters and one syllable too, right? But I'll tell you this, Mick, if there's anyone in my life I would use that word with—and it probably wouldn't be in the way you wanted it used—it would be you. Only you.

MICKEY
(trying very hard to sound lighthearted)
Yeah, well, I fuck you very much, Ad.

ADDIE
(laughing as her eyes fill up)
I fuck you too, Mick.

Someone bangs on the front door. Addie jumps. Mickey watches her smooth her skirt and wipe her eyes with the heels of her palms. He squeezes his bleeding finger.

ADDIE
(cupping Mickey's face)
You saved me from my father. Maybe you could save me from my husband. But you can't save me from me.

Mickey turns off the burner and the kitchen light as Addie runs to the front door and opens it for ALAN, a thin man with thinning hair and wary eyes. He wears a brown leather blazer and a dress shirt with enough buttons undone to reveal a gold crucifix.

Mickey walks into the living room with the kitchen knife. Alan looks around as if nothing is wrong but stays near the door.

ALAN
Hey, babe. Mick. Helluva place. Thanks for the effort, man. She's a special lady. Am I right?

MICKEY
I didn't do much of nothin'.

Addie hugs Alan who doesn't hug back—his eyes have settled on the knife in Mickey's hand.

ALAN
Things ain't always what they seem, Mick, am I right? From the outside, a marriage might look one way or,

for my Addie here, in the heat of a marital agitation, another. But even the devil's got more than two faces.

Mickey knits his brow: *what the fuck does that mean?* Alan and Addie kiss fervidly and sloppily. Mickey does his best not to look away.

> ALAN
> Ah, not what you expected, Mick? I know you ain't seen me for a while, and after listenin' to this one run her trap, you probably figured I'd walk in here twirlin' my moustache, talkin' De Niro. Am I right? You figured 'cause I run with a rough crowd, connected guys—uh-huh—sell a little bouncing powder to make ends meet, I'm the bad guy. Am I wrong? Well, in domestic disputes, lughead, the cops gotta take *someone* in. It's the law. So a disagreement gets a little loud, Addie does one of her "cries for help" on her arm, and the nosy neighbors call the boys in blue. But appearances are perceivin', Mick.
> (to Addie)
> You got your bags, babe?

Addie pulls her overnight bag from behind the recliner.

> ADDIE
> (trying to not look at Mickey)
> I just got the one.

> MICKEY
> Cries for help?

> ALAN
> (quietly to Addie)
> Still got the stuff, right? Tell me you still got the stuff.

> ADDIE
> All but a little, yeah. Most of it.

Alan tilts Addie's head back by her chin, taking in her raw, red nose.

ALAN
You look like fuckin' Rudolph.

He smacks her face—hard. Addie's lips begin to bleed. Mickey wipes
the knife on his apron and takes a step forward. Addie's wet eyes go
wide. Alan grabs her arm and pulls her close, her back to his chest,
putting her between the two men.

ALAN
(hissing to Addie)
Double dippin'. Tsk tsk. What I tell you?

Addie sniffles something that sounds like, "I'm sorry."

ALAN
We need that stuff to clean the slate with Mr. Foster.
Then, you and me, babe, we get that money back
from the bondsman, and we'll be in like Flynn.

MICKEY
You bailed him out. Dropped the charges.

ADDIE
I'll pay you back, I swear, but, Alan, he's my husband.
I'm sorry.

ALAN
She got you to give her some cash, huh? Well, I didn't
think she earned it sellin' skid-marked panties.
(to Addie)
Louie said you were shacked up with Special-Ed here
when he picked me up at the PDU, but I didn't
believe it.

Mickey briefly looks down as Alan continues to speak, but when he
raises his head, his face betrays his barely controlled rage as he glares
at Alan. The record skips.

ALAN
Guess it paid off in spades—and blue balls for you,
big boy, 'less she gave you the all-tunnels pass.

Alan squeezes one of her breasts. Addie doesn't react.

ALAN
You 'bout ready to blow this Popsicle stand, babe?

MICKEY
What about the Protection from Abuse order?

ALAN
Again with that shit? Christ. Well, if she did file, she'll
rescind when the hearin' comes up, just like before.
Ain't that right, babe?

Addie flinches. When she looks up, Alan smacks her again, sending
her to her knees. *Don't worry now*, Bruce sings from the turntable, his
voice a whisper. *Don't cry now…*

ADDIE
(between the fingers covering her face)
I woulda bought you that CD player, Mick. I woulda.

Baby, don't cry now. As Mickey starts towards Alan, the stomp of his
work boots makes the tonearm skate into the record's last song.
Addie looks up at her friend, her face pleading. Mickey stops and
puts the knife behind his back.

ALAN
(grabbing the bag from Addie)
See you 'round, Mick. Love what ya done with the
place.

Addie gets up, takes her jacket, and follows Alan through the door
without looking back. Mickey is motionless for a few moments
before throwing the knife to the closed door where it lodges in the
wood.

The violence of his throw causes the needle to jump into the run-out groove. Mickey pushes his sleeve up and traces his scar with his bloody finger before walking to the stereo and turning the record over. Distracted, he misses the lead-in groove as well as the intro and once again drops the needle into the first verse of the first song.

Mickey reaches for the knife but just taps the handle, watching it quiver. After turning off the lamp, he heads to the kitchen. The knife remains where it is. When he reaches the doorway, he notices he is still wearing the apron. He takes it off and tosses it into the relative darkness of the living room behind him.

In the kitchen, he turns off the burner and switches off the light. He sits at the table, extinguishing the candle nearest him with his fingers. The house is dark except for the candle on Addie's side of the table. Bruce is singing:

> *You wake up and you're dying*
> *You don't even know what from*
>
> *Well, they shot you point blank*

CURTAIN.

Pinkly Gets Shown the Door

Pinkly liked to think of herself as being more sophisticated than her mother, but after seeing Carl kissing a man, she thought maybe not. This was one of those things, she knew, where she was *telling* rather than *showing*, a big no-no according to her creative writing professors back at college—her therapist had the same opinion—but Pinkly's idea of being sophisticated was easier told than shown in the early days after the kiss.

She *told* herself she hadn't seen what she'd seen.

She *told* herself it was a figment of her overactive imagination—Carl didn't go around kissing men.

She *told* herself she wouldn't tell anyone else, and if she did, she *told* herself she wouldn't be drunk and crying but, it turned out, she was a little guilty of both.

And she *absolutely told* herself she wouldn't tell her mother, another promise she broke, this time after the nightly news ended and before a comedic monologue began.

Drunk and crying were wayward forms of showing, she knew, but the most conducive way to spilling the beans.

"I saw Carl kissing another man," she'd told her mother, and her mother *pooh-poohed* the thought, then almost fainted dead away. (At least that was what she told her daughter over the phone.) It must have been something Pinkly had done, her mother said once she recovered. Men have certain *needs*. Were those grad school classes getting in the way? Was Pinkly not attending to those nightly intrusions? "It only took a few minutes with your father. *Poof!*—and then done. No big deal." By the end of the conversation, Pinkly was defending homosexuality (which she didn't think was unnatural like her mother did, just unnatural for her husband). When she found herself also defending her own methods in the bedroom, sense caught up with grief and she hung up.

Pinkly was the one to move out of their apartment in the city, the apartment where she'd imagined raising their first child. (It was never the right time, according to Carl.) She didn't want to move closer to her mother, but that was exactly what she did. Pinkly's moving out was part of what her mother called her independent streak—like the streak of pink in her otherwise light golden hair.

She'd been Pinkly ever since she declared the color pink to be pinkly in the first grade. Her teacher treated her like a dangerous rebel and removed all the pink implements from the communal crayon and colored pencil collection. Pinkly's father, God bless his soul, went to the school and confronted the teacher. What the fuck else would you call the color pink, he asked. (Her father worked the docks, and his language was as colorful as a box of Crayolas.) The pink crayons and pencils magically reappeared the next day—in fact, they seemed to have multiplied.

In the year since moving out, Pinkly avoided dating completely. Carl came around, of course, begging forgiveness, trying to explain—something about playing G. I. Joes when he was little with Albie Mish—but divorce was the path he had put them on, and it was a path she followed to the end. She took nothing that wasn't hers, but she left the living room set which wouldn't have fit in her new little apartment. (Carl claimed not to want it since it had been purchased by her mother; regardless, it was now his to sit upon or not.)

No one in her cubicle set brought up Carl much after she moved out unless she did first. After all, she moved out the day after Christmas. Nosy old Judy Pawlowski tried to give her marital advice, but the afghan she draped over her shoulders every morning "to fight the draft" smelled so strongly of Marlboro cigarettes whenever she leaned over the cubicle wall, that it was all Pinkly could do not to throw up on her knockoff Jimmy Choos. Eventually Bonnie "Bon-Boom" Munch, who sat next to Ellie Strunk, the office's perpetual lonely heart (probably unaware that she now had competition for the title), tried to fix her up (having given up on Ellie a while ago, probably much to Ellie's relief), but Pinkly politely declined. She thought Bonnie was a little fast—short skirts (despite thick thighs and a hint of cellulite), lots of freckled cleavage, a tattoo on her ankle (Hot Stuff the Little Devil whom Bonnie insisted on calling the angry Casper), and a husband with a salt-and-pepper crew cut, a long black (dyed) goatee, and earrings in each ear, whom she habitually cheated on. (He also had a small trumpet tattoo on his left cheek, despite the fact that, according to Bonnie, he didn't play; she said he'd gotten it to remind her to "get to blowing"—*lovely*.) The thought of doing shots all night in some dive bar with a scruffy associate of Bonnie's spouse made her want to contemplate kissing a girl. Most nights, she listened to AC/DC or the Cure at an insane volume (or as insane as her apartment building rules allowed) while she made a salad or, if she was feeling daffy, some fettuccine alfredo. Then she'd watch a movie and go to bed early. She rarely felt frisky.

Then came this year's office Christmas party, held offsite at a huge banquet hall near the mall. She swore, after last year's debacle, that she wouldn't go, but Bonnie and Judy wore her down; this would be time away from their husbands, and they were planning on getting plastered and would need rides home. Pinkly caved with a (inward) groan. The office Christmas party was a ghastly, gaudy affair where their company's owner flashed his financial well-being by catering the event and providing an open bar. The owner's requisite speech would frequently be interrupted by cheers and applause from lit employees who otherwise cursed the man 364 days a year. Alcohol, Pinkly, observed, could turn any narcissistic charade into an act of largesse, and this one included a loquacious DJ in skinny jeans who was planted in front of the small dance floor. A special kind of hell, in other words. Secretaries and administrative assistants who acted primarily as lackeys for their bosses were suddenly shaking their booties freely regardless of booty size. Spouses drank too much and aggressively hit on young interns. Uptight supervisors undid a blouse button or two to celebrate Jesus' birthday. Pinkly was hugged often at these parties and told how much she was loved, adored, cherished, and worshipped by people who after the holidays would go back to pretending not to know her name. (Some people refused to say it just because it sounded childish and called her by her last name instead; she told no one her real first name unless it was absolutely necessary.) At least the food was good, but she preferred to eat alone rather than among the hungry hordes whom she suspected were bulking up just because they felt it was their earned right to do so—like the office Christmas party was a stated job benefit.

She was in line for the punch (which she hoped wasn't spiked; she wasn't much of a drinker) when she was shoved—almost tackled—from behind by a tall, younger man with dark hair and a shadow on his face. In the middle of the shadow was a smile.

"Pinkly—I'm sorry. Hank and those guys from the mail room. They get a little rowdy waiting for punch."

Then it *was* spiked. Pinkly frowned.

"No harm done…I'm sorry, do I know you?"

"No, no you don't. Not officially anyway. Gregory—Greg—Salvatore."

"Italian for savior."

Greg held back another bum-rush from Hank.

"That's what my mother says." He grinned, and his grin shifted the shadow on his face into new shapes and pushed it into new crevices. "She claims two fellows wanted her hand back in Palermo, but my father's last name boded well. What did she know? They came over here, and my father was a garbage man till the day he died, which was early."

"Mine was a dockworker."

"Ahh."

End of conversation. Pinkly poured herself some punch despite knowing that she wouldn't do more than sip it. She scanned the room for a place to sit. "Celebrate" had started on the dance floor, and all the other office ladies went *wooo!*

"*And the colored girls go, 'doo, doo-doo, doo-doo, doo-doo-doo,*'" Greg sang into her ear. Apparently the conversation was not over.

"Lou Reed," she said automatically.

"Ahh, a connoisseur among us."

Greg took a seat at the nearly empty table she'd found.

"Up until *Metal Machine Music*," she said. "Lou lost me there."

"Feel the same way about Dylan's *Self Portrait*."

Pinkly laughed.

"I can't even listen to that one."

"But I bet you own it, music geek like yourself. You just can't help   it.'

"Three copies," admitting what she admitted to no one. "One on vinyl, one on CD, one download."

They sat in bemused silence until a slow song played. She knew he'd ask her to dance like they were at some soph hop, and she knew she'd say yes. She was correct on both counts. All that was missing was a wrist corsage. The song was the Bangles' "Eternal Flame," not terrible as slow '80s numbers went. Better than "Take My Breath Away" or "Total Eclipse of the Heart."

Greg smelled good. It wasn't cologne. It was just good, strong soap. Her head barely reached his shoulders, but somehow they fit comfortably with none of that nasty hard-on-poking, grinding type of slow dancing she'd been subjected to at proms and a couple of weddings. She forgot she'd wanted to be alone. She even forgot her husband had kissed another man in front of her.

"Susan," she whispered, but she didn't know if Greg heard her or not. It didn't matter. It just felt good to say her secret name. If only for this moment, Greg deserved to know it.

"Eternal Flame" ended and "Shout!" began. She was in no mood to fast dance. Besides, sometime between the Lou Reed comment and the slow dance, she'd downed her punch and was feeling less than human all of a sudden. She needed air and fast.

"I'll be back, Gregory Greg Salvatore," she told the tall man, and he nodded, letting his long arms slowly release her into the swirling mass of dancers through which she made her way with difficulty.

Pinkly used her back to push open the first door she could find, hoping it wouldn't lead to a clutch of smokers. She found herself in a near-mirror image of the office Christmas party—only this one was decorated with 45s and CDs, strung from the ceiling with fishing line, instead of Christmas balls. A menorah sat on an empty table. There was a sign near a far door that read, "Annual Christmas Party" (the word annual made her smile briefly), along with the name of the failing music retailer that employed her ex-husband. What were the odds, Pinkly wondered. About the same as catching Carl kissing a man at his company's Christmas party last year.

Pinkly wandered around the music retailer's soirée for a bit, willing her nausea to take a back seat to her curiosity. Some besotted employees patted her shoulders, told her what a good job she was doing; it's all streaming now and nothing else; and Merry fucking Christmas. The music wasn't much better than at her company's party, which was surprising, but she should have remembered. She'd caught Carl doing his thing to a Steely Dan song—and not even a classic one, but a reunited Steely Dan song. Could have been worse. Could have been Styx, she thought. She'd lost her virginity to "Babe" and regretted the song more than the guy.

Pinkly was about to turn back when Carl's secretary ("your doppelgänger," he'd always said though Pinkly never saw it) caught her eye and waved. At least Pinkly thought she was waving. The secretary was draped across what appeared to be an ice machine, a thick crowd gyrating and singing in front of her ("*I always feel like somebody's watching me,*" so it went, "*and I have no privacy*"), and Pinkly walked towards her, not knowing why. Was she going to tell or show when she reached the woman who'd worked for Carl longer than

Pinkly had been married to him? The secretary was clearly showing—that washcloth that passed for a skirt would be appropriate if she were working a street corner and not three months pregnant, news she'd picked before it grew ripe and fell from the storied vine—she'd rather have swollen info than stale scuttlebutt, even if it came without indication of paternity. What would Carl's secretary know? Everything perhaps and Pinkly asked herself: what did *she* want to know? All of it of course. After all, who was Gregory Greg Salvatore? He was already in her past. More Carl—in the form of information on the man-kissing incident—was in her future.

As Rockwell faded out and the rhythmically-challenged crowd in front of the ice machine dissipated, there he was—there was Carl, his balding head and roguish chin buried in his secretary's neck. The secretary now had one pantyhose-clad leg wrapped around her boss' thigh. She hadn't been waving at Pinkly. She'd been shooing her away. To spare her the indignity? Such shooing was an enticement to watch. Pinkly was no mere fly at this picnic; she felt, momentarily, like a swarm. Carl went in for a kiss, received one (with tongue, Pinkly could see through her returned nausea), then the doppelgänger pointed her way. Pinkly ducked, and the swarm dissipated.

"Pink! Pinkly!" Carl shouted, but Pinkly, in the only response her tipsy mind could muster, dropped to all fours, then in a crouched sprint, rushed here and there, looking for the door she'd come through—running straight into the legs of a large man who was accompanied by another gentleman of equal size.

"Where's your name tag?" the first man asked as he lifted her to her feet with little effort.

Pinkly smiled what she hoped was her prettiest smile. "In the punch?"

"Out. You don't belong here. Wrong party."

"Wait—how do you know?"

The two behemoths looked at one another.

"Because you're smiling," was the answer.

The cold air hit her before she realized the two men had been standing before a door—and *not* the one she'd been hoping to find. *Slam!* She was without her jacket, and she backed away, ignoring Carl's face at the door's window, a rerun of the previous year's Christmas party, only then she hadn't been shown the door by two giants. No, the preceding year she'd run through the front door of the facility. But just like then, Carl never opened the door when she turned around; he just stared at her dumbly through the window.

Pinkly went to find her car. Bonnie and Judy would come looking for her eventually for a ride home. Her keys were in her jacket, which was somewhere in the complex. Hopefully one of the women would notice it on the back of a chair. Shivering in the wind, Pinkly decided she would wait and *show* the end of the story rather than try to find her way in and *tell* it. Showing was better after all, even if it hurt more, *especially* if it hurt more. And what was more sophisticated than being hurt twice by the same man? Her mother would be so proud.

-end-

The Sanctus Bells

Running up to the church on Thursday nights was always unsettling for Robert. The stained glass windows in front flickered hesitantly under the power of distant flames, while the ones on the second story were dark, ominous even, as if some plague had blighted them out. The narrow stone steps, the tall wooden doors, the century-old masonry—all of it in the dark made the mysteries contained within seem extremely real, which to Robert, during stressful parts of the day or when he passed a bar, they most certainly did not. But this wasn't an AA or NA meeting inside Assumption of Our Lady this time of night. (He attended both but in the basement of another church.) This was Sola Fide—By Faith Alone—the group of parishioners in search of *more* led by Father Judah. Not quite a Bible study group, not quite a self-help group (although it certainly numbered among its members recovering alcoholics and drug abusers like himself), it was, as Father Judah put it at their first meeting, a mystery group. Not the Agatha Christie or Arthur Conan Doyle variety, Sola Fide plumbed mysteries of faith and tried to bring them out into the light, so that the group could admire and understand them even in the dark. Sola Fide was for those few parishioners who wanted more than Mass, who needed more ritual for ritual's sake, and Father Judah was the right priest to lead this motley assembly of the spiritually hungry and the seemingly morally bankrupt. The pastor, Father Dave, was too friendly and happy, but he allowed Sola Fide to exist because he was young enough to think outside the (confessional) box. The other parish priests were too old or too set in their ways. But not Father Judah. Mysteries of faith were his specialty and so too, it was whispered among Sola Fide, were the dark arts, long forgotten or maligned by the modern Roman Catholic Church: exorcism, it was said, and so much more. But these were just hopeful rumors spread among a not-so-hopeful bunch. Father Judah, until quite recently, had been their spiritual leader, their confessor, their confidant, their friend. But tonight faith alone wouldn't help the priest, Robert knew.

He shivered in the late autumn air.

Robert was running not because he was late (which he was, as usual), but because he wanted to make sure a public lynching hadn't taken place during his brief absence. He didn't think the others would take action without him—he'd become something of a leader himself since the crisis went down—but there were a couple of members, Graham and Clea among them, who were anxious for blood, influencing those precariously perched on the fence, like James and Susan. Graham was a self-righteous richie from Anchor Hop who drove all the way west to the borough of Mondauk Proper to go to meetings (there was nothing like Sola Fide in his parish) only to tie his sweater around his neck, cross his arms, and declare, while looking to the side (rather than meeting anyone's eyes), that he had no crisis of faith and didn't know what he was doing there. Clea would jump right up to the painted ceiling if you said boo to her, and, as a single mother, the protection of her child (and by extension all children) was of the utmost importance, especially as one who had obviously not been protected as a child. The situation tonight was dire, to be sure, but it was as complicated as it was simple. Father Judah had been their point man in a tunnel of darkness. It wasn't easy to fell a giant; it wasn't simple to kill a god.

It went like this: two months ago, Father Judah had been implicated in a crime, in great detail, by a member of his parish. The victim had already been interviewed by the police—more than once. According to a loose-lipped legal clerk in Robert's Tuesday night AA meeting, the district attorney's office was set to bring charges as early as tomorrow; the process had only taken this long because it involved a priest; everyone wanted to have their ducks in a row. The situation had become common knowledge within Sola Fide, and Robert let them know his inside knowledge—something had to done. "If he's innocent," Marybeth had said at their secret meeting outside in Mondauk Common two nights ago, "then we need to warn him." Clea had scoffed, her freckled face dancing in the candlelight. "*If* he's innocent? What are you deaf, Marybeth? He's as innocent as my ass." The impending charges would leave little wiggle room—they had to confront the situation now or never. James spoke up: "Marybeth is right. But if there's a hint that he isn't innocent, we'd be guilty of sitting on our hands if we didn't press him. No sense tripping into quicksand ourselves." (James could be a bit dramatic if given half a chance) Robert simply listened. He was only there because he just didn't want to see anything get out of control; Graham and Clea were instigators, and a couple of members needed little instigation for their fists to curl. There was a time and a place for everything. Better to let a professional handle a situation such as this.

Robert pulled open the large wooden doors and, upon entering the narthex, blessed himself at one of the fonts. The vestibule was dark. After opening the inner doors, he could see the church wasn't much cheerier—as usual. Even the recessed ceiling pin lights were off. The only light came from the prayer candles on either side of the chancel and the pillar candles on two small tables on either side of the chair facing the group. Father Judah's chair. An ornate set of three connected bells sat on the left table. They were all here, all twelve of them. Robert was the last to arrive. Father Judah hadn't exited the sacristy yet, but it wouldn't be long. Robert took a pew behind Clea, Graham, and James. There was usually a little whispering between pew mates, but no one spoke, not even Marybeth, who probably chattered her way through sex, Robert imagined, so when Father Judah walked across the chancel and down the steps towards his chair, only his footsteps and the swish of his cassock were audible.

Robert looked up to see if there were nooses dangling above their heads. He allowed himself an inward grin: the group's sense of drama was catching.

"The night's running right up to our front doors." Father Judah started as he always did. "Something is rotten in Mondauk."

Being born into a Jewish family gave Father Judah an excellent viewpoint of Catholicism. Like Christ, he had been raised in the Jewish faith and, after his BA in theology, had even gone to rabbinical school for a time before finding Jesus—or before Jesus found him. About a mile or two up the road from the rabbinical school was a seminary, and before long, he was enrolled. The transition, he said, was easier than he'd expected. "God is God, Robert," Father Judah had said. "He doesn't *just* speak Hebrew—or English for that matter." Sola Fide was a natural extension of those beliefs in the transmutation of God. Sola Fide, Father Judah explained, had sprung from a basement study group in the seminary whose members were more interested in mysteries of faith than Church doctrine; they were fascinated with how those mysteries applied to everyday lives. They often immersed themselves in discussion instead of burying their heads in books. For the young seminarian and his friends, the night was always running right up to the church doors.

The priest allowed a moment of silence after his opening remarks. Robert wondered if he knew, if he had any idea of the impending darkness about to knock on his own door. Clea shifted restlessly in the pew and Graham snickered. Marybeth broke the quiet and whispered to Peg.

" 'Friends, Romans, countrymen,' " Father Judah joked, "lend me your ears.' "

Even Peg, who giggled at everything, was silent.

Father Judah was undeterred, although Robert thought he saw the priest try to catch his eye. Robert usually sat up front alone; maybe that was it. Despite being the last to arrive, the group had saved his pew again.

"The Holy Spirit, the Holy Ghost. What is it? What is its function? How is it part of the trinity with the Father and the Son? Is it a bird? Is it a plane? It *is* a kind of spiritual Superman. It is also one of the dividing points between our Church and the Orthodox Catholic Church, especially the *Filioque* controversy, as we discussed last week. Another difference can be viewed in the approach to a prayer called the epiclesis, said during the consecration, calling upon the Holy Spirit to bless the bread and wine. The Orthodox Catholic Church believes that the epiclesis, the invocation of the Holy Ghost, is when transubstantiation is completed. In our faith, transubstantiation occurs during the Words of Institution. Nonetheless, the epiclesis is still part of the sacrament." The priest lifted the set of bells from the side table. "When we celebrate the mystery of transubstantiation, it is during this prayer that you will hear the first of three assemblies of bells."

Robert bowed his head, and the three connected bells rang out in the nearly empty church.

Oh God...quiet!...don't you dare—

Robert shook his head.

Like the bells echoing in Assumption, he knew there would have been very few ears to hear someone scream in Scout's Copse, a stretch of woodland in the southernmost part of Mondauk Proper, not far from the creek the locals called the Puddle. Separated from the bulk of Pennypack Woods by a small stream with steep banks, the copse was so dense that kids rarely partied in there; it was said to be haunted and there were plenty of good drinking spots in the adjacent tracts of tall yellow weeds and electrical towers, an area known as the Fields, just below the Recreational Center. Yes, there would have been very few ears to hear someone scream in Scout's Copse—especially if it was a little girl. It was a miracle that screaming was even a possibility.

"Those, Sola Fide, were the Sanctus bells. At the risk of sounding like Marley's ghost, you will hear the bells two more times before this night is over, and each time I want you to picture the Holy Ghost, in whatever form pleases you, descending to my hands. The priest is the conduit. That is why we need priests. We need someone who is not scared to perform the ritual."

He was pleading his case in front of a hangman's jury, Robert thought. Clea bit her lip and shook her head, lowering her eyes. James leaned his elbows on his knees, his muscles pulsing beneath his red salmon-colored knit shirt. Graham appeared to be checking his messages. All the others had met a couple of hours ago to make a final decision on what to do; he had no idea if they did. Clea had called Robert before the meeting and spun a blue streak, but Robert begged off—working late and all, and he'd wondered if this would be seen as an abdication of his leadership role. They'd become a sensitive bunch. But he wanted no part of this jury. Their initial meeting, the one in Mondauk Common, had convinced him of that. He didn't want to be seen doing anything out of the ordinary. Only he among Sola Fide had the facts; he was poker buddies with Detectives Cotten and Welles of the Special Victims Unit. Let the rest of them shout from their high horses and doubt themselves when they were alone. He had no doubt about what had happened, only about what he was going to do. He was a Christian. Wasn't forgiveness supposed to be second nature?

"The Sanctus is the last part of the prayer of consecration of the bread and wine," said the priest. "I am sure you all know it by heart if not by name. Clea?"

Clea looked away and shook her head no.

"Okay, but boy is your face going to be red when you hear it, because I know you know it. Burt? Peg? Graham, surely. *No?* Marybeth?"

Dead quiet except for maybe the auditory illusion of the faint echo of bells.

"Robert, my Robert," Father Judah said, rubbing his hands together. There was sweat on the priest's forehead.

Robert closed his eyes and recited the prayer in Latin to himself.

Sanctus, Sanctus, Sanctus,
Dominus Deus Sabaoth,
Pleni sunt caeli et terra gloria tua.
Hosanna in excelsis.

He cleared his throat and said, "It's not coming to me."

Clea turned around and scrunched her face at him, making her freckles jump. He fought the urge to shrug—he didn't know what her odd facial expression meant.

Little Veronica (a woman in her early-to-mid twenties with the body of an emaciated twelve-year-old) opened her mouth:

"Holy, holy, holy Lord,
God of power and might.
Heaven and earth are full of your glory.
Hosanna in the highest."

Veronica had barely spoken two words since Sola Fide was founded. At any other time, Robert would have thought the reedy sound of her voice auspicious. But things were so bad, Veronica was not just speaking, she was reciting part of the Sanctus. (And to think, he suspected her of catnapping through Mass despite her ardor.) He assumed that Clea and Graham had brought her over to their side— this was Veronica being bold—though he was sure none of them had a plan of action besides ignoring the priest or maybe walking out.

"Very good, Veronica." Father Judah said. He looked pleased; everyone knew that Veronica was one of his favorites. "I like surprises, and I like hearing the youthful sound of your voice."

The girl screaming in the copse hadn't been heard by anyone other than two teenage burnouts sharing a joint in the Fields. The teens, who were later dragged to the police by their parents and who then shared the screaming with any law enforcement officer who would listen—the screaming and who they saw emerging from the trees when they went to "investigate" and before they ran away. (On the surface, not the most credible witnesses, but the detectives ran them through the ringer before accepting their statements.) The screaming emanated from a little girl the stoners never saw. Her name was Margaret Murray, an only child, and she was in the third grade at Assumption of Our Lady Elementary School. Margaret had blonde hair that was frequently tied into pigtails. Her skin was creamy white, her eyes pale blue. Margaret's parents were big churchgoers, and when the local papers reported that sources said the priest had been questioned not once but three times, their shock and anger was immeasurable. They blamed themselves; they blamed the diocese. What they'd thought was after-school pre-confirmation instruction (Assumption offered no such class) turned out to be private lessons with Father Judah. It was, according to Detective Cotten, as if the parents had lost their daughter, as if Margaret were dead.

Father Judah had submitted to police interviews without a lawyer being present. He must have thought he successfully pulled the wool over the detectives' eyes because he *requested* a polygraph—which was inconclusive. Detective Welles told Robert he thought the priest must have had a thumbtack in his shoe.

The assembly of bells rang for a second time.

"*Benedictus qui venit in nomine Domini,*" Father Judah said. "Blessed is he who comes in the name of the Lord."

Comes in the name of the Lord. Robert thought that was almost funny.

It was as he'd thought: no one was going to say anything. Clea scowled and scuffed her shoes. Graham kept his eyes on his cell phone. The rest of the twelve seemed equally occupied. All their talk had come down to this: nothing. Not a one of the mighty verbal warriors spoke up and leveled an accusation. No one walked out. Nobody tried to sabotage the priest's talk.

"The Sanctus prayer is adapted from Isaiah 6:3, which is prefaced by two verses describing the Lord sitting on a throne surrounded by seraphim, each with six wings. '…with two they covered their faces, with two they covered their feet, and with two they hovered.' So what is the mystery of transubstantiation all about, really? What do we mean by saying these prayers as this most sacred of sacraments is being performed? Let's hear from the peanut gallery. Simon? David? Brianne?"

Robert turned his head. The peanut gallery, the three who always sat in the back and usually said little in group (only Veronica said less), now silently stared straight ahead. Brianne looked like she was in shock. Simon and David looked frightened—at what Sola Fide would do as a whole or at what had happened, Robert didn't know. (*Allegedly* had happened, Marybeth had stressed at their meeting in the Common—*allegedly* for none of the group had the inside scoop Robert had.)

Father Judah shrugged off their stares.

"The elevation of the chalice is the last time we hear the Sanctus bells. *Vinum de vite*. We're asked to share in His sacrifice. His blood. A little water is added to the wine. This is His sweat *and* His blood. Tonight, as we look at the sacrament of Holy Communion, I ask you to think of sacrifice. I ask you to think of forgiveness."

The priest rang the assembly of bells a third time.

Margaret Murray had been violated sexually in every orifice. Her legs were stained with blood. She'd been left in Scout's Copse until the uniforms arrived. There was blood on her scalp from where he had pulled her hair out. Her school jumper, found in some nearby underbrush, looked as if it had been ripped apart by savage, hungry animals. She was torn up so much down there, the doctor in the emergency room had to sew her up. There were hickeys on both sides of her neck and bite marks on her chest and thighs. One nipple was bleeding. Until the forensic lab came back with definitive results that pointed in another direction (believe it or not, it appeared the perp had worn a condom, although Cotten said, without explanation, that it had been inexpertly donned), the police had only one suspect, one name, and, one piece of physical evidence stained with the bloody fingerprints of the child: a strip of white plastic about six inches long and one and a quarter inch wide. A clerical collar. From the moment the detectives told him about it, Robert didn't have to wait for the DA's office to know the priest was damned.

Robert wondered for a brief moment if the naming of the priest hadn't been some sort of sick cosmic joke played by his parents and God. Judah. Jude. Judas. The betrayer. After many assurances of her safety, Margaret Murray had whispered his name to Detective Cotten, and it was the name of the person the stoners had seen emerging from the copse. Her rapist has attempted to strangle her with her underwear; she'd been left for dead, tied to a tree—only this little girl God had left breathing to speak for the other two dead Catholic grade school girls, who'd been found in Mondauk County in the past three months: one in Fox Chase, the other in New Hope, both discovered on nights when the Assumption girls' basketball team played the local elementary school. Until Margaret Murray, Welles said, they'd never even considered the priest, who never missed a game, though Cotten said they figured it was a matter of time before the perp hunted in his own backyard (there was too much evident rage, rarely controlled for long), though they never expected to find a victim alive.

Robert's anger grew with every word the priest uttered, at every nervous shuffle of one of the twelve. It was anger that had first driven him back to the Church and then to Sola Fide. But as a young man, under another name, his real name, anger had served him well. He'd been a button man for certain old men of power in Philadelphia. As the cliché went, when these men wanted someone's button pushed, they called Robert to do the pushing. Only it wasn't as clean as in the books and movies. Sometimes the vics screamed, begged, cried, wouldn't die after one bullet, two bullets, a blade to the belly, a blow to the head. After a while, Robert could sense the souls fleeing their bodies, their tendrils brushing his cheek, not in desperation but in gentle, understanding love. And this from some of the biggest scumbags in the Commonwealth and South Jersey. He split after his twentieth, hung 'em up; he could no longer stomach the work, and the souls were scaring him, showing up in his nightmares and daydreams. His twentieth made him realize that it wasn't just the souls that disquieted him, the souls and their tender caresses as they made their way to wherever they belonged. No, it was a lack of purpose. While he knew most of those he put down deserved to feel his handlers' displeasure, it almost always had to do with money. He'd been raised Catholic, and with the departure of every soul, every one, he heard the jingle of Judas' thirty pieces of silver.

He no longer wanted to kill or even maim at the whim of those in power. When he'd used a garrote on a drug dealer (called Licky) who sold to grade school children (a big no-no in the family's territory), he stopped just short of killing the motherfucker when his eyes took in Licky's filthy apartment—spoiled food, used condoms, and what appeared to be random piles of dog shit calcifying on the threadbare rug, even though he'd previously ascertained that the mook didn't have a dog—finally settling on...a little girl, so dirty, it was as if she was wearing camouflage; but she wasn't staring in horror; no, she was trying hard not to smile, and he'd finished off Licky, leaving a thick roll of bills next to the body. He'd wept in the car and punched his shower wall again and again, watching his blood mix with the water and swirl down the drain. He should have taken the little girl to—where?—*anywhere*: the ER, even a police station, maybe a supportive relative, if one existed.

As he dried off and examined his torn knuckles, he told himself: he'd done what he could. That roll contained at least five hundred dollars, if not more. She could if nothing else, she could get out of that hell hole and find herself a nice...*SLAM!* She was probably eight years old, maybe ten. *SLAM* went his knuckles again. When the skipper palmed him a little extra, Robert went out, bought a new suit, and threw up in the gutter when he left the tailor's.

The fact that he didn't run far, just to Mondauk County, some fifteen miles outside of Philly, betrayed a bit of reluctance on his part to leave the life, but since he wasn't really on the run (the powers that be just assumed he'd been clipped), a change of identity had sufficed. A quick visit to Chinatown for a new set of IDs and a little cosmetic surgery—and *bam!*—he had gone from being a member of a certain Italian-American subculture to being a member of Sola Fide, the main difference being he no longer saw any departing souls and was no longer responsible for their dispatching. Otherwise he still served a higher master.

The priest prattled on blindly.

"God the Father didn't imbue his only begotten Son with the Divine Nature. No, Christ was *of* the Divine Nature—and the Son of God, the Word made flesh, spreads the Word to us through the Eucharist. The bread doesn't *represent* His flesh—after the transubstantiation, it is the *actual* flesh of our Lord Jesus Christ. The wine may have come from the grape, but, in the end, it is blood, blood of the sacrificial lamb. Let us meditate on these mysteries—or use contemplative prayer. Remember, Sola Fide, it's whatever gets you *there*. We want to let all the facts come to the surface; we want our faith to buoy those that don't."

And nothing happened. The rest of the twelve closed their eyes and prayed or meditated. When the appropriate amount of time had passed, Father Judah spoke at length on the mystery of transubstantiation with a few side roads on the topic of forgiveness. There was a closing reading (John 6:41-58) and finally a prayer, muttered by the whole group except for Robert. The other eleven, impotent with anger or muddled with indecision, exited single file down the nave when the meeting was finished. Robert sat in his pew as Father Judah, oblivious to his presence, blew out the candles, checked the transept doors, and carried the chair back to the side of the chancel. Robert waited until the priest had entered the sacristy, then pulled on his gloves, walked up the aisle (stopping to kneel and bless himself), and with much care, lifted the Sanctus bells from the pillow near the edge of the chancel where Father Judah had placed them.

There was doubt as to whether Margaret Murray would ever be able to bear children or even enjoy a normal sex life as an adult (aside from psychological scars). Her parents were shell-shocked. They'd removed their daughter from Assumption's elementary school. According to Detective Cotten, they were thinking of moving. Catching the perp, prosecuting him, seemed a distant second in their thoughts. "God will provide," Mrs. Murray had said to Detective Welles. *Provide what? The doer? Peace for Margaret?* Welles didn't ask; he simply nodded his head but later told Robert he wished he replied, "There's not a whole lot of God left in the world, ma'am." The detective shook his head. "It's the only way she'd understand." That was when Robert realized he'd been called to do God's work; there was more than one way to atone for his sins.

The sirens were still in the distance, persistent, their volume increasing—there was no doubt that they were coming to the church. Robert didn't have much time. The priest had entered the sacristy through the door on the left, so Robert leapt onto the chancel, muffling the bells, and shuffled past the altar and the tabernacle. He entered through the door on the right as quietly as he could and closed it behind him. The priest had already begun to unbutton his cassock and was standing with his back to Robert. Robert gripped the Sanctus bells in his right hand, pressing the assembly against his body to dull any sound.

"*Hosanna in excelsis*, Robert."

The priest turned around, slow, confident, careful.

"I never thought it would be you. Clea and Graham, maybe. James. But not you. Your life did such a 180; I never figured you'd leave."

"I thought you liked surprises, Father."

Robert's stomach took a turn. The smell of incense was so strong.

"I do, my son, I do. But you should look deep into your heart. Matthew 7:1, remember? You know not what you do."

"I just want to hear you say it."

"Say what, son?"

Robert thrust his free hand into his pocket and clenched, then relaxed his fist. "I just want to hear you tell me how tight her pussy was. How *good* she was. Can you give me your confession, Father? Can you do that much?"

The priest went about changing out of his cassock, his face serene and trying for contrite. Robert had seen that look many times when the vic knew his number was up. If they didn't beg for their lives, they turned meek and humble, sinners in the confession box.

"Papias is a saint in our Church, Robert, an Apostolic Father, and he lived in the first half of the second century, roughly. He wrote much which is lost to us, but some fragments have survived, like this bit: 'His genital was larger and presented a more repugnant sight than has ever been seen; and through it there seeped from every part of the body a procession of pus and worms to his shame, even as he relieved himself.' That was Judas Iscariot he was writing about, that whole tradition of Judas not dying by hanging but rather expiring when his bowels exploded upon the earth. I think I'd rather go with hanging myself, wouldn't you?"

"You don't have that option," Robert said, bored with the conversation.

"Oh, but I could. You hear the sirens growing closer. Who do you think they're coming for? The priest or the hit man? No, no, don't worry: the sacrament of confession prevents me from speaking of such matters."

"But the Word of God isn't enough for you to—"

"If you were I, Robert, what would you choose? Hanging or having your bowels explode in public?"

"I think I'd choose a girl my own age, vow of celibacy aside."

The sirens were so close. The priest smirked: *what did he have to lose?*

"You would? When presented with such fine specimens as they were? I think not, Robert. The appetites of men are universal (if you factor out the homosexuals). We all want a taste of whatever we can't have. Your best friend's wife, his daughter, your niece or cousin, the girl skipping rope down the street, the young novitiate sweating through her wimple."

The sirens were right outside the church.

"So what's it going to be, Robert? Let me take my own way out or—?"

Robert smacked the side of Father Judah's face with the Sanctus bells. The priest fell to the floor writhing, holding his hand over the gash one of the bells had opened on his right cheek.

"Robert…"

Robert knelt down and with the bells hit the priest over and over until his face was full of open gashes and blood seeped from multiple wounds. A piece of flesh hung from the priest's cheek, and Robert tore it off and stuffed it into Father Judah's mouth. He then pulled the priest's pants down, his underwear too. He almost grinned at the peanut of a penis nesting in an unruly ball of pubic hair.

"Robert…for God's sake…"

"One last thing, Father."

Robert brought the edge of one of the bells down on the peanut penis, severing the head from the root. Blood squirted wildly.

"*Domine non sum dignus*," Robert said, and he meant it. Lord, I am not worthy.

Taking the Sanctus bells with him, Robert fled the sacristy, jumped from the chancel, and took the stairs down to the church basement. In the dark, Robert found the side door he'd scoped out the previous night. He kept his head down and crawled up the stone stairs to the grass. Police lights flashed at the front and back of the church and rectory. Robert crept across the side lawn until he reached the elementary school, then ran as hard and fast as he could past the Rec and the through the Fields beyond it. He ran until he reached Scout's Copse.

At night, the copse was an exquisite meeting of moonlit radiance and impenetrable shadows, an oasis between the rest of the woods and the yellowed Fields. It was hard to believe something ugly had happened here. In places, the leaves were tinted by the moon and their veins looked delicate, almost pulsing. He could hear the Puddle in the distance, its dirty water tumbling over rocks and debris. From the police report in his pocket, he located the tree and tore off the remaining police tape. Using his hands, he dug a hole for Margaret Murray and buried the assembly of Sanctus bells, careful to tamp down the earth when he was finished. But that wasn't the only thing he'd buried. Next to the bells he'd laid the tip of Father Judah's penis.

A finger of one of the gloves had split from digging, and tiny pieces of quartz had lodged themselves under his nail. Rivulets of sweat had found their way into every crevice of his body, and his back ached like it always had in the old days when he'd cover a body with lime after pulverizing the teeth.

Robert prayed:

Sanctus, Sanctus, Sanctus,
Dominus Deus Sabaoth,

Pleni sunt caeli et terra gloria tua.
Hosanna in excelsis.

Robert stood up, removed his gloves, and wiped his hands on his pants. He could see the police lights, like fireflies, flashing at Assumption. He smacked his lips and that decided it. He needed a drink. Fuck AA. They didn't know from this and what was a couple of pints? Robert walked back to his car, which he had parked two blocks away from the church, and drove to McCullough's for a cold one. On the television hanging above him to the right, the newswoman spoke in staccato sentences about the arrest and possible mutilation of Father Judah. He knew the ambulance would reach the church before the priest bled out. The justice of the thing was what kept Robert from finishing him off: a murdering pedophile priest in prison without a penis. Father Judah will wish he was dead. After a while, money would change hands, and a couple old friends inside would do the priest in, without knowing the order came from a ghost.

When the newscast was over, Robert drove home. He needed a good night's sleep. And when he arrived at his apartment that was just what he got. No phone calls, no cops, just sleep. Tomorrow, before he left, he'd visit Margaret Murray in the hospital—he was a stranger to her, so he'd just stick his head in, and even if her parents or a nurse was in the room, he'd leave a roll on the bed (he'd made plenty of dough when we was in the life, and he'd been a good saver); if the kid was alone and awake, maybe he'd smile and say hello, nothing too stressful—for either of them—but tonight he would sleep the sleep of the dead. He'd sleep with the satisfaction of a job well done. *Benedictus qui venit in nomine Domini.* He'd come in the name of the Lord, and he knew now that he'd do it again, oh yes, to every one of those sick bastards. He'd do it again. An avenging angel. Mondauk County was a temporary stop after all. He'd found his calling.

Another name, another town.
Hosanna in the highest.

-end-

Midge for Marjorie

The Soul selects her own Society –
Then – shuts the Door –
Emily Dickinson

File #CA-44

From the subject's notebook #17, dated October, 20—
For never was there a tale of less woe
Than this of me and my Romeos

Take #—
Cue Miss Lee!
Action!

Never know how much I love you
Never know how much I care
When you put your arms around me
I get a fever that's so hard to bear
Peggy Lee

There was no sixty-seventh chapter of Isaiah, just as there was no twenty-third chapter of Revelation. Marjorie didn't know what kind of trick her date was trying to pull, but it wasn't very funny, and he wasn't terribly interesting, trying to impress her as if she gave a whit about his Biblical knowledge. (She was sure it was a test of some sort.) Although she had to keep up appearances, she'd sworn *last* time that she wouldn't let her former college dorm mates fix her up, but here she was again with the adjunct professor of something or other from a college Marjorie wasn't familiar with and was beginning to think didn't exist. While her date was fairly good-looking in that squinty sort of way, his joking manner and slight jowls accompanied watchful eyes that seemed to take in everything and nothing at the same time.

"And how do you know Kimmy?" she interrupted.

He sipped from his club soda and flashed a gash of a smile. He had to teach tomorrow, he'd said, so no drinks for him, even though tomorrow was a Sunday—and she highly doubted he was a Sunday school teacher. Maybe he had another date later that night.

"Your old roomy? Well, Kimmy and I had a freshman course together. Chem maybe," her date said. He had mussy brown hair and his casual attire (no tie, two shirt buttons undone, silver chain, boat shoes) seemed *desperately* casual. "We had a course or two later on together as well. Maybe a grad course. I don't recall." He stabbed a piece of broccoli, and Marjorie cringed. Her date already had many little pieces of the vegetable in his teeth. "Kept running into each other though. At parties and such. Readings."

"And that's how you know Judy and Madeline too?"

Her date nodded and sipped the club soda. A couple of pieces of broccoli dislodged from his teeth and floated on the top of the drink.

Marjorie gathered her purse and shawl and wrapped a scarf around her conservatively styled yet vehemently red hair. (Scottie called her a ginger, which never failed to elicit a smile.) "I think I want to go."

Her date looked surprised, sort of mock offended. "Okay, let me settle the check, and we'll go."

"No thank you," she answered. "I'll take a cab."

"This time of night…"

"The pleasure was mine, Mr.… I've forgotten. Apologies."

"Ferguson," her date said, extending his hand, which she pretended not to see, although she took note of his large gold ring with a shield on the side.

Their table was near the door (her choice), and she turned to the maître d' and asked him to hail her a cab. He did so and one pulled to the curb immediately. Only then did Marjorie extend her hand.

"Thank you for a lovely dinner, *Detective* Ferguson," she said, then left the restaurant and hopped in the cab. As the taxi pulled away, she watched her date in front of the restaurant stamp his foot and curse and pull off his police ring. She had never had a roommate named Kimmy. Kimmy had lived down the hall.

+

You give me fever
When you kiss me
Fever when you hold me tight
Peggy Lee

I consider myself a student of physiognomy. One edition of Webster's defines physiognomy as "the art of discovering temperament and character from outward appearance." It has much to do with the face. My old American College Dictionary defines it as "the face or countenance, esp. as considered as an index to character." (An index to character—now *there's* a name for a book!) That is my true art: I study people's faces and gestures and from those I infer certain character traits, specific likes and dislikes, demeanor, even fantasies, fulfilled and otherwise. All writers people-watch, but I read between laugh lines and crooked smiles. That's how I know Scottie Steward is in love with me and that he's just waiting for the right time to reveal his devotion before betrothing. His actions may say one thing to the untrained eye, but his facial expressions and body language, to one skilled in such arts, say another thing altogether—I can read his secret language. When I was young, I trained as a ballet dancer at the Bundle-Theseus School of Movement Identity. The body says more than anyone realizes, and the face says just about everything else—but it reveals nothing about the soul. Although I write novels, my favorite writers are poets, for only poets know the true nature of the soul. Me, I always feel that my life is like a movie that gets shown over and over but never in the same order, which sounds pretty soulless to me and not very poetic.

As a writer, I am able to discern certain secrets that others may or may not know about themselves. This ability developed when I was a stringer for the local paper, and now that I exclusively write fiction, I use it almost everywhere I go. Generally I don't attend cocktail parties despite the abundance of simmering secrets. I abhor blind dates. (Necessary evils; my last one ended in a most bizarre fashion.) I don't go to bars. Oh, I'll pop in the Ritz for a nightcap with Scottie or my agent, Henry Elster, after a late night heart-to-heart (or, in Henry's case, a brainstorming session—though these were more for Henry's benefit than mine; I am never at a loss for ideas). I'm just not the social type, really. The only cocktail parties I attend are those thrown by Scottie—he's quite the social cat—or the obligatory book release parties. The latter are truly tedious and just awful experiences. Everyone is nice enough, but I'm always expected to read; to choose one small pinch of a new book to *perform* somehow seems demeaning to the work—the Cliffs Notes version of Marjorie's latest. But it is at these very events (and others like them) that people, knowing I'm a writer or upon learning it, start down one of three paths. The first possible path begins with a polite and sometimes sincere question: what is your book about? (In ten words or less, or the interrogator's eyes glaze over.) Or the variant: what do you write about? Or: what kind of writer are you? (I always want to answer: the kind that uses words instead of eggs, but I'm far too polite to give free reign to my id.) Sometimes, when I answer fiction, the inquisitor scrunches his or her face, as if only dead people wrote fiction or just Stephen King. At these events, I am often regaled by the dreaded utterance: have I got a story for you! (The beginning of the second path.) These stories usually revolve around a humorous (to the teller) fishing accident or something that happened to the speaker's crazy Aunt Madge. I've learned when to smile or tilt my head or furrow my brow. I've learned how to throw the concerned, open-mouthed look to Scottie. I've even gone as far as to take out my notebook (a holdover from my press days) to jot a line or two as the story wound down. These notes, flashed to Scottie, usually read something along the lines of, "Help me!" or the longer, "If I hear one more squirrel in the attic story…" Scottie is always amused—he has a fractured smile that's hard not to adore. He finds me "darling," he has said, "if a bit on the camouflaged choleric side." That always makes me laugh. Scottie frequently cracks me up. He's a real card. Sometimes I think Scottie's crowd must know how I feel about him, but it was recently revealed to me that I'm thought of as a lipstick lesbian who will grow old alone (forgetting that redheads don't grow old—they rust).

The third path these conversations take is the most intriguing and it affords me the opportunity to use my skills. "Oh, a writer, how interesting," someone will say, or "I enjoyed your last book; looking forward to this one," and then the talk will return to whatever passes for normal conversation (usually with someone other than me). I used to think that perhaps this type of person is used to being around artists and is not easily impressed—but, consciously or subconsciously, as the conversation continues (especially if it's not with me), they will begin to perform ever so slightly (gestures writ large, or awkward but sincere comedic attempts), as if they know that

I'm keeping an eye on them. And while their behavior is a mess of exaggerations, there is truth in them there hills, and these incidents give me fodder aplenty. Let's say someone is asked a question, even one as simple as, "How ever did you land that position?" If the answer is accompanied by the person's eyes looking to the right, then he or she is pulling out a memory of an image, a sound, a scene, or perhaps an emotion. If the eyes look to the left, then the one under the glare of the spotlight (or the one grabbing it with both hands) is constructing the answer, often out of whole cloth. Physiognomy. Fairly common knowledge perhaps—not exactly a superpower—but a knowledge I've heard few confess to utilizing. The way a hand is placed during a conversation: on the table, laying in a lap or fidgeting there, or constantly picking at (and thus pointing out) a real or imagined flaw—these are often clues to what is really going on behind those flapping lips. People's stories were interesting enough (as long as they weren't of the Aunt Madge variety), but physiognomy told deeper stories, sometimes previously hidden ones, and it is from that well where I pull out my most memorable (to me at least) characters—from their secrets.

Now Scottie—there's a character worth studying! So of course I follow him. (*They* were following me, after all.) I couldn't have laid my plans if I didn't surveil him. Now, Scottie's not his real name. His given name is John, but at the university he attended, nicknames were still the rage among the male matriculants. (Often these nicknames were titles, such as the Frenching Doyen, the Twice a Day Ace—a reference, I assume, to self-pleasure—and the Sarcasm Master.) John became Scottie. I knew him then, and he never looked like a Scottie to me. He wasn't Scottish. He didn't drink scotch (at least not then). But Scottie he became. I prefer to call him John—long to call him John actually, but I refer to him as Scottie to fit in. To dissimulate. It was difficult initially. My first real boyfriend (maybe my only real boyfriend) was named Scott, and he died when he went through the windshield of a car I was driving. (A Ford Thunderbird.) We were teenagers. It wasn't my fault, really, though who else's fault could it have been? Turns out I had my own squirrel story: I swerved to avoid one and collided with an oncoming vehicle. Scott's head, severed by the shattered windshield or a piece of the other vehicle, went in one direction, while the rest of his body rested on the hood. The casket was closed, and I was asked to leave the wake, so I have no idea if they were able to sew Humpty Dumpty together again.

(The intellectually curious and the hopelessly morbid occasionally overlap.)

The thing of it is, Scottie never grew tired of nicknames: early on I became Midge, which was cute enough in a little sister kind of way when we were undergrads (at different schools, which we were close enough for us to hang out at a local coffee shop three or four nights a week) but downright infuriating as an adult. (At least it's not Midge Master.) My book jackets have the name Marjorie on them, but just about everyone calls me Midge. I can take it from Scottie though; I can twist it into a pet name, but not when the bartender at the local watering hole calls me the same thing. If Scottie and I are to be together forever, it can't be as Scottie and Midge. It must be as John and Marjorie. And strike "if" from two sentences ago. The "if" phase has long passed. If women have internal clocks, then mine has a second hand devouring every instant of time—moments count. But I don't desire a baby (although a child with Scottie would be divine); I only desire Scottie. And Scottie desires me. (I can read his secret language, remember?) So it all works out.

Except for Andrea. Andrea isn't part of the plan. Where this horny hellhound, this false Psyche came from, I could never discover. One day she was just there among Scottie's crowd at one of his many cocktail parties. Busty, striking eastern European face, and with what I overheard one partygoer describe as "legs that don't stop until they reach her ass and pitch a tent." And whoever saw hair that red? She laughs easily, if maybe a bit too loudly. She tries hard to be one of the boys but obviously wants attention of the sexual kind. She leans over them when they play poker, all cleavage and Chanel No. 5. Andrea is forever putting one foot up on the ottoman to adjust her strappy Louboutins; she never wears stockings, so everyone can see right up her skirt. She once described what type of underwear she was wearing (a thong!) and went so far as to perform a trick where she removed her bra without taking off her shirt. Once Andrea even suggested strip poker, an idea seized on by the men in the room, but their escorts wisely and quickly demurred, and the idea was abandoned, much to Andrea's consternation. One or two of the boys asked Andrea for a date, and she acquiesced, but nothing came of those, I understand, although there was a great deal of bragging (and eyes shifting to the left). But when I came out of Hal's Typewriter Shoppe (the only one in town; I needed to buy another Royal, the Junior model; it's best, I discovered, to have several spare Royals around; if something breaks down on mine, I can always cannibalize another one), I almost walked smack into Scottie and Andrea *holding hands* as they left the Brew-Ha-Ha, the coffee shop where I was headed. I was so startled that I dropped the Royal. (Hal, bless his heart, saw this and took it back, giving me another and telling me not to worry, that he would fix up the one I dropped and make it as good as new. I promised him I would buy it as soon as it was ready.)

The typewriter exchange took several minutes, but I was able to catch up to Scottie and Andrea, mainly because they were lazily window shopping. Lugging the Royal, I hid behind trees and a mailbox and even a very large man who took his time extracting a jelly doughnut from the front of his shirt. Then it happened: at the corner of Butler and Ridge, she actually lifted one leg, leaned in, and administered a kiss that lasted forever and appeared to involve tongues. Then she lowered her leg and pressed her body into his and whispered in his ear. I followed them all the way back to Scottie's apartment. By then it was getting dark, but I stayed outside, clutching the Royal, until the light went out in Scottie's bedroom window—and in my heart too (almost).

But men will be men. My mother told me that, and she should know. My father was a pipe smoking, sweater vest wearing, barbecuing-in-the-backyard dad, a perfect husband, until one day Mother discovered a stash of swinger magazines in Daddy's bowling bag. She threw him out but after a bit took him back. They went to counseling. Mommy told me my father said he'd never gone swinging; she didn't believe him though. But she chose to forgive and get on with the task of raising me. Men will men, she said. I was twelve when the swinger magazine incident occurred; it was truly the only blip in an otherwise blissful, almost '50s style upbringing. (I did manage a quick study of one of the swinger magazines—Mother had thrown them out on trash day, unconcerned for some strange reason that the neighbors might see them. I took one out and hid in the shadow of our shed, paging through photograph after photograph of men wearing masks and women with incredibly hairy pubic regions bent in every sort of position with any number of partners. I saw my father behind every mask and eventually threw up on the magazine and buried it in the backyard.)

Scottie was just being a man. I am no match for Andrea physically, with her glistening doe-like eyes, dangerous curves (to choke on a cliché), ginormous breasts, and apparent sexual eagerness.

(However, I suspect the color of her flaming locks originated in a bottle). I am short; I wear glasses and dress conservatively—and I was born a ginger. I am not particularly religious, but I rarely use profanity and avoid those that do except for Scottie; he curses like a sailor sometimes, but men will be men, as I've said. I cross my ankles when I sit. I don't wear pants to a cocktail party. But I don't expect others to adhere to my strict principles, and I try not to judge. Also, and this is important I suppose but not as important as one would think (by which I mean it doesn't explain my character), I have never been with a man. Oh, I've danced around the subject, and I've had a few kisses. Some chaste, some not so (though I could never get used to Frenching—all that drool). Once, Bradley Stevens, who was, I daresay, just about humping my leg as he jammed his teeth against mine and sent his tongue dancing along my molars, reached over and fondled my left breast. I will admit that for a second—and *just* a second (or two)—my body tingled all the way down to my toes and back up again. My nipples, I'm embarrassed to say, grew very knotty. But then the slobbering and the leg humping brought me back down, and a well-administered move of my knee put Bradley out of commission for the rest of the night. (I brought him a bag of frozen peas before settling in my favorite chair with *Wuthering Heights*.) Now one might surmise that I am saving myself for Scottie, and while that is true, it is not how my chastity began. (Blame Orthodox Catholicism and a healthy fear of the male apparatus for that.) So I'm a virgin—*virgo intacta*—and I know Scottie isn't. (We were tight even back in our college days when we were both knee deep in other people's books: fiction for me and philosophy—that was Scottie's major—for him.) I just don't know *when* he lost his virginity or with whom. But I know Scottie is the one, *the* one for me. Yes, I know *exactly* when it hit me. In truth, I think I knew the moment we were introduced at an incredibly boring "cotillion" that our being together was inevitable. I'd felt like I'd known him since we were little. But, still, men will be yada yada yada, and the Andrea fascination continues unabated.

I know this because I keep careful notes. What time Scottie picks her up. Where they go for dinner. What movie they see at the Ambler. (Twice I sat three rows back and noted that they shared one bag of popcorn and one soda with two bendy straws.) Which of Scottie's books she's read. (He writes mysteries and thrillers—so much for philosophy!) How often Andrea stays over Scottie's apartment. How often he stays at hers. What time the lights shut off. Scottie's apartment is on the second floor, but Andrea's is on the first, so, using the investigative skills I'd honed as a reporter, I was able to ascertain what sexual positions they prefer and how often, on average, the act is performed. One night when they switched to doggy style, I almost gave myself away. I was so startled that my notebook and pen flew out of my hand and hit the window, but the should-be-illicit couple was too involved in their barnyard activity to notice. The Whore of Babylon held sway.

Now, I don't write mysteries or thrillers (although I am often encouraged to do so by Henry because of what is perceived as a "dark element" in my work), but Scottie once told me, as we sat side by side, just the two of us (the way I always want it to be) in one of those semicircle booths at the Ritz, that while the perfect murder doesn't exist—even lye heated to three hundred degrees, effective as it may be (don't leave home without it, he said) cannot remove *all* the DNA left on the scene by the perpetrator(s)—a murder executed in a perfect *style* could come damn close to being aesthetically perfect. (The profanity was his.) "Write about that, Midge," he told me, "and we'll be drifting in a Venetian gondola eating cheese off the back of a serving boy in no time." (I didn't know, and still don't, if the "we" part of that sentence referred to him and me, or his whole gang; I prefer to believe the former.) "That kind of murder," Scottie continued over martinis, "I could get behind. An act of passion, a calculated *amour fou*. I'm not talking about some domestic dispute where the husband and wife use cans of Schlitz as projectiles. I mean passion, Midge, *real* passion. Not heat of the moment. Planned. Meticulous, tenacious, and dedicated as only an artist can be (like Balzac or Trotsky chaining themselves to their desks), for only aesthetic passion could drive a person to erase another without thought of themselves other than the original fervor that brought them to this point; in other words, to render regardless of consequence. But done at the perfect time with the perfect weapon in the perfect place. There would no doubt of the love there, and that's the beauty of the thing, Midge, don't you see? I'm talking *style*—that's the real test. Even if one partner dies or the husband's lover takes two in the head and the wife goes to prison, love is splattered all over the walls. The great American contradiction. 'I love you.' Blam blam blam." I nodded, taking it all in, pretending to sip my martini while Scottie worked on his fifth. "I couldn't write that sort of thing," he said. "Too literary. My publishers, they'd never go for it. I can hear 'em now. 'Too conceptual.' They want my recurring characters solving intricately plotted puzzles. My books are almost goddamn procedurals. But you, Midge…" He kissed my nose, and I breathed in his boozy breath. "…you could do some damage with the idea of aesthetic murder. Really knock 'em dead."

I love listening to Scottie ramble when he had a few; unlike most people, he becomes more insightful, albeit elliptical, but within those spaces, it's beyond telepathy: we are one. That's what love is: not finishing each other's sentences but taking up real estate in each other's skulls. I feel for sorry for Scottie, for I'm always filled with either expectation or dread—often both, meaning what I expect is the absolute worst. But listening to Scottie that night weaving his way through his aesthetic murder number, I thought: here was my love threading my dread into one expectation: that out of a death will come our life.

"A warning though, Midge," he said as he finished that fifth martini, "sometimes down is up and up is down."

So it was only a matter of planning. I don't chain myself to my desk and I don't have any real hobbies; my only passions are writing and Scottie—not in that order—but I believe I can pull off the meticulous obsessiveness necessary. As far as style, well, Scottie *was* inebriated that night, and it's likely that the concept of style only made sense in his beautiful head, which meant it made sense in mine too, even if I could barely grasp its rounded corners; I take it to mean putting my own distinctive mark on the act, so that as I watch what I hope is bottle-red hair slip slidin' away, I'll have dispatched not only with extreme prejudice but with acute expression (and Andrea will know what I've known my entire life: *the nearer your destination, the more you're slip slidin' away*). The only obstacle (and it was a pretty big one) was *them*. I don't know who put *them* on to me or why. Maybe I'm on some list because of something in one of my books. Or maybe, somehow, *they* got a glimpse at my notebook, and *they* know the details of the plan. Maybe Andrea caught on, realized she was playing defense—but she is a physician's assistant in a urologist's office (the girl is all about penises)—what connections did she have? (Maybe there is a penile connection!) It had to be Andrea who betrayed her. *Their* attention can't be politically motivated; I have never been very political. The charities I give to are non-ideological. Animal rescues mostly—though I would never have a pet. How could I love anyone or anything as much as I love Scottie? Scottie may be able to put off the love he feels for me by playing footsie or Farmer in the Dell with Andrea, but I can only love one person at a time—and I've only loved Scottie; giving my body or my mind or my affection away indiscriminately is an impossibility for me.

Nothing is impossible for *them*!

They even try to trick me; this has happened at least once that I know of, but I'm sure there have been other attempts of which I am not aware (although it's not like me to miss many details.) But neither *they* nor anyone else will deter me. Scottie told me what to do. He wants me to prove my love. Men will be men. He's sowing his wild oats, or maybe he's just testing me. But I can do some damage with Scottie's idea. Then I will rise above *Midge* and truly, in *John's* eyes, become Marjorie.

I can hardly wait.

+

I said to my soul, be still, and let the dark come upon you...
T. S. Eliot

They were in a boathouse. She was tied to a piling, her bottom half submerged in the cold water. Marjorie could hear the moored vessels bumping into each other. She couldn't have seen them if she wanted to, even though the blindfold had been removed—the unwanted tears that followed the latest slap stung her eyes and refused to dissipate or fall even when she blinked.

"Your *real* name, red," the man standing in the shadows behind the thug doing the slapping demanded for the umpteenth time. "We know it, *Marjorie*, and we know it ain't Marjorie."

"If you know it, then why don't you just say it, smart guy?" she countered.

Nobody spoke. She shook her head and asked, "What makes you so sure I'll break?"

"Same way I know I'll make it with the wife every night even when she feigns a migraine or a stomach cramp. Sooner or later, you all give in."

"Then your wife is married to the kind of man who prefers habit to happiness?"

She thought for sure that would earn her a slap, but the slapper wore a confused look, as if he was chewing over what she'd just said. His face was the first she saw clearly when the tears finally dropped from her eyes.

The man in the shadows struck a match to light a cigarette, and it didn't surprise Marjorie a bit that it was Franco, who earlier this evening had been her date at the bistro around the corner from her apartment. (She'd chosen the place so that if her companion turned out to be a stiff, a bore, or a spy, she wouldn't have far to run.) One thing was clear: he should have eaten the onions.

Marge, Margie, Marj, Jorie, Maggie, she recited to herself.

"Marge, Margie, Marj, Jorie, Maggie," Franco the shadow man said after another slap. "Which is it?"

Darn it to hell! *They* could hear her thoughts, or at least some of them. This was going to be difficult. She wasn't sure how she could carry out her mission under these conditions.

"The mission—what is the mission?" Franco asked. "What conditions?"

"Name, rank, and serial number. That's it, right?" she sputtered. Her mouth was full of blood. "Well, I'm not in the service, so I don't have a serial number or a rank, and you already know my name. It's Marjorie." She swallowed some blood. "I can spell it for you if you like."

"We ain't gonna get spit from her, boss," the slapping man said, directing his assessment not to Franco but to one of the boats. The slapper was oafish and had moles all over his face. Franco kicked him. "Hey," Moleman said, rubbing his back. "I was just sayin'."

"Say a little a less and slap a little more," Franco commanded. "We don't have much time. Word is *l'ange de l'assassinat* here's gonna pull her job by the weekend."

Marjorie had to laugh. "*They* teach thugs French now? Part of the new agency curriculum?"

Moleman raised his hand, and Marjorie raised her face to meet it. She deserved another slap: she should have known *they* would know everything about her, including her food preferences: red grapes, apple juice, burnt hamburgers…and onions.

She had told Franco to meet her at the bistro, and she went early, but he was already there. A bad sign, but Franco was a perfect gentleman, standing when she entered, pulling her chair out, ordering the wine. At first she thought he was from Puerto Rico, but after a couple of sentences, he didn't have a trace of an accent. (Nothing more than a poorly drawn character, she thought.) The conversation was a tad banal but more interesting than her usual dates. She often had to remind herself that all this dating was just a cover, although it had become more and more obvious that *they* had caught on. But she couldn't suddenly change her modus operandi without arousing even more suspicion, so she sometimes accepted the offers of young men she encountered at museums or at cocktail parties.

By the end of the date, the only thing Marjorie worried about was that it had gone swimmingly. Would Franco insist upon walking her home, kissing her goodnight even? She couldn't allow either to happen. But he might catch on if she didn't relent at least a little. A walk to the corner and a kiss on the cheek, she decided. That was it.

But then, as they were nearing the end of their meal, he offered her his onions. He had removed them from his salad, which oddly he'd saved for last. She was still working on her burger. (She ate slowly and counted each chew.) In retrospect, it was surprising that she didn't think anything at first when he proffered the onions— not about what they could reveal anyway. What she thought was that she didn't want her one true love, her Romeo, her Scottie, to smell them on her breath, which is why she didn't get them on her burger; she wanted to be fresh for him in case they met up later for a nightcap. (Not that he'd ever done more than kiss her on the nose.) Plus her Romeo's dislike of onions was well known among his friends and fans. She, of course, knew *all* of his likes and dislikes and picky ways. What she hadn't counted on was that *they* knew hers. And she adored onions. Red onions especially, which were the variety offered by Franco. Turning them down led to her being half-submerged in the brackish boathouse water, her arms tied behind her around a piling, slaps stinging her cheeks, Moleman's rings cutting her face. She realized now that the onions had been *their* test. Not to ascertain her identity—that much *they* already knew (if not her name)—but to use the onions, one of the few differences between her and her beloved, to positively identify Romeo (whom she hadn't ended up meeting later after all, thank God). They'd obviously already confirmed the existence of a mission, or they wouldn't have bothered with the charade. But the nature of the mission, she guessed, was still a mystery to *them*, or she wouldn't be in the boathouse. She wouldn't still be alive.

"It's gotta be a dye job," Moleman said. "I ain't ever seen hair *that* red before." He shook her, as if he wanted to make sure she was still conscious. "Hey lady," he said, "do the curtains match the drapes?"

An exaggerated sigh came from one of the boats.

"Why don't we start with your family name, red," Franco said, flicking his cigarette past her head so that it landed in the water with a *sssp*, "and work our way up from there?"

She spat blood. "I suspect you already know that too." Moleman raised his hand, but she stared him down. She was starting to get the idea that Moleman didn't like to bat women around, but a job was a job; these were tough economic times. "Or at least you *think* you do."

"Oh, Miss Corday, we know a great many things," Detective Ferguson said as he emerged from one of the moored boats. "Much more than you think and much less than we'd like. Which is why…you're gonna cut the shit…and tell us, yeah…what we want to know." Each pause in his speech contained a whack to Marjorie's head by his shoe.

Her vision was beginning to get fuzzy, and she fought against the urge to close her eyes and slump forwards. "My name's not Corday, *Jean-Paul*," she said. "Yeah, I got the reference. I went to college too."

Ferguson squatted down next to Moleman and smiled. His smile was worse than she remembered. He had broccoli stuck in his teeth again. "And what did Miss Corday do, babe? What's she famous for, smarty pants?"

Marjorie couldn't see his watch (and she doubted she would be able to read it in the darkness of the boathouse), but she knew it was very late. She needed to be at her post, watching Romeo's house. It was her job. It was what she did.

"Charlotte Corday stabbed Jean-Paul Marat in his bathtub. Marat was a leader during France's Reign of Terror, a member of the Jacobin faction. Corday held him personally responsible for the September Massacres of 1792, during which about half the prison population of Paris was executed, including non-political prisoners, women, and even children. Marat had a skin condition which required him to conduct his business from his bathtub, and Corday talked her way into his chambers and stabbed him with a six-inch knife while he soaked in the tub."

Ferguson looked at Franco and back at Marjorie. "Impressive, red, really." He smiled once more, and Marjorie looked away so she wouldn't have to see the broccoli. "And Marat's final words supposedly?"

Marjorie was tiring of this. She was tired period. She would never be able to stay awake during her Romeo stakeout if the boathouse games went on much longer. But she had earned her degree, summa cum laude, and had taught for a while before turning to the writing life and the sometimes guilty joy that came from making things up and telling a story. But her pride in her education was such that she wasn't able to *not* answer. " '*Aidez-moi, ma chère amie!*' "

" 'Help me, my dear friend!' " Ferguson translated, standing up. His knees popped like two cars backfiring. "How sad, no? Corday stabs the poor bastard, and he asks for her help, calling her 'friend.' "

Marjorie swung her head in an attempt to fling the hair out of her eyes. Moleman reach down—she recoiled—and moved the few remaining strands back for her. "Marat could have been calling to someone outside the room," Marjorie countered. "His wife Simone most likely."

"Perhaps." Ferguson paced slowly and seemed to study the dock. "But it at least *suggests* he knew his assassin."

"He didn't," she said much too quickly. "Corday wasn't a 'dear friend.' "

Without looking at her, his hands suggesting she apply the brakes to her brain, Ferguson said, "I know, I know, sweetheart. But to someone less schooled than you and Franco and I—like Moleman here—it *could* seem that way: that Marat knew Miss Corday."

"The point please, Detective Ferguson," she said, thoroughly irritated now. "Places to go, you know. People to see."

Ferguson stopped pacing and placed both his hands in his trench coat. He nodded his head and bit his lip. "That we know, babe. That we know. People to see. A *person* to see. And what will you be telling us next: you're expected somewhere, you'll be missed, et cetera?"

"Something like that." Marge, Margie, Marj, Jorie, Maggie, she recited in her head.

"And your *real* name?"

Marge, Margie, Marj, Jorie, Maggie.

"I grow tired of asking the same question over and—"

"Marge, Margie, Marj, Jorie, Maggie," she blurted out.

Ferguson sighed. Franco reached a hand into his jacket pocket, but the detective waved him off. "Gingers. Jesus. Cut her loose," he ordered Moleman. "Cut her loose."

"But, boss—" Franco started.

"No, no. Our girl here doesn't want to admit it, but her trail will be easy enough to pick up. She's a creature of habit, more like the doomed Monsieur Marat than Mademoiselle Corday, aren't you, red?"

Marjorie climbed to the dock, gathered herself, and walked past the three of *them*.

"Sooner or later," Ferguson called after her, "we'll catch her in the tub—if she doesn't drown herself in the meantime."

"Not if I catch *her* there first," she called over her shoulder. "Ta, ta."

+

Romeo loved Juliet
Juliet, she felt the same...
Thou givest fever...
Peggy Lee

The first sentence I typed this morning was, "This is a story of hate," but I pulled the sheet of paper out of the typewriter and burned it. (Leave no evidence, Scottie had said.) I had woken with what felt like a hangover but one earned without drinking. It was a long night last night, watching, waiting outside Scottie's apartment.

What bugs me most is that I missed Andrea's departure. I hope she didn't see me. It's hard to be so fake, so nice, around her; it's a lot of work. Her "just-one-of-the-boys" laugh annoys me. Her pointy nose annoys me. Her C-cup chest annoys me. The way she pronounces her name, as if the accent is on the second syllable (and the first "a" is pronounced with an umlaut)—än-DRAY-uh instead of AN-dree-uh—annoys the living hell out of me. I imagine that her hands smell like the penises she touches all day long at her job in the urologist's office. So "This is a story of hate" isn't far from the truth—but I don't hate Andrea because of her pointy nose, the regal pronunciation of her name, or her penis-scented hands. I hate her because I love. So really this is a story of love.

What I'm supposed to be working on is a novel of passion. A literary thriller, I suppose one would call it. My first toe anywhere near the waters of the thriller genre. (My agent Henry likes to pigeonhole my books, but I'm usually lumped in the vague "literary genre" graveyard.) I want to finish the first draft before things go much further—before I prove my love to Scottie, which will be a difficult act, I'm sure (if I can go through with it), but a defining one, an act that may very well land me in the hoosegow. So it would be nice to have at least the first draft complete, something for Henry to chew on while he figures out how to turn my new found infamy into dollars. When my agent first asked me what the book was about, I told him: a woman is being pursued by a nameless entity she suspects is a contract killer (which this person may well be), but the heroine remains resolute in her mission: to protect a man whom she loves unrequitedly. The man is being stalked by a deranged woman with a pointy nose. But then the protagonist discovers the stalker is actually the man's lover, and it turns out that it's this wanton woman who set the nameless entity on her trail, so she then puts aside the role of protector and assumes that of the assassin in order to go head-to-head with both her pursuer *and* her rival. Henry practically wet himself with joy—a book that might actually make the bestsellers list, I'm sure he thought. A literary thriller, he declared.

If there is a moral structure to the universe, if there is a God, then I could be in for a heap of trouble. Here's the thing: being raised in the Greek Orthodox Catholic Church, I was taught to pray. I was taught to pray for the dead (which I never understood; wasn't the fate of the dead already a done deal?), to pray for lost souls (which I confused with the dead; I didn't think, as my pew mate Agnes thought, that they were souls that were not very good at directions), to pray for the impoverished in Africa (made sense), and to pray for our families. But it was the praying for Africa bit that stuck in my craw. Because we more often than not prayed for something we desired: please make my mother better, please ease grandfather's pain, please make so-and-so come back to me, please keep Johnny safe in the war, please make sure Santa gives me that shiny red bicycle for Christmas. God as Santa Claus (a conceptualization that comes with startling implications). We were told, when distressed, to "pray on it." But why would God listen to a prayer about a sick grandparent when thousands were starving to death in parts of the African continent? Doesn't God have more important things to worry about (hurricanes, the opioid crisis, the Middle East) than whether or not Jenny gets that new job or Dottie wins the lottery? Yes, I can read Scottie's secret language, but indoctrination is hard to break. So I pray for Scottie to love me, and, against all logic, I know he will—nay: I know he *does*. Because I prayed on it.

But the cocktail party tonight at Scottie's is fairly devoid of God, I am quite certain. Not that I'm one of those right-wing Christian nut jobs. It's just an observation. People sneak out—well, not *sneak*; it's fairly obvious what they're up to—to smoke marijuana. I believe that cocaine is being snorted in Scottie's back bathroom. Men are hitting on women. Women are leaning on men. Cleavage is in abundance. Thighs are flashed. (My buttoned up pink cardigan is conspicuous and out of place. I'm like a Victorian writer in the midst of the lost generation of the '20s. I am definitely *not* keeping up appearances.) Men light cigars and the ceiling is alive with their smoke; it crawls and undulates and makes shapes, gives signals that only I can read. Even the people who arrive as couples purr up against other potential partners. It's like a '70s key party. I watch one man lick salt from a woman's shoulder (not his wife's) before taking a shot of Cuervo. I see another woman cup a man's genitalia over his pants while she converses with his apparently approving spouse. A tall man pretends to reach for an ashtray and rubs his arm against a short woman's enormous boobs. I'm no prude, but as a writer, I can't help but notice that the room reeks of sex—or what I imagine sex smells like: sweaty pubic hair and hot breath and acrid dreams of death.

Andrea is here of course. She has no idea that the guillotine's blade is hanging over her head and the time of the chop is coming, but I'm getting ahead of myself. (Yes it was Corday that got the guillotine, not Marat—the guillotine metaphor just sounds better; down is up, up is down, right?) Andrea is dressed in her typical harlot attire. If she's wearing a bra, it must be one with holes for her nipples, for they poke at her blouse with a notice-me insistence. I doubt she is wearing underwear; they are, I assume, too passé. She floats through the party—well, *tromps through* is what it seems like—rubbing this man's shoulder, touching that one's elbow, but always making physical contact, as if she needs to remind herself (and every male at the party) that she is corporeal, that she is real and could easily be had. Her perfume should be enough of a giveaway: I can smell it from across the room, as if it is on my neck not hers. I am almost overcome by a strong desire to demonstrate Andrea's doggy style to the revelers, but it is Scottie's party, so I restrain any canine impersonations. (Besides, it would be out of character, I think, but what is *in* character is starting to get fuzzy.)

Soon I am overwhelmed by the surrounding frivolity and eventually lose track of Scottie. It is late, and just about everyone is drunk and loud except for me. I am sure I will find Scottie at the center of one of the floating, mutating circles, guffawing to beat the band. Scottie is wry but once his drink is on, he can bray with the best of them. But he's nowhere to be seen as I haunt the circles, trying to be more of an impression than a presence—a tactic that fails. A woman I don't know very well—big-boned with frosted hair teased like some ancient video vixen—thinks I can't hear her (or doesn't care if I do) when she refers to me in a smoker's croak as a "dowdy Vera Miles." As I can only assume she is referencing the actress from Hitchcock's *Psycho*, I walk right up to her (I have to crane my head) and inform her that Vera Miles' real name was Vera June Ralston and that she had to change it because Republic Pictures had a Czechoslovakian actress named Vera Hruba, a former ice skater, whose name had been changed to Vera Ralston and who, despite having little box office appeal (the American public couldn't get past her thick accent, it was said) and limited acting skills, was kept on at Republic Pictures for seventeen years because the studio chief was in love with her. Brassy Miss Big Bones is unimpressed and appears to have no idea who Vera Miles actually is; quite possibly she was just repeating something she'd heard. But, Lord, if I were to repeat what I've heard about *her*, well, it's safe to say that she makes Andrea look like a monastic nun.

I'm left alone after that little display. (It is quite possible *I* was too loud.) It's good though, gives me time to catch my breath and reflect. I had a stage name once. Oh, I didn't tread the boards very long. A little in college, some amateur theater, summer stock. I was too self-conscious. I was acutely aware of all those faces staring at mine and of the sweat patches spreading under my arms. I was easily distracted too. All of this drove one director, during a local production of *Twelfth Night*, to actually growl at me from the side of the stage during a performance to break me from my spell. Was it during act 1, scene 2, where Viola says to the captain, "Conceal me what I am, and be my aid / For such disguise as haply shall become / The form of my intent" or during act 2, scene 4, where she tells Duke

Orsino, "She never told her love, / But let concealment, like a worm i' the bud, / Feed on her damask cheek"? Despite the general negativity my acting aroused, a drama professor once told me that if I studied and worked at my craft enough, if I really wanted it, I could someday lose myself, inhabit a role, and see the others in my company as characters rather than actual people, but I think he just wanted to sleep with me. (Doesn't mean he wrong though, I decided later.) Taking a stage name wasn't a pretentious act on my part, and I suppose my given name isn't a bad one, but choosing a different name helped to remove me, just a little bit, from an extracurricular activity that I was drawn to and repelled by in not quite equal measure. (It depended on the day.) Choosing a stage name was easy. A dowdy Vera Miles I was not, but I did use the name of a character in another Hitchcock film, portrayed by Barbara Bel Geddes, the actress who'd been blacklisted (but Hitch didn't care). The real problem for me was that I spent most of my time on stage looking out to see if Scottie was among the theatergoers. (I'd only taken up acting because he'd told me once, when he was in his cups, that I belonged before the footlights.) He always claimed to catch every production I was in, but I never saw him at any. So I eventually quit the stage (he never said a word) and hid behind my typewriter. It was easier to watch Scottie from there anyway.

But where, oh where, is my dear Scottie now?

It strikes my brain like a brick being dropped on my head. I had traveled through every circle before resting by the vintage 1960s Naugahyde bar, and not only didn't I see Scottie, I didn't see my blazing-haired nemesis Andrea. Not caring who is watching (and the carousers are too red-faced to give me more than a glance: I am neither a swinging wife nor a tawdry possible pickup), I dash from group to group one last time, throw open the front door, and run back to check the balcony. I then look up at the ceiling, and my stomach churns. I take the stairs slowly, careful not to hit a creaky board. (Though how it would be heard over the boisterous noise downstairs, I don't know.) Halfway up, I see through the banister that Scottie's bedroom door is only partially closed and that the lights are off. I duck when a sound like an animal expiring escapes the room.

"Shhh!" I hear Scottie say. "What if someone hears? What if *she* hears?"

I can only assume *she* is me. I have become that lowliest of all female companions: the pronoun.

Andrea scoffs. "Ha! She wouldn't recognize the sound."

I run down the stairs and out of the house, forgetting my shawl. The plan, Scottie's passion plot, must be moved forward. I know the players, I know the schematics, I know the risk, and I certainly know the rewards awaiting me in the end. The perfect time, the perfect weapon, the perfect plan. The aesthetically perfect murder is one of passion, Scottie said, *planned* passion, unrestrained at just the right time. And a perfect murder is one in which the perpetrator is suspected perhaps (unrequited love does sometimes exude an aroma of desperation) but is never caught, because the passion is quite well hidden—in this case, by popular opinion: *at least she's more femme than butch, right?* All of which is the opposite of my love for Scottie: never suspected but about to be caught.

+

I said to my soul, be still, and wait without hope...
T. S. Eliot

If jealousy can only exist with desire, she had plenty of both in spades. It hadn't taken many stakeouts outside Romeo's, watching his shadow and safeguarding it (for that was her duty) to discover that her Romeo still danced with Rosaline, as portrayed by the Whore of Babylon. (What had made her believe that particular dance was over? Wishful thinking? Denial?) That finding led to several self-lacerating moments (literarily), but she had a job to do (protect Romeo at all costs)—and maybe a new undertaking as well. (*Snuff!*) This new mission became a reality when after a little poking around (very little, for this Rosaline was not careful at all in covering up her trail of Trojan wrappers and K-Y Jelly receipts), Marjorie discovered (how?—does it matter?) that it was this interloper, this bookmark, who had indeed set *them* on her trail. It was Rosaline who had loosed the dogs (Rosaline or whatever the tramp's true name was—something with an annoying accent on the second syllable, wasn't it?—names being irrelevant in the new millennium, as she'd heard someone say at a cocktail party). It was Rosaline who had spotted what Marjorie thought had been a careful, innocuous infiltration of her Romeo's life. And if this Rosaline had been skilled enough to spot Marjorie, then the hussy was into Romeo for more than his bed. While the harlot had sicced *them* on Marjorie—and *they* had tried to pin the label of would-be assassin on Romeo's guardian—the true villain, *le voleur de coeurs*, the thief of hearts, after photographing his bank statements and sharpening her red-handled switchblade, was probably hanging her stained panties over Romeo's shower rod at this very moment.

Sometimes, Marjorie knew, people pigeonholed her as being prudish, repressed, uptight, a schoolmarm. Well, for all *their* sins and shortcomings, *they* had pegged Marjorie right—only in advance. She hadn't been an assassin before, but she was going to become one now. (Plots change; things happen on the job, and writers know to follow the story wherever it may go.) Charlotte Corday, indeed. Marie-Anne Charlotte de Corday d'Armont to you, mister. But: "What's in a name? That which we call a rose / By any other name would smell as sweet." Juliet said that. Romeo's Juliet. A few lines later, Romeo replies to his young love, "My name, dear saint, is hateful to myself, / Because it is an enemy to thee. / Had I it written, I would tear the word." The young Montague never came up with poetry like that for his previous female interest, the crush, the unseen (by the audience) Rosaline. The words Romeo expended on Rosaline were merely practice for the poetry he presented to Juliet.

Again: it would take meticulous planning. *They* would surely be watching: Detective Ferguson, Franco, Moleman, and who knew how many others? The job was further complicated by Rosaline's admittedly impressive and easily accomplished disappearing acts. Oh, she could follow this meddler, this trespasser for a bit when she stepped out of Romeo's apartment, but Rosaline had a way of slipping between the lines or becoming just an indistinct head in a crowd; her trail of lube only led to Romeo's, never away from it. Even though Romeo spent nights is what appeared initially to be Rosaline's first floor apartment, the woman didn't seem to actually live there, and Marjorie could never pin down the exact address of her living quarters or even where she worked (if she worked). All of which only meant one thing: the hit would have take place at Romeo's. Marjorie agonized over this for days: what if some shrapnel hit her Romeo? What if he saw her dispatch Rosaline and didn't like what he saw? (Seeing Marjorie standing there with a smoking gun or a bloody knife just might upset him.) She wasn't worried about Rosaline seeing her before she saw Rosaline; the strumpet would never expect an attack at Romeo's. One thing was for sure: Marjorie couldn't enlist any accomplices. This was the kind of job so personal in nature it could only be handled by the one truly in love, for love and death are two sides of a tossed coin.

A knife was risky, it being an up close weapon, but a gun was noisier. Sure, she could buy a silencer, but a gun could be as unwieldy as a knife for a novice like herself. Bullets sometimes ricocheted. Knives glanced. (Better to bring both, she decided.) From her notes made as she perched in a tree with binoculars, details added from the one time she sneaked in and felt enough like a shadow to blend into the shade), Marjorie was able to construct a typical Rosaline night visit at Romeo's. First the obligatory opening embrace (that could last several agonizing minutes). Then either right to the bedroom or, more often lately, dinner in, sometimes with candlelight (sickening), sometimes not, sometimes cooked by Romeo (or both), sometimes ordered in. But retiring to the bedroom would not be far behind in the night's activities. Used to be each lights-off session lasted between forty-five minutes to an hour, but it was getting shorter and shorter as of late. Visits used to culminate with a dual shower. Then Rosaline would leave and vanish or stay and watch a movie in Romeo's bed. (The last film they'd watched was Hitchcock's *Spellbound* with Gregory Peck and Ingrid Bergman—eyeballs, scissors, and cards, oh my!) But lately, after the lights came back on in the bedroom, her Romeo would hop in the shower solo, then watch some TV while Rosaline lounged in the bath. It was there, in the tub, Corday-style, that Marjorie decided the assassination would take place. It would be easier to clean up too. Just let as much blood as possible drain away and follow it up with a gallon or so of bleach, keeping an eye out for any bodily fluids that may have landed elsewhere. (This would be *after* she disposed of the body.) As far as *when*, she would have to play it loose. There were a few pretty big ifs. (Perfection is often conditional.) If she wasn't followed, if Rosaline took more than a whore's bath (which she did more and more often, as if she knew) and actually got in the tub, if her Romeo was safely tucked into bed watching television, then Marjorie would at least have a little time to do the deed before he discovered her, scrub brush in hand (which, she had to admit, would be as damning as finding her wielding a just-discharged hand gun). But by then, it would be too late—Rosaline would finally have a hole in her that couldn't be easily filled (if she wasn't already dissolving into a sodium hydroxide soup).

The one downside to the plan would be if Romeo's repulsion at the act blinded his true feelings. (The feelings she knew he had for her, not what little he felt for Rosaline.) The upside was obvious: her Romeo would know that she, Marjorie, was his red-haired Juliet. In less flowery terms, he would know she was in love with him and had been for a very long time. Since time immemorial. Since the beginning of time itself, it seemed. It was just unfortunate that she (or they if he truly recognized Marjorie for who she was) had to be bothered with getting rid of the body before they took their place in the sacred bedroom, cleansed now by Rosaline's death. Her work (body disposal aside) would be done: she would have protected her Romeo from a not-so-clever thief of hearts, and she would do a better job shielding him from future harm when she was by his side. So to that end, to speed the romance along, she'd purchased four gallons of lye. (She'd still have to scrub the tub afterwards.) She'd already decided that to cut Rosaline up would be too messy and more than likely would take too long, and dragging her body out of the apartment to bury it could attract unwanted attention from *them*.

Either side of midnight, she waited through the turning of calendar pages, and the only soundtrack to her vigil was what she sang softly to herself over and over; funny—she didn't even like Dylan:

> *Early one mornin' the sun was shinin'*
> *And I was layin' in bed*
> *Wonderin' if she'd changed at all*
> *If her hair was still red*

Then a night presented itself. All the necessary pieces fell into place. (Marjorie reminded herself again to change the sheets before lying down with Romeo; she'd even brought along a fresh set just in case, like a typical man, he had only one. Men will be men.) The knife was well hidden on her person but easily accessible; a gun *sans* silencer (she didn't have the extra cash or room on her credit card for accessories) was behind her back; and bleach, lye, scrub brushes, rope, and trash bags were in the trunk. She was out of the car when *they* emerged from the bushes and from behind trees. Ferguson, Franco, Moleman.

"Didn't I just leave this party?" she wondered.

"Going somewhere, Miss Corday?" Detective Ferguson asked.

She thought the gumshoe had said before that she was more Marat than Corday Well, well, well—somebody decided to remove his head from his posterior and actually study the clues.

Moleman slid around so that he was almost behind her.

"As a matter of fact," Marjorie said, tapping her chin, "I was just about to visit your wife."

Ferguson blanched.

"Your police ring wasn't the only ring I saw that night on our 'date,'" Marjorie said. "I also saw the pale band of skin around your left ring finger. You not only forgot to remove your police ring, but you forgot to cover up the shadow of your wedding band. Not that I believe you are actually working for the police now. But by the look on your face—don't play poker much, huh?—there's a Lady Ferguson, and I wonder how she would feel about our little date. Not official police business, that's for sure: no, *their* business."

The men looked at each other.

"Would it be more appropriate to call you *Agent* Ferguson?"

The men then stared at her, and no one spoke.

"Opposition research, gents, look it up. But a date's a date. Franco's girlfriend, a curiously pale Rita Moreno—I bet she doesn't like it when you eat onions. Oh, she and I could have a whole discussion about *Allium cepa*. Onions were your test for me, but by the careful way you removed them from your salad, you wouldn't haven't dared to eat them anyway."

They retreated a little now. Moleman came back around and sat on the curb, once again looking confused. Marjorie gestured towards him. "You gentlemen really ought to fix up your friend here with a nice girl," she said. "Even a moleman needs a good woman. Just look at him."

The man with the moles smiled weakly. Marjorie resisted the urge to smack the smile off of his face.

"And if a man has a bad woman?" Ferguson asked, in an effort to recover.

"'And if thine eye offend thee, pluck it out.'" she answered.

"I think," Ferguson responded after a bit, "that the verse is referring to *self-plucking*, not what you have in mind."

She rested her weight on one leg and hoped the knife sheath didn't peek out of her cardigan jacket sweater, which she didn't think was practical for the job, but it *was* October, and the chill in the air reminded her of the death inherent in the fall. "And what do I have in mind, Detective-Agent Ferguson?"

Ferguson shook his head wearily. "Look, red. We didn't request this assignment. *You*—"

"*They*," she corrected.

"Have it your way," he said, dismissing her with his hand, but then rebounding, "but *you* sign the checks, *you* give us our marching orders, *you* instituted the inviolable rule that we are to follow the assignment to the letter no matter how dangerous—to *you*."

Her knees buckled. "To *me*...?"

Ferguson raised his arms in the air as if he was surrendering. "*You* said it was research! A book, a novel, something. Hell, *you* told me to call you 'red' and 'babe.' *You* gave him moles and made Franco vaguely Puerto Rican."

"I *am* Puerto Rican," Franco said, indignant.

"And I'm the Pope," Ferguson said, his eyes dime-store-novel-detective tired. "It's all you, babe. I've been in better stories. Ya think I'm really this clichéd? It's all *you*."

"*Me?*" she asked, squinting her eyes. "But *they?*"

Ferguson sighed and looked at Franco who shrugged. Moleman put his head in his hands. "*You* are *they*," he said gently. "*You* are the instigator of *us*, not Rosaline or Andrea or whatever you're calling her now." Then he appeared to blow his stack and shouted, "Goddammit, *you* are *they*! *You* are *us!*"

"Why...why are you telling me this?"

"Because, babe," Ferguson said, looking haggard, "because we like you. We don't want to see you get into any trouble you can't get out of. And we don't want to be a party to it. I know we're paid—by *you*—to tail you, watch your every move, but we can't do that if you're going to commit a crime as heinous as...well, as heinous as what you're planning on doing." Marjorie noticed for the first time the bags that had settled beneath the detective's eyes and how purple they were; she made a mental note to make his eyes bloodshot next time too—then shook her head: *what was she thinking? Next time? What next time? She wasn't here to create...she was here to destroy...this was absurd to the nth degree. Just more mind games courtesy of*—

She thought she would faint. She looked from face to face. "And I'm going to..."

"Miss Corday, in the bathroom, with the dagger," Franco said. Ferguson glared at him, and Franco shrugged again. "*Clue.* Played it a lot growing up in Minnesota. Made me want to be a cop."

Since when was Franco from Minnesota? *Since she thought it just now. No—wait…*

"And instead you became the *boricua* Colonel Mustard," Ferguson growled, "or is it Señora Peacock?"

"What's in a name?" Marjorie whispered.

"Speak up, red, or…"

She blocked out Ferguson's voice. It was booming, and she hoped it didn't alert Rosaline, but somehow Marjorie doubted it. *They* were in league with Rosaline, no matter what *they* said. *They* were trying to confuse her, telling her *she* was *they*, and by doing so, *they'd* shown their hand. The only mystery that remained was why *they* just hadn't taken Marjorie out right then and there or at least physically removed her from the scene. She couldn't listen to anything *they* were saying; it was a disinformation campaign, that was all it was. Or maybe *they*, at least this particular manifestation of *they*, were nothing more than figments of her over-adrenalized neocortex. If she just closed her eyes…

She heard Ferguson sigh again. (He was especially adept at the overly dramatic sigh. *She had written him well. No—wait…*) "Open your eyes, Miss Corday."

Marjorie did: *they* were gone and the knife was in her hand.

Confucius said, "If names be not correct, language is not in accordance with the truth of things."

Oliver Wendell Holmes wrote, "Fate tried to conceal him by naming him Smith."

The French writer Octave Mirbeau wrote, "Murder is born of love, and love attains the greatest intensity in murder."

Marjorie, or whatever her name was—she no longer cared, not now, not when she was so close to taking her Romeo's name and his lover's life—smiled and licked her lips. Nerves. She didn't know what sex felt like, but she imagined the anticipation of the act must feel something like this. Feverish. Flushed. Fantastic.

Alfred Hitchcock said, "Someone once told me that every minute a murder occurs, so I don't want to waste your time, I know you want to go back to work." While she couldn't confirm his secondhand statistic, Hitch was right about one thing: it was time to go to work.

+

He gives me fever
With his kisses
Fever when he holds me tight
Peggy Lee

I pray hard for Scottie to love me—Scottie, John; I pray for both of his names—and if he doesn't love me back, I tell myself, then there can be no God. Yes, God has His hands very full, but I pray so darn hard so darn much, a little has to have gone through. Surely God must see that Scottie and I belong together, that this is how the story must end, like the stories of Sleeping Beauty and Snow White and *The Princess Bride*.

But perhaps God is waiting for me to make my final move, to deliver checkmate. To that end, I go forward with my plans. I don't fear prison. How could prison be any worse than the place I currently inhabit? A little less sunshine maybe? A few more lesbians perhaps? But I hedge my bet. I purchase a wee bit of insurance, which will hopefully create a temporary smokescreen, as well as provide a patsy.

Wallace B. Ambrose is the first private detective listed in the phonebook, so he's the lucky guy who gets the first call. His office is above an insurance agency. It is small with two windows that don't allow enough ventilation; it's stuffy as hell and smells like the inside of an old man's shoe after a long day at the track. Mr. Ambrose— "Wallace, I insist; Wally if ya really like me"—is a nice enough man, a once-thin man, it's obvious, whose gotten lazy and thus chubby. (His wastebasket is filled with empty potato chip bags, and his belly strains against the waist of his pants.) He agrees to take my case for a substantial deposit. His assignment is simple enough: spy on Scottie's house from the end of the working day to just after midnight. Start a file. Jot down a few notes. File regular reports. Take some pictures if anything of interest happens—if Scottie has a female visitor, say (unless that visitor is me).

Hiring Wallace serves a few purposes. The first is minor, but important: I'm tired, and as the big night of passion approaches, I need a few nights off. Not that I end up using them anyway. Most nights I'm in my usual perch. (I instruct Wallace exactly where to park his car—so he can't see me.) But on the very few nights where I'm simply too exhausted to even lift a knife, Wallace can give me the skinny. The second purpose is of far more import: to confuse those I know who follow and watch me. If *they* think I've given up on Scottie—even if *they* think I've hired Wallace (I've paid Wallace enough for the flabby dick to keep his trap shut)—perhaps *they* will focus all their efforts on staking out my place (if *they* weren't already) or maybe even looking elsewhere. There was always the chance that *they*, who'd seemingly climbed right out of my book into real life, weren't targeting me but were protecting Scottie. Maybe *they* would start tailing Andrea instead. I mean, how much do I really know about Scottie? Everything, I think, but could it be possible he is involved in something far more dangerous than writing mysteries and spy novels? Who is Andrea *really*? Has Scottie perhaps, in one of his convoluted plots, stumbled across a truth the government doesn't want broadcasted, so *they* keep their eyes on him—possibly because he is too valuable a resource to knock off? Whatever the case, Wallace's presence is a misdirection.

The third reason for hiring Mr. Ambrose is a far more sinister reason, I must admit, but I see no way around it. It's sort of a safety measure, just in case. See, Wallace, for all his superior detective skills (he's actually not bad and his reports are surprisingly thorough), tends to fall asleep on the job, usually just a catnap. So it would be no big thing to ease open his passenger door and plant the same exact knife currently strapped to my person under the seat (I'd bought two for this express purpose), along with some spent shells, courtesy of target practice in the woods. (I've appeared out of nowhere and climbed into his car a couple of times, so if he woke, he wouldn't think twice about me being there.) Of course, there wouldn't be any blood or DNA on the knife, but it would match the stab wounds (and if I use the revolver, the shells will speak volumes). I don't want Wallace to take the fall; I just want him to be the prime suspect for a bit, a temporary patsy. The authorities would detain him, question him, maybe toss him in the can but eventually let him go. (Who knows what *they* would do?) That would give me enough time to clean up anything I've missed. Scottie would help me by then, I'm sure. He would see the lengths to which I've gone. He would fulfill the prayers I've sent up to God.

Speaking of God, maybe it's time for a confession.

Andreas is my family name. It's Greek. It's pronounced with the accent on the second syllable (and an umlaut on the first "a"), which used to annoy the hell out of the nuns at the Roman Catholic school I had to attend for a couple of years. Since the nuns couldn't see the primary accent mark, then it wasn't there. (Talk about doubting Thomases!)

Greek women, Greek-American women too, are supposed to exist to marry (Greek men preferably), have babies (lots of 'em), and cook (Greek dishes of course). Writing is not considered a viable occupation by my mother or my aunts. They've never read a word I've written. "Why make stuff up, Charis?" my mother asks. "Just open a newspaper" (as if I hadn't written for one). My father has been dead for over ten years, but Mother invokes his opinion as if his ghost is in the next room with his smelly feet up, just home from work, reading the sports page. "Your father, bless his soul," she says, crossing herself or touching one of the many Mary statuettes that dot the house, "he doesn't believe in made-up stories. He only watches the news. He says made-up stuff is nonsense. 'How could anyone care about a detective show when police are being shot in the bad neighborhoods right here—when they're not busy harassing Greeks? How could anyone watch a show about army surgeons when all you have to do is open your front door to see blood?' He knows, Charis, he knows things. 'Fake blood,' he says. 'What do I need to see *fake* blood for? I prick my finger ten times a day down the deli. Blood I can see for free.'" (Her use of the present tense drives me to distraction sometimes!)

Greek women can be fiery. My mother says it was because of Aegea, a queen of the Amazons, who converted and was drowned in what is now called the Aegean Sea, but I think she is mixing up the Amazon queen with Aegeas of early Greek mythology. Regardless, I think my mother and my late father would have agreed that, although Greek women could be hot-blooded, they don't (normally) commit murder. They don't plot and scheme and find patsies and sharpen knives and buy gallons of lye and store it in their car trunks next to the bleach and a bag of lime (just in case). And they certainly don't Americanize their first names. The list of my sins is long and about to get longer, and no amount of crossing myself is going to change that; I just have to trust that God backs *this* passion play.

I think of all these things as I first check Andrea's first floor apartment (she isn't home), then drive over to Scottie's place, and I have to shake my head to physically clear my mind. I try to think of the good times Scottie and I have had together. The late night study sessions which usually turned into movie watching marathons. Scottie loves old movies, and he's very into directors: Orson Welles, Otto Preminger, John Ford, Billy Wilder. But mostly Hitchcock. He started calling me Midge after a character in *Vertigo*, he said, which was where he got his nickname too, but he never watched it with me. He said it would put too many ideas in my head. Before that, he used to call me Norma because of my favorite song (a fever indeed!), the only song I ever really liked—I think; I do seem to own a lot of records. When I told him my real name, my Greek name, Charis, he laughed so loud, I thought someone was going to call the cops.

In the vestibule, I force myself to breathe evenly, then I make my way slowly up the stairs to Scottie's, taking a step every couple of minutes in case I hit a loose board. The apartment below is empty, so there are no extraneous noises to break my concentration. I know Wallace is snoozing in his car, so there would be no record of my entering the building (unless *they're* watching). The knife is in my hand, which may be a mistake; keeping it hidden might give me an edge and what if, God forbid, Scottie somehow stumbles into me first, but I am far too shaken and stirred to worry over such fine points. Slice and dice. Those are the watchwords of the night. But just a few seconds ago, I heard footsteps walking across Scottie's apartment. And not the heavy, thudding footsteps of a man. Scottie is sweet and well-meaning and gentle, but men don't tiptoe when they can clomp. Not unless the man is one of *they*, and even *they* can be heavy-footed at times. No, this is Andrea, has to be. She is being cautious, moving quickly on her toes like a dancer but in a roundabout way, as if she doesn't know the lay of the land—and she shouldn't. There is the chance Wallace double-crossed me, sold me down the river for a song and all that, tipped Andrea off—it's possible but unlikely. Before zonking out, the man had just tucked into a pizza with mushrooms and red onions while sitting in his twenty-year-old car, which is to say he didn't seem particularly motivated; it was hardly the behavior of a turncoat or a man easily bought (unless he was well-trained and the car was agency-issued). What if it was *them* instead of her? Well, *they* would have had to escort Scottie out of his apartment in order to plant *themselves* inside. (There's no way *they* would dare risk dealing with me having Scottie there.) But I would have seen the exit go down or Wallace would have (pre-pizza). Two sets of eyes; there had been no evacuation. The footsteps can only belong to Andrea, forewarned (by *them* or Wallace or her own killer instincts) and possibly forearmed. A drop of sweat falls on the blade, and I sheath the knife. There is a plan two. A far noisier plan two.

Squeak, squeak, squeak, squeak, squeak, squeak, squeak.
Pause.
Squeak, squeak, squeak, squeak, squeak, squeak, squeak.
Pause.
Pant. Pant. Long moooaaan. Pant.
I listen to the bedsprings sing:
I love you, Midge.
I love you, Midge.
I love you, Midge.

The light from the streetlamp out front glinted off the gun, which was steadier in my hand than I thought. Going to be hell to clean up—a head shot—though not as messy as it would be if I had to use my knife, I suppose. Blood in the bathtub, like my adopted namesake achieved, is one thing: a generous amount of heated lye, then a few scrub brushes, a gallon or so of bleach, and some significant elbow grease—plus copious amounts of dissolving acid. Presto chango! But brains on the wall? Heck, there could be little scattered pieces of skull everywhere. A fractured mind.

I know then I'm going to have to kill Scottie too. (How's that for style?) Cleaning a bloody bathtub is one thing, easy enough to get behind (assuming he understood everything the way I understood everything), but a splattered brain? I don't think so. Scottie wouldn't stand for it; his innate goodness wouldn't let me get anyway with it. So despite my best efforts, his death will be on my hands. There'll be at least two shots which means Wallace just might wake up, ignore that last slice, and call the police. Which means if *they* are out there—and why shouldn't *they* be; every other part of the plan is going to hell—then *they're* going to get *their* hands on me. Catch me red-handed literally. Which means…I don't even want to think about it. Picturing my own brain matter as some crimson Rorschach test is a stomach-churning exercise. What if my brain fluid mixes with hers? What then?

As I listen the footsteps above execute a perfect *battement frappé* three times (*frappé* means "to strike," and I can practically hear the dancer's pointe shoe brushing the floor) followed by what I imagine is a halfway decent *fouettés en tournant*, I know God is dead or that He never existed at all. I was taught that if one word of the Bible was untrue, then the entire Bible was false. The argument: because every word has been proven true through faith, our faith was rewarded with the knowledge that the Testaments were nothing less than the Word of God. So if Scottie doesn't love me (and my faith is based on the belief that he does), then God is just so much fairy dust, a Santa Claus, an Easter Bunny, a Great Pumpkin. That He could be more than this conceptualization, that He could be busy in North Korea, the ghettos of Baltimore, or the badlands of North Philadelphia doesn't faze me. I am beyond that argument. My love for Scottie is truer than most anything else, and if God is omnipotent, then He is capable of juggling tsunamis, terrorism, and me.

I love you, Midge.

I love you, Midge.

I love you, Midge.

Only that's not my name, is it? And if it's not Midge (I finally watched *Vertigo*—alone), it's certainly not Marjorie, my pen name. Norma—Peggy Lee's real first name? Not even close (but cute—however *my* fever is palpable and has lasted longer than three minutes and twenty-one seconds; Miss Lee's fever spins towards a finite end at forty-five revolutions per minute). *Wait—isn't my name Agent something?* Only Scottie—John—knows my *real* name and even the name behind that one. It's funny in that sort of head-hanging, aw shucks kind of way: despite the fact that I am sure he'd never read my first novel or anything I'd written, Detective Ferguson had it right in a way with his Miss Corday this and Miss Corday that. My name, my *American* name, is Charlotte. And no, not after Charlotte Corday, the infamous tub assassin. Charlotte was my Americanization of my Greek name, Charis. I thought Charis was too…ethnic. After all, I don't look Greek in the slightest. If it wasn't for my red hair, I could pass for a WASP with no trouble: my skin tone and facial features aren't "Greek-looking in the least," as my mother puts it. Just a genetic hiccup. My father used to joke that my mother must have been fantasizing about ginger Robert Redford while stuffing grape leaves. So phallic, his joke—not like my father at all, as if who I am is a mystery to him too.

Charlotte for Charis. Midge for Marjorie.

I reach the landing, and the .38 is heavy in my hand, heavier than it was when I bought it. I flick the safety off.

Charlotte was the only name change. (Pen name aside.) I couldn't Americanize my last name. Then I would be Charlotte Andrea (still with the annoying accent on the second syllable.) Who needs two first names? (Okay, maybe I do—but my parents would never forgive me for dropping the "s" from the end) So Charis Andreas became Charlotte Andreas who then became Midge for Marjorie. The name Corday I borrowed for the surname of the protagonist from my first novel, a woman bent on rooting out the cause of the tragic nature of her life and assigning blame.

Midge. Charis. Marjorie. Andreas. Corday. Charlotte. Andrea.

I break in the door even though it's not locked (it's old, wooden, and who knew?) and land in a perfect split in the middle of the empty floor. The room is dark, and I crouch and spin slowly, my gun pointed into the darkness, as I my eyes chase elusive red streaks (of hair). A car squeals to a halt in front of the building. The light of its headlights seems to reach up and illuminate the parts of the room that the streetlamps or even the moon can't reach.

I am surrounded by floor to ceiling mirrors. There is a wooden bar (barre), about waist high, running the length of the room. I turn, pointing my gun at each of the women.

Charlotte Andreas. Charlotte Corday. Andrea. Charis Andreas. Midge for Marjorie.

They all look the same.

Hair so red, it's like blood in a river. Blood in a tub. No hair can be that red. Red that goes slip slidin' away from mirror to mirror.

Scottie runs into the room, and I point the gun and shoot.

Click. Click. Click. Click.

"Scottie...where is...? Why is your apartment covered in mirrors? Scottie?"

He takes the toy pistol from my hand and gathers me up in his arms.

"You've been lurking outside for so often, dear, you are the very definition of a suspicious character. Anyone could have seen you 'break in.' We have to get you out of here before someone calls the police. Damn good thing I disabled the studio's alarm."

I look up at his face. It is lost in the shadows.

"You were the one following me?"

He nods his head. "You kept flashing me notes everywhere I was: parties, the Brew-Ha-Ha, the bistro around the corner from your apartment, the Ritz even. 'Help me' written on your palm. 'Help me' scrawled on napkins in red lipstick. 'Help me.' Once there was even a note about squirrels that I didn't understand: a squirrel in the attic, a squirrel in the middle of the road. The last note had the name of a supposed dance studio. 'The Bundle-Theseus School of Movement Identity.' That was a good one." When we reach the stairs, Scottie carries me and we descend slowly. "Hume's Bundle Theory of Self," Scottie, the old philosophy major, says. "The Ship of Theseus. Theseus' paradox, which raises the question: if all the component parts of Theseus' old ship are replaced over time, is it still the same ship? That was Plutarch's baby originally—and then David Hume, the Scottish philosopher, ran with it and noted that we think we're the same person we were five, ten years ago and that person appears as present as it did way back when." A small laugh escapes his lips. "Impressive, red—really." He carries me through the doorway (back over the threshold, as it were), looking both ways. "There's only one dance school in town. Even though I didn't follow you the entire day today—I couldn't, especially all night long, and besides: most of the time you were following me, so I thought you were perfectly safe— when I couldn't scare you up tonight at your place, you were easy enough to find using your last note."

I nod excitedly. Scottie is catching on; he's getting it. "Did you see, Scottie? In the studio? Did you see *them* all?" I narrow my eyes to slits. "Andrea was there too, wasn't she?" I shudder and ask again, "Did you see *them* all?"

Scottie lowers me to my feet with care. "The question," he asks as he helps me into the passenger seat of his (my?) Ford Thunderbird, which is comfy and makes me instantly sleepy, "is did you?"

I remember seeing flashes of red hair in the mirrors of the dance studio, but just now I'm too tired to care—much.

I yawn as he starts the car. "Did I what, Scottie?"

Scottie cups my face and kisses my nose. "I'm not Scottie, Charlotte."

I blink.

"I'm John. Just plain John. Scottie—Scott died a long time ago, Charlotte. The car accident, remember? I never really knew him. I just know what you told me, what your mother told me. No one knows how it happened."

"October," I say, as if that explains everything. I rub my eyes. "If you're not Scottie… Why are you calling me Charlotte? If you're not Scottie, who are you?"

"I'm just the lucky recipient of your undeserved attention," he answers, smiling that cracked smile of his I love so much. "We've

294 · *Everything's Ephemeral: Stories from the Workshops Volume I*

known each other since we were kids; we lost touch for while after you met Scott."

Before we take off, I lower the window, and the crisp air slaps my face, as if trying to bring me to my senses, at least temporarily. I'm not even sure we're in a Ford Thunderbird. I look around for squirrels anyway.

"And I don't write mystery books. I help solve mysteries— sort of. I'm a psychologist, Charlotte. Not yours, still one nonetheless. But I've been talking to yours. Or the one you used to see before you quit therapy. He couldn't tell me much, naturally, but because of the potential danger, he pointed me in the right direction, and your mother filled in the rest."

"So you're not…"

The good Samaritan shakes his head. "Afraid not."

"And I'm not…?"

He smiles again. "What you are, Charlotte, is a complicated woman, which is exactly the kind of woman you should be. You just need a mental health professional to help you put the pieces together again, and you'll be good as new. A lot better than Theseus' old ship, as a matter of fact. Philosophy wasn't my major, it was Scott's, but I'm well read." He grins.

We pull away from the curb, and I dare a look behind me, and while I don't see another redhead crouched down in the backseat, I do see *their* car pull away a few seconds later, *their* headlights off, and I know everything is right with the universe. Whatever he is babbling on about (he's always babbling away about some subject or another), I am here with Scottie. We are together again. The old team. Maybe tonight will finally be the night he gives me a kiss before we part. But if not, I can wait. Someone (not Miss Lee, I'm sorry to say) sang *"waiting is the hardest part,"* but I beg to differ: waiting is the *best* part. If a rival (or two) needs to be dispatched, then I am ready and willing to do the dispatching. I'll do anything and everything. Whatever it takes to be with my Scottie. Whatever it takes.

I can't wait to get home and write all of this down. It's so absurd, it's almost fiction. Almost.

They give you fever
When you kiss them
Fever, if you live you learn

Fever!
Till you sizzle
Oh what a lovely way to burn
Oh what a lovely way to burn
Peggy Lee

<u>Closing file #CA-44</u>
Re: Operation Former Flame
Condition: grievous
Recommendations: abort and dissolve
Conclusion: expunge asset CA
Special Agent Scott J. Steward

-end-

The blazing fire makes flames and brightness
out of everything thrown into it.
— Marcus Aurelius

Thank You

Thank you, my Readers

Much gratitude to
Beth Meier, my copyeditor,
for setting my words on the straight and narrow
and for being my good friend

and

Steve Brandsdorfer & Dominique Messihi
of Pepper Lillie who designed the cover

Warmth goes out to Michael, Karin, & Danielle Berson
for their mightiness

Thank you so much:
Craig Do'vidio—for the movie we never made
Krisy Paredes—for your publicity guidance
Kelly Stengel, CRNP—for keeping the lantern raised
Flora Westbrook—for your photograph

Thank you, Sir Duke—for coming home

I wouldn't be half the person I am without
my mom, Kathleen Rose Harrington
and my sister, Kathleen Rose Cronk

Patti Cline—we shall forever miss your smile,
and your laughter will echo throughout our lives

Acknowledgements

My writing workshop professors, Arcadia University:
Gretchen A. Haertsch
Jeffrey Ingram
Quincey Jones
Larry Loebell
Dr. Richard Wertime

My literature and writing professors, Arcadia University:
Dr. Pradyumna S. Chauhan
Dr. Hugh Grady
Dr. Thomas Hemmeter
Dr. Sandra Hordis
Dr. Jo Ann Weiner

About the Author

Dreams, they complicate my life.
— R.E.M.

Michael-Patrick once owned a record store called:
  a) Disc/Connection
  b) Disc/Combobulation
  c) Geeks & Gawds
  d) Championship Vinyl

When the author used to gather the neighborhood kids to perform
West Side Story in his backyard, which character did he always play?
  a) Tony
  b) Bernardo
  c) Maria
  d) Riff

Michael-Patrick was born in _____ and now lives in _____.
  a) Castle Rock & Mondauk
  b) Bethlehem & Nazareth
  c) Philadelphia & Ambler
  d) Camelot & Middle-earth

In grade school, the author once had a t-shirt made that read,
  a) Boys Rule, Girls Drool
  b) Frodo Lives!
  c) Awww, Freak Out!
  d) When You're a Jet…

When he was a boy, Michael-Patrick ran scared out of a theater
during what movie? (He later returned.)
  a) *Jaws*
  b) *Terms of Endearment*
  c) *Animal House*
  d) *Close Encounters of the Third Kind*

E-mail answers to:
michael@michaelpatrickharrington.com

www.michaelpatrickharrington.com

Michael-Patrick supports the following charity organizations:

o   National Multiple Sclerosis Society: nationalmssociety.org

o   Brookline Labrador Retriever Rescue:
    brooklinelabrescue.org

o   RAINN (Rape, Abuse, & Incest National Network):
    RAINN.org

o   National Education Alliance for Borderline Personality
    Disorder: borderlinepersonalitydisorder.com

o   Borderline Personality Disorder Resource Center:
    nyp.org/bpdresourcecenter

www.ingramcontent.com/pod-product-compliance
Lightning Source LLC
Chambersburg PA
CBHW060849250626
47159CB00008B/2658